Falling Leaves of Ivy

FALLING LEAVES OF IVY

YOLANDA JOE

LONGMEADOW PRESS

Published by Longmeadow Press
201 High Ridge Road, Stamford, CT 06904

Cover design by © One Plus One Studio
Interior design by Donna Miller

Library of Congress Cataloging-in-Publication Data

Joe, Yolanda.
Falling leaves of ivy / Yolanda Joe. —1st ed.
p. cm.
ISBN 0-681-41396-4
I. Title.
PS3560.O242F3 1992
813′.54—dc20 92-14376
CIP

Printed in U.S.A.

First Edition

0 9 8 7 6 5 4 3 2 1

This book is dedicated to my grandparents, Bernice and George Barnett, who raised me to always do the best I can, to love God, and to be fair to everyone. And to Mom, Dad, and my sister, Donna, who are always there for me. Much love; everything good pales in comparison to you all.

Acknowledgments

Special thanks:

To Rhinold Ponder, big brother, friend, agent, and attorney all rolled into one.

To Reginold Ponder, who was the first friend to see my writing and gave me at age fourteen the ultimate compliment: "Cool."

To my publisher, Adrienne Ingrum, whose invaluable help made this book possible and my dream a reality.

To Malaika Adero for being that second set of caring editorial eyes.

To my cheerleading friends, Clark, Mark, Toni, Elise, Jennifer, Sonya, Val P., Dorothy, Val W., Lee Ann, Andi, members of the Ponder clan, and Doreen, who cheered the loudest. Love y'all!

To Carla, for helping me understand the thrills and ills of the investment banking world.

To the University of Chicago Libraries, the Alderman Library at the University of Virginia, Media Relations at the Chicago Police Department, and Mary Schmidt of Illinois Bell.

There is a tide in the affairs of men,
Which, taken at the flood, leads on to fortune;
Omitted, all the voyage of their life
Is bound in shallows and in miseries.
On such a full sea are we now afloat,
And we must take the current when it serves,
Or lose our ventures.

—*Julius Caesar,* Act 4

Chapter 1

THE inside of his throat clenched and unclenched. Despite the bitter winds, tiny beads of sweat ran down his brow as he faced his destination. The sky was carpeting the university plaza where he stood with thick snow. Kayo seemed to be shrinking in the midst of great expectations: the gothic structures with their grey stone and coal-colored streaks had aged gracefully, defeating years and upholding traditions.

Kayo jammed clammy hands into his pockets, pulled out the note that was the source of his dilemma, and began unraveling it like a kitten fighting a ball of yarn. The message read: "Please don't . . ." Kayo balled the note up and tossed it as far across the plaza as he could.

A group of people were trudging an oblong trench in the snow at the western end of the plaza. The wafting flakes settled gently on their hands, backs, and shoulders. They reminded Kayo of the trapped figures in a child's Christmas toy; a toy just like the one and only gift he had received on Christmas Day more than ten years ago. Now, just like then, he didn't want to break it.

Kayo started to run. There was no urgency in his stride, just the swishing thud of determination.

"Kayo, not you. Not you!"

Kayo turned toward Rodney Anderson, a thirty-five-year-old dining hall worker. They had worked in the kitchen there together, washing dishes. Rodney would even cover for Kayo when he needed to study for an exam, punching out his card at the regular time even though Kayo had left early.

"Listen, man . . ." Kayo's voice trailed.

Rodney's brow was withered with worry lines that stretched and meshed with his receding hairline. His skin was a dark smoke blue. Rodney's eyes were generally bright but today the hours out in the cold had iced them. "Man, how can you cross our picket line?"

"Don't put me on the spot. I've got to work, Rod!"

Rodney grabbed him by the back of the neck. Kayo jerked his elbows and broke the hold. "Don't touch me like that!"

Rodney moved in, fists cocked, eyes thawed and flashing with anger. Two of the workers grabbed his arms. "Be cool. You don't want to get arrested," one of them said. "He's a Yalie and the cops will always take his side. He's not black, he's a Yalie."

"I'm both, dammit!" Kayo shouted. He could feel their stares clawing his back as he turned inside the entrance of Commons dining hall. Frustrated, he glared at the people amassed at the seemingly endless rows of cherry oak tables. Hundreds of energetic voices buzzed in his ears like radio static on high. Kayo hurried to the back. The food was overflowing nickel-colored trays that lay in a wooden bed. White steam shrouded the four student servers who dished up the food with huge tin spoons and planted it on china plates embossed with the Yale crest. Kayo slipped off his parka (he had already put on his dining hall shirt before leaving his dorm room) and stomped back out into the dining hall. He began picking up the brown plastic trays littering the empty tables.

Elizabeth, Connor, and the others seated at their table

watched Kayo stretch his long, taut body across a chair, reaching for more trays. His skin was smooth, shiny, and the color of a new penny. His muscular legs were graceful and bowed like the body of a cello. Kayo's eyes were big, black, and moist. Tightly knit curls coiled on the top of his head. Elizabeth stared while Connor cleared his throat and barked, "Hey, busboy, how much are they paying you to do that hard labor?"

"Aww, Connor," Elizabeth joined in, "it isn't polite to ask an indentured servant what his bond is . . . in his case though I believe it's safe to say it's stupidity." The others at the table began to laugh; some even threw their arms up in a goalpost position and snapped their fingers, a time-old Yale tradition of approval.

Kayo glared at the table full of people. Elizabeth and Connor were seated in the center, flanked on each side by four others. Elizabeth's branchlike torso was well above the tabletop. She wore the traditional Yale blue sweater, frail and faded by too much bleach, pushed well up to the elbows of her long arms. Her blond hair rested on top of muscular shoulders. Bangs, neat and parted like a fish's fin, hung just shy of her eyebrows. Elizabeth had a boxer's square jaw and the other features of her face were just as strong and plain. Her blue eyes twinkled when she was happy, sparked when she was under stress. Elizabeth wasn't pretty by anyone's standards, but there was something attractive, immensely sexy about her. She nodded to Connor, seated at her right.

His soft brown hair was cropped close behind his ears. The strands were intricately interwoven. Connor's skin was flawless. His eyes were the color of spring grass and his features were keen and drawn. When he smiled the brightness of his teeth, the long, even rows, gleamed. His upper body made a V above the tabletop and the Italian handwoven sweater he wore hugged his body.

Kayo reached out and grabbed a tray while still looking at his friends. He brought it high under his chin as if he was exercising, and dropped it loudly on top of the other trays:

Crash! Elizabeth leaned forward and shouted, "Look at those nostrils flaring. I-I think we're supposed to get frightened."

"Oh no. See," Connor explained, "he's a scab. He only scares poor workers who don't make enough money for their families."

Kayo slammed down another tray, threw his hip against the garbage can, and took a step toward the table. His foot slipped and Kayo was down on one knee, splattered with cold potatoes and gravy. The entire dining hall joined in a chorus of laughter. Kayo scrambled to his feet, the laughter ringing in his ears, and pushed his way through the crowd of students in line. "Look out!"

"Hey! What's his problem?"

Kayo grabbed his coat from behind the counter, strode through the dining hall and out into the plaza.

"Hey, Kayo! You're supposed to serve the food, not wear it, buddy!" Rodney jeered.

The cold wind gripped the sides of Kayo's face and flared his coat as he tried to close it. Anger forced his mouth open and the inside of his throat stung from swallowing the frigid air. Kayo's tongue rubbed against the roof of his mouth and set it afire. He cleared the plaza, crossed the street lined with frosted oak trees, and stepped into the heart of the campus.

The campus was pulsating with the sounds of students hurrying from one building to another. Kayo headed north on the crosswalk that stretched in each direction. To his right was the main library, preceded by a grassy yard just large enough for about two dozen students to play Frisbee football.

Kayo crossed and entered Old Campus. It was where all freshmen were required to live so they could get to know the other members of their class. A few upperclassmen who were lucky enough to draw high in the dorm lottery also stayed on Old Campus. Kayo turned the corner quickly, opened the door to entryway A of Durfee Hall, and sprinted up the stairs.

Michelle looked through the peephole. She could tell by the rivers running across his brow that Kayo was angry. She tightened her plush white bathrobe and flicked the doorknob with a sharp turn and tug. The door crept halfway open and Michelle was already on her way back to her study cubby.

Kayo followed her down the short, narrow hallway. The floor was polished hardwood, the walls painted a stark white. On the right were two large wooden cabinets, on the left the door to the bathroom which was shared by the students on the other side of the hall. Kayo stepped into the doorway of the study cubby. It was big enough to house a desk and chair, one bookshelf, a small student refrigerator, and a box-shaped window that overlooked Old Campus.

Michelle was sitting at the desk, her head already buried in the pages. Kayo could not see her face, just the long, roped strands of hair doubling down her spine. Kayo couldn't help but notice Michelle's pert, mahogany breasts that were filling out the top of the bathrobe. A single crossed knee parted the bottom of the robe and her foot wagged nervously, thumping against the third drawer of the desk.

"Michelle, I swear . . ."

She knew by the tone in his voice that this was going to be a long and dramatic conversation, if she let it be. "Listen, I don't have time. First-semester senior grades are important for grad school. I've got to study for these exams."

"Ain't that a bitch! I guess if I were Connor you would have thrown the door open and that bathrobe you got on too! I came here to talk about a problem. Some friends I have! All y'all are pitiful!"

"What's the matter with you?" Michelle looked up from her book. Her eyes were moons of black, her nose full, her lips pouting.

"You don't care," Kayo accused as he walked over to the small refrigerator and leaned on it.

"C'mon, you know I care about you. What's up?"

"Well, I was working in the dining hall today and Connor and Elizabeth embarrassed me in front of the whole place!"

"What were you doing in the dining hall?"

"I just told you, working."

Michelle shook her head in disbelief and picked up a piece

of paper off the desk. "This note is from the union and the student committee that Elizabeth is heading up. She's worked really hard on organizing the protests and writing letters to the faculty. I mean, she even talked Connor into helping. Now you know, as conservative as he is, how much effort that took! I mean, did you even read it?" Michelle shook the note at him viciously.

"I fucking *got* it!"

Michelle began reading: "Please don't work in the dining halls. We know you must eat, but we ask that you cause as much disturbance at mealtime as possible to help."

"I mean they dogged me out in front of everybody!"

"They should have. You're taking food out of those people's mouths."

Kayo dug his hands deep into his pockets, threw his head back, and spouted air as if he was blowing out a candle.

"You know better."

"What-a-bout-*my*-family?" Kayo said, snapping his head forward, locking it tight as a loaded shotgun. "If you think that I'm going to let my brother go to the hole so somebody can buy their kids a pair of gym shoes from Kmart, you're crazy! Crazy as Rod, Elizabeth, and Connor!"

Michelle leaned forward, hands clasped in a praying fashion. "Ben's in trouble?"

"When is he not in trouble?" Kayo questioned, drawing his hands out of his pockets. "This time I think he's going to the hole. Ben's a goner unless he gets one hell of a lawyer, which costs lots of money. And guess what? Money don't grow on trees in the projects. In fact, trees don't grow in the projects!"

"Why didn't you say something to somebody?"

Kayo shrugged his shoulders.

"If you have a problem, you should have talked to me or Connor or Elizabeth about it! You should have come to one of us."

"It's my problem. I can handle it. I just don't like the way Connor and Elizabeth chumped me off in front of everybody! They're against me."

"That's not true and you know it! You know how hard they've been working. All those meetings. And that protest in front of the dean's office. Elizabeth could have gotten kicked out for that!"

"She cares more about her causes than she does her friends!"

"Boy, you sure can act crazy sometimes, you know that? We're all your best friends. If you weren't so stubborn, you wouldn't forget that!"

Kayo leaned back on the refrigerator and peered out the window.

Michelle stood up and walked over to him. "I have an idea. My Dad knows a guy who's a serious criminal attorney. They were Freedom Riders together back when Daddy was at Morehouse. He's in Chicago now and I'm sure he would help for *free* as a favor to Dad."

"I don't know, Michelle."

"You don't know?" Michelle shouted, stepping back. Her hands dropped and formed handles against her hips. "First, you come in here with your face mopping up the floor because Connor and Elizabeth balled you out—and rightly so. Then you piss and moan about needing money to help your brother get a lawyer. Now, when the solution to the problem is right at hand, you big, tough Kayo have to think about it? *Ignorant*!"

"Who you callin' ignorant?"

"Who am I looking at?"

"If I'm so ignorant, how did I get to Yale?" Kayo remarked snootily.

"Honey, some of the biggest fools I have ever met have been hiding behind these ivy walls."

"Okay," Kayo couldn't help but smile—"you win."

"Good," Michelle said, returning the smile. "I'll call Dad tonight and have him work it all out. I'll give him your home number so he can talk to your Mom about it. Don't worry, Kayo."

"Who's worried?"

"Some nut in an ugly dining hall uniform. Please! Go take it off!" Michelle scooted Kayo toward the door. "Go!"

She waited until the door slammed, then she looked at the closed book and debated. Michelle drummed her fingers on the desk, stopping only when her decision was made.

Twenty minutes later, she was standing on the front step of her entryway, looking out over Old Campus. The high-beam lights that outlined the glistening snow gave the grounds a mystical atmosphere. The crisp air felt good circulating inside her lungs. Michelle stepped down, turned the corner, and began jogging toward Elm Street.

The late hours of the day, forced by winter to share its time with the night, blanketed the sky in deep blue-black. It seemed thickest over the arching pyramid of stone. Michelle hurried toward it. A bulky wall encircled the hulking tomb that looked like something out of ancient Egypt. Broken tree limbs wrapped in icy gauze rested limply against the sides of the tomb. She grabbed the gold knocker that hung like a bone from the mouth of the lion roaring at the door.

Slowly the door inched open, giving way to a ray of light. "Come in," a voice boomed in a false bass. Michelle struggled to adjust her sight. Instinctively she stepped forward and when her vision cleared, she was inside, the door was shut, and Connor was standing in front of her, grinning. "Hi, you've got great timing. I just got here and the rest of the guys in the society just left to go to a beer party. What's up?"

Michelle lit into him. "Why are you so cheery after the way you and Elizabeth treated Kayo today? Huh?"

"Whoa! Whoa!" Connor said, grabbing her arms, pulling her close to him. Michelle pulled back, but not out of arm's reach.

"Connor, I know Kayo was wrong but you didn't have to embarrass him in front of the whole dining hall. You know how sensitive he is!"

"Well, Kayo wasn't being very sensitive when he crossed that picket line!"

Michelle snatched her gloves off and gestured. "We know

that he was wrong and he knows that he was wrong. But there is a way to point that out without holding him up to public ridicule."

Connor stood there admiring the black sparkles going off in her eyes.

"You know how long it's taken for Kayo to trust . . . to trust, ah, people. We've got a special friendship and you guys could have ruined it."

"Michelle, you're going overboard now. C'mon, let's go downstairs and talk about it."

"You think you're slick," she said, crossing her arms.

"Slick, nothing! It's cold in this doorway," Connor said, pulling Michelle along.

They walked down a long hallway. The floor was bumpy, made of stone. The walls were high and sponges for the cold. There were olympic oars, muskets, frontier rifles, and pinup calendars. As they entered a narrow stairwell, light dashed against their bodies from candle-shaped electric fixtures. This was a semiformal dining room. She squinched her face up, "You know, I hate this room."

"But this is my favorite room!"

Michelle pointed at a row of jagged teeth, hanging fur, and vicious growls. "Gross! Look at all those ugly stuffed animal heads! No wonder you guys won't let any women in this secret society 'cause those would surely have to go. I mean, is this Yale or *Wild Kingdom*?"

Connor inhaled deeply, then pulled out a chair from a long oak table. He sat on the table and put his feet in the chair. "Tradition. The society is called the Lion's Den. Now how is it going to be the Lion's Den without lions on the wall?"

"Back to what I was saying . . ."

"Coat?"

Connor took it and motioned toward a chair in the corner, stopped, and tossed the coat on the floor.

"Boy, are you crazy, throwing my stuff on the floor?" Michelle demanded, following the coat with her eyes as Connor mischievously pulled her close between his legs. He stared at her, trying to use his eyes to chip away at the anger that was sculpting her features. He kissed Michelle passionately but she pursed her lips tightly.

"What's wrong?"

"I'm trying to talk to you about Kayo and you just want to fool around."

"Damn you, Michelle! Forget Kayo for now. I want you."

"Connor, I'm trying to talk to you."

"I'll fix it. Forgive me?"

Before she could answer, he kissed her again. Connor felt her body relax against his. She wrapped her arms around his waist and squeezed. He slowly slid off the table, still holding her firmly. Connor ran his hands along the back of her thighs. Squeezing.

"Not here," Michelle whispered.

"Here and now—I love you," Connor said, his words coming in quick, short breaths. He nibbled her eyelids and then traced the inside of her ears with his tongue. "I love you."

Michelle dropped her eyes for a long moment before saying, "Then why the secret?"

"You know why. It won't be much longer," Connor said fluidly, having used the words many times before. "Be patient, Michelle. You know I love you."

"I love you too." Her voice trembled with fatigue from bringing the words all the way up from the heart.

Then they began grabbing at each other's clothes. Each knew a quick avenue to nakedness and the material gave way to their fingertips like confetti. They stood embracing. Connor planted powerful, hot kisses on her lips, neck, and breasts. Michelle's hands stroked his back, thighs, and the central point of his desire. The pores of their skin opened and became magnetized. They slid on top of the table, the sweat from their bodies oiling it. Michelle's arms fell back above her head and she opened her legs wide for him. Connor ran the palms of his hands down the inside of her thighs. He leaned up and into her as if he were easing into a hot spring that was bubbling all over his body. Michelle felt the entering warmth as light thrust inside her body. They were consumed with each other, their breathing and their pleasure one in the soft solitude of passion and darkness.

Kayo pulled up the white shade and looked out over the yard at half-finished snowmen and students running and sliding in the snow. The laughter, the yells, sounded like the hip arrangement of a jazz classic. It was reading period, a week meant for exam study, not for fooling around. Kayo rested his head against the windowpane, the chill ironing a crease in his temple. He watched as a group of students greeted Friar Pete, who was standing in one of his old familiar spots. He was a homeless man who had carved a niche for himself on the campus. Friar Pete was lanky, in his late fifties, and a man with a busy personality, always stirring some emotion in whomever he came into contact with. Kayo watched as the students patted him on the shoulders, their pale hands a contrast to his knobby brown bones. Someone handed Friar Pete a beer. He screwed off the metal top with his mouth, balanced it on the tip of his tongue, then floated it inside his jaws, working them ever so slightly. Within seconds, Friar Pete rolled his tongue out again, and there resting on the tip was the top, molded into a perfect pyramid. The students applauded. Friar Pete the perennial Yale scholar, Kayo thought to himself.

Kayo turned and looked around the room. There were two beds, one on each side, narrow and flat like sticks of gum. On the right above his bed was a photo montage of his favorites: early Jesse Jackson, Black Power button, Afro, and all. There was Bogart on the airfield from *Casablanca*; Public Enemy, the rappers, holding fourteen-carat gold record discs in their palms; Magic Johnson spinning a globe as if it was a basketball; John Johnson holding up the first issue of *Ebony* magazine. Lavender, red, green, and orange pillows decorated his bed. Kayo jumped from the window onto his bed. He reached under one of the pillows, pulled out a plastic bag with a dozen rolled-up joints. Kayo lit one of the marijuana cigarettes and inhaled deeply.

"Now news and weather from WYBC in New Haven. Weather forecasters say a big warm-up is on the way, accompanied by rain. . . . Driving is expected to be hazardous tomorrow . . ."

Kayo's jaws ballooned. He leaned up and looked into the dresser mirror and wondered if Dizzy got started playing the horn this way. Kayo took another pull and then glanced over at Connor's side of the room. There were several color photos of his family arranged by years. Connor, his brother, his father and mother on a vacation in France in '77. Connor, his brother, and his mom making a snowman in the Swiss Alps in '79. His mother and father shaking hands with Vice President George Bush at the Yale Club in New York in '82. On the wall facing the foot of the bed was a poster of Larry Bird in a leprechaun hat twirling a basketball. On the wall over the headboard was a montage of The Grateful Dead, Phil Collins, and one huge photo of Marvin Gay from a live concert back in '74. The bed itself was piled with dirty clothes and the sheet was hanging to the floor. There was a teak nightstand and next to it was a basketball with all the Boston Celtics' signatures on it.

Kayo took another hit and thought back to the first time he saw Connor with the basketball. It was freshman year at Payne Whitney Gym . . .

A group of guys entered the basketball court, all wearing leather gym shoes, shorts with matching shirts from Nike, Adidas, and Olympic. Kayo watched them come in. Six hundred dollars' worth of stuff on each one of them! Welcome to the Ivy League, boy, he said to himself. Kayo was sitting on the floor, lacing up his Converse gym shoes. The group of guys chatted loudly and clowned around. They stopped just about five feet away from Kayo and plopped down, one right after another. Kayo continued to lace up his shoes. One of the guys opened a red gym bag and pulled out a ball. "Guys, here is *thee* ball—the Celtic Special," the brown-haired guy bragged. He started pointing out different signatures to his friends: "Larry Bird! Robert Parish . . ." The back of his shirt said "Connor."

Kayo finished lacing his shoes and was standing up,

stretching, when one of the other guys walked over. He had fire-red hair, a long angular nose, and freckles that filled his face. He tapped the bridge of the wire-framed glasses he wore and held up the same hand to Kayo, saying, "Hey, man, wanna get down with some ball?"

Kayo looked at the clammy palm held up for a high five. Too easy. Kayo grabbed the palm, turned it sideways, and shook it firmly. "Sure, let's get a full-court game."

Some of the others had already gone out onto the court. Stretching, Kayo braced an extended leg against the wall and pushed. Kayo noticed that "Red" was talking to Connor. He stepped over a bit and listened as he continued to stretch.

"Hey," Red said, "I'm choosing against Michael. With me, Bud, you, Kile, and the black guy we're a cinch to win."

Kayo picked up a stray basketball and began bouncing it, pretending not to hear but listening all the while.

Connor grabbed a towel out of his bag. "You've seen him play, Mick?"

"No, but he's black," Mick said, running his hands through his red hair. "He's got to be able to play. He didn't get those worn-over shoes from being a runner on the stock exchange."

Kayo bounced the ball.

"Come on!" one of the other guys yelled from the floor.

Connor waved the towel. "Hang on!"

"I'm going to bet Bud fifty on this game! He always wins because he picks the same guys over and over. But today, with *him*, we'll win."

"Mick, that's bullshit. Just because he's black doesn't mean he plays like Magic Johnson."

Mick glanced over at Kayo. Kayo suddenly got a mischievous idea. He spun the ball with one hand and placed it on the tip of his index finger.

"Look!" Mick's face lit up. "Look at that."

"Ssh, not so loud. He'll hear you."

"Come *on*!" Mick said, running out into the court. "Let's go!"

Kayo walked over to Connor and picked up *the* basketball. He twirled it in his hands. "Celtic fan?"

"You know it," Connor said, standing up, extending his hand. "My name is Connor. What's yours?"

"Kevin. But everyone calls me Kayo. K-O."

"How do you like freshman year so far?" Connor asked.

"Not bad. Where did you meet all those guys?" Kayo said, pointing with his head.

"Choate. They're cool. C'mon, let's play a little ball."

"I guess you think Larry Bird is the greatest player in the NBA?"

"No! Magic is. But I still love my Celtics," Connor said, grabbing the ball out of Kayo's hand and stuffing it back in his bag. He jogged out on the court. "Let's go, Kayo!"

The choosing of sides went just as Mick planned. Michael was the husky guy, really hairy and muscular. Mick grinned at him and shook his hand as the "skins," their team, gave the "shirts" the ball first. Pounding feet sent sounds echoing throughout the court. Grunts. Pushing. Holding. Picks. Nets swishing. Fouls. Shouts.

Kayo threw the ball away every chance he got. Two of his shots hit the rim and went up and over the backboard. He double-dribbled the ball twice, bounced it off his foot once, and overthrew his open teammate three times.

"Damn, Kayo!" Mick yelled angrily. "You can't play worth shit!"

Kayo smiled innocently, shrugging his shoulders. "Well, I'm on an academic scholarship, not an athletic one. Sorry."

The game ended with Kayo's team losing by four baskets. Connor had five buckets, three assists, and stole the ball twice.

Connor was wiping his sweat-drenched body when Kayo walked over to compliment him. "Nice game, man."

"Th-thanks," Connor panted. "Listen, let me give you a few tips. Now, no problem about the loss—"

"Yeah, it is too a problem! Jesus! You suck!" Mick yelled coming up behind them. He grabbed his bag and followed the other guys out the door. "Shower action. You guys hurry up, it's time to eat!"

"Don't mind him," Connor said, slapping Kayo on the back. The wet T-shirt against his skin made a loud, sucking sound. Just Connor and Kayo were left in the gym now.

"Show me some of those B-ball tips?" Kayo said, smiling.

"Now? It's almost time for dinner."

"Hey, we'll make it three baskets. Every time you hit, you get the ball back. It'll go by quickly the way you play."

"Okay," Connor agreed, knowing he could take Kayo easily. "I'll let you have the ball first."

Kayo took the ball out and watched as Connor gave him about five feet. "You better tighten up on that D."

Connor smiled. "I got it."

Kayo took two steps and he was at the top of the key, shot: *swish*! Connor ran and grabbed the ball bouncing under the net. He tossed it back.

Kayo grabbed the ball and bounced it between his legs, took two quick steps to the right, stutter-stepped, and drove right past Connor for a reverse lay-up.

On the last shot, Kayo ran under the net and picked up the bouncing ball.

"You fucking heard!" Connor laughed. "You dick! I like you."

Kayo twirled the ball on his finger and laughed too . . .

Now Kayo took another pull and laughed out loud at the memory. He lay back, propping his feet up against the wall. Pictures flashed through his mind. Connor taking him to the infirmary when he had the flu last year. Elizabeth bringing him soup from home. Michelle massaging his back with some smelly stuff her grandmother sent from Georgia, stuff that would "kill a cold quicker than a pig can squeal." Kayo smiled to himself and his gaze fell over at the empty bed. His mind told him: Connor's spending the night with Michelle. Slowly his smile disappeared and Kayo questioned himself: Why does that bother you?

Chapter 2

THE next night Michelle was picking out a table in the back of the Raven's Nest Club. It was big and drafty but the students loved its huge buffed wood dance floor and the lax attitude toward ID cards. Watching a small crowd of people dancing, Michelle could feel the music's bass line against the bottom of her feet. She looked around impatiently for the person she had come to meet. On the phone the voice had been near the breaking point, urgent. Now Michelle wondered if maybe something terrible had happened.

"Wanna dance?" a deep voice behind her said.

Her thoughts broken, Michelle looked up. The man weighed at least two hundred and fifty pounds and had to be a grandfather already. She forced a smile. "No thank you. I'm waiting for someone."

"Oh," the dancer said, rolling his hips. "Well, I'll sit down until your company comes."

"No," Michelle said, bracing the chair with her foot.

"The hell with you then. You're not so hot!" He turned and sauntered away.

Michelle was thinking about catching him to apologize, when someone touched her shoulder from behind.

"Michelle!"

Michelle turned to Elizabeth and knew. "Dinner at home with the folks was rough, huh?"

"It was a nightmare." Tears filled Elizabeth's eyes as she plopped down in a chair. "The same old bullshit! Mom was pissy drunk. Dad came late for dinner and she screamed and cursed. I mean it hurt hearing her talk to him like that. Daddy's had an emergency, you know? After all these years of him being on the force she ought to know that things will come up! But no, she acted like a maniac. Daddy is a good guy, always loving and supportive . . ."

"I know, I know," Michelle said, patting her hand.

". . . and she treats him like dirt! It's the liquor, I know. I told her to leave him the fuck alone and then she turned on me! It's my fault. Everything is my fault. She even tried to blame me again for Meghan's death."

"Stop it." Michelle leaned up. "You know good and well that wasn't your fault."

"That's what Daddy said. But Michelle, Mom just went crazy! She threw the knife and fork at me, dumped the peas in my lap! But Dad stopped her and put her in her place right then. He'll take Mom's shit but he protects me. I-I just couldn't stay there anymore. I called you and got the hell out of there."

"Try to calm down."

Elizabeth took a deep breath and more memories of the night's battle came creeping back. She shook her head and pushed them away. "I don't want to talk about it anymore. Let's just have a good time."

"Okay." Michelle squeezed her hand. "That's the Liz I know! Let's have a good time. It's kind of empty here tonight though."

"Yeah, it is but the music is good," Elizabeth said, bobbing back and forth. She scooted up and tossed the raincoat she was sitting on onto an empty chair at a neighboring table. The coat was a sloppy yellow sea slicker more than forty years old. It was made out of beaten sealskin that was both soft and rubbery. There were little square eyelets around the cuffs of the baggy sleeves, and the hood was lined with thin fish netting.

Michelle pointed at the coat and laughed. "I was looking for that! I thought you didn't like it."

"Hell, it was better than getting wet. It's warm now, I didn't even have it on in the cab."

"Cab? I thought you'd have your father's car."

"No, my mother was making a big deal out of my using it. So I just said screw it, I'll get a ride back with you in Connor's car."

"I took a cab too. I spent my last dime on it."

"Uh-oh! I'm broke too," Elizabeth said, laughing. "Here in a club with no men and no money."

"Oooh, that's too depressing. Hey, let's call Connor and Kayo."

"Think they're at home?"

"They ought to be," Michelle said, smiling up at the waiter as he reached the table. "They didn't come in the library. I was there almost all day. They both have that big Econ exam coming up and I know Kayo likes to study in their room when it's late at night."

"What will you ladies have?" the waiter asked. He wore jeans and a T-shirt that said "Roost at the Nest."

"I'll have a piña colada," Michelle said, standing.

"Same," Elizabeth said, rocking and swaying in her chair.

The waiter reared back and peeped at her shuffling feet under the table. "Well, with you here things will start jumping tonight."

A slight smile spread across Elizabeth's face and she pouted her lips slightly. "I like it when it's jumping."

Michelle headed for the pay phone in the hall. "I'll call the guys."

Elizabeth continued to smile and flirt with the waiter.

* * *

Kayo heard the key in the door and quickly slid off the bed. As soon as Connor stepped inside the doorway, Kayo let loose. "Why did you make a fool out of me in front of the entire dining hall yesterday?"

Connor didn't answer. Instead, he dived on his bed and landed face down in a heap of dirty clothes.

"What the fuck was the deal in the dining hall—huh?"

Connor flipped over. "Look, we had been giving everybody shit that came in to work yesterday. Now, how would it look if we didn't say anything to you?"

"It would look like you guys were my friends."

Connor opened his mouth, then decided against saying he was sorry. "Forget it already."

"That's easy for you to say. You don't give a damn about the strike anyway," Kayo said, moving to stand over him.

"Back off. You know Elizabeth nagged me for weeks to get on that committee. You know how she is, gets an issue and just won't let go. I thought it was an okay cause and got on the committee. I mean you always said Rodney wasn't getting paid enough money and his family needed better health insurance, right?"

Kayo started to squirm at the mention of Rodney. His friend had looked so angry and hurt. Sulking, Kayo moved to his bed and opened an Econ book. "Just leave me alone. Stay on your side of the room. Don't ask me to tutor you in Econ. Matter of fact, don't talk to me, period."

RRrrrrng! RRrrrrng!

"Hello," Connor snapped into the receiver. A bowing-down tone crept into his voice. "Oh, hi Dad. How do you know I was on the committee?"

Kayo instinctively looked up.

Connor's eyes bugged. "Mick told his father . . ."

Kayo grabbed his crotch at the mention of Mick's name.

". . . and his father mentioned it at the Yale Club? No Dad, I wasn't trying to embarrass you. No, it didn't take away from my study time. The only reason I got on the committee was because Elizabeth asked me to."

Kayo watched Connor nervously wrap the telephone cord around his wrist.

"Okay. Okay. I'm off the committee. I-I-I've got to study now. 'Bye."

Now Connor was sweating. He threw a punch into the pile of dirty clothes on the bed. "God! He's pissed. Said I embarrassed the family by going against the university. He's up for a seat on the board and I'm going to fuck around and blow it for him."

Kayo felt sorry for Connor because his father was always riding him about his terrible Econ grades. But he refused to say a word.

"Study! Study! All this studying is killing me!" Books and papers were scattered around the head of Connor's bed. He doubled up a pillow, wrapped it around his fist, and punched it underneath his stomach. He watched Kayo read and check his notes. "You don't even have to study this hard, Kayo. Man, what are you trying to pull—an A plus?"

"You need to shut up and get back to work!"

"Aha! You talked to me! Still mad?"

Kayo rolled his eyes.

"I'll take that as a no," Connor said with mock seriousness.

It took all Kayo's remaining self-control not to smile.

"I need a little pick-me-up," Connor said, reaching inside the top drawer of his nightstand. He grabbed a small packet and then reached under his bed and grabbed an old album cover—Parliament in platform shoes and blown-out Afros. Connor dusted it off with the sleeve of his sweatshirt. He opened the packet of coke and dumped it on the album. He took the sharp edge of his notebook and made neat rows.

"You're neat as hell when you do that coke," Kayo noted. "You could be a little neater around the room. I keep telling you there are no maids here."

"You're talking to me again! You can't stay mad at me, buddy."

Kayo swung his legs down off the bed. He kicked one of Connor's sweaters high in the air. "Three points!"

It came wafting down on top of his roommate's head. "Hey, man, this stuff is bad!" Connor said, careful to keep the sweater off his makeshift coke tray. "Want some?"

"Naw, you know I only do weed."

"I know, I just didn't want to be rude," Connor said with a wink.

"RRrrrrng!"

Kayo lunged off the bed and answered the phone. "Um, hello? Mrs. Bellington."

Connor dropped his pillow, jumped up, and grabbed the receiver away from Kayo. "Mom?"

Kayo grabbed the pillow and rolled away toward the window, laughing.

"What are you guys doing, Connor?" Michelle asked.

"Kayo's being a jerk. I'm studying."

"Yeah, right!" Kayo laughed.

Connor heard music playing in the background. "Where are you?"

"I'm at the Raven's Nest with Elizabeth. We don't have a way to get back to campus and we don't have any money. You guys come on down and let's have a little fun."

"Hey, Kayo. Michelle and Elizabeth want us to meet them at the club. They don't have a ride or any money."

"Call 911!"

Connor relayed the message and Michelle shouted, "Both of you get down here and fast!"

"I guess we can come down and get you two off the hook," Connor said, hanging up the phone. "Let's go!"

The air outside was crisp and misty. Connor was a few steps ahead of Kayo, looking down the long line of parked cars. "I'm trying to remember where I parked!"

"I thought it was on the other block."

"Hell no, I don't park over there. The street is too narrow. Somebody might hit it."

Kayo spotted the vanity plate. "Con Man One," he said, pointing at the back of the car.

It was a 1950 black BMW with a custom-made top trimmed in oak. The unique handmade tires from Germany were slightly narrow with triangular grooves in the tread. Inside the triangles were little number ones. Connor stepped around the back and wiped the slush off the back fender.

"Let's go!" Kayo said, drumming the top with his thumbs on the passenger's side.

"Cool out, man."

"You're crazy about this car!"

"Hey," Connor said, opening the door and sliding in, "it's a family thing, you know?" Connor reached over and opened the door for Kayo. "Granddad gave it to Dad and Dad gave it to me. I want to pass it on to my son."

"Well, let's roll, man," Kayo urged, hopping inside.

"Yeah, I'll take the shortcut down by the river. I'm ready to party!"

Multicolored lights flooded the club with energy. Giant speakers hovering high overhead sent down pulsating beats as the people jammed below.

Kayo spotted them first. He tugged on Connor's arm and they made their way to the back table. Connor and Michelle exchanged glances, resisting the urge to hug because there were too many other students around. Their love had to be kept secret; too many people on campus knew Connor's prominent family. His father would not approve.

"Hi, Michelle. You're looking good!" Connor said, caressing her with his eyes.

"Thanks," Michelle said, playing along.

Kayo's jaws tightened. Elizabeth took another sip of her drink and studied Kayo's face.

Kayo sat down across from her. They hadn't talked since the dining hall incident. His face started to burn at the thought of it.

"I'm sorry. Wanna call a truce?" Elizabeth said, knowing she couldn't stand another fight tonight.

"Okay." Kayo cracked a smile. "But don't ever embarrass me like that again. Ever."

"Truce," Elizabeth said, smiling. She looked up at Connor and Michelle, who were still standing. "What are we waiting for? Let's party."

For the next few hours they danced and drank and sang out loud to the music. Connor even grabbed the mike and sang off-key to Marvin Gaye's "Got to Give It Up." The DJ let it slide once he found the twenty-dollar bill Connor slipped him, spinning on one of the turntables. When Connor was done, Elizabeth and Michelle cheered. Kayo whispered, "Man, I can't fuckin' take you nowhere."

They sauntered back to the table littered with near-empty glasses. The liquor and the music, the laughter, energized their bodies. Michelle and Elizabeth were ready to go to bed but ready to dance more, all at the same time. Kayo's eyes were drooping in a rum-reddened face. Connor didn't look a bit better.

"Um, you guys are the last ones here and we are about to close," the waiter announced.

"So soon?" Elizabeth smiled.

"Wow, the place sure is empty." Michelle looked around the club and laughed. "Let's go."

Kayo got up and shouted at the waiter, "Beam me up, Scotty!"

They all laughed. Connor stood up now, weaving a little bit. "Now I *know* it's time to go."

Outside, a dusting of warm rain had spread a film across the front and back windows of Connor's car. Elizabeth and Kayo were walking in front with Connor and Michelle a few steps behind.

"God, it's warmed up a lot out here tonight," Elizabeth said, watching Kayo lean up against the car. She was holding the raincoat by the sleeves. Elizabeth went to toss it over her arm and her ring got caught in the thin netting inside the hood.

She fished it out and tossed the coat over her shoulder. "Boy, am I going to sleep well."

Connor wobbled his way around to the driver's side.

"Um, Connor, let me drive," Michelle said softly from the passenger's side.

"I'm fine," Connor said with a reassuring wink. He got inside and let everyone else in. "Pick 'em up! Move 'em out!" Connor said, juicing the engine. He looked at Elizabeth and Kayo in the backseat, then reached out and hugged Michelle around the neck.

"Hey, no screwing in the front of the cab—unless I'm in on it!" Kayo shouted from the backseat.

"Shut up and mind your own business!" Connor said, reaching back to shove Kayo's knee.

"Alright, don't get violent . . . don't get violent."

Connor flicked on the defogger and began pulling the car out. The back wheels spun a little, then the car lurched forward.

There were no other cars out. It was early morning but still quite dark. The white light from the streetlamps cast an eerie glow over the street. Connor rubbed his eyes.

Michelle turned on the radio and hit only annoying static.

"You can't find anything?" Elizabeth moaned.

"Nothing really," she said, fiddling again with the dial. Michelle locked into Country & Western and winced.

"Please, if that's the best you can do, turn it off!" Kayo said.

The car wheels skidded. Connor turned in the direction of the skid, then straightened the car out. "It's slick out here."

Kayo started to sing the Yale fight song: "When the sons of Eli . . ."

"How come it's the sons of Eli instead of the sons and daughters of Eli?" Michelle questioned, turning sideways to face Kayo.

"What do you want them to do? Change a more than one-hundred-year-old song cause the place went coed?" Kayo asked, his head bobbing with laughter.

"Hell yes!" Elizabeth said. "I think I'll write a letter to the dean."

"You would," Kayo sneered.

Elizabeth slapped Kayo on the back of his neck with the palm of her hand. Michelle reached back and threw a punch at his leg.

"Help!" Kayo said, hanging his hands over the front seat.

Michelle was now tickling him under the knees. "When the daughters of Eli break through the line . . ." she sang.

Connor could feel the wheels occasionally losing traction in the slush. He sang over his shoulder, "That is the song we hail . . . Bull-dog! Bull-dog! Bow, wow, wow . . . E-li Yale!"

"Look out!" Elizabeth yelled.

Connor jerked back around. The car was lurching to the left. He twisted the steering wheel hard to the left. The right wheels rode the curb and the car spun forward.

Thud!

Connor pumped the brake up and down, up and down, trying to stop.

"Lord!" Michelle screamed as she was thrown forward. Her mouth seemed cold and frozen like when she sucked ice-cream bars as a kid. She bounced back, clutching the dash in pain.

Kayo and Elizabeth were tossed back on their seats like rags.

The car jerked to a stop.

"What the fuck!" someone said.

Michelle wiped her mouth and tasted blood.

Connor's hands gripped the steering wheel. The leather seemed to eat at his palms. The pressure made his knuckles bloat. He tried to speak. He turned to Michelle and saw a thin stream of blood running down her upper lip. Connor touched her face and found his voice. "Are you alright?"

She nodded yes.

"What? What happened!" Kayo sat up and began squeezing his shoulders. He worked his neck. Elizabeth's eyes were wide from fright but she looked unharmed.

"My God!" Elizabeth screamed as she pointed out the window. She opened the door and jumped out of the car.

The three inside the car turned around and watched her. She was now several feet away, hunched over a body in the street. "Get out!" Kayo yelled, kicking the door open with his foot. He jumped out of the car and only stopped long enough to bang on the front window. "C'mon!"

Connor thrust the door open. His heart raced as he stumbled toward the body.

Michelle was the last one out. Her knees buckled. She grabbed the top of the door and got her bearings. She could smell the murky water and saw that they were by the river. Michelle looked at the three hunched over in the street. She saw what looked like baggy pants and shoes dangling beyond their kneeling bodies and ran toward them. She reached her friends and over Kayo's shoulder she saw his face. It was calm and serene. His hair was standing on end, thick and long. There were speckles of snow mixed in it and pieces of paper. A gash in his forehead sent blood cascading through the salt-and-pepper eyebrows. "Friar Pete!"

Elizabeth felt her teeth chattering. Her hands began to sweat and she wiped them on her jeans. She knew he was dead. His chest neither filled nor rose. His throat lay exposed, motionless and brown as a log. She ran her hands through her hair. "Jesus!"

Connor was sweating. "I-I-I didn't see him!"

Dead . . . Man . . . man . . . *Man*! Kayo looked at the lifeless body in front of him. He reached out to touch Friar Pete's shoulder but stopped himself. A picture of Friar Pete holding two dollars flickered through his mind. Kayo stared into the eyes, looking for a sign of anything, but all he saw was cold, motionless death.

Elizabeth rocked on the back of her heels. Her stomach turned over; she fought to keep from throwing up as she stumbled away.

"Where are you going?" Kayo said, grabbing her.

"I'm going to call my father . . . police," Elizabeth blurted out and the words seemed to hurt as they left her mouth.

"Are you crazy?" Kayo tightened his grip on her now. "No way! No police!"

"Som-some-bo-ody, close his eyes," Michelle stuttered.

Connor rocked forward on his knees. "I had slowed down! I had! It's slick out here. Where'd he come from?"

Elizabeth tried to take a step, but Kayo wouldn't let her move. "Lemme go."

"Listen," Kayo said, his chest heaving. "He's dead and there's nothing anybody can do about it."

"My father—"

"He ain't fuckin' God! Unless he's God there's nothing he can do!" Kayo said, shaking her. "Okay, chill. Okay everybody, listen up for a second. We've got to do something and fast!"

"What?" Elizabeth said.

Michelle reached forward, hand trembling, reaching to close Friar Pete's eyes. "Our Father who is in heaven . . ."

"I can't believe this! Somebody do something!" Connor groaned.

". . . holy is they name . . ."

Kayo spoke loudly, trying to drown out Michelle's words. "If we call the police, we'll all get into serious trouble. We've been drinking and that's the first thing they'll check for!"

". . . thy kingdom come . . ."

"They won't be fair. We could all go to jail for this!" Kayo pleaded.

". . . thy will be done . . ."

Kayo leaned down and shook Michelle hard. "Listen to me! Snap out of it and listen!"

"Connor ran him over," Michelle said drowsily.

"I tried to stop! I did! It was you guys fucking playing in the car." Swelling tears magnified Connor's eyes as he screamed, "How am I suppose to drive the freaking car with you guys playing around the wheel?!"

"We killed him," Elizabeth said, staring down at the body.

"Listen, that's what I've been saying," Kayo said trembling. "If we go to the cops, we'll all have records and maybe even go to jail! Listen! We're all in trouble. We gotta dump the body in the river and get outta here! Nobody—but nobody—can know."

"No!" Elizabeth shouted.

"Yeah!" Connor said, grabbing Kayo by the shoulder.

"My father—"

"Listen," Connor began, "if word of this gets out our whole lives are ruined."

Kayo balled up his fist. "They'll make an example out of us because your father's a cop and because we're Yalies! They're sure to throw the book at us! They're not going to be fair. Do you want all your dreams to go down the fucking tubes because some bum didn't watch where he was going?"

Elizabeth imagined the problems it would cause. "Alright."

Michelle stared down at Friar Pete.

Kayo turned to Michelle. "Nothing can bring him back."

"Don't look at me!" Michelle was standing now, trembling. "Y'all do what you want."

"Hell naw, Michelle! We were all in the car and we're all in this to the end," Kayo said sternly.

Connor looked at Michelle. "Please, Michelle, please."

Michelle nodded her head furiously. Tears ran down her cheeks.

"Okay." Kayo licked his lips, then coughed nervously. "Get his feet."

Connor gingerly grabbed the worn-out heels. A cold stickiness oozed through his fingers. Connor thought it was blood and dropped the heels. He stared at the sludge on his hands.

"C'mon, it's getting lighter!" Kayo said, his hands hooked on the body's shoulders.

Connor grabbed the heels again and lifted.

"Follow me back," Kayo said, walking backward. He stopped.

"What are you stopping for?" Connor hissed.

"Elizabeth, Michelle, he's heavy. Both of you grab the ends with one of us. Hurry!"

"No! I can't touch him!" Michelle said, trembling. "I can't!"

"We're doing it!" Connor shouted.

"C'mon Michelle, so we can get it over with! Close your eyes if you have to," Elizabeth whined.

Michelle stepped over by Kayo and grabbed the shoulders. A bitter taste jumped into her mouth. She turned her head and spit.

At the edge of a small platform where small boats would dock, the body hit the water with a tremendous force. The river accepted the gift of chaos and in return sent a cold, oily splash over the four numbed friends standing at the edge.

Chapter 3

"I didn't mean it. I didn't . . ." Connor groaned from the edge of fatigue. He squeezed the sides of the bed with his hands.

Fear became a mirror in his mind, it reflected everything and everything reflected it.

Rivers ran across the ceiling. Remorse, heavy and cold like sand, sank his body deeper and deeper into the hot, sweaty sheets.

Connor's emotions were scraped raw. The tape reran in his mind over and over again. What if someone finds out? Stop-don't-think-it.

I was driving the car!

The returning thought sent vibrations of pain gushing throughout his body. Connor sat up and sweat streamed past his navel. He looked over at Kayo who was still asleep and wondered how he was doing it. Connor threw back the covers and swung his feet out of bed and onto the floor. He feared sleep and thought maybe a hot shower would relax him.

Inside the bathroom, waves of cold wafted up through the tiled floor and Connor shivered. The bathroom was very bright. There were two sinks, one on each wall, facing each other with about ten feet of space in between. Connor stepped to the shower, kicked the door open, and stuck his hand inside, instinctively turning the right knob for "Hot." The water sprinkled his retreating hand; Connor shook it, then popped open the mirrored cabinet above the sink. He grabbed the can of shaving cream and lathered up. Connor looked up into the mirror and the sight terrified him. Instead of his own face he saw dark brown skin, a broad nose that commanded the entire face, eyes that were droopy, puffy, and open in half-moons like a beat-up fighter.

"Friar Pete," Connor whispered in disbelief. He grabbed his eyes with both hands and began frantically pinching and massaging them. All he could hear was the rushing, splashing sound of the hot shower. Connor took deep breaths and his chest fought him with every inhale and exhale. "No! No!" He pounded the sink with his fist. The lather was now in his eyes, burning. Connor grabbed the doorknob. His sweaty palm slipped off. He lunged at the door with both hands. His thoughts accused: Your fault! Your fault!

Finally the door opened and Connor stumbled into the hall. "Kayo!"

Elizabeth stood next to the bed, fully dressed, staring outside, unable to sleep. She picked at the chipping paint on the windowsill. A pile of the shattered white shells lay at her feet. She stared out the window, trying to keep from thinking. The recent events had put death on her mind and conjured up guilt from the past. It began to rain outside and the drops against the window rolled and curved and turned into a muddy brown color. The strings of color whirled and formed the outlines of an empty chair. She shuddered. It was Meghan's chair. God, I miss you, Meghan. I only wish that . . . that it hadn't happened.

But it had happened. They had been sitting out in the

backyard, Meghan and Elizabeth. The chairs were made of wicker that had gotten ratty over the years. If you leaned too far back in the center chair, you'd find yourself taking a slow tumble backward. That was Elizabeth's favorite chair. It was like being on an amusement-park ride. Meghan was sitting in the chair that wobbled to the left, playing with her blocks. It was exceptionally hot that day. Meghan was using glue and blocks to build a bridge. She stuck her tongue out of the side of her mouth in intense concentration. Sweat was pouring down her face and Meghan licked at the salty bitterness.

Elizabeth could see herself and her sister Meghan so clearly. She could smell the grass as she rolled closer and closer to the table. Head or feet. Elizabeth watched herself get up and bounce in her favorite chair. Meghan was so stingy and antsy when she started playing with those silly old blocks. Once she started, she wouldn't stop to play tag or dolls or anything. Elizabeth watched her small body rocking the chair from side to side. Time for a ride! Her feet went back, heel after head. She felt a snag, just for a moment. "Look, Meghan," she yelled from the ground, "see how much fun it is?" Meghan was crying, running in the house. "What's wrong, Meghan?" Scattered in the grass beneath the lawn table were the remains of Meghan's bridge. "I didn't mean to do it, honest."

Her mother was now running toward the table from the house in staggered, rushed movements. Her blue eyes were shooting sparks. She was wearing an apron and the pink bunny slippers Elizabeth had given her last Christmas. Her long blond hair bounced and flickered in the sunlight. She stopped at the table, grabbing Elizabeth up from the ground by the elbow.

Big wrinkled hands, gooey and hard from being in dish-washing liquid, slapped Elizabeth. The cool hardness left a wet spot on her cheek. Tears added more wetness. That shattering voice: "How many times has your father told you not to play in that chair like that?" Before Elizabeth could answer, she spanked her wrists. Elizabeth could feel the stinging now against the back of her hands. Now she could see herself parallel with her mother and she could smell that stuff Daddy told her mother not to drink in the apron strings. Why was it okay for her to disobey? Meghan was gloating from behind their mother's hips. Their mother forced Elizabeth back into the chair and told her not to move until Daddy came home. She kissed Meghan and walked back to the house. Elizabeth just sat there and stared at her little sister. A big crybaby. Elizabeth turned away and crossed her arms. I'm telling Daddy on both of them.

Meghan began playing with her blocks again. Elizabeth angrily stared at her smudged shoelaces. Meghan grabbed her and began waving her hands back and forth frantically. Elizabeth turned away. "I'm not playing with you!" Meghan grabbed at her own throat. Squeezing. "I'm not playing with you I said!" Elizabeth crossed her arms. Meghan's face seemed to blow up in front of her eyes. Cheeks straining, blue-black. Her eyelids snapped closed, popped open. Her neck scrunched up and she reached for Elizabeth, pleading.

Something was wrong! Elizabeth got up from the table and ran into the house. By now she was frightened, terribly frightened. She grabbed her mother and tugged. "Meghan is looking weird!" That's all she had been able to say, and the way she said it had been enough.

Everything that happened next was a blur. The only thing Elizabeth could remember after that was the men who came with the narrow bed on wheels. They put Meghan on it and put all these plastic tubes everywhere. They even gave her a shot, and Elizabeth started to tell them that Meghan didn't like shots, that shots made her cry. Don't make my sister cry. But she didn't and they gave Meghan the shot. And Elizabeth had been amazed because Meghan didn't cry, she didn't even flinch. Nothing. Meghan wasn't doing anything, except turning colors. When she turned white, Mommy started to scream. Elizabeth fainted.

Later, the doctor said that it was a piece of dried-up glue that had gotten caught in her throat. The strain of the heat and the dryness of her throat made it lodge there. She had choked to death. Death by choking. All these years, Elizabeth had disputed that. It was death by pettiness.

The sound of the phone ringing snapped Elizabeth to attention. She looked at Michelle all balled up into a knot in her bed and answered the phone.

"Hello?" She spoke in a cracked voice. She grabbed the receiver with both hands, eyes widening. Her teeth gritted against each other. "Oh Connor, no!"

Michelle's body drew in even tighter.

"You must be scared to death. Yeah, she's here." Elizabeth touched Michelle. "Connor needs to talk to you."

Michelle pushed the phone away.

"Michelle!"

She jerked the covers over her head and rolled up against the wall.

"Connor," Elizabeth said into the receiver, "um, she's too upset to talk. Yeah, okay, I'll meet you now."

Michelle heard Elizabeth's feet dragging around the room, then the door slamming, and she buried her face in the pillow. "Lord, please forgive us. We didn't mean it. Help us make it through this, Lord, please. . . . Amen."

Michelle squeezed the pillow tighter. And for a minute, a soothing tranquility blanketed her. But before she could burrow into that calm, her teeth began to chatter and her eyelids stung as if someone was poking them with hot daggers.

She saw her father: tall, stocky, his robes snug and sleek around his body. His soft, sleepy eyes seemed to know all. Michelle saw herself as a child standing in front of him in the church basement, her six-year-old hands clawed around two silver dollars, asking herself why she had to put one of them in the collection plate.

"Now baby," she heard his deep, gravelly voice, "I'm going to tell you nobody, not even God, can make you do the right thing. All God can do is make you *know* the right thing. The choice is up to you."

Michelle looked at the tray, which was the same shiny color as her silver dollars. She looked up at her father and knew what she should do. She leaned up on her tippy-toes in squeaky patent leather shoes. Her tight little fist popped open and the coin clanged as it hit the bottom of the tray.

"God loves a cheerful giver," Daddy said. The three missing teeth seemed to enhance Michelle's smile. "I knew you'd do the right thing."

Michelle felt the sob building up in her throat and she fought to hold it back. But the swelling and aching bouncing against her vocal cords was too much. Her lips gave way and sobs erupted from her body, filling the infinite space of guilt.

Squad cars were everywhere. Smoke rising from the hoods and beams of flashing red lights swirled up into the sky. The police officers were searching everything with their eyes and fingers. Their voices mingled and flowed freely, competing with the murmur of the river.

"Pull! Whoa! Let some of that water run off."

"Okay!"

Radio static in between messages: "Sizz. . . . Unit Four . . . possible robbery in progress. . . . Sizz . . ."

The slick, oily cables squeaked from the pressure of the load, and water dripped down freely.

"Drop it!"

Grey water gushed from his mouth along with small bits of paper and a penny. His entire body was bloated and huge. All the exposed skin was black, rubbery, and slick. Water dribbling out from under puffy eyelids looked like pus oozing from boils. The policemen stepped back, then stepped forward. Death was more outlandish than anything in life and that attracted and repelled them at the same time.

Sergeant Mike Nickelson stopped his car at the opening of the street. His face was flabby around the jaws. His eyes were a deep, expressionless brown. The bridge of his nose had a big hump in it, courtesy of a ticket scalper who had resisted arrest outside the New Haven Coliseum some three years earlier.

He looked down at the five squad cars scattered along the narrow road and shook his head. "Dumb rookies!" Their cars were parked haphazardly, cutting each other off and preventing a quick exit. Nickelson craned forward and spotted one vehicle parked on the side, wheels turned out for a quick exit. He smiled, knowing that it was Jim Brady's unit, the smartest rookie on the force. Nickelson began driving toward the ones who were kneeling down by the swollen body. He couldn't believe that he was getting stuck with training all the rookies by himself. The old shields knew no mercy. "Here comes the kindergarten teacher!" Nickelson had gone to the chief and begged for a new assignment but instead got a rebuttal: "Break 'em in, Nickelson. And this next case is perfect. It looks like it could be a cheap murder or suicide so that'll be a good chance to sharpen the rookies up."

Nickelson lit a cigarette and got out of the car. His police hat was covered with used plastic from the dry cleaner's. He wore an old, tight, beige trench coat that made his body pouch in spots. It was his lucky coat. He had escaped death twice while wearing it: a dope addict misfired at point-blank range and a robber got his knife hung up in the lining. Nickelson sauntered over to the rookies.

They all scrambled to their feet.

"You guys get this body out?"

"Yes, sir!" they voiced in unison.

"Yeah, Sarge, it was rough," one rookie named Maxwell added. "But I told the guys all we had to do was get those cables and hook them up across that fishing beam over there and slam-bam-thank-you-ma'am."

Nickelson wiped his mouth and looked at Maxwell's blue eyes and flat, tiny red ears, his thin body and chubby face. He still had pimples. "Well, Maxwell, that was a way to get the body out, but did you ever think that there might have been some evidence in, say, his pockets? Maybe there was a gun and you just fucking put it at the bottom of the river!"

Maxwell looked around wild-eyed. "Yeah, we-we thought of that but we just didn't think this was that kind of a case. Right, fellas?"

The other rookies nodded, except for Jim Brady.

Brady was short and small built, but his arms, back, and legs were muscular. His thin black hair stuck out from under his cap like straw, crowning his pale face. Brady's small, piercing eyes stared ahead and he remained silent with his hands folded across his chest.

Nickelson looked down at the body for the first time. "What?" Nickelson got down on one knee and examined the face closer. His mind took him back weeks before when he had routed this same man outside the Yale campus . . .

"What are you doing hanging around here all the time? Look, I don't like it!" Nickelson said, grabbing Friar Pete by the arm. He examined Friar Pete's torn, weathered jacket littered with holes big enough to put your feet through.

Elizabeth came running through the gate. "Hey, Daddy, that's Friar Pete. He's okay!"

Friar Pete turned and smiled at Elizabeth. He knew all of the seniors. He was so soaked that the light rain was now beading him from head to toe. He placed his hand over his heart and said in a jolly voice, "Elizabeth, how are classes going?"

"Fine, Friar Pete. This is my father—Sergeant Mike Nickelson," she said, walking up beside him.

Nickelson had a way of licking his lips before he was about to speak, as if he was greasing them so the words would slide out smoothly. "This is police business."

"But Daddy—"

"Listen, fella. I want you to stop hanging around here."

"But I am a part of this institution. I am a professor of Yale and my course of expertise is Life."

"Listen, the parents of these kids are paying fifteen thousand dollars a year for their kids to go to this school and they don't need a bum to teach them anything!"

"I prefer the term 'displaced refugee,' thank you. And please, I *have* had a home since my mother's womb. Surely you don't think I was born into this? I am one of millions with a disease. It's not terminal like cancer and it's not contagious like leprosy. It's a disease that rots society and there is a cure—they just haven't bothered to find it yet."

"Maybe you need to go down to the station. There's a couple of doctors there who'd like to talk to you."

"Just because someone has lost their home and their job does not mean they have lost their marbles too."

"He's got you there, Daddy," Elizabeth said as if she were keeping score.

Nickelson frowned at his daughter, then addressed Friar Pete. "Listen, you have nowhere to stay, so it looks like you're loitering."

"Looks can be deceiving. All that glitters is not gold. Shakespeare. Do you know which play?"

"Um-huh." Nickelson looked at Elizabeth.

"Police business, remember?"

Nickelson sighed. "Alright, you better watch yourself around here or I'll personally come and bust you myself, understand?"

"Sir, your concern about my welfare gives me faith in the world. I thank you." Friar Pete bowed from the waist, then turned toward the university. "And my public thanks you."

"Aww, give me a break!" Nickelson said waving Friar Pete away . . .

"Sarge?" one of the rookies asked, bringing Nickelson back to the present. "Hey Sarge, you know him?"

"I saw him bumming around town a couple of times." Nickelson took a penknife out of his pocket and began probing the insides of the soggy pockets. He fished out two dollar bills, two playing cards, a small book simply titled *Sonnets*, and a tiny burlap pouch. Nickelson peeled it open and two pristine pearls rolled out into the palm of his hand.

"That's a weird collection of stuff," Maxwell noted.

"Bag it," Nickelson grunted, then stood back up. "Somebody brief me."

"Well, Sarge, it's like this—" Maxwell piped up.

"Anybody but you, Maxwell."

Grant stepped forward, pulled out a pad from his back pocket, and began, "At about six o'clock this morning, a Hart Jenson was showing his grandson where he used to come fish as a kid. Jenson and his grandson threw in a couple of hooks and snagged the body. They called the police." Grant flipped his pad closed and stepped back.

"Say, Bates!" Nickelson picked out a rookie hiding in the back.

"Um, me?" Bates asked timidly.

Nickelson took one huge step and was nose to nose with him. "You can't be hard-of-hearing. All rookies are tested up and down before they hit the street. You ought to be able to hear a dog pissing a block away!"

The other rookies started to snicker.

Brady seized the opportunity to shine. "Sarge, I would like to offer my assessment."

Bates glared at him. Nickelson nodded the go-ahead.

"The victim looks to be between fifty to fifty-five years of age. At first I thought he was drunk and fell into the water, drowning by accident. But on closer inspection I believe the deceased was a victim of a hit-and-run. I spotted some unusual tracks and skid marks on the way in."

"Fuckin' good! I spotted tracks too," Nickelson encouraged.

"I'm sure there was more than one person involved too."

"How do you know that?"

Brady walked around two of the other rookies and headed for the feet of the corpse. He picked up the heels and twisted the legs over. "See? The back of the shoes have scuff marks that show the body was dragged at some point. It'd take more than one person to drag and dump this guy in the river."

"I'm likin' it," Nickelson said admiringly.

"Sizz. . . . Unit Ten . . . emergency. . . . Sizz."

Nickelson pointed to two rookies in the back. "Roll!"

"Yeah, but we're not done here," one of them spoke up.

"We can handle a dead bum without you, I guess. This ain't Jimmy Hoffa here! Get going," Nickelson yelled, stuffing balled-up fists in his pockets. "And don't disappoint me."

The two officers turned and jogged toward their unit. Nickelson barked at the other rookies. "Look down by the river and see if you can find anything. And one of you call back to the station and get a man out here to get a cast of these tire tracks."

They all scattered. Brady and Maxwell headed for the nearest unit. They both grabbed the door handle at the same time and glared at each other. Nickelson chuckled to himself. "Maxwell, let Brady make the call. He found the tracks!" Maxwell sneered at Brady and slowly made his way over to the river. Nickelson watched as Unit Ten finally drove around the last car and pulled away, siren now blaring. He glanced back at the cars and something caught his eye.

It looked like a yellow ball. He walked over to it and knelt down. It was dirty and tousled, with tire tracks running all over it. Nickelson yelled over his shoulder. "Hey, you guys!"

The wind and Unit Ten's siren muffled his voice to a whisper. Nickelson began unraveling the yellow ball. He pulled the arms out. A yellow sea slicker of beaten sealskin. Fish netting in the hood. Decades had weathered the arms slick; the square eyelets around the sleeves were slightly tinged with rust. The outline of something blue was shading the right pocket. Nickelson pulled out a thin sea-blue exam booklet, half the length of a standard notebook. On the cover it read "Elizabeth Nickelson. Senior. Quiz. American Lit 335." His heart fluttered. What would she be doing down here? Nickelson looked at the unique sea slicker in his hands. He didn't recognize it at all. He glared at the exam booklet; recognition of her handwriting nearly blinded him.

Brady was now standing beside his car watching Sergeant Nickelson. "Hey, I've seen that coat somewhere," Brady mumbled as he began walking over. He scratched his head, absorbed in thought.

Nickelson stuffed the booklet back into the pocket, crunched the coat up into a ball as tight as a fist, braced it against the side of his leg, and began walking toward his car.

Brady stopped and watched him.

Nickelson opened the back door of his Malibu and tossed the coat on the floor. He turned the collar up on his trench and walked over by the river where the rookies were. "Hey, you guys, come on over here."

They began walking over.

"Just leave Unit Twelve on this assignment. The rest of you will go back on general roster to do regular patrols."

They grumbled.

"Um, Sarge, by the edge there we found a lot of footprints. That means there were others down here," Brady said.

"I just fucking told you that Unit Twelve is going to handle this case! You're not in Unit Twelve."

"Yes, sir."

"Unit Twelve, take over and the rest of you report in for patrol."

Brady walked back to his car with Bates. "This stinks. Even a hit-and-run bum deserves a decent investigation. What gives? Hey, I'll bet Sarge is testing those guys. Hell yeah, and those nuts will screw it up for sure and make us all look bad."

"Aww, let 'em have it," Bates said, opening the squad car door. "It's too much work!"

Brady got in the car and a question pounded inside his brain. I know I've seen that coat somewhere, but where?

Kayo opened his eyes and stared at the ceiling of his bedroom. What Connor had just experienced was terrifying and Kayo had tried to calm him but all he could think to say was, "Don't think about it. It'll be okay!" And Kayo knew that it hadn't been enough, but he was having a hard enough time dealing with this tragedy himself. Right now his heart was beating so hard he could hear it. "But what else could we do?" he whispered to himself, grabbing a fistful of hair and tugging. Kayo turned on his side and buried his head in a small corner of the wall. The darkness, the cool air seeping up through the floor, soothed his face. Dirty cops would have done us in just like they did my Daddy.

Kayo pictured him: tall as a streetlamp, wiry, square-jawed, and always tired from work but not too tired to play with his two sons. Swing me, Daddy! As soon as he picked Kayo up, Ben would come and jump on his back. Kayo could see them all rolling around on the floor. The small rugs from Woolworth's doubled up behind their heads. He could hear their laughter. "I bet Daddy's got something for us!" Tiny hands searching through pockets. Daddy yelling, "Help I'm being robbed!" The last time it was lollipops. "Look Ben!" Ben was riding his father's back like a cowboy on a bronco. His brown eyes got big. Ben reached out and grabbed the lollipops. Daddy snatched them from Ben and held them out to Kayo first. "Ah-ha! Ah-ha! That's what you get!" Kayo smiled at the memory now. Suddenly a tightness gripped his chest. Don't get up, Daddy. Man, just stay there and play with us. If you get up, the cops are going to get you and you'll never come back.

Daddy set Ben aside and straightened up, elbows out resting on his knees.

Kayo tried to lift himself out of the dream but couldn't. The unfolding memory had him caught in a vise.

Daddy rose and headed for the door.

Kayo sucked in air with open-mouthed gasps, kicked his legs, and tried to use his arms that were heavy and round under his body.

Daddy waving 'bye to his boys.

The motion propelled Kayo's body to attention like an electric shock. Kayo looked around the room, chest heaving, sweating, then slowly he dropped his head.

The green across from Phelps Gate was glistening from the brief rain. The back of Connor's pants was wet and sticking to the park bench. The roar of traffic was faint. Connor dropped his head back and hugged the shoulders of the bench.

I can't believe I hit him. Driving too damn fast. No I wasn't! He should have been more careful. I should have been more careful. It was dark. It was slick. The road was not salted. Oh, God, I wish I could talk to you, Mom. And the thought of her nudged Connor's mind back to years ago.

He remembered how he and his brother Timothy as kids would snap at the workers. Connor was only playing a game, imitating his father. He would scrunch up his little brow and bark out orders. He pictured their driver, Wallace, standing there smiling at him. Laughing. But when Timmy joined the game nobody thought it was fun anymore. He was too serious, too much like their father for there to be any humor in it. One day Mom caught them at it and shook them both hard. Connor could see the anger in her eyes now. "We were just playing," Connor sobbed. Timothy just pulled away from her, his eyes flashing guiltlessly, and ran.

I'm sorry, Mom. Connor's eyes were burning with tears.

She looked down at him and brushed the long strands of brown hair from his eyes. "I know you meant no harm, darling. But you have to remember everyone has feelings and you and Timmy have been given a lot of special things so you have to care even more about people's feelings." The warmth from her hands seemed to draw the hurt from him. "You won't forget?"

The memory made Connor rock forward and rest his head on crossed elbows.

"I'm sorry I'm late," Elizabeth said, touching him on the shoulder. "I had a hard time getting to sleep last night."

"Me too. I really need to talk," Connor said, looking up.

Elizabeth plopped down next to him. "Maybe we shouldn't talk just yet . . ."

"Fuck, we killed a man last night!"

"I didn't deserve that," Elizabeth mumbled as her stomach lurched.

"I know. Elizabeth, I just feel so bad I wanna scream."

Elizabeth took her hand and rubbed the back of Connor's neck. "You know, when you called I thought Michelle was wrong for not talking to you."

"I know she's hurting, but so am I." Connor paused. *"I-I was driving the car!"*

"Don't take all the blame, Connor. We were all in the car too. We all had a part in it."

"But I was behind the wheel! That's the same as pulling the trigger. The same as holding the knife!"

"Stop it! It wasn't like that at all. You're making me feel worse!"

"I'm sorry. I'm sorry. I'm just upset." Connor grabbed her hand and squeezed it. "I just feel like . . . well, you know when we used to stop and talk to Friar Pete? Out of everybody, you always seemed like you were really listening. The rest of us were just being entertained, like we were watching a skit on *Saturday Night Live* or something. I can hardly believe it all happened. It felt like my body wasn't mine. It was like I was there but I wasn't there."

"You've got to put it out of your mind, Connor," Elizabeth said. She thought about Meghan's death. "The way to get through it is to not think about it."

"I'll try, but it's going to be hard for all of us."

"That's what I'm going to tell Michelle. She just needs a little space. We all need a little space."

"No, I want us to talk about it so we can all be of one mind about this thing. I don't want one of us losing it."

Elizabeth thought for a second. "Look, we've got to be together whatever we do. If we all feel we should go to the police and 'fess up, then let's do it. We all need to decide together. Let's meet at your society at the end of the week, make it late. Make sure it's empty, okay?"

"Alright, tell Michelle when you go back."

Elizabeth stood up and touched Connor's shoulder. "We've got to live with this hurt, you know?" Again she thought back to her sister's death. "It'll stop. You just pray that it stops hurting soon and then you just hold on till it does."

Connor stood up, they embraced, and neither said anything more as they walked away in opposite directions.

Elizabeth reached the corner and began crossing the street when a car came roaring toward her. She jumped back onto the curb.

Nickelson pulled the car over. "Get in."

Elizabeth sensed his tension, jogged around to the passenger's side, and got in. "Hi Daddy."

He looked at her strangely but said nothing as he pulled the car back into the traffic. "Where'd you go last night?"

"I'm sorry I forgot to call, Daddy. I went over to the Raven's Nest for a while," Elizabeth answered nervously.

"With who?" Nickelson said hitting the gas, speeding through a reddish-yellow light.

"What's wrong, Daddy?"

"Answer me! Who were you with?"

"Michelle, Connor, and Kayo! Who am I always with?"

"How long did you stay?" He stopped at the light.

She didn't answer.

He looked at the way she held her jaw. He could see her nervously puffing air on the inside of her mouth. Nickelson slammed on the accelerator when the light changed. The motion jerked her forward. He asked again: "How long did you stay?"

She wanted to lie, but couldn't. "Till the place closed."

"Your mascot Friar Pete was killed last night."

The words exploded in Elizabeth's mind, then ricocheted around her brain. She closed her eyes and said as calmly as she could, "I'm so sorry to hear that."

Nickelson slammed on the brakes, swerved the car over to the side, and parked. "What happened?"

"Nothing happened," she managed to whisper.

"Don't lie to me," he said, gripping the steering wheel tighter.

"I don't know what you mean. We-we went back to school, that's all."

Nickelson reached down under the backseat and pulled up the yellow sea slicker. "This look familiar? It's yours."

The sight of it slapped Elizabeth senseless. There were mud stains on it and tire tracks. She swallowed and regained her composure. "It's not mine. It's Michelle's. She found it at one of those antique shops she's always browsing in."

Nickelson ripped the exam booklet out of the pocket. "And I guess this isn't yours either? This is your exam book and your handwriting!" Nickelson said, shaking it in her face.

"I-I must of left it in the pocket when I-I borrowed the slicker," Elizabeth offered no more.

"Well, I found them this morning down by the river where that bum got killed! You were there! What happened?"

A sob burst from her and emotion exploded inside the car. "We swore not to tell," Elizabeth stuttered. Strands of hair stuck to her cheeks looked like scars. "We swore!"

Nickelson grabbed her shoulders. "Let me help. I'm not mad. So help me I'm not! I know it had to be an accident."

"It was, Daddy. I swear to God it was! Connor was driving and Friar Pete just stepped out of nowhere, Daddy! He-he did! And Connor tried to stop—he tried, but we hit him! And then he was just there, *dead*! Then we got scared, everybody was so scared 'cause-'cause we killed him. But God, we didn't mean it."

Nickelson took her hands and held them against his cheek. "Baby, why didn't you call me? I could of done something."

"I-I wa-was! I-I mean I tried, bu-ut Kayo wouldn't let me . . . he-he grabbed me and said no police . . ."

"So you all threw the body in the river? Thinking nobody would find it?"

"Yeah-ah," she moaned childlike.

"Ssh. Ssh. It'll be okay. Now, you said Connor was driving the car?"

"Mmmm-huh!"

"Okay, think. This next answer is real important."

Her body was now hiccuping up and down as she struggled to stop crying.

"Honey, did you touch the body? Did you help throw it in the river?"

Elizabeth threw her head back and let out a loud, soft moan, then nodded.

Nickelson pulled her toward him. She buried her head in his neck and her tears ran down his back.

"Don't tell your friends that I know anything about this. That's the best way. You all keep this a secret just like you're doing. Don't worry. I'll fix everything."

Chapter 4

BRADY spent the next couple of days trying to remember where he had seen that sea slicker. He walked around talking to himself, kicking garbage cans, and swearing. Where the hell did you see that yellow slicker before? He got a marker and pen and sketched the coat, hoping he could doodle up the answer: long sleeves with little squares around the cuffs. That big hood, with a net or something. Yeah, netting inside. He stared at the drawing.

That night, at home, Brady decided that he was too tense, so he got into his beat-up old Datsun and headed down to the Strip.

"Look out, girl. I need to be seen!" The prostitutes strutting up and down the avenue spotted the car and started jockeying for position.

"Um-un, no! This john is a big tipper and he ain't no freak neither."

Brady slowed down and stared at the five women poised

for his approval. They were all tall. And each one was decked out in bright colors—cherry red, orange, yellow. There was slush around their feet. "Humn," he said, scratching his head. "Aah, the winner is baccalaureate number three." Brady rolled down the window and held up three fingers so they could see.

"Shit!"

The third woman stepped out. Her long blond hair hung just an inch above the slanted back pocket of her pink mini skirt. There was a rip in the black fishnet stockings she wore that exposed the fullness of the inside of her right thigh. Winnie had a girlish face and she was tastefully made up, one of the reasons many of the men chose her. She did and didn't look like a prostitute. As she opened the door to get in, one of the others yelled, "Why don't y'all get married and you can give it to him free?"

Winnie yelled back laughing, "Jealous!" She slammed the door. "Hey, Jim. I've been thinking about you, baby!"

Brady started to rub her thigh hard. He liked the way the net and the flesh combined for a rough yet smooth feeling.

"You're really ready. That's the way I like it," she said, thinking, He'll really tip big tonight. "C'mon, now. Let's go. I don't want to give away any secrets to my competition!"

"Okay, let's go take care of some serious business."

Brady lay flat. His shirt was open, his pants at his ankles. Winnie hovered high above him, licking her thick tongue across hard, huge lips. She blew air through clenched teeth and her lips shook and vibrated like a blender.

Brady caught his breath.

Winnie continued her game, running her motored lips from his navel on down until she whipped up an erection. Then without panties and in a skirt too short to hoist, she straddled him. Winnie began a deformed bump and grind, as if she had been born without bones in the lower half of her body. Her mindless, pedestrian movements caused the muscles around Brady's eyes and cheeks to twitch into funny faces. Winnie cradled a chuckle deep down in the recesses of her throat. Brady moaned softly, feeling his hip bones grinding in their sockets.

It was in the middle of his release that the answer popped into his mind.

The next day Brady walked into the antique shop.

Hanging from the ceiling were posters of Hollywood leading ladies—Garbo, Monroe, Horne. On a row of shelves lining the right side wall were lamps from China with gold sash braids and shades made out of pressed silk and eggshells. On the other side of the room was a clothing rack with everything from hand-tailored waistcoats to poodle sweaters. A long counter in the back held hand-carved jewelry beautiful in its simplicity.

"Can I help you, officer?" Mr. Harrington, the owner, asked while dusting one of the counters. The top of his head was as pale and shiny as a cue ball. He wore round horn-rimmed spectacles that were just coming back in style. "I've seen you in here before. I don't think you were in uniform though," recalling the short, muscular build and the small eyes. Then it hit him: this is the young man who asked whether the place was a junk shop. Harrington spread his hands on the counter palms down. He was not so cheery anymore.

"I'm patrolman Jim Brady. About six months ago I came in here . . . and I saw a yellow sea slicker. Do you remember it? It was real unusual."

"Yes, of course I remember. It was a beautiful old sea slicker. That coat was popular with seamen back in the forties and fifties. Very practical, sturdy. You could hang fishhooks in the little eyelets around the wrists . . ."

"Yeah, yeah. Who did you sell it to?"

"That coat, as I was saying, is a real piece of craftsmanship. It was a rare find."

"Look, I don't fucking care. I just want to know who you sold it to and when!"

Mr. Harrington took off his glasses and searched his back pocket for his handkerchief. "I sold it a few months ago and I don't remember to whom," he said, turning abruptly.

"Listen, old man," Brady said, his right hand latching onto

Harrington's worn collar, "don't be snooty with me and don't disappoint me."

Harrington raised his hands slowly, appealingly. "Um, listen. Just calm down, Officer Brady. My memory comes and goes. I don't remember. So many people come in and out of here."

"You're disappointing me!" Brady said, his anger brewing hotter now.

"Listen, I'm going to call your superiors and complain about your outlandish behavior, young man. I'll have your badge! I know important people!"

"Um, look," Brady said, slowly withdrawing his hand, "I just want a straight answer!"

"The nerve!" Mr. Harrington raged, freedom boosting his courage. "Get out of my shop now!"

"Okay, okay. I'm sorry, alright, I was a little rough there but this is serious business, you know." He started walking backward, facing Harrington. Brady forced a smile as he reached for the door behind him.

It slammed against his knuckles.

"Shit!" Brady brought his bruised hand to his mouth.

"Oh, I'm so sorry," Michelle said, concerned. "Are you hurt?"

His mouth made a sucking sound as he took his knuckles out to speak. "I'm okay!" He examined the pretty girl in front of him, noticing the Yale sweatshirt under her open jacket.

Michelle stepped inside and held the door open for him. "I'm really sorry, officer."

Brady nodded and left the shop, planning to go check on the tire tracks.

Mr. Harrington waited until the door slammed and said, "That is the rudest young man I have ever met!"

Michelle had been trying to study for her exams but couldn't. She had dodged her friends and refused to talk about "it" with them for two days. This morning when Elizabeth went to lift weights she had lowered the boom: all of them were going to meet at Connor's society tomorrow night to talk. Nobody else would be there.

Mr. Harrington was still talking over her thoughts. "That punk comes in here so big and tough and then questions me about a yellow sea slicker I had in here. He wanted to know who I sold it to."

Michelle froze.

Harrington rubbed his bald spot with his hand. "I don't remember who I sold the slicker to. For Christ's sake, that was months ago."

"Listen, um, uhuh, I have to go, Mister Harrington. I'll come back later and browse."

Michelle rushed out of the shop and began running, trying to remember if she had seen the sea slicker around the room at all this morning. She reached the entryway door out of breath and once upstairs she could hardly get the key in the door, her hands were shaking so badly.

Michelle opened the door and yelled, "Elizabeth?" No answer. She threw her jacket off, tossed it on the floor, and examined the coat rack in the corner. Coats, jackets, sweaters, and windbreakers were piled on top of each other in a hulking lump. Michelle began grabbing coats, shaking them, then tossing them over her shoulder. She heard the door open but didn't stop.

"What are you doing?"

The rack was stripped bare. There was a pile of colors in the middle of the floor, running together like brackish water. Michelle fell to her knees and rummaged through the middle of it; the material seemed to swallow her up.

"What is the matter with you?" Elizabeth said, kneeling down beside her. She grabbed Michelle's arm and began pulling her out. Michelle's body was limp from fear and Elizabeth dragged her to the side. She could hear her friend sobbing.

"We're going to jail! You musta dropped my slicker that night! It's not here!"

Elizabeth sat back on the floor and thought of her father pulling the sea slicker up from under the car seat.

"A policeman went to the antique shop asking about it!" Michelle said, closing her eyes.

"My father . . ."

"It wasn't your father, it was some young guy!"

Elizabeth grabbed Michelle by the shoulder roughly. "You talked to him?"

"No! I saw him on the way out. Mister Harrington told me he was asking about the slicker. I was hoping that it was here! God, I was hoping."

"Listen, don't worry," Elizabeth said.

"This is serious! This isn't some protest or boycott of the Co-op. You can't write a letter about this! We are in big trouble."

"Shut up and listen! Daddy has the coat and he said he would fix everything!"

Michelle's eyes snapped open wide. On her hands and knees, she began backing away from Elizabeth, whispering, "You told! You told!"

Elizabeth pleaded with her eyes and voice, "I had to! Daddy had the slicker. He found it by the river! I had to tell. Daddy can protect us. My father can fix it!"

"Maybe we should just go to the police and confess," Michelle said wearily.

"No!" Elizabeth said in a low, menacing tone. She crawled over to Michelle and turned her. "It's way too late for all that. We're all in it. Daddy's in it. Now, he said he'd take care of it and he's the biggest guy on the whole force. I'm going to call and tell him what happened to you right now."

"Give me a break! This isn't a scraped knee!"

Elizabeth reached out and shook her hard. "Daddy said he'll fix it and he will."

Michelle looked into her eyes and saw confidence behind the anger there. She nodded.

"And we will not say anything about this to the guys, *understand*?!"

Elizabeth released Michelle when she nodded Okay.

* * *

The door to the evidence office was ajar and through that crack Jim Brady could see Kurt Connelly reading the newspaper with his feet up on the counter, his shirt open four buttons down, a cigar hanging out of the side of his mouth. His pants legs were too long and the hems were dusty. His shoes were caked with slush and mud. His stomach was as round and firm as a potbellied stove.

"Yeah, kid, who sent ya?" Connelly mumbled gruffly.

"Nobody sent me." Brady leaned the flat of his knuckles on the countertop. "I'm Officer Jim Brady and I'm here to check on some evidence for a case I'm working on."

"Case number?"

"Three-one-three. I'm interested in—"

"You're not interested in nothing on that case," Connelly said, folding the paper up neatly.

Brady held his pad over to where Connelly could see. "It's case number 313 and I'm interested in the molds of the tire tracks."

Connelly didn't even bother to look. He stood up and said, "You're not assigned to that case. Do your own work."

"I came down here to check on something, alright? You take care of your business and I'll take care of mine!"

Connelly leaned across the counter until his face was three inches from Brady's. "Kid, I was doing this when you were trying to learn how to piss standing up. Don't come in here in your new uniform trying to tell me how to do my job, boy. Don't you do it!"

Brady felt his face tighten. He didn't want to back down and give Connelly something to brag about to all the other old shields. "I want to see the evidence for that case."

Connelly smirked and sat back down. "Regulations. Only the supervising officer and the officers working on a case review evidence."

"Regulations also say you're not supposed to smoke back here and that an officer should be neat and clean at all times. You don't tell, I won't."

The chair slammed against the floor, his cigar popped out of his mouth, and Connelly's hands were now in Brady's collar. "Listen, asshole, don't fucking threaten me unless you're ready to go all the way. I've given this department a hell of a lot of years and I've gotten nothing but a kick in the ass and a bullshit assignment for it. If you think you can kick this old man's ass, then you can look at anything you want back there in that cage."

Brady felt his knees buckle a little bit as the hatred flew in his face. He slowly threw out his arms. "Okay, man! Okay!"

Connelly stooped to pick up his cigar, righted the chair slowly, and sat back down, never taking his eyes off Brady. He put the cigar butt back in his mouth. "Little prick!"

Brady eased away, letting the door slam behind him while vowing to return.

Connelly waited a few seconds, then picked up the phone under the counter. "Hello, Mike? Kurt. Yeah, that young pup was down here. I gave him what for and sent him on his way. You're right. He's too cocky. I took some of the starch out of him. My pleasure. Need anything else, just give me a call."

Nickelson hung up the phone and leaned back in his chair. His office was small; just a box-shaped room with a desk, phone, two chairs, and a file cabinet. On his desk were baby pictures of Meghan and Elizabeth and his favorite family picture of them all on the hayride at Boone's Farm amusement park. A clown dressed in faded denim overalls had taken the picture just as their car pulled up to the bottom gate. Elizabeth was laughing, showing all mouth, tickled by the speedy, jerky movements. Meghan had cried through the entire ride despite her Daddy hugging her tight and she squeezing his index finger. The clown saw her tears and did a back flip, his red hair flopping, his big yellow shoes like huge gourds spinning. Meghan had let out a loud, deep laugh that echoed the fear she had just endured and the amusement and relief seemingly suspended in midair before her. Her mother and father, both smiling, looked and touched her at the same time. The yellow gourds landing and the bulb flashing sounded like a drum and cymbal. Nickelson traced the outline of Meghan's smile and then Elizabeth's curls with the eraser of the pencil. I lost one baby, he thought. I'm not going to lose two.

Nickelson pushed his chair back and opened the file cabinet. As soon as he got the call from Elizabeth about what happened to Michelle at the antique store, he knew what he had to do. They didn't know the cop's name, but it had to be Brady. The complaint from the shop owner was confirmation; the call from Kurt, the clincher. He slammed the drawer shut and threw the file on the desk. He kept one on all his men. He wanted to know what he was dealing with. Weaknesses. Strengths. Nickelson couldn't rely on their on-the-job character alone, he needed to know where they came from and how they acted when there wasn't a shield hanging on their chest. Nickelson flipped open the file: Jim Brady, age twenty-five. Childhood in an orphanage. Good grades. Nickelson read a note he had penciled in on the side: "Got lost on outing, found and befriended by Officer Sam Monroe. Monroe later killed in a boating accident." He fumbled through the pages until he got to the handwritten notes in the back. Nickelson had tailed all the rookies under his command. Just making notes of their habits and who they saw. (Everyone else was pretty boring, although Maxwell loved to play poker.) Nickelson had tailed Brady for almost a month after he had joined the force, shocked that he had a thing for prostitutes. He figured a young guy like Brady could find a nice girl without a problem, but all his action was with hookers. That was bad news. But he'd planned to school the kid. Brady was smart and had the nose and guts to be a detective. A habit like whore hopping could leave a big hole for somebody to put their foot through. Nickelson never thought he would be the one to do it, Nickelson shuffled through the loose sheets of legal paper, cab receipts, and finally found the slip of paper with the information he wanted. He read the name aloud: "Winnie Stelman."

The wheels made a grinding sound on the pavement and the Malibu's muffler alternately spit and scraped the ground.

Nickelson saw the prostitutes milling around and he pulled up just enough to let the front of his car be seen. He spotted Winnie. He opened the car door and held up the appropriate fingers, just as he had seen Brady do. Winnie came running toward the car.

"Hello, honey, what can I do for you?"

Nickelson looked at her exposed thighs, red as a fire from being in and out of the cold. He felt a stirring inside but checked himself.

"Now, honey, we can talk price later . . ." Winnie said, hunching her skirt up higher.

"Police officer," Nickelson hissed, flashing his shield.

Winnie hit the window with her fist. "Fuck me."

"That's why you're in trouble now," Nickelson said with a laugh.

Winnie leaned forward, her breasts straining against the tight half T-shirt she wore. The coat of rabbit fur fluttered under her chin. "Listen, I just got busted awhile ago. Why don't you guys pick on somebody else?"

Nickelson cranked the engine. "Let's take a ride and work something out." She got in and the car began pulling out. "There's a short, stocky guy with stringy black hair that likes you a lot."

"I think I know him. What'd he do, spend all the alimony on sweet Winnie here?"

"That's my business. All I want you to do when he comes to get you is drive down this street here and go in that alley. Do that, and I'll make sure your next bust doesn't go on your sheet. I'll be watching the next few nights."

"Well, if watching turns you on, baby . . ."

"Cut the shit and do like I say, bitch!"

"Well, what are you going to do?" Winnie asked. "I don't want no trouble."

"Don't worry about it. It's nothing that will get you in trouble and nothing you need to know about."

"I've got to cover my ass—this is risky! If he finds out I

helped he might come back and get me. A little cash would help me hide out awhile,'' she said with a pouty smile.

''Look, Winnie, do it or I'll bust your ass so fast and so often you won't know whether you're coming or going. Just get the guy to pull into the alley and cut the shit. He won't know you had anything to do with it. He won't bother you either. Here's, ah, fifty dollars for your trouble. Just do like you're told and keep your big mouth shut.''

Winnie took the fifty. ''Um, Jim never comes until real late so, um, wanna kill some time? Loosen up?'' She took her hand and rubbed the inside of his leg.

Nickelson felt himself getting hard. He swerved the car and took a wide left.

''Wait a minute—don't kill us!'' Winnie screamed, now halfway down in the seat, clutching the seat belt strap and trying to pull herself back up.

''Just go back and wait for him, do like I told you, and keep your hands to yourself until I drop you off!''

''Okay! Okay!'' Winnie said, sticking her hands into her jacket pockets.

After Nickelson dropped her off, he circled the block and parked on the side to wait. Nickelson looked over at the few prostitutes still trying to catch. He shivered for hours in the car.

The next night, sitting in his car was even colder. Get horny Brady. I'm ready to fucking get this over with. ''Hel-lo!'' Nickelson said as he eyeballed the car pulling up. Brady's Datsun. Nickelson cranked his engine as Winnie made her way over to the car. They drove off. Nickelson hit the gas pedal and followed.

''Well you're in a bad mood,'' Winnie said, turning sideways in her seat. ''And you sure took your sweet time getting here tonight!''

''Why? You got something else to do?'' Brady said sarcastically.

''I got something special in mind, a little different than our usual, and I *know* it'll get you to smiling again. Pull into this alley coming up.''

He did as she asked.

"Honey, let me give you a little something new . . ."

"I've told you before, no freak stuff."

"Nothing freaky, babe. It'll loosen up those tight jaws of yours tonight."

Nickelson slowed his car and parked. He reached down and pulled up his right pants leg. He pulled out a small bag stuck down in the side of his sweat sock. He had taken a few packets from a small drug bust last year. In the heat of the moment, while the other officers were busy rounding up the suspects, Nickelson had palmed a few packets. At the time, he wasn't sure why. It was risky. But something told him he might need the stuff one day to drop on somebody, like the throw-away piece most of the cops had in their cars.

Nickelson got out of his car, walked over, and banged on the Datsun's window. It was pretty fogged up, so he pulled out his badge and stuck it in the only clear spot in the upper right corner.

He heard Brady say, "Oh shit!"

"Open up!"

Slowly, the door opened. Brady was looking down, stuffing his shirt in his pants. Brady, still not looking up, began: "Hey, listen. I need to talk to yo—"

Winnie was getting out on the other side of the car.

"Sarge! I can explain . . ."

"Shut up!" Nickelson barked at Brady. He looked at Winnie on the other side. "Don't let me catch you around here again!"

"Yes, officer." Winnie made sure she showed a frightened eye to Brady, then she turned and ran.

"Sarge, let me explain," Brady begged, getting out of the car.

"Move," Nickelson said, pushing Brady aside. He leaned into the car and stuck his hand that had the package of cocaine palmed in it under the driver's seat. He fiddled around and came out dangling the package. "Dropped your stuff, Brady."

"That ain't my stuff, Sarge! That lousy whore! It must be hers."

"You're out," Nickelson said, pointing a finger. "I want a resignation in the station tomorrow and I want you packed and gone by the end of the day. Give any reason you want, and take your shit with you," he said, tossing the coke at him.

Brady caught it. "Please, Sarge!"

"That's it!" Nickelson said, turning to walk back to his car.

Brady slammed his fist on top of the car and cried: "It's not mine! Hell, you're going to kick me off the force for getting a little pussy? I'm sorry, Sarge! Okay? Goddamn it, can't you see I'm sorry!"

Nickelson kept walking.

"Motherfucker." Brady looked around and grabbed a beat-up can. It whizzed past Nickelson's ear.

Nickelson stopped, stiffening with the thought of starting back, but instead he began walking away again.

"I idolized you! I thought you were the end-all! The best fuckin' cop around! I wanted to be like you, *motherfucker*! It's not over! You're not going to finish me!"

The inside of the cellar of the Lion's Den was misty and damp. It was well lit with small shaded lamps. The room was circular and made of stone. King-sized wooden chairs, evenly spaced, lined the wall. Connor pulled out four of them and motioned for Kayo, Elizabeth, and Michelle to sit down. Michelle was the last to sit, her face frozen with dread.

Kayo straddled the chair backward and thought it best to say something, anything. "Man, Connor, what do you guys do down here?"

Connor sat down. "It's our induction room. A secret ceremony is held down here."

Elizabeth pulled at her bangs. "Oh, that's interesting."

"Yeah," Kayo spoke up.

Michelle rolled her eyes, folded her legs, and looked down at the floor.

Connor got up, walked over, and stood behind Michelle.

He put pressure on the back of the chair with his body. She ignored him.

Kayo hung both arms over the top of his chair and rested his chin. "I don't guess we all came down here to just stare at each other in this ugly, cold-ass cellar. So why don't we get to the point. I'll start."

Connor sat down next to Michelle and his shoulders slumped in relief.

"We did something that—"

Michelle stood up.

"Where are you going?" Elizabeth shouted.

"Sit down, girl!" Kayo commanded.

Michelle sat back down and crossed her legs.

Connor touched her ankle. "If we talk it'll be better."

Michelle clenched her lips tighter.

"What we did was terrible," said Kayo. "But it was an accident."

"It's something we'll have to live with!" said Connor.

Michelle was rocking back and forth in her chair, clutching her elbows.

"But it was an accident!" Kayo continued. "So we can't let it ruin our lives. Nothing can bring Friar Pete back. You can't let death ruin your life, you just can't."

Michelle sucked her teeth.

"You got something you want to say?" Kayo challenged.

Michelle simply wagged her foot and looked down at the floor.

"Look at us!" Connor shouted. "You've been distant like this ever since it happened. Talk to us, Michelle!"

"Michelle"—Elizabeth scooted her chair over closer to her best friend—"we're all feeling really bad."

"If we all just talk about it for one last time, then it'll be easier to put it behind us. Don't you see?" Kayo pleaded.

"Right," Connor said, nodding his head.

Michelle continued to look at the floor.

Connor yanked her chair, then tilted forward and spoke low and angrily. "I tried to talk to you and you just blew me off!

We're all hurting in this room. Your feelings aren't any more precious than anyone else's! We've got to live with something ugly here''—Connor stopped to take a breath—''or else we can decide differently. I was driving.'' His voice cracked. ''I'll take the whole responsibility.''

Stillness crept into the room like an early-morning ache in the bones. The words shaped the self-sacrificing moment. Everyone was numb and only their eyes seemed able to judge. Connor looked at them with complete giving. They looked at him with an all-encompassing admiration as if they were seeing something rare and fleeting like an eclipse or a comet.

''You'd do that,'' Elizabeth stated, weighing the nobility and the consequences of it.

''We can't let him do that!'' Kayo said, glaring at Michelle.

''I-I don't want that! I'm just scared!'' she whined.

''We're all scared,'' Connor said, clawing the air.

''Because it's all our faults and we've got to stick together and keep this secret,'' Kayo said urgently, leaning forward.

''Forever,'' Connor said.

''And,'' Elizabeth nodded, ''no matter what nightmares we may have, we will not talk about this again.''

''Alright!'' Michelle sobbed, looking around at her friends.

Connor moved and hugged her around the neck. Elizabeth and Kayo went to them and they all huddled together in comfort.

Chapter 5

THE campus was quiet; only the wind rushed about the grounds. Elizabeth was standing just outside Phelps Gate with her suitcase, waiting for her father. She was one of the last students to leave for Christmas break. She was dreading three weeks at home with her mother and the clashes that surely would arise. Elizabeth promised herself now that she would do everything possible to avoid them. "I'm going to have a great Christmas," she willed out loud to herself.

"You are," Nickelson said, picking up the suitcase. "You are going to have a great Christmas, honey."

The drive home was quick. When they stepped inside the house, the smell of cooking food greeted them at the door. She turned and spoke over her shoulder, "Daddy, how did you talk her into fixing dinner?"

"He didn't have to talk me into it. It was my idea," her mother, Mary, said from the doorway of the kitchen. Her square jaw was set firmly in a face that liquor had aged too quickly. "Hurry and set the table."

"Is this a trick?" Elizabeth whispered to her father.

"Trick? She's been off that mess for two weeks. Maybe it'll last," her father laughed nervously.

Elizabeth saw something in his eyes. She wasn't sure whether it was hope or relief or . . . excitement. Yes, he was excited about possibly having a wife again.

"Hurry up," Nickelson said, steering Elizabeth into the dining room. "I have to work later."

"Aww, Daddy, the first night I'm home!"

"It's just tonight. I'll be home tomorrow morning, early."Nickelson grabbed Elizabeth's arm and spoke firmly in her ear. "Listen, the two of you should talk."

"Okay. I just don't want us to be disappointed again, is all."

Elizabeth set the table and the food was brought out.

"Real, real nice," Nickelson admired. "I'll say grace."

The words seemed to fade away behind Elizabeth's thoughts: God, let her stay straight. Please God. Let her stay straight.

". . . Amen," Nickelson said, raising his head.

Mary handed him the lasagna. "Try this first. I used a special recipe."

"Okay," he said, taking the dish from her. "Oh Elizabeth, we have to pick out a tree."

"Let's do it tomorrow afternoon," she said, taking the tray from him.

"Shoot, I have an appointment," Mary said, uncovering steaming french green beans.

Elizabeth scooped the food out and onto her plate. "That's okay. Daddy and I always do it by ourselves."

Nickelson kicked her under the table.

"Um, but we can wait for you, Mom."

"No, that's okay."

"No, really I-I *want* you to decorate the tree too."

Mary looked up at both of them and said with feeling, "Alright, wait for me."

The rest of the dinner went quickly, Elizabeth telling her parents about the Yale-Harvard football game, her father sharing stories about the station. It all seemed relaxed, spontaneous, and just plain wonderful. Before Elizabeth knew it, it was time for her father to go back to work. He kissed both good-bye and whispered in their ears, "Talk."

The door shut behind him and there was silence. Loud. Empty. Awkward. There was five feet between them and Elizabeth stepped back, adding more distance. The clock on the wall struck ten and she sat down. "Gee, it's ten o'clock already."

"Yes, I heard the chime," her mother said, brushing back her shoulder-length blond hair. She jammed long, slender hands deep into her apron pockets.

"Um, the food was really good."

"Thanks. I wanted you to have a really good dinner since the last time you were home things weren't so nice."

"I know." Elizabeth winced.

"Exams go well?"

"Mom, I told you that at the table," she laughed nervously.

Mary tugged at her ear. "I'll go in and wash the dishes."

Elizabeth nodded okay, but then remembered that there was liquor in the kitchen cabinet. "I'll help you."

"No, I'm sure you're tired."

"No, I want to help," Elizabeth said, following her mother into the kitchen. Mary went right to the sink and began running water over the food-stained dishes.

Elizabeth opened the right-hand drawer at her waist and took out two dish towels. She couldn't help glancing at the top cabinet, a favorite hiding place for her mother's liquor. No matter how hard she tried, Elizabeth's eyes kept floating back up to that cabinet.

Out of the corner of her eye, Mary watched her stare up at the cabinet. "Elizabeth, get the dishwashing liquid. It's in the *bottom* cabinet."

Elizabeth hesitated, then opened the top cabinet. "Is it in here, Mom?" No liquor.

Mary stomped over and opened the bottom drawer. She pulled out the white bottle of Ivory Liquid and pointed it at Elizabeth. "Here it is. *It's always in the bottom drawer.*" She slammed the plastic bottle down on the counter. A grey, soapy stream spurted in the air. "I'll do it myself!"

"I'm sorry."

Her mother turned the faucet on full blast. The extra burst of power set the old sink to moaning.

Elizabeth picked up the dish towels, then tossed them onto the counter. "I'll be upstairs."

She stayed upstairs for another three hours. Her mother didn't come into the room to say good night although Elizabeth heard her pass the door. The downstairs clock chimed out twelve, and Elizabeth went to bed.

Every way she turned—on her side, on her back, on her stomach—was uncomfortable. Sleep became a trance of partial truth. There was no rest, just pictures of people, places, and things flashing in front of her eyes. High school graduation. Cross Campus library at Yale. Daddy in his uniform, Mom, and Meghan for a family portrait. Her sister's funeral. The funeral . . .

It was dark, rainy, and quiet that day except for an occasional blast of thunder. She hoped that Daddy would say she couldn't go to the funeral because it would be too scary. When her father did come into the room to get her, he tried to smile but only the corners of his mouth turned up. "Daddy, you look so sad! I don't wanna go. But I'll go and keep you company, Daddy." Elizabeth held her arms out to him. And he bent down to pick her up off the bed and she noticed his socks. Daddy, you have on mix-matched socks—one brown and one black, Daddy, she wanted to say. Elizabeth pointed down at his feet but something told her that it wasn't really important, so she had hugged his neck instead.

The casket. Everything was so wet! I know Meghan is in there. C'mon out, Meghan. You better hurry up or they're going to lower you down in that hole! It's dark down there, Meghan, honest, I looked. Elizabeth was holding her father's hand. Her mother was on the other side of him. The umbrellas crowded around the plot looked like mushrooms. "Ashes to ashes," the minister said. There was a click and it started to move. Elizabeth pulled her father's hand. "Daddy, all the way down there?" He didn't hear. His body was racked with sobs. Elizabeth bent over and looked down into the hole again. "Dust to dust." And the darkness fell. Then out of the darkness of her mind, she saw another image, ghostly and ravaged. It was Friar Pete: the image of his body floating in Meghan's grave.

Elizabeth screamed. She didn't stop screaming until her mother shook and slapped her out of the nightmare.

"What's wrong? What is it?" Mary asked, sitting on the bed beside her.

Elizabeth stared blankly at her.

"You dreamed about Me-meghan. God, tell me, I want to know . . . to understand," her mother pleaded, for she had recurring nightmares as well but felt too isolated to tell anyone about them.

"I-I can't tell you! Where's Daddy?"

Mary let Elizabeth's drained body drop. She stood up. Her knees buckled, but she forced herself to stand anyway. "Just like that night Meghan died. The two of you crying and comforting each other, and just leaving me out. It's always you and him. Jeez, I need a fucking drink!"

Elizabeth lay paralyzed, staring up at the ceiling.

"Wake up, darling."

Connor turned over and took in the smell of hot cinnamon rolls which instantly told him it was Christmas morning.

He opened his eyes and the fuzzy outline of his mother, Jennifer, sitting on the side of the bed wobbled before him. "Come on, Connor," she said, patting his stomach, her hands trembling slightly.

His vision started to clear: her body was flat and thin. The bones in her chest made it look like a washboard. She had swept back her brown hair and the lines of her face, long and curved, revealed that this beautiful woman had been very sick for a long time. Connor leaned up and hugged her. He could smell the cinnamon in her hair. "Merry Christmas, Mom!"

"Merry Christmas!" she said, hugging him back with the all-encompassing touch of someone living with the constant possibility of death. "You'd better come down. Your father and Timmy have been up for hours. I had to hide some of the rolls I baked for you."

"I knew you'd take care of me," Connor said, brushing a strand back from her face. "Are you taking treatment this week?"

"Well, Doctor Nexan says I should—but I'm not. I'm feeling pretty good and I want to stay home more," his mother said, making her decision right there.

"Is that a good idea?" Connor said, slipping on his robe.

"I don't worry about it," Jennifer said, looking at him, "and you shouldn't either."

Connor wanted to tell her that he did worry, that at times he would be in class studying and the image of her in a crisis would come to him out of nowhere. The image of her looking like corn in a drought; weak limbs, cracked skin, and brittle hair. But why should he tell his mother what she already knew, what she hated to hear? After so many years she was now about to remove worry and toss it away from herself like a piece of dirty clothing, something he couldn't find the stamina to do. So instead, Connor did what he always did to cope—he placed his head on her shoulder.

But this time she stepped away.

What's wrong? Connor said it with a look.

"Connor, you've got to stop worrying about me so much, clinging so much."

"What'd I do?"

His mother wanted to renege, to slip the words back inside, but instead she played it out. "There's nothing wrong, Connor. I'm just saying that you can't baby yourself and me every time you come home."

Connor had the look of a lost child unable to find his mother. "I don't understand!"

Now she wanted to put her head on Connor's shoulder; she sat down on his bed instead. "I just want you to take things on the chin more and let me do the same. That's what life is about and you can't expect to be babied or baby somebody else every time things go bad. I'm saying that you need to take things as they come more, deal with them head up."

"That's what you want?"

"No, that's what you should want and do for yourself. That's the next step, in maturing, in going out into the real world."

"I see," he said, keeping his face turned away.

A faint voice from the hallway broke the impinging moment of silence. "Hey, Jennifer! You and Connor come on—Timmy and I want to open the gifts!"

"Coming down," Jennifer said, heading for the door.

"Yeah." Connor turned and spoke thoughtfully. "I want my cinnamon rolls."

She smiled.

They stepped into the hallway and Conrad and Timmy were standing at the end, at the top of the stairs.

"We were wondering what happened to you guys!" Conrad said, smiling. His father's hair was a glowing, aged color like the mercury in a thermometer. It was thick and cut low on the sides and in the back. Half-moon glasses perched on the tip of his nose. His body was muscular and showed that he worked out every week at the club. Little bags of flesh hung from his cheeks. Connor's younger brother Timmy was standing under his father's arm about two steps down. He was the image of his father's youth. His hair was dark brown and his eyes were blue. He had the same high forehead and even now as a teenager you could see the beginning pout marks on his cheeks.

"Hey, Connor . . ." Timmy said, pulling on the Choate T-shirt he wore, then with a devilish smile, "how about a slide?"

Their father, remembering how his sons would run and slide down the long hallway, mused, "Give it a go, Connor!"

That was all the encouragement he needed. "Watch this!"

"Hey—" his mother said.

Too late. Connor took three quick steps and jumped in the air; gravity was transformed into an impish helper tossing his body higher than he anticipated and slamming it down harder than he remembered. His body hit, hips down, legs up squared and twisted. He was now spinning down the shiny hardwood floor of the hallway . . . past the mahogany tables with antique vases . . . past the oils hanging . . . past the giant plants trying to outgrow their pots.

Connor felt hands jolting his body to a stop.

"Whoa!" he heard his father laugh.

Timmy slapped him on the chest. "Not a bad slide. But I've always been better." He moved around his father and brother. "Watch this, Dad!"

Jennifer caught Timmy by the waist and turned him around. "No. You guys broke at least a dozen of my Staffordshires doing that! One trip to the past is *enough*."

"Aww, let me show you a real slide!" Timmy urged, his ever-present competitiveness surfacing.

Connor grinned to himself, knowing their mother wasn't going to give in a second time.

They all headed down the stairs. Below was a huge room with sanded oak floors. Tasteful red oak furniture was sparingly placed throughout. On the east wall was a hand-carved cabinet full of Baccarat crystal and a Bergues carriage clock. In the center of the room was a giant Christmas tree beautifully decorated with gold, blue, and white satin balls. There were porcelain Santas, wooden reindeers, and candy canes hanging from the tips of the branches. Connor watched as Timmy jumped with a basketball-like motion, tipping peppermint canes off the branches. He shoved one in his mouth and tossed the other two to his father and Connor.

"Let's go, Dad," Connor said, standing by the Christmas tree eyeing the boxes he wanted to open first.

"Sssh! Hang on—" his father said, sitting in a recliner with a pad and pen. "I'm just making a few notes."

Jennifer was already sitting on the floor, legs tucked underneath her body, waiting. "Well, this one has *your* name on it!"

Conrad looked over the top of his glasses, then tossed the pad and pen on the floor. He looked at all the presents. "Let's get organized! Um, let's work right to left."

Timmy grabbed a big grey box and tossed it to Connor. "For you!"

Connor grabbed it and started ripping it open.

Jennifer grabbed a box with her name on it and began ripping it open; finally Conrad did the same.

They spent a wonderful, exhausting hour opening gifts.

"Well, I'm going to take a little nap! I want to be fresh for the theater this evening," Jennifer announced, a spell of pain overcoming her. She worked hard to mask it.

Timmy began setting up the grey marble chess set Connor had given him. "Hey, Connor, let's get a game."

Connor was putting on his new Movado sport watch. "Nah."

"I'll let you go first," Timmy said, putting the knights on the board.

"I don't want to play, I said."

"Just play," Timmy ordered, putting the kings on the board.

Their father, sensing a fight coming on volunteered, "I'll have a go, Timmy."

"Well, I really wanted to play Connor, Dad."

Connor sneered at him, "You know Dad'll beat you!"

Timmy slammed down the queens. "Let's go, Dad!" He aimed his annoyance at Connor, who now had in his hand the lesson plan books that his mother had given him.

"Great! I need these to organize for the computer class I'm teaching. Hey, Dad, Tim, you should of seen the kids. They were so excited!"

Connor's father looked up and took off his glasses. "You're

teaching computers and you're the assistant director of the tutoring program. That's too much. Connor, you've got to let that tutoring stuff go."

"I can handle it, Dad," Connor said, letting his voice drop off.

"I don't think so. Your Econ grades were terrible *again*, and this is your last semester—you need to go out strong."

"I *am* going out strong. I'm a finalist for the Wheaton Cup for History."

"That's great, but that won't help you in the firm next year. Now, you've been teaching at the U.S. Grant Program for three and a half years—that's enough. Drop it!" his father said, making an authoritative move on the board.

"Yeah, Con. What's the big deal?" Timmy said, scanning the board searching for a move. "Dad's right."

"Shut up, Timmy!"

"Hey." Timmy glared at him. "Not my fault you can't handle the books, man."

"Prick!" Connor said, throwing a clump of ribbons at his brother.

"Hey! Settle down, Connor. I'm telling you to quit tutoring and spend that time on your Econ."

"Yeah, that's a great lesson for business. Quit something after you put all your time and effort in it. That'll prepare me real well for the firm, Dad."

"You know good and damn well I'm not saying that! I'm saying get your head out of that program and into the books where it belongs! You know this last semester is important."

"I've promised the kids."

"They'll get over it. You've got a responsibility to yourself to get ready for next year. I don't want you coming in half-baked."

"I'm not dropping the tutoring," Connor said firmly.

"What?" his father's attention turned from the chessboard to Connor's face.

Connor turned and faced him. "I'm not dropping it. I've got a responsibility and I'm going to see it through."

"Oh, and I guess your responsibility to this family takes a backseat."

"Aww hell, Dad—this hasn't got a thing to do with the family."

"Bullshit!" his father said, slamming his fist down. The marble pieces flew in the air and several came crashing down on the floor like hail.

"Hey!" Timmy yelled.

Connor looked at the pieces scattered around the floor, then at his father. "I'm not quitting," he said finally, and then just walked away. His father's angry stare was like heat on his back.

"Connor!" his father yelled.

He kept walking, whispering to himself, "I'm not quitting. I'm not!"

The Chicago wind flapped its jaws and sent pangs of cold nipping at the people trying to walk down the South Side street. Faces ached with the sting of what seemed like a thousand prickling needles. Three young men—Kayo, Shorty, and Marty—stood shivering in the doorway of a liquor store.

The bib on Shorty's White Sox baseball cap reached to the tip of the awning under which they were standing. His body was long and curved around the back and shoulders. He had tiny bumps all over his face and a long neck. Shorty smiled and a flicker of light bounced off two gold front teeth.

Marty was dressed in a black wool coat with fur around the collar and sleeves. His black hat was neatly creased in the middle and was tilted back on his head, the wide brim taking away some of the heaviness of his face. Marty's fingers were neatly manicured and swift as he counted his bankroll of mostly tens and ones.

These were Kayo's "boys." Growing up, Shorty and Marty had taught him how to pop his bike up on the back tire and do a wheelie when they were ten. When Kayo's father got killed, Marty and Shorty took a two-hour bike ride to the North Side and stole a beautiful plant out of one of the shop yards for his mother. In high school, when they couldn't get enough money from their parents for the kind of clothes they wanted, they started playing Three Card Molly. Marty ran the game itself. Kayo played the mark, the guy who would win big and then egg someone else on to play. Shorty was the troubleshooter; he watched the bus driver, in case he wanted to call the police, and he watched the losers in case they got any rough ideas.

"Yo-yo bus!" Marty yelled.

People ran from the doorways of the different shops lining the block.

"The posse is moving out!" Marty commanded, leading Kayo and Shorty as they ran to the bus. Marty turned and spoke directly to Kayo. "My man, we gonna make boo-coo dollars today!"

Shorty sat in the front. Marty sat in the back and Kayo sat near Marty on the side. At the stop in front of the Illinois Institute of Technology, they picked up people switching from the El train, students from the university, and students from a nearby high school. Marty waited for them to get settled, then he pulled out a Chicago *Sun-Times* newspaper and unfolded it on the floor. From his side pocket he pulled out three cards.

"Yo-yo-yo!" Marty called out in a lyrical voice. "We got a game to play here, y'all. It's a game about royalty, about kings and queens," Marty said, turning over the three cards and revealing carefully colored-in brown faces.

Many in the crowd laughed.

Marty roared back. "Y'all ain't hip! We had kingdoms and fabulous civilizations before anybody else. Benin. Songhai. Ghana and Egypt had gold, sculpture, and an alphabet while the white folks were still living in the dark! Just because we're not in the history books doesn't mean we don't have a history."

Murmurs raced through the crowd.

Marty smiled as he bent the cards in the middle until they resembled little tents. "Two black kings and a queen. Now, Miss Queen Thang is the one you have to find, and she is a real slick chick." He began shuffling the cards, bringing his hands high and slow in the air so that everyone could see where the queen was. "Bet ten, take home twenty. Somebody find the pretty lady!"

A crowd started to gather. Marty turned over one black king. "You got a fifty-fifty chance. Come on, all you players in the house!" Marty pulled out his roll of bills. "Anybody see it? Just point to it and win ten!"

The people watched but no one said anything.

"Y'all scared to win some money? Y'all help me get rid of some of this money—I'm 'bout to get a hernia!"

The people in back started to laugh.

Kayo was looking around the crowd. He saw a blond-haired guy in Gucci penny loafers looking at the cards intently. Premed, thought Kayo, scanning his one science book; thinks he's smart. Kayo pulled a ten-dollar bill out his coat pocket and moved through the crowd. "I saw it. Bet ten."

"Lies!" Marty peeled off a ten. "Turn the card over and get up off my ten."

Kayo turned over the queen and snatched the money. "Ha! I made me an easy ten!"

"Damn, y'all too sharp. I got to win my ten back!" Marty began reshuffling the cards.

The blond-haired guy leaned forward. He had seen the dealer palming the queen and making it look like he dropped it left, when it was right. Out of the corner of his eye he saw where the queen landed. He slammed the book closed. "Bet fifty!" he said, reaching into his wallet. It was sleek and the alligator gave easily as he peeled the lips back with his index finger and thumb. He pulled out a fifty-dollar bill and laid it like a trump card on the floor next to the other cards.

Marty dropped five tens on top. "Turn over the card."

The student smiled and flipped over the card on the left. "Queen!"

But it was a king.

"N-N-o! You cheated," the student started to stutter.

Marty flipped the cards back over, reshuffling them again.

"He's cheating!" The student's face started to lose color.

"Give me back my money or I'll have the bus driver buzz for the police."

Shorty started to move over to where the guy was sitting.

"You gonna fuck around and get hurt, college boy," Marty said, pointing his finger. "Just cut your losses and break, my man!"

Kayo wiped his mouth.

Shorty was now next to the student, smiling, gold teeth shining, his hand in his coat pocket.

Kayo reached over and grabbed the fifty out of Marty's hand.

"What the—" Marty wheeled around.

"Here," Kayo said, handing over the money. "Let's make a move, y'all!"

"What the fuck y'all doing?" Shorty whined.

"Bring your ass on!" Marty said angrily over his shoulder. "Nobody's going to play after that shit."

The three got off the bus and stood in the middle of the street.

"What the hell is your problem, nigger?" Marty said, grabbing Kayo by the arm. "Giving that fool back fifty. You musta lost your mind up there at that chump-ass school!"

"You limp-dick, pussy-motherfucker!" Shorty snorted from behind him.

"We could've got arrested!" Kayo shouted back in self-defense.

"Arrested!" Shorty mimicked in a white boy's voice.

"You scared of a honky! Honkies got you running scared! I can't believe my homie dis'd me. Later for you!" Marty turned away and grabbed Shorty's arm. "C'mon!"

Kayo fell in behind them.

"Step off, Kayo," Shorty turned to warn. "You done lost your game, man."

"Later for y'all," Kayo shouted angrily. "I have not lost my game. Y'all just too stupid to see trouble coming, is all!"

The bus ride back seemed to take hours. Kayo watched as the burned-out storefronts and boarded-up buildings just kept coming and coming. He rested his head on the glass window and listened to the vibrations of the wheels, the crunching bottles and pieces of paper slapping against the window. The projects where he lived came into view. They were brick dominoes lining the street, stretching for blocks, and only the dried-blood color changed occasionally to a dirty gauze color. His home tumbled out before his line of vision and whirled up into his mind's eye.

In sociology class freshman year, this had been pegged as a slum, a breeding ground for violence and discontent. But to Kayo, this was his home. There was nothing in the books about the good feelings that could be found here. There was nothing about mothers armed with buckets and paint who went around at midnight scrubbing stairwells and painting walls the city neglected. Nothing about Grandma Pete on fourteen who opened her apartment to preschool children to come play and learn their ABC's at no cost to their mothers. Nothing about neighbors who pitched in and bought Kayo a typewriter when they heard he was going off to college. No, this was not in the book. There needed to be a footnote that said Yes, there is bad here but there is good too, just as there is good and bad everywhere.

Kayo got off the bus and entered his building that had a series of blue and red graffiti circles on the door. He slammed the elevator button. I want to get Momma out of here, Kayo thought as he got on the tin-walled elevator. The pungent smell of urine penetrated his senses. After nearly four years at Yale he had seen that there was better; and better was what he wanted for himself and his mother. In front of the apartment door, Kayo searched for his keys as the faint sounds of Miles Davis played softly inside.

The living room was shaped like an L. There was a flowered loveseat covering in cracked, yellowed plastic by the window. There was a coffee table and matching end tables with marble tops that his brother Ben had bought hot. Oval, square, and irregular-shaped rugs were placed in different spots on the tiled floor where it was puckering or torn. There was not a hint of dirt anywhere and Kayo could smell pinto beans cooking. His mother was seated at a small dining table in the living room just off the kitchen. She was at her sewing machine making beautiful full scarves of silky blues, avocado, and reds. The elderly ladies at the neighborhood beauty shop liked to buy them to fancy up their old dresses.

"Hi, Momma," Kayo said, hanging up his coat.

"Hi, Kayo. I didn't think you'd be back so soon. Come sit by me," his mother said, pulling out a chair. Emily Watson was a tiny yet shapely woman. Her back was muscular and she had big legs and round hips. Her hair was cut short in the back and curled high in the front. There was no fat on her body and the wrinkles in her forehead and around her neck were the only signs that she and age were acquaintances.

"Momma, I'm ready to go back to school."

"Why? Did you have a run-in with Shorty and Marty?"

"Yeah, they're acting funny."

"Aww, they're just jealous 'cause you're so smart. They're nice boys, don't get me wrong, but they're not like you!" she said proudly.

"Yeah, baby brother is so precious!" Ben said sarcastically, tossing his leather bomber jacket on a rocker by the door.

Neither of them had heard him come in.

"Don't start teasing, Ben," Emily said staring at her oldest son.

Ben was an older version of Kayo, tall and muscular. He had big brown eyes and thick, curly hair. He walked over to the table and sat down next to Kayo. "Thought you was hangin' with your boys."

"Changed my mind."

"Decided to do something college-y instead?" Ben laughed harshly, his drilling stare aimed right at his brother. "Anyway, I was just down at the pool hall and you know that old man that used to sit outside by the playground all the time? Well, he got busted for molesting some little boys."

"That's a shame. Need to throw that dirty old thing up under the jail," their mother said, shaking her head.

"Hey," Ben said, laughing, nudging Kayo, "guess what they saying down at the pool hall?"

"Tell me later," Kayo said, nudging Ben back, knowing it was dirty and not wanting his mother to hear it.

"The old man was giving it to 'em in the back, you know. And the guys are saying the old man was passing out free fudge bars to the kiddies! Get it?"

"Ben, don't talk like that in front of Momma."

"It's a joke, man. We all grown sitting here."

"Aww, Kayo I don't pay any attention to Ben," their mother said, barely looking up from her work.

"Yeah, only Kayo is worth any fuckin' attention."

"Hey, man, I just told you . . ."

"You don't tell me nothing, Kayo!" Ben snapped. "You a college boy—that's it! I'm a man running this. I'm out here hustling every day while you're off playing Einstein."

"Stop arguing!" their mother said to both of them.

"You think college is easy? I'd like to see you try it."

"Boy, please. You up there eating cake. We got mud pies down here, remember? See, you up there with your white friends, the ones that call here talkin' all proper, and you think the world is some girl waitin' for you to get over—but it ain't! Just wait."

"Yeah, wait." Kayo's chair made a popping sound against the floor. "When I get my degree, I'll be out there on Wall Street *doing it.*"

"Baby brother"—Ben struggled to keep from laughing—"everything is cool now. Y'all studying together and the world is ebony and ivory. But only the ivory gets over in the real world. That world out there is gonna be kicking your young black ass and it don't matter what kind of *dee*-gree you got attached to it."

"Stop it, Ben! Kayo's trying to *do* something!" Emily said, pointing her finger at him.

"I'm trying to do something too. I'm trying to school him."

"Man, you can't tell me nothing! I'm the one who kept you

out of jail, and I'm getting a fifty-thousand-dollar education, thank you."

Ben leaned forward and said softly, "You ain't did shit more than blood s'posed to do for blood. I'm trying to save you some pain, man."

"Stop it. And I mean right now," their mother said, standing up and slamming down her sewing.

There was a long silence.

"Now both of you take this scarf down to Carol at Tootie's Beauty Shop and bring me back my ten dollars."

"Momma, we not little boys anymore to be sendin' to the store," Ben complained, lolling back in his chair.

"Don't my boys want to do Momma a favor?" she said, squeezing Ben's hand.

Always got to baby him, Kayo thought as he stood up and walked over to get his coat.

"C'mon Ben," Emily said, motioning with her hand. "The two of you haven't spent any time together since Kayo's been home."

Kayo now had his coat on and was handing Ben his jacket.

"Now that's better!" she said. "Act like brothers and don't take all day now, dinner's almost ready."

"Alright, Momma," Kayo said.

"Check, old lady!" Ben said, kissing his mother on the cheek. He flipped the collar up on his jacket and held the door open for Kayo. "Brains before beauty!"

The neighborhood courtyard was full now. A group of teenaged boys with matching jackets were huddled in one corner. A dozen kids were climbing black steel monkey bars, the only structure still intact on the playground. The beauty shop was about five blocks down the street. Every other person they passed they knew from the building, from grammar school, or from high school.

"Hey Ben! Hey Kayo, didn't know you was back."

The greetings came and were returned. Suddenly Ben stopped. "Hey Kayo, it's Zeke."

Kayo turned around and in the doorway they just passed

was an old man crouched down on the stoop. Mud caked the unlaced black brogans he wore. Zeke's face was gaunt and scarred with pox marks. His hair was wild and full of lint and dust. One bottle of Thunderbird stuck out of his pocket while his fist was wrapped tight around another bottle of the same. Zeke motioned for Ben and Kayo to come to him with a hand as big and brown as a baseball mitt. "My boys! My boys!" he called in a gravelly voice.

Ben jogged back to the doorway.

"Kayo, come here!" Zeke motioned again. Ben was now holding him up under the arms.

Kayo waved but didn't move, thinking Now I've got to hear the same old thing from him. "Hi Zeke. I got an errand to run for Momma."

"You ain't got a minute, Kayo? Me and your Daddy go way back!" Zeke said, wiping his mouth.

"Yeah, Kayo," Ben shouted.

Kayo cleared his throat. "I'll see you later, Zeke."

Zeke glanced down at his clothes and kind of rubbed them with his hands. "Guess I do look kind of bad . . . wouldn't wanna be seen with a bum like me, neither."

"You ain't no bum Zeke," Ben said. You always a big man in my book. Don't pay any attention to him! I'll come by later and buy you something to eat."

"Thank you, boy!" Zeke said, sliding back down to his stoop. "Your Daddy got some fine boys. He'd be real proud."

"Thanks, man," Ben said, waving as he walked away. Ben walked faster, turned the corner, and then started to run after Kayo. He grabbed him by the neck and threw him against the wall.

"Damn, Ben . . ."

"Just shut the hell up! Who do you think you are?" The words rode on a wave of passion and bits of saliva sprinkled Kayo's face. He tried to speak up but Ben's forearm was stretched across his throat.

"What I do?" Kayo coughed the words out dryly.

Ben eased the pressure he was putting on Kayo's upper

body. "Did you forget? Man, you must have forgotten. *Please*, let me jog your memory some here. Them cops put Daddy in jail over some traffic bullshit, right? Lying, talking about Daddy pushed them and had to be restrained. Then . . . aww man, then what lie they tell next?"

Kayo tried to break away.

"Wait." Ben slammed him back against the wall. "Now let me get it right. Yeah, they said they changed shifts and the new guy didn't read the sheet. They knew that man was crazy when they put him in the cell with Daddy. Zeke was in jail too. He heard the fight when it started. Zeke say you had to be dead not to hear it. He yelled for somebody to come and save Daddy! After it's all over, them lying motherfuckers had the nerve to come around ducking their heads, 'We so-oo sorry. It was all a mistake. Just sign this, Mrs. Watson, and we'll give you your first check and you'll always get a check every month.'"

Kayo tried to push him away, but Ben just kept leaning.

"Yeah, a check comes every month alright, a welfare check—ain't that a bitch! The only person that really went out their way to help Daddy, to help us, was that man you chumped off back there. Yeah, well, piss on you, little brother!" Ben said, suddenly moving from him.

Kayo dropped like a coat from a hanger.

"You make me tired, you know that?" Ben said, walking away.

The sun was rising in the burnt orange sky. The grass was green, wet, shiny, and spent, bordered by open flowers that were a mix of hues. The Georgia winter spread color like a rainbow. Michelle opened her bedroom window. The crisp, rustling air made her body shiver under the bathrobe she wore. The tree limbs did a slow bump and grind with the wind. Michelle stole the moves to help her get dressed for Sunday school. She hummed as she glided around the room. She reached under the canopy bed and pulled out a small bag she had packed last night, the baptism stuff. Michelle peeked inside: rubber slippers, Danskin bottoms, and a robe.

Michelle's wonderful vacation was almost over. Her mother and father had looked as if they were going to cry in the beginning when they picked her up at the airport. All Michelle's favorite foods were cooked and waiting, fighting to get out of the pots. She had gained five pounds over the break. Michelle dressed quickly, hearing her mother's rich alto voice humming downstairs. She took up the melody and carried it with her to the steps. Her mother, Ella, was in the kitchen debating over a pan of homemade buttermilk biscuits. Her face was the color of the dark brown pan they were baking in. Her eyes were big and a soft, sandy brown. Ella pushed the pan of biscuits back in the stove. She wore a white apron that said "Jesus Saves."

"Well," she said in a voice that seemed to chime, "I thought you were going to try to sleep in today too. I baked us a few biscuits just to have before church. But they'll be plenty of food there today, too."

Michelle walked over and hugged her mother. Even when she wasn't cooking them, she smelled like sweet potatoes.

"Well, we are having a great morning today!" Ella said, hugging her daughter back. She swung her out, holding her palms. "Got my good looks."

"Daddy gone already?" Michelle said, hopping over to a table in the corner of the kitchen.

"Now you know he is. He went to open up and set the chairs up for Sunday school. I told him we'd be right behind him to help, but *somebody* didn't make it snappy getting up and out of bed," Ella said, peeking at the biscuits. Out of the corner of her eye she saw that Michelle was shaking salt into her palm. Ella warned: "I've told you since you were a child not to eat salt plain like that—bad for you and most certainly is bad luck!"

"Aww, Momma, that old-time stuff!"

"Aww, Momma, that old-time stuff," she put her hands on her hips and mimicked. "Um, that tree out back still bears strong switches."

Michelle put the salt down. "And you would go grab one in a minute."

"Don't you know it!" her mother said with a smile. Then thoughts of her daughter's upcoming graduation popped into her mind. "Your Daddy and I are so proud of you. You're just doing so well at school and all my friends talk about how nice and polite you are."

"Thanks to a certain tree out back."

"Aww, don't you even try it. You have really grown up to be a wonderful young lady. And you're going to be a big-time professor at one of those fine colleges out East there. The first professor in the family, not just a high school teacher."

"You and Grandma are wonderful teachers!" Michelle said, surprised.

"Oh, I'm not downplaying that, baby. It's just that you'll be doing something more . . . having it better than the rest of us, that's all. I'm just so proud of you."

Michelle could see it gleaming in her eyes. "I won't let you and Daddy down." She reached out and embraced her mother.

The basement of the church was full of people milling around. A group of deacons, all in dark suits and crisp white shirts, were taking down folding chairs that had just been used for the morning devotion. Off to the side was a large kitchen area. The smell of simmering collard greens, peach cobblers, and black-eyed peas filled the air. Reverend Howard, a commanding presence in his white minister's robe, was lured by the smells. His stout legs took him straight to the kitchen counter where he leaned over, coveting a pan of freshly baked ginger cookies. His stomach under the robe was as round and solid as one of the pots. "Let me have some of those cookies!" Reverend Howard pleaded to the three elderly women moving swiftly about the kitchen.

"You don't need any!" a voice behind him shouted.

Reverend Howard turned around laughing, knowing it was his wife. "Ella, Michelle, y'all are late! Where have you been?"

"D.Z., don't even look at those cookies! You know the

doctor says that you have to watch your weight and stop eating all those sweets."

From behind her mother's back, Michelle rippled her fingers in a wave at the ladies basking in the smells and heat of their own cooking.

"Hi baby!" Miss Hudson shrieked with glee. She was toasty brown, thin as a wafer, and looked nowhere near her seventy-two years. She turned and swatted her hands with a dishcloth while speaking to the rival cook in the kitchen, Mama Lockheart. "Michelle's here!"

"Chile, chile!" Mama Lockheart said, her bottom lip quivering. She spit a stream of black juice into a dented paper cup strategically placed off to the side on the floor. "C'mere, baby, and give Mama Lockheart some sugar."

Michelle rushed over, feeling the old women's love gushing around her, and she hugged them both.

Reverend Howard reached for a cookie.

"Don't!" Ella shouted, smacking his hand with hers.

Reverend Howard spotted two of his deacons as they finished folding up the chairs. He winked at one and said loudly, "Now, woman, if every time somebody said don't, I didn't, I wouldn't be married to you."

"Whooo-wee," Michelle teased, cutting her eyes at her mother.

"Lord, it's getting hot back here and it sho' ain't these black-eyed peas and collards cooking!" Miss Hudson laughed, tapping a Crock-Pot with an old wooden spoon.

"Am I right, deacons?" Reverend Howard bellowed in a deep baritone.

One of the grey-haired deacons straightened up and smoothed his striped polyester suit. "My name is Jess, I ain't in this mess."

"I haven't heard that one before, Deacon Tyler," Michelle said.

"Me neither, chile," Miss Hudson said, grinning into a frying pan of green tomatoes and onions.

"Humpf!" Mama Lockheart snorted. "Old as you is, you heard Eve tell Adam to take a bit outta that apple."

Miss Hudson rolled her eyes at the older woman and sucked her teeth. "Jealous 'cause I'm younger than you and can outbake you."

"Help me Lord! The girl done go stone crazy."

"Ladies," Reverend Howard intervened, for he knew these two could go at it until the end of time. "The service is about to start!" He began walking away, holding the cookie.

Ella took it out of his hand. Reverend Howard kissed her behind her ear. "I'm just a slave for the Lord and for my wife."

"Oh, go on!" Ella said, pushing him away. She followed him up the steps.

"Michelle, your Daddy tells me you graduate this May. Has it been that long?" Miss Hudson asked, taking the top off a big black pot. Sweet curly steam shrouded her face.

"Yes, Miss Hudson, it's been almost four years."

"Wait till you taste my greens, child."

"Aww, pooh," Mama Lockheart said, her dentures slipping forward slightly. "I'm eighty-three years old and got a recipe for greens that's older than that! I cooks 'em with a little brown sugar and chives. I made these black-eyed peas special for Michelle too. My college baby up there at Yale."

"You know the church ought to have some extra bake sales and get a bus and ride up there for the graduation!" Miss Hudson said, dabbing salt into her pot.

"Too much salt." Mama Lockheart squinched up her face, folds of skin creasing her cheeks in wrinkles. "You always put too much salt in your greens."

"This my pot over here, yourn over there. And last time, New Year's, your black-eyed peas was mushy!" Miss Hudson winked at Michelle out of the corner of her eye.

"I ain't studyin' you," Mama Lockheart snorted. "Michelle just done grown up into a fine young woman."

"Now, you telling the girl something right!" Miss Hudson

said, walking over to the counter. "The whole church is talking about you, all of it good. Keep it up now, hear?"

"I promise you all I will," Michelle said smiling.

Crowds of people were seated in wooden pews that were divided into three main rows. There was a balcony hanging over a quarter of the church and people were sitting in the pews and in the aisles there. It was First Sunday and Baptizing Day. Family and friends were packed into the church to see loved ones taken into the folds of religion through an immersion in water. The sound of patent leather shoes running up the stairs, alternating with the step and thud of orthopedic shoes and padded canes, could be heard in the halls. The sun projected the Resurrection through stained-glass windows onto the faces poised in prayer. Candles flickered, shadowing red satin rollers leading up to the altar. The choir swayed back and forth like flowers in the breeze, flowing robes rippling red and white, palms up high and waving in the air.

"Can I get a witness!" Reverend Howard shouted into the microphone.

Outstretched hands clutched the air above them. "Witness, Reverend!"

D.Z. Howard was the son of the son of the son of a Baptist minister. Spitting fiery words of praise was as natural to him as waking up in the morning. His head was balding and shone in the lights above the pulpit. "We are here today to bring found sheep to the Holy Shepherd. Not lost, I say, but found. Found in the spirit of repentance and ready to witness for the Lord!"

"Tell the story!"

"Aww, y'all sinners don't wanna hear it," Reverend Howard shouted. His mouth was strong, spitting out syllables like sparks. He spun around, ran down the pulpit stairs, and then sped up the aisle like a meteor from heaven on a mission from God.

Michelle watched her father from the baptismal pool in back of the choir stand. "Preach, Daddy!"

"Here are the sheep! God's sheep!" Reverend Howard

shouted, pointing to a row of people sitting in white robes fashioned out of cotton sheets. They stood: five children, one no more than six, a woman of middle age, and an elderly man. "Are you ready?"

"No!" one little girl mumbled; the cold floor on her bare feet stung, making her hop around.

"Sssh! You not supposed to answer and you supposed to say yes," said her big brother of ten next to her.

She frowned. "I'm scared. I don't like Reverend Howard when he get all scary like this."

"C'mon sheep, come to the water to be baptized," Reverend Howard said, turning, and they followed him as the choir took up the words and made them into a processional for the soul.

"Take me to the water!"

Michelle watched them come, looks of apprehension sculpting their faces. She turned and got ready. The pool was about three feet deep with steps leading down and up and out on the other side. The warm water slapped at her legs as she went down two steps. Her job was to help them out of the pool after they were baptized.

"Take me to the water!"

Michelle watched as her father stepped down, the water bunching his robe up around his waist. He stood center and held out his hand to the flock waiting at the top of the steps. "Come on to the Lord!" The first child stepped down into the pool. The water was almost to her throat. Reverend Howard held her trembling hands. "Do you believe Jesus died for your sins?"

The shivering girl nodded.

"I baptize you in the name of God Almighty!" the Reverend shouted. Hands over the forehead, under the small of the back, he let the water swallow the body beneath the floating robe.

"Amen!"

Michelle froze. Her mouth went dry and her legs felt as if they couldn't hold her. Under her father's hands she saw a face floating under the water: Friar Pete. She shook her head. No! She leaned back and let her head rest against the plywood wall. The plastic smell stuffed her nostrils like cotton and she opened her mouth to breathe.

"Take me to the water!"

Michelle covered her ears to squelch the sound of dragging heels and the splash of Friar Pete's body.

"Take me to the water!"

She felt faint, then a hand pulling at her waist, clawing. Michelle pushed it away.

"Help me out, please?"

Michelle strained and saw water dripping in the little girl's face. Her hair was matted over her closed eyes. Her hand was outstretched. Michelle leaned back and as darkness enveloped her she felt someone take her by the shoulders and lead her upstairs.

"Are you alright?" a distant voice asked.

It was Deacon Robinson. His strong old hands were picking her up, laying her down on the couch. Michelle opened her eyes but white light beat them back closed.

"Just struck by the spirit, I guess," she heard someone say.

Chapter 6

CHRISTMAS break was over. It was the beginning of the second semester, known as the shopping period. Students roamed the campus with blue book catalogues in hand, looking for required classes and the one and only "cakewalk" course at the school—especially the seniors. Kayo and Elizabeth were standing outside at the top of Science Hill. Kayo made a mark in his blue book and said gleefully, "Connor took this Bio 110 class last year and got an easy A. Hell, it's the only gut on campus. We've gotta take that!"

Elizabeth was thumbing through her blue book of classes. "Yeah, no need for second-semester seniors to kill themselves just to get out of this place."

"I wish you would tell Michelle to take it easy!"

"I know! She's geared up already and the semester has barely started. She's taking all the toughest Lit seminars."

"Some people like it hard," Kayo said with a smirk.

"Ooooh, I'm telling!"

Kayo and Elizabeth were standing at a rest point on Science Hill, leaning against a bike rack. Kayo watched now as dozens of students with heads down, legs bent, bodies leaning forward, made their way up. "I'm going to meet Connor for dinner. You coming?"

Before she could answer, a tall, stout, blond guy walking up the hill stopped at Elizabeth's side. He had on a blue jacket with a Seattle high school seal. His hands swelled the grey knit gloves he wore until you could see the pink of his fingers. The muscles in his arms made an M. His nose was sharp and he traced the inside of Elizabeth's ear with it. "Hi."

"Hi Greg," Elizabeth said, still reading.

Kayo watched as Greg began rubbing Elizabeth's back. Slowly he began making his way down, massaging, squeezing the right cheek of Elizabeth's butt.

Kayo heard a car horn blow approval and turned to see a black Chevy with "Elvis Lives" bumper stickers. He turned back and leaned up off the rack. "Get your hands off her ass!"

"What's it to you?" Greg asked, rubbing his chest with an open, flat palm.

"Just take your hands off her ass!"

Greg dropped his hand and squared off.

"Kayo, calm down," Elizabeth said coolly. She faced Greg. "It's no big deal."

Greg looked from Elizabeth to Kayo. "Okay, fine. I'm gone," he said, turning and walking away.

"Greg! Greg!" Elizabeth called behind him but he wouldn't wait. She turned to Kayo. "What was that about?"

"That was about letting him just feel all over you in the middle of the street. He just disrespected you."

"A little feel? Disrespectful? Don't be so old-fashioned!"

"I know you like your little reputation for being wild," Kayo said angrily, "but don't let anybody treat you like that!"

"Don't start preaching. I get enough from Michelle," Elizabeth said in a soft yet guarded tone.

"I should of just popped him right in the mouth," Kayo mumbled.

"It's over!" Elizabeth said, punching his arm playfully. "Go to dinner. There's a seminar I want to check out."

"Alright, we'll see you later then," Kayo said, walking backward slowly, making his way down the hill until he reached the back entrance of Commons, the dining hall. He was grateful the administration had settled the strike over Christmas break.

"Yo! Ka-yo!"

He turned. Connor was standing up at a table about three rows back from the center aisle. Kayo waved.

"Get your food and come over here!" Connor shouted.

Kayo waved at Connor, who was sitting with a table full of students he had gone to Choate with. Kayo picked up a tray and walked through the doors. Inside, behind the counter, the trays were full of soul food: black-eyed peas, fried chicken, mustard and collard greens, candied yams, and barbecued ribs.

"Can I have some of that?" the woman in front of Kayo asked. She brushed back a strand of hair making a scar down the middle of her face. She had on white cords and a tie-dyed shirt from India; little beads the size and color of green peas adorned her neck. The anthropology book on her empty tray made one side pop up. "It's spinach?"

A wiry-built black woman was serving behind the counter. Her hair was swept back in a bun and her neck was creased with wrinkles that seemed to fade away into her chest. "No, these are mustard greens and they are very good and good for you. Lots of iron!" she explained while loading up the plate. Her arms were speckled with little black spots from where hot juices had scarred them.

"It looks kind of greasy. Are you sure?" the student asked, fiddling with her beads.

"I've been eating greens all my life and I'm damn healthy."

"Thank you," the woman said, putting the plate on her tray, moving on.

Kayo stepped up. "Hi, Alana."

She stared at him, not forgetting he had crossed the picket line. She slopped the food on his plate.

"Kayo!"

Kayo turned to his left. A few rows back there was a table full of black seniors. Richard was standing up, waving him over. "Man, where have you been hiding?" Richard asked, playing with the loose threads of his blue-jean jacket. He was slender, wafer-colored, with small, serious eyes.

"Been around man, been around!" Kayo put his tray down at the edge of the table and held his hand up for five. Richard reached up, slapping it hard. Kayo reached around and did the same with Arthur and Tim, who were also sitting at the table. He squeezed Carol's hand and kissed her on the cheek. Kayo waved to the other black students too far down the table to reach. "I'm just stopping by for a minute. I told Connor I'd eat dinner with him."

Over at Connor's table, Mick leaned over and said, "Guess Kayo is going to join the NAACP meeting."

The other five students at the table laughed, except for Connor. "Shut up, Mick! Every time you open your mouth something stupid comes out."

"Stupid?" Mick said, looking around in mock confusion. "Let your eyes be the judge. Is that not a table full of black people segregating themselves over there?"

A stocky, brown-haired student in a faded polo shirt named Michael said, "Yeah, why do they sit by themselves like that? It's like they think they're different or something."

The others at the table nodded; a few grunted.

"They're all here on affirmative action anyway," someone else said.

"Bull! Everyone who gets in Yale has been measured on the same scale!" Connor balked.

"Not the blacks!" Mick said, stuffing food in his mouth. "They let them in because of the sixties. My Dad says that's why they're lazy and expect things to be handed to them all the time."

"That's right, Con!" two of the other students said, speaking up.

"I guess Kayo's lazy and stupid, that's why he'll be graduating with honors in Econ, huh?"

"He *seems* to be different from the rest of them," Michael said, shoving food in his mouth.

"I'm telling you guys," Mick said, jumping in, "blacks don't want to work and the majority of them are on welfare, taking all our tax dollars. The jails are full of them. I know you guys are pretty close, but hey, facts are facts. You can't count on him!"

"What's that supposed to mean?"

"That means that a black will grin in your face but he doesn't care about you. He's just friends with you trying to get your contacts, your family connections. When it comes down to it he'll chose his own kind over *you*!"

Connor looked down at his plate and scooped up a mouthful of candied yams. "You guys know Kayo is cool! He's not like that at all. He's hung out with us before!"

"Man, I'm telling you. They're different!" Mick said.

"Ssh, here he comes," Michael said out of the corner of his mouth. "He's not coming over here to eat either. *He hasn't got his tray*!"

"Hey fellas, what's going on?" Kayo said casually.

"Hi Kayo." The voices mingled together.

"Kayo, check this out, man," Mick said, grinning. He stood and rolled up the sleeves of the baggy lacrosse sweatshirt he wore. "We went to the Caribbean over the break. Check out this tan." Mick put his arm up against Kayo's. "Looks good, huh?"

"You look like human toast."

"Son of a bitch!"

Connor threw his head back and laughed. "You asked for it, Mick!"

Kayo chuckled to himself. He leaned down and clasped Connor on the shoulder. "Listen, I'm going to eat over there with Richard and the guys. I haven't really spent any time with them lately so . . . well, you know."

Connor looked at Kayo, then down at the people sitting at the table. "No problem."

"Come over with me?" Kayo asked.

Connor looked over at the table full of blacks and instantly felt intimidated. "Naw, go ahead."

"Well, get me when you're ready to go back to the room, alright?" Kayo said, seeing that Connor was getting angry.

"No problem. Chill."

Soon after, Connor got up from the table, bused his tray, and made his way to the door.

Kayo noticed him leaving and told his friends he would catch them later. "Connor! Wait up!"

Connor turned back around but kept walking. Once outside, he felt a hand on his shoulder slowing his stride.

"What is wrong with you?"

"You know," Connor said, cutting his eyes at Kayo.

"Who was sitting at your table?" Kayo asked coolly.

"Me and the guys!"

"Who are all white," Kayo stressed.

"That's different," Connor said angrily. "You know it's not the same."

"Listen, we are already integrating this university, okay? Every waking moment it should not be on us to integrate every classroom, every table in the dining hall. Why is it always on us to make the first move?"

"You guys act like you're different when you're together like that. It's this excluding black thing. It just looks and feels different, Kayo, like no whites are welcome."

"You could come over there and sit and eat. I've introduced you to everyone over there."

"You don't understand how bad it looks to everybody . . ."

"Okay, Connor. Some things I don't expect you to understand, and vice versa. I'm sorry I stood you up for dinner."

"No, don't just give in. I want to understand," Connor said angrily as he opened the door to their room.

Kayo didn't want to deal with it and the phone ringing was the perfect excuse. "Hey, get that."

Connor grabbed the receiver. "Hello? Hi Dad."

Kayo threw his coat on the bed and then fell right on top of it. "Tell your father I said hello."

Connor threw up his hand. "C'mon Dad, I told you over Christmas that my Econ grades were the same as before. I do too try!"

Kayo took two joints out of the bag. He lit one and took a long pull.

"Look, it's time for a late seminar I'm taking. I'll talk to you later. 'Bye!"

Kayo took another pull. "Boy, this is some good weed. Take your coat off and grab one of these joints, man, and chill."

"Breathing down my neck! Breathing down my neck all the time!"

"You're repeating yourself, Connor."

"So what?" Connor said, pacing the room.

"Fine. Drive yourself crazy." Kayo took another hit.

"Fuck you—you and everybody who sits at the black table!" Connor said, turning abruptly, heading back out the door.

"Michelle, everybody is driving me crazy!"

Michelle looked at his pouting face and said as always, lovingly, "What happened?"

Connor fell on the bed, face down. "Kayo and I had it out about him eating at the black table!"

"Con, just because he sat and ate with other black people does not mean he and they are planning a revolution!"

"That black table stuff is racist! You believe in that?"

Michelle laughed, falling back on the bed. Their faces were parallel. "How could I be racist and sleep with you?"

"Yeah, you got a point," Connor laughed.

"Speaking of racist, how's the old man?" Michelle said as easily as she could.

Laughter died in Connor's throat. "He is not a racist!"

"Then tell him about us."

"I can't."

"Because?"

"Because he just isn't ready for it."

"You mean he isn't ready for me, little ole black me from Georgia?" Michelle said sarcastically and a bit sadly. "He's okay as long as he thinks we're friends, but romance, marriage . . ."

"Don't push me, Michelle! I've told you and told you that as soon as I get to the firm and start working, doing well, I'll tell my parents about us!'' Connor moved to her and gently ran his fingers across her tensed brow. ''I've got to take on one battle at a time with him. I've got to prove to him that I can piss with the big boys at the firm. Tonight he called and balled me out because my Econ 325 grade was bad. I hate that I'm just not into Econ like him and Granddad. But I'm going to prove to him that I've got the Bellington stuff. I'm going to lick this thing! I've got to know you'll hang in with me. I need your support.''

Michelle bit her tongue and forced her heart to once again give in. ''Come here!''

Connor slipped into her arms. ''What can I say that I haven't told you before? I love you. You're the reason I can keep going, dealing with Dad and this Econ, family stuff. I'm going to do well. He doesn't think I can but I am!''

She stroked his forehead. ''You don't have to convince me. Just do your best and that will be plenty good enough, Connor.''

''With you encouraging me, I can't possibly go wrong.''

Michelle took strands of his hair and began twirling them into little knots. ''Connor, don't count on me being in New York next year.''

''Why not?'' he said, sitting up.

''The Ph.D. program at Columbia is the toughest one to get into. The Lit Department is small, so it's harder to get into. Stanford, Iowa, and Washington are tough but they have bigger departments. I'll be sure to get into one of those.''

''You don't think you can get into Columbia?''

''It's going to be tough! But getting in would just be fabulous. I'd go crazy, but I'm not setting my heart on it. Just be prepared for the possibility.''

''I've got confidence in you! Look at your grades and the essays that you sent—they'll snap you right up. They'd be fools not to. Wait and see!''

''Thanks,'' she said, bending down and kissing him.

''No way, lady, am I going to let you get away from me.'' Connor kissed her back. Michelle stroked his forehead, her eyes filling with hope.

Chapter 7

ELIZABETH sat in a weeny bin at the library, tired, her thoughts loafing. It was exam period at the end of the year. The back of her head ached against the top of the metal chair. Her torso was stretched, stiff as a board, across the chair. She had no energy. The white walls of the study cubicle seemed to wobble and push in. She turned from them and looked out into the library itself through the narrow glass of the door. Bodies were stretched out on the floor. Arms dangled over the sides of chairs. Paper was scattered all around. Vietnam without the blood, she thought. Elizabeth caught her reflection in a strip of metal in the corner. Her ponytail was bunched up off to one side. Strands of hair were all over her head. Darkened half-moons punctuated her eyes. Her sweatshirt was stained with cola.

"Hey, Elizabeth!"

She turned. Peering into her cubicle was Whitney, whose sleek brown hair was swept up and neatly curled on the sides.

Her face, taut and round like an olive, was a palate of colors. She wore a salt-and-pepper dress with a matching sash. "Look at you!" gasped Elizabeth.

Whitney pulled the door open and then stepped back, doing a little curtsy, "Thank you! You look like shit though."

"It's exam period, Whitney! Who has time to get all done up?"

"Honey, if angels woke me up in the middle of the night and said 'Time to meet the Maker,' I'd say, 'Hang on a minute while I put on my face.' You should want to do the same."

"Well, I guess I'd try and do something to keep myself cheery too if I didn't know what I was going to be doing next year. It must be worrying you to death! Me, I'll be at ABC in New York, so I'm just kind of tying up a few loose ends here before moving on."

"Well, I'm not really worried. It does take time to hear from the better law schools," Whitney said, nervously stroking her long neck.

"I guess," Elizabeth said, seeing that she had drawn blood. "Are you sure you'll get into Harvard or Yale?"

Whitney dug in for the competitive war of words so common on campus during senior year. "Well, I'm graduating cum laude, so I guess I don't really have anything to worry about. Is broadcast journalism going to your *real* career? Or are you just working a year so you can take the LSAT again?"

Elizabeth suddenly felt fed up with the conversation and began quickly clearing her books and papers off the desk. "I've got to run. My Daddy's coming to pick me up for lunch."

Whitney, sensing victory, added, "Is he still a police officer? How does he stand it?"

Elizabeth looked at the neat creases in Whitney's pleated dress and said, "You know, I don't know. I keep telling him he needs to stop putting his life on the line protecting ungrateful, undeserving people." She snatched her bookbag off the table. "Know what I mean?"

"Um huh," Whitney hissed. "Well, see you later."

Elizabeth rolled her eyes and thought to herself, Bitch!

* * *

"Where are you going?" Connor asked, walking into their bedroom.

"To my job interview in New York—I made the second round!" Kayo answered while fidgeting with his clothes. Kayo was dressed in a double-breasted, dark blue suit. His shirt was powder blue and his tie was striped, navy and burgundy. Kayo was clipping in a pair of gold cuff links, round and thick as grapes. His shoes were burgundy and elaborately wing-tipped.

Connor walked over closer to Kayo. He eyed the burgundy silk handkerchief hanging from his jacket pocket. "Aachoo!" Connor yanked it out, covering his mouth with it.

"Damn, Connor," Kayo said, angrily snatching it back.

"Sorry!" Connor said, snatching the handkerchief out of Kayo's hand and blowing his nose with it. "Whoosh! This cold is killing me!"

"I can't wear that handkerchief after you blew your nose in it," Kayo said, pushing him hard. "This isn't playtime. I'm not guaranteed a spot like you—"

"Sorry man, I wasn't thinking."

"Where did my cuff link go?" Kayo began looking around the floor.

"Hey, finish getting dressed and I'll look for it for you."

Connor was now down on the floor. He saw the cuff link and palmed it and slipped it into the cuff of his pants. "Kayo, I don't see it, man!"

"Aww, it's got to be there. It just didn't disappear!"

"Tell you what, wear my cuff links with the Yale crest. That'll go well with your suit."

"But they're so plain!"

"No," Connor said, opening his drawer quickly, pulling out the cuff links. "See," he said, stopping Kayo as he started to kneel. He quickly flipped them in.

"Hey, looks classy," Kayo admired.

"You look sharp, except for one thing."

"What?" Kayo said nervously. He looked at himself in the mirror.

"The shoes."

"Boy, these are Stacy Adams steppers. I paid two hundred dollars for these kicks. Two hundred and *fifty* dollars. Read my lips—two hundred and fifty dollars. My favorite color and my favorite style."

"These investment guys are older, Kayo. They don't have much taste. They're not cool like us. They're not going to appreciate them."

Kayo pictured Connor's father. "You got a point."

"Say, the other day I caught a shoe sale but they only had them a half-size smaller, but I got them thinking they would stretch—and I've walked around in them and they're still too tight. They'd go perfect!" Connor headed for the closet. "Here they are!" Connor held up a shiny new pair of Gucci burgundy penny loafers.

Kayo took them and carefully slipped off his Stacy Adamses. "These bottoms are clean," Kayo said, looking up at his friend.

"Take a look in the mirror."

Kayo slipped the shoes on. "I look like . . . like I'm supposed to look. Thanks."

"Don't mention it."

Kayo looked down at the empty pockets of the shoes, "I'll put some slugs in these—later."

Connor rolled his eyes.

The conference room was lavishly furnished with Early American furniture and plush gold carpeting. A secretary had brought Kayo in and instructed him to wait for Mister Flagstaff, who would be in shortly. When the door slammed, Kayo felt the latch catching in the middle of his chest. He pulled out a chair from the glass-topped table. The seat cushion looked new. The chairs next to it, across from each other, were worn. He pulled out one of those instead and sat down. Just then the door opened.

The first thing Kayo noticed about Jerry Flagstaff was that he was very short, about five foot four inches tall. The freckles on his face made him look much younger than he actually was. His eyes were small and very blue. His skin was smooth, white, and oily. Flagstaff wore a dark grey Brooks Brothers suit with a white shirt and a grey and burgundy striped tie. Kayo stood up as he walked over to the table. He glanced down at his feet and noticed they had on the same shoes. Kayo smiled, stepped forward, and gave him a steady handshake. "Kevin Watson."

"Jerry Flagstaff," he said. Flagstaff motioned for Kayo to sit down as he pulled out a chair for himself. He opened a folder and began glancing over the material. "Your grades are outstanding! Probably get cum laude?"

"At least. If I remain consistent, and I plan to, I should get magna cum laude."

"I only got cum laude at Harvard," Flagstaff said. "I guess that means I didn't work hard enough."

Kayo wasn't sure what was going through Flagstaff's mind. "Not necessarily. What was that I read? Harvard's Econ Department has more Nobel Prize winners, I believe, so it's probably a lot harder to get A's."

"Yes, it does have the most Nobel Prize winners on staff in the Econ Department. That's why it's consistently ranked number one. Always over Yale."

"Our program is ranked third. And we just hired a professor from Duke who shared in the 1982 Nobel Prize—we're strong and getting stronger."

Flagstaff nodded. "Well, tell me. Why do you want to work for Baker and Neiman?"

"Baker and Neiman is a quality firm which—"

"Quality?" Flagstaff asked.

"Quality, yes. That is my own personal value system. I look at the maturity of the company for one. Now, Baker and Neiman is the fifth-oldest investment banking firm; that means there is a strong tradition here. Second, Baker and Neiman has the largest support staff of all the other firms, more analysts, associates, secretaries—even the mailroom staff is twenty-five percent bigger than the largest firms—meaning that I will have a larger team to work with and those urgent reports, those overnight proposals, will get out just a little faster than our competitors'. I feel that every part of the team is important." Kayo noticed the college ring on Flagstaff's hand. On the side was a crew emblem. He's so small—had to be a cox. "Every person on the team is important. It's not just the big guys who pull all the weight. Like in crew, the cox that guides them, keeps them on the right track, is just as important."

"I like that," Flagstaff smiled. He saw eagerness, strength, and potential in Kayo. He leaned back in the chair and made the offer. "Forty thousand to start. Bonuses range from twelve to fifteen thousand. We will provide you with full health and dental insurance. There is a company investment plan and, let's see, three weeks' paid vacation, and we always provide for membership to your college club here in the city as well as the health club of your choice." Flagstaff stood up and extended his hand. "Welcome to Baker and Neiman."

Kayo looked at the hand and he wanted to yell, to shout. This was the opportunity he wanted, the one he had been working and hoping for. The money, the perks, all that the company represented itself, said he was a player, a mover and a shaker, what he wanted to be, what he demanded of himself to be. Kayo was on his way and he knew it. Kayo shook Flagstaff's hand.

"Thank you. This is a great feeling."

"Stop! I have finally figured it out."

Michelle looked up at Edmond, one of the handsomest men on campus. He had jet black, satiny skin. His nose was powerful and perfect, his eyes full and almond-colored. Edmond was as conceited as he was gorgeous, standing now with his palms hooked in his blazer like Washington crossing the Delaware.

"What, Edmond?" Michelle said, standing on the steps to Yale Station. "I have to check my mail."

"I know why you won't go out with me."

"Because you're conceited and you've slept with every woman on this campus."

"Except you!" Edmond smiled, leaning down. "But I've figured out why. You, Elizabeth, Connor, and Kayo all hang out together. Everybody on campus figures Elizabeth and Connor have a thing and you and Kayo have a thing. But Kayo has got other women he's seeing. You, daughter of a Baptist minister, wouldn't go for that."

Michelle began walking down the stairs.

"I think you've got something going on with that Connor guy. And Kayo's covering for you."

Michelle stopped and looked up at Edmond. "Get a life."

"Am I right? Give me a hint?" Edmond called after Michelle.

She ignored him and wasn't even concerned about his revelation. He was always gossiping and most people never took him seriously.

Michelle bent down and peered into the mailbox. The letter on its side cut the space into triangles. She sighed and looked around Yale Station. The narrow hallways led to the mazelike room full of mailboxes. Hundreds of students, packed into the small space, buzzed around the tiny squares like bees in a honeycomb. It was exam period, the end of the year: grades, jobs, and grad school.

Another student walked up next to Michelle and peered into his box. His face was tanned from days of lying out on the campus lawn under the sun. His hair was bleached the color of a clamshell and pained anxiety marked his face as he stared into the box.

"Yes!"

They both turned.

The student's face was covered with a straggly beard that looked like two weeks' worth of growth. His hair was long and stringy and stuck out from under the Dodgers baseball cap he wore. "Harvard Law!" he screamed at the top of his lungs, his clenched fists beating the air, long thin legs kicking, his tattered shirt tail flapping up and down.

"Alright!" a voice from around the corner yelled.

"Drop dead!" another voice countered.

Michelle looked back at the key still dangling from her mailbox.

The student next to her opened his box. "I want good news! Good news!" he mumbled, grabbing the letter out. "Shit!" he shouted and fell back into the mailboxes. *"Awwww."*

Michelle rushed over to him. "Are you okay?"

"Harvard Law rejected me!" he moaned.

"How do you know? You haven't even opened the letter!"

"Are you blind? It's a thin letter!"

"So?" Michelle said before she could stop herself.

"Acceptance letters are thick! This is thin! Thin!" he said, his voice straining to a hoarse moan. "Four generations of Harvard lawyers and it stops with me!"

Michelle reached for his shoulder.

"Leave me alone!" He jerked away from her, crumpling the thin letter, and folded his arms across his chest.

Michelle turned the key and grabbed her letter—neither truly thin nor truly thick. She shoved it in her back pocket and started walking away quickly, determined not to make a scene like the one she had just witnessed. Michelle had told her friends she would meet them at Connor's room before dinner. They'd all be there.

At the entryway door, she stepped inside and used the nails of her middle fingers to rip the envelope open:

> Congratulations. You have been accepted to the Ph.D. program at Columbia University. . . .

Michelle closed her eyes and swallowed. "Columbia, yes!" She ran up the steps and pounded on the door with her fists. The letter felt like gold in her hand. "Hey, open up!"

Elizabeth opened the door and with a look, knew. "Columbia, yeah!"

Michelle grabbed her hand and began dancing. "We'll be in New York together. Alright! Alright!"

Kayo grinned at them. "Way to go, Michelle!"

Connor hugged her. "I told you it was possible! You'll be in

New York with us! Congratulations! We'll all be together—me at the firm, Kayo at Baker and Neiman."

"And me at ABC," Elizabeth said, taking over.

Michelle and Elizabeth grabbed each other by the shoulders and screamed, "AAAAhhhh!"

Connor winced at the shrill sound, put his hands to his ears, and laughed, "Chill out a little. People will think we're killing somebody in here."

The clouds were dressed in formal black for the special occasion. The warm rain soaked the windowpanes, the rafters, and more than one thousand chairs that stretched from one end of Old Campus to the other.

Streams of black from all directions trickled through the paths and emptied into the center of campus. There the students wearing their caps and gowns and their hearts on their sleeves lined up for the traditional processional through the city into the middle of Old Campus.

Rain beaded on top of the caps and left trails down the backs of the young people bouncing with excitement at the culmination of four years of driving oneself to the limit with intense study and partying.

The graduating seniors marched down the street, up through the green. Slow, intense steps. Graduating: the thought constant in all their minds. Their movement was patterned and engrossing like lightning striking above a hill. Their black robes were soaked through but they didn't care. Flags representing each of the residential colleges were held high and floating on the wave of invisibility as the students paraded through the arch of Phelps Gate into Old Campus.

Connor keyed himself into the sounds of the processional. "Old Blue! Old Blue!"

Kayo looked at the cracks in the arch. He'd never noticed how worn it looked. He felt himself slow down, almost to a stop. Elizabeth pulled him on gently.

Michelle sighed, looking at the old place for the last time.

They cleared the arch and walked out to their seats. Old

Campus was full now. All that could be heard was the sound of the President's voice over the drenched speakers, fighting the sound of the falling rain. The smell was of crisp spring mixed with tobacco as graduates smoked clay pipes, indulging in the tradition of old. There was something special about the moment that they all felt. It wasn't one thing or another but, like flowers in a bunch, it was all things together: the excitement of accomplishment, the reverence of tradition, the promise of a rich future, and the confidence of a unique comradeship that would last their lifetimes.

With the end of the speech, the standing, now cheering, students, many waving white handkerchiefs over their heads in the Yale tradition, let out a final rousing cheer. They were still to proceed to their individual residential colleges to get their diplomas, but this was the last time the entire class was to be together. It was their last hurrah before they would embark on their individual missions to save or conquer the world.

"Bulldogs! Bulldogs! Rah! Rah! Rah! E-li Yale!"

Chapter 8

THE cab darted between cars on the Manhattan street. Elizabeth stiff-armed the window to break her fall. "Shit!" She straightened herself back up and caught the cab driver's face in the rearview mirror. His nose was long and curved. His skin was badly pockmarked. His hair was a thick, curly Afro and his complexion was the color of whitewash. The driver looked up and winked at her.

"Hi baby. How are you?" he said with an accent that made the words fall out of his mouth and hit the floor like bricks.

"Fine and how are you," she answered, uninterested. The drab buildings and jitters about her first day held her thoughts hostage.

Through the rearview mirror, the cab driver used his vision to paw her body. "So, you secretary?"

"I'm in a hurry, running a little late."

"Okay baby, but how you like me to pick you up after work? Take you out for drink and real good time."

"No, thank you!"

"Stuck-up bitch!" he hissed, slamming on the accelerator.

"Wait a minute I—" Elizabeth's body slid all the way across the seat to the right, crashing into the window handle.

"Here's your stop," he said, slamming on the breaks. "Twelve-fifty, secretary!" The driver was facing forward, his hand back like he was holding a waiter's tray.

"You must be losing your mind," Elizabeth said angrily, straightening her clothes. "Look at me!"

"Not my problem! You in hurry, now I'm in hurry!"

She dug into her wallet and pulled out twelve dollars, and then fished around the change compartment until she found fifty cents. Elizabeth dropped it in his hand, and climbed out of the cab.

"No tip?" he asked, leaning across the front seat.

"Yeah, learn how to drive, you dick!"

He flipped his middle finger up.

"I'm going in here looking like I've been in a fight," she cursed. She stepped into the hallway and went to the elevators. During the ride up she begged herself to relax. Elizabeth got off the elevator and could hear the noise from the newsroom.

"Hey, you're the new writer—uh, Elizabeth!" a voice from behind her called. She turned, and standing there was a middle-aged man with a slight pouch. He was bald on the top and his hair was very thin on the sides. His sweatshirt sleeves were rolled all the way up and packages of cigarettes folded inside adorned him like military decorations. "I saw the memo on the back of the door saying you were coming today. My name is Rick but everyone calls me Flash," he said, extending a hand.

Elizabeth took his hand and winced, feeling that he was missing two fingers.

Flash sensed her uneasiness and held up his right hand. "The best thing about missing the two fingers is that I can flip management the bird without them knowing it!"

Elizabeth laughed away her discomfort.

"I lost the fingers in Vietnam. I was there on a special assignment with a reporter. We caught a unit of U.S. soldiers torching a village full of women and children. Shit . . . just mowing em' down like moving ducks in a carnival–*man*! Anyway, a funny-looking soldier saw that I was rolling on the whole thing—I mean I had gotten a spot in the trees and was hanging, getting it all—and he reached up and yanked me down. Well, I fell out of the tree and landed on my stomach so I kept rolling. A good cameraman never stops rolling. He didn't take too kindly to that and slammed down a machete he had taken from a village farmer—pop-pop! Off went the fingers, but I got the story. Got that fucking story and an Emmy too." Flash looked at his hand. "And after thirty years in this business, I've decided that I'd rather have my fingers!"

Elizabeth stepped back amazed. "What a story!"

"We're in a storytelling business, kid. Remember, always tell the story fast and true—get it fast."

"Is that why they call you Flash?" Elizabeth asked.

"No," Flash said with a grin. "I got that name because after I lost my fingers, I was a little camera shy, you might say, so I switched over to editing, matching those great pictures with the writer's words, which was film at first and now it's videotape. Anyway, when I cut my first piece on videotape, I couldn't get the damn machine to lock up right. So I had gaps that weren't covered with pictures which shows up as flashes on black—a definite no-no. I had twelve flashes in that two-minute piece, a station record, hence the slug Flash."

"Well Flash, you are the bright spot of my day. Everything's been a little crazy already," Elizabeth said, her shoulders slumping slightly.

"Well, wait until you get in the newsroom—it's really crazy, kid! What time are you supposed to meet Flap?"

"Mister Fletcher?"

"Yeah, Flap—fucking lousy-ass person. And there are no misters around here—he's Fletch to his face and Flap behind his back."

"I'm supposed to meet Mister, ah, Flap, in a few minutes but I want to freshen up a little bit first."

Flash glanced at his watch. "Let me introduce you to some newsroom guys real quick first!"

"Like this?" Elizabeth said, looking down at her clothes.

"Naw, you look fine—we all dress like normal folks around here. C'mon!" he said, pushing her through the newsroom door.

The room was full of people hustling about. The room itself was shaped like an octagon and there was a square wooden anchor desk in the middle with four padded chairs. Pointing at each chair was a studio camera. Set back from the anchor desk and all around were office desks with typewriters and telephones. From the ceiling were suspended studio lights of all different sizes. Elizabeth and Flash walked down an aisle that separated a block of desks and a high, paneled platform that looked like a judge's stand. Sitting in the center was a tall balding man listening to police scanners. Around him were four chairs with people answering phones. Hanging overhead was a huge clock surrounded by three large television sets mounted in the wall, all tuned in to the network channels.

"This is the assignment desk," Flash said, pointing. "The guy in the center, in the slot, is the assignment editor. That means he checks out stories and assigns the crews that go with the reporters on the story. The assignment editor and the executive producer and sometimes the show producers decide which reporters will cover which story. The police scanners are to pick up breaking stories like fires and murders and stuff. The folks sitting around the assignment desk are assignment researchers. They call the police stations around the city and make beat checks—you know, to find out if anything is going on in that area that we don't know about. If they miss a story and the other stations have it—they hang the guy in the slot from the ceiling by the thumbs!"

"You're teasing," Elizabeth said.

"I wish he was," the assignment editor said. He stood up and was barely taller than the ledge in front of him. "My name is Gordon. And I hope you have the good sense to get out of this business while you've still got all your teeth, hair, stomach lining, and mind."

Elizabeth looked at Flash.

"Listen to the man, he's been in this business longer than I have."

"Hey, here comes Flap!" Gordon said, sitting back down quickly.

Flash sat down on the counter just under the assignment desk. "He looks bad—but don't let him scare you, kid."

Elizabeth watched the man marching across the room. He was dressed in a tattered plaid suit jacket and dirty grey painter's pants. A cigar hung from the corner of his mouth and a pair of horn-rimmed glasses were fighting to stay on his nose. His shirt was open at the collar, showing off little black hairs. He pointed at Flash first and barked, "If you want to socialize all day, then go work in a massage parlor. Get busy!"

Flash threw up his hand, giving his favorite management sigh, "Sure thing." He winked at Elizabeth.

She smiled and thought, I like you, Flash.

"And are you going to smile all day or are you going to come to my office? You were supposed to be there thirty seconds ago! We are in a time business, young lady—never miss your air slot!" he said, looking at a stopwatch on a string around his neck. "Let's roll!"

Elizabeth walked behind him through the newsroom. She noticed the eyes staring at them as they made their way through.

The office was made of glass and faced the newsroom. Fletch sat down in the chair and Elizabeth took the seat across from the desk. There was a bookshelf full of videotapes; bits of paper marked each one with a reporter's name and the city they were in. There were four television sets in a wall unit and several framed press passes from different political conventions. Fletch's desk was piled with show scripts from the last week. He picked up one. "I want nothing in my shop but good writers with balls. Understand? I know you don't have any experience but I like the way you write. I know you went to Yale so you must be smart as hell. You probably want my job already. There are just three things to remember and you can go and fill out your papers and get your writing assignments. Those three things are: Always double-check your facts. Second, attribute everything you write—to the police, the fire department, the person, to authorities—to somebody, so if it's wrong we don't get sued. And third, I'm the news director here. I make your life heaven or hell, so whatever you do, don't piss me off or I'll eat you alive. Now, get out there and work your ass off."

"Yes sir," Elizabeth said. Her silk blouse was clinging to her underarms now.

The rest of the day started to pass quickly. Another writer laid the groundwork, showing her where the copybooks to type stories on were kept. She had been given a desk, a typewriter, and the first rundowns of stories for the six o'clock news. Elizabeth wrote and filed her first story.

"Rewrite!" the executive producer said, giving Elizabeth her copy back. The sound of people around her seemed to magnify rather than drown the words.

"I need a crew, dammit!"

"And I need a life, blow me."

By now, Elizabeth had come out of her suit jacket and she was rewriting her story for the third time. Elizabeth looked over at the executive producer, Helen. She was a short woman with long blond hair. Her face was beautifully shaped to a point and smooth. Her eyes were a faint green. She was standing there with her hands on her hips, holding court while a reporter explained the new slant on his story. Elizabeth could see that the reporter was sweating. She felt herself getting queasy as she remembered Helen's voice the second time she gave her back the same story: "This isn't college so we don't need a thesis—just tell the story, short and conversational!"

Short and conversational, Elizabeth kept telling herself over and over again. She checked her rundown, finding that the story played in the third section just before the commercial break. Elizabeth reread her copy. Unsatisfied, she balled it up and dunked it in the wastebasket just under her typewriter.

"Breaker . . . got a triple murder in the Village!" Gordon yelled from the assignment desk.

"New lead!" the six o'clock producer shouted.

Elizabeth watched as people started jumping up—two writers headed over to the producer, who sent one to the assignment desk and the other to the edit rooms where tape was cut. Gordon got on the two-way radio that linked him to all the camera crews out in the city. "Base to unit three!"

Elizabeth typed faster, wanting to finish so she could help. She was going over it for typos when she felt a hand on her shoulder.

"Elizabeth? Got a minute?" Flash asked, a solemn look on his face.

"Well, not really," Elizabeth said, frowning slightly. "I want to help on this new story."

Flash cut her off. "It's just that there's been a death in our newsroom family and I thought you'd like to sign a card."

"Oh, sure. Where is it?" Elizabeth asked, standing.

"It's across the hall in the planning office where they set up stories for the week. C'mon, I'll show you."

Elizabeth followed next to him. "Was it sudden?"

"It was murder!" Flash said, clutching his throat.

"That's terrible—did they catch the person who did it?"

"Yep, got him trying to dump the body . . . guy claims it was an accident!"

They turned inside a room with stacks of newspapers and magazines on the floor. There were two desks with phones and a series of file cabinets against the walls. Sitting at one of the desks, an intern, a pudgy kid with a faint mustache, was looking as if he were going to cry.

Elizabeth followed Flash to a desk with a large handmade card. It was about three feet by four and was sitting on top of a table next to an old, stained coffee machine. There were hand-painted roses and several signatures under the heading "We love and will miss you!"

"The art department made the card special," Flash said, handing her a black felt-tip pen.

Elizabeth took it and looked for a spot. Suddenly, out of the corner of her eye, she saw something and jumped back. "What the hell is that?"

"That's the deceased," Flash said. "See?" Flash grabbed the corners of the laminated shoe box that had been cut into quarters. There were rose petals all around inside. In the center among the petals was the smashed body of a cockroach three inches long. "Old Scoop is dead and gone—only been in this business a year but he had endeared himself to us all. That's the guy that murdered him and tried to dump the body into the trash can!" Flash was now pointing at the intern.

"I just stepped on him by accident," the young man said, sweating. "I-I sprung for the flowers, didn't I?"

"A minor point," Flash said, turning his back. "These young kids today have no values. Ha!"

Elizabeth looked at the card full of names. "Everyone in the newsroom must have signed this. You guys are nuts," she said, smiling.

"In the news business it's called being creative."

"There you are!" Helen said, touching Elizabeth on the shoulder. "I can't believe you're in here goofing off with Flash while we're trying to put a show on!"

Elizabeth cringed, suddenly remembering the copy still on her desk. "I . . ."

Helen threw up her hand. "I was looking for you to help with this breaker but after I saw this copy on your desk I changed my mind. My dear, you couldn't write a bad check. I suggest that you take the rest of the day off—go home and get yourself together and come back tomorrow."

She watched dumbfounded as Helen walked away.

"Hey kid, don't pay any attention to Mount Saint Helen—she's always erupting!" Flash said, trying to be consoling.

Elizabeth walked out of the room, ignoring Flash's call. She went back in the newsroom and grabbed her purse out from under the desk. She headed down the hall, thinking about her rough start. As Elizabeth stepped onto the elevator and muscled her way to the back, she vowed never to have a day like this again.

Connor looked across the desk at the empty chair. He crumpled the corners of the papers in his hand, then looked around his father's office. It was expensive and full of traditional American furniture. There were two bookcases on the west wall full of volumes on economics. On the top shelf was a marble sculpture of an eagle that his grandfather had commissioned back in the forties. There was a huge picture window facing east. Connor forced his eyes back to the papers that seemed to be burning the tips of his fingers.

I can't believe it! Connor looked at the top line, a question. Just under that sentence there were four lines of an answer. I know training class is the starting block but I don't need any favors like this! God, he's assumed I'll fail before I ever get started. "Bullshit!"

"What'd you say, son?" his father said, entering the room.

"Nothing, Dad."

His father sat down behind the desk that was full of paper. His suit hung on him the way it did on the hanger—perfectly. Connor shook his head and wondered, how come he looks so untouched all the time?

"Now, which associate did I give that computer disk company deal to? Fucking idiot, undersold it!" he said, rummaging through the papers. "You should be studying those papers."

"It's not fair."

"Is that what's bothering you? Listen, Connor, I have a lot of things going on, today in particular, and I don't have time to baby you. Just learn what you need to know so that you'll be placed in Mergers—where the money is! You are going to do well here. And you have got to learn to do whatever it takes."

"Have a little faith, Dad. I don't need these!" Connor said, holding up the sheets of paper.

His father sat down and slid the papers off his desk, folding his hands. "What were your grades like last semester?"

"I got two A's in history," Connor pointed out quickly.

"Your Econ grades were a joke."

"That's old hat now, Dad." Connor started slouching down in his chair.

"Sit up!" Body language is very important," his father shouted. "Playtime is over!"

Connor sat up.

"Listen, son," his father said, easing up, "it's just that everyone here knows that you are a Bellington—that you are part of a legacy—and no one likes anything better in this world than to see somebody with a leg up fall. Understand? It's like this: If a cripple falls, it isn't funny and everyone runs to help him up. But if a man in a grey flannel suit hits the ground, it's funny as hell and everyone laughs and keeps walking. Now that's how it is in the real world. I just want to make sure you get off on the right foot. If a father can't help his son, who can he help?"

"But I don't need this kind of help, Dad!" Connor said as he held up the cheat sheets.

"You don't know your ass from a hole in the ground. You're a man and I'm a man. But I'm your father too. You are going to kick ass in this company if I have to kick *your* ass. Now get out of here and get ready for your training class!"

"First you tell me I'm a man, then you treat me like a kid," Connor said, his voice breaking.

"Connor," his father said, holding out a palm as if to push him away, "just go and do as I say, son, alright?"

Connor spun out of the chair and left the office. He made his way to the bottom floor of the building. He headed through the glass doors and down the short hallway into an open space. The floor was a maze of white plastic. Connor could hear the voices murmuring. The light clicking of computer terminals could be heard as well and every few seconds the bated hum of a telephone broke through. Connor checked his watch. Almost time for class! He picked up a clipboard and pen. He stuck the papers under the first few clean sheets of his tablet and attached it to the board. He headed for the bathroom, pumping himself with confidence as he went inside. I am going to do well. I've got to show Dad that I can do it on my own. Connor looked into the bathroom mirror. The cold water and liquid soap gave his hands a cool, crisp feeling. Connor shook them hard and then began looking around for a towel but couldn't find one. He went inside one of the stalls and grabbed a handful of toilet tissue.

"Listen, I'm telling you, Craig, that old ass Bellington is a big prick! I went over and introduced myself to him at a restaurant last night, just to say hello, and the old shit dismissed me like I was the waiter."

Connor peeped through the hinges of the stall door. He recognized Steve Fretstein, a new analyst in his class, and Craig Maston, an associate.

"Maybe he'd had a bad day or something," Craig said, putting a finger to his lips.

"Good morning, gentlemen." Connor stepped out of the stall.

Both of their jaws dropped. Craig recovered first, extending a stiff right hand. "How are you today, Conrad?"

Connor shook his hand. "Fine. But I'm Connor. My Dad's Conrad or Big Prick, depending on who you're talking too."

Steve was now leaning over the sink, his palms clutching the sides. His sandy brown hair was falling in his face. Steve looked up into the mirror. His eyes were the syrupy-brown color of cough drops. He struggled to breathe through his pinched nose. Steve spun around, offering, "Hey, Connor . . . didn't mean it. You know?"

"You meant every word," Connor said, fiddling with his hair.

Craig stepped up to the sink and started washing his hands. He was short and powerfully built, with big arms and shoulders. He had played college football and had made it to the second-to-last round before the Jets cut him. His face was broad with fine features. His skin was the same shade as the soap lathering his hands. "Hey, Connor. We all have bad days and say things we don't mean." Craig stared at Steve, branding the words in his back.

"Maybe," Connor said, walking out of the bathroom, wanting them to sweat over it.

"He's going to screw me over now every chance he gets! And we're in the same training class too!" Steve said, turning around and sitting on the sink.

"Hang on, Steve. He might not say anything to his father. Don't make unnecessary enemies." Craig went to grab a paper towel and didn't find one. "But now you know to keep your mouth shut. You don't know who'll be where around here."

"Fine," Steve said, straightening his tie in the mirror. "I'll just have to get me some allies. I already have you! I'm not worried." But already Steve could feel the muscles in his legs cramping. He twisted his feet like a baseball player in the batter's box.

Craig recognized the nervous habit from their days on the football team at Princeton. He decided to give Steve some space. "I'll see you later. Good luck in your training class."

"Right, no sweat," Steve said checking his face in the mirror, looking for chinks in the armor. "Get tough."

The conference room was oval-shaped. There was a coffee machine on a table in the back corner and a few people were back there sipping and chatting. Chairs were in a semicircle in two rows with a short aisle in the middle.

Connor took the third seat in the second row and balanced the clipboard on his crossed knees.

A man with an enormous black briefcase waltzed in. He set it down on a table in front of the chairs. His hair was the color of a shiny new dime and his face had liver spots all over it. Big creases cut across his jaws and worry lines crowded his forehead. His eyebrows were white and grew like weeds in a little patch above each eye. His glasses were half-moons and by the time he had wiped them clean and cleared his throat, everyone in the room had taken a seat. "Good morning to everyone," he said. "My name is Carl Weems. "It is a beautiful, money-making day!"

The door opened and all heads turned. Steve hurried into the room, almost bowing to Weems as he went. "Very sorry!"

"Mister Fretstein, time is money—a much-used saying that never loses its value. You will miss the deal of your life, young man, if you don't get where you're going when you need to be there."

"I'm sorry," Steve said loudly to the entire class. He wanted to sit down quickly and the only empty chair was beside Connor.

Weems cleared his throat.

Steve sat down.

"Now," Weems began, handing out the packets, "here is a financial profile of a dummy company. It's a company that your firm is asking you to assess and to sell. I want to ask you a few questions about the information to get an idea of your instincts."

Got to get into that Mergers division, Connor thought.

I've got to be sharp, Steve thought, taking a packet and passing the last one to Connor.

Weems leaned back on the table and fired the first question.

Connor looked down at the profile sheet. His hand shot up and his answer was strong and confident.

"Good," Weems said, smiling.

Confidence goosed Connor up in his seat.

Next question.

Connor dug his nails into his pen. He quickly began scanning the numbers.

The hand next to him went up.

"That's correct, Steven," Weems said.

Steven smiled.

Connor glared at Steve.

Weems slowly walked up their aisle, stopping momentarily by Connor. "This is a very sharp class. Try this . . ."

Panic gripped Connor's body. He knew he didn't know the

answer and out of the corner of his eye he thought he saw Steve move. Connor gritted his teeth and lifted the pages.

"Young Conrad?"

Connor felt the words tear at his throat the first time. Then for the next four questions he answered, it became easier and easier. He felt the envious stares and felt ashamed and powerful like someone who puts a dollar in a change machine and then gets too many coins back. Connor flipped the pages over and the clipboard hit the floor.

Steve leaned down to pick it up, trying to be polite.

"I got it!" Connor snapped.

"Let me help!" Steve said, snatching the papers up. Instantly, he saw what they were.

Connor froze, his stomach tight from holding his breath.

Steve handed the clipboard back to Connor without a word.

Connor prayed that no one would see his hands shaking.

"Time for a break. Fifteen minutes!" Weems said, heading out the door.

Connor sat motionless, trying to figure out what Steve was up to. He turned and caught Steve standing at the coffee machine with the others. Connor picked out Steve's voice, then he heard the other voices shrink to a murmur, then a loud roar of laughter. Connor felt a hand on his shoulder. "Outside?"

Connor shook off Steve's hand. "Let's go!"

They walked until they reached a small foyer where many of the secretaries hung their coats. Connor turned inside, then grabbed Steve's collar and pulled him in behind him. "Listen, you didn't have to go flapping your mouth off to the rest of the class, asshole!"

"I told them a dirty joke! I didn't say a word, alright?"

"Why?" Connor questioned in disbelief.

"Because we got off to a bad start in the bathroom, me calling your Dad a prick. I'm just trying to square things, alright? But you got to be square too, and stop using those cheat sheets."

"You don't want anything?"

"Did I ask for anything?" he said, holding out his hand.

Connor stared at Steve for a long moment, then shook his hand.

Michelle looked at all the boxes scattered around the living room of her off-campus apartment. There were two windows with bars going across the west side of the room and there was a fire escape ledge big enough to sit out and read on. Michelle had already put some of her plants out to catch some sun. Under the window was a radiator, burnt red from cheap paint and rust eating away at the pipes. The kitchen had just enough space for her to jump back in if the bacon frying got too feisty. Michelle stepped around two boxes marked "Books," grabbed her jacket and notebook off one of the suitcases, and headed out the apartment door.

West 119th Street sloped down toward Amsterdam, making Michelle's feet move in a fleet cha-cha step. She turned the corner and there was a restaurant and a bookstore, university buildings—International Affairs and Law—along the street. There was a ledge, made of concrete, that people would sit on. There now, a group of construction workers were sitting, eating sandwiches and talking. Three spaces down, a man in a suit was sitting drinking bottled water while two more young men, who seemed to be law students, sat next to him comparing notes. Michelle began walking toward them and instantly, self-consciously, checked her clothing. She had on a fitted blouse, bright red, with matching slacks. Nothing at all too tight or seductive. But as soon as she stepped past the first construction worker it started.

"Babe, nice, *nice*, ass!"

"Yeah, girl . . . those tits are talking to me!"

"Whoa! Slow down! Come here!"

Michelle cringed. The words flowing from their mouths were filthy and dense and powerful and cutting. She wanted to rip her ears from her body. Michelle walked faster. She cleared the construction workers and thought her ordeal was over but it was not. The man in the suit took a swig and added his thoughts: "I'd love to take you home with me!"

The two students whistled, laughing, joining in by making sucking sounds with their mouths: "Wthehf! Whtheyf!"

Michelle felt cheap. The men looked at her as if she were a thing, a disembodied sex organ with no emotions. She wanted to die and fade away right there. Michelle was on the verge of running when a hand stopped her from behind. She thought it was one of the men—her mind feared rape even though it was daylight on a public street. "No!" she turned and shouted.

But standing there, with compassion in her eyes, was another woman. Her hair was brown, pointy, and shiny like the extensions of a desert flower. Her face was rich, soft brown. Her jacket was a bright red and lined in white fleece. It flapped in the breeze. She wore flat shoes with tassels made of soft suede. Her body was slim and shapely. "Don't take that!" she said and turned Michelle around. She held her shoulders tightly as they walked, "I'm Val. Don't be afraid. I'm tired of this!"

They stopped in the middle of the sidewalk, in front of the men. Val spoke up loud, her voice throbbing with anger. "Who said it was okay for you guys to sit there and assault this woman?"

All the men laughed uneasily. One challenged. "What assault?"

"It's not funny!" Michelle said, gathering strength from Val. "You have no right to make dirty comments about how I look! About my body!"

"Hey, what's up with you two?" one of the students asked, confused.

The man in the suit added, "It's a compliment! Take it as a compliment!"

"Would you compliment your mother, your sister, or your girlfriend like that?" Val asked, scanning the row.

"What, y'all don't like men or something?" one of the construction workers bellowed, trying to be macho.

"Men yes!" Michelle shouted, "Dogs no! What you're

doing is scary and it hurts! How do I know one you won't rape me one day when I walk past here?"

The men were quiet, their words finally hitting home. A couple of them left, one mumbled a "Sorry."

"Don't be sorry, just don't be dicks! Act like real men and respect women," Val said, and she grabbed Michelle's arm and they walked away.

When they were out of earshot, Michelle stopped and propped herself against a wall. "I'd never have had the guts to tell those guys off if you hadn't been here. What's your name again?"

"Val, Val Jemison. And you are?"

"Michelle Dubois Howard. Girl, you've got guts!"

Val was breathing heavily now too. "I was scared. But that has happened to me so many times, that when I saw it happen to you I just couldn't stand it anymore. I thought, Kid, if you're going to be a lawyer defending people, you'd better start now."

"I'm in the Ph.D. program for Lit. First year."

"Huh, Ph.D.—that's the Pretty Hard to Do stuff." Val took Michelle's arm and they started walking. "So, like, where were you going before we had our day in court?"

"To the Financial Aid office. I've got to get some more money out of those tightwads."

"Don't we all? It's tough too."

"You're an expert, huh?"

Val winked. "That's right. I'm in my second year here and I'm an expert on what to say to those stiff-asses at the Financial Aid office. Tell these folks you are poor and don't have thousands of dollars lying around to give to them."

"That works?" Michelle asked, waiting as Val opened the door to the Financial Aid office for her.

"Nope, but you've got to attempt something to keep yourself amused while you're getting screwed in there."

"You're going to let me go at it alone?" Michelle said, feigning distress.

"Yeah, girl. One fight per day. Besides, I saw enough of

those money-grubbing dragons yesterday!" Val winked at her. "Got a class. I'll look you up in the directory and we'll have dinner, alright?"

"Okay." Michelle watched as Val walked swiftly away.

Inside the Financial Aid office was a room full of tension and disarray. There were pieces of paper and envelopes all over the floor. There were cages where you could pay your tuition bills that looked like the ticket booths at the old sporting arenas. People were standing in lines that curved around the corners to the offices where the loan handlers were. Michelle could hear the statements ripping at each other like a hammer and tongs.

"What?! I have to wait until the end of the month to get the money credited to my account?"

"That is procedure, sir."

"When I owed *you* guys, it was right now. Now *you* owe *me* and it's the end of the month—bullshit, lady."

Michelle stood balked by dread. Finally, she began walking to the one empty seat across from a woman busy flipping through papers on her desk. The woman's fingers were thick and pink. She wore a white cotton dress with prints of red roses all over it. Her face was shapely and pale and otherwise nondescript. Shiny premature salt-and-pepper hair hung in folds on top of her shoulders. Her nameplate said "Kitty Bloom."

Michelle cleared her throat and extended her hand. "Michelle Dubois Howard. I'm a first-year grad student working on my Ph.D."

"Hello, Michelle," Miss Bloom, said shaking her hand. "How can I help you?"

"I got these papers for this year and the difference between my fellowships and the school costs is ten thousand dollars."

Miss Bloom didn't bother to look at the papers. She sent them. "You'll have to take out loans every year to make up that difference unless your family can pay for it."

"My family hasn't got that kind of cash. My father's a minister and my mother's a teacher."

"Well, then it's the loans. The university does not have any money to give you in the form of scholarships but we do have plenty of loan sources."

"C'mon!" Michelle leaned over and spoke softly. "I'm in for literature, which does not translate into big cash. I need just a few thousand more from the university—these loans are just piling up."

"It's loans or go to another university. There are plenty of people who would love to be in your shoes," Miss Bloom said, her thoughts traveling elsewhere. "I'm sorry, there's nothing I can do for you. Here are some loan applications."

"This is pretty shitty!" Michelle said angrily.

"I can't help you," Miss Bloom shot back. "You students get these off-campus apartments for five and six hundred dollars a month while I'm paying almost half of my take-home pay for a cold-water flat. You'll survive. All you students do. I'd advise you to take out the loans. Good day!"

Michelle walked slowly outside, threading through the crowd, trying to calm herself. She headed down College Walk. The sun beating down on the top of her head made her scalp sizzle. Michelle walked up the steps that led to Low Memorial Library. The students were laid out, sunning, reading, listening to music. Michelle found a little corner on the fourth step and plopped down, sulking. She unfolded the papers and tuned everything else out. Ten thousand dollars a year! It was more than she had borrowed during the whole four years at Yale! She couldn't ask her mother and father for more money, they had already taken a second mortgage on the house to help. Connor would give her the money, but Michelle was much too proud and independent to ask.

"That was quick!" Val stepped up and stood in front of Michelle.

"Look at these papers!" Michelle opened her notebook.

"No thanks, I've got my own hate mail. Just sign them and concentrate on getting your degree. See, it's all a game. This whole academic setup is designed to try your patience, your realm of sanity, and your sense of human decency. In more

Harlemized terms—they throw a lot of bullshit in the game, hoping you'll slip and fall."

"I'm so mad I don't know what to do!"

"You walk over to 121st and Broadway with me and have some nice herbal tea at this little shop I've got picked out. They even have a juke box with fifties tunes on it. I promise to show you how to do the twist." Val bent her knees and started to twist down the steps.

Michelle smiled. "It's better than sulking, that's for sure."

Kayo felt his insides popping like firecrackers. He looked around the room at the other first-year analysts in his training class. They wore more fine versions of blue suits than he knew existed. He pinched down the crease of his pants leg like checking the sharpness of a knife, then he touched his tie. Satisfied, Kayo looked ahead at the two rows of people in front of him, staring straight ahead. He dropped his pencil on the floor but the thick, plush carpeting swallowed the sound. Kayo bent down and picked it up, stopping to wink at his polished shoes. The first person he had met today, Danny the shoeshine boy, had done a fine job.

The instructor was a tall woman with a long neck, sloping shoulders, and spreading midsection and hips. Her name was Beth Gonzalez and she was immaculately put together. Her suit fit every contour of her body and her makeup was perfect—not too heavy or too light. She twirled a solid gold pen between her fingers and the reflection from the light made a windmill on the wall. She had taken her suit jacket off and rolled up the sleeves of her silk blouse. A Rolex watch was pushed down on her wrist. Kayo watched as her reddish-brown hair bounced from side to side as she talked to the class.

"In front of you is a breakdown of a company. Take a look at it quickly because I'll have a few questions for you." She stood up and stretched her legs a bit, walking to pour herself a glass of water from a pitcher set aside on a refreshment table. She took a sip, then looked around at the people in front of her. In the first row was a young woman with long, black, stringy hair and slightly buck teeth. Her blue suit was too tight and she had a habit, like now, of wiggling her foot. Beth took a sip and evaluated her. You're too nervous, Kelly. At times I can see you know the answer, but you hesitate and in this business it'll cost you dearly. Now, that Harold sitting behind you is going to be a superstar right out of the starting blocks. He's got the Ivy League tie—Penn—and the suspenders. Confident and charming all the time. Beth took another sip of water. And Kevin. He's got the answer but doesn't want to seem like this class is too easy for him. Doesn't want to make any enemies and that's smart. He answers questions like a bat out of hell—always on top of it. "Okay everybody"—she began walking back over to the center of the room—"on what basis would you value . . ."

Kayo's hand went up.

". . . this type of company. Kevin?"

"I think it best to value this company on an EBIT basis, Earnings Before Interest and Taxes."

Beth glanced down at her sheet, "Why not on an Earnings basis only?"

"In this industry, the companies are characterized by varying degrees of leverage and maturity. EBIT will give the truest evaluation."

"That's correct. Listen we've been at it all morning. Why don't we take a break, back in say, twenty?"

The room began clearing quickly. Beth flipped through her papers and called over her shoulder, "Kevin, come here for a moment."

Kayo walked over.

She put the paper clip on a few sheets. "Would you go upstairs and drop this off at the receptionist's desk for me? I'd appreciate it."

"Sure, I'd be happy to," Kayo said, feeling like a flunky.

"Thanks," Beth said, knowing he'd run into Ed Morrow.

Kayo decided to take the stairs. He stepped out into the next level and headed for the receptionist. He handed her the papers and turned to go. Out of the corner of his eye he saw someone he knew had to be Ed Morrow, the first black investment banker hired by the company.

A short, thickly built man, he was standing by the big picture window near the hallway entrance. He had a white mug in his hand and he sipped while staring outside. His hair was the beautiful, shimmering color of the pebbles on a beach. It was cut very short, almost in military style. His face was dark like tree bark and his Adam's apple was big and lumpy. Kayo began walking over to him. Apprehensively, he stopped a few feet from Ed's back.

"If you have something to say, say it!" Ed said, taking another sip of coffee without turning around.

"My name is Kevin Watson and I'm an analyst here. I just wanted to meet you, Mister Morrow."

Ed turned and extended his hand. "Hello, Kevin. It's nice to meet you. I've heard some promising things about you," he said and started walking away.

Kayo looked puzzled, not knowing whether to follow or not.

Ed turned. "My grandfather walks faster than you do! He turned back around and continued walking, smiling into his cup.

Kayo caught up. "Mister Morrow, I heard you were the first black investment banker they ever hired here."

"That's right. They hired me reluctantly in the fifties and had me working in the mailroom, then pushing paper. In the late sixties they decided to tap my potential and I helped them make a ton of money. Then when their consciences started bothering them back in the early seventies, they began promoting me."

"Wow," Kayo smiled, "you're a trailblazer!"

Ed stopped and looked. "I'm a witness."

Kayo stopped. "Of what, all the changes?"

Ed started walking again. Kayo took two double steps to catch up. Ed looked into his cup. "Everything and nothing has changed."

"Huh?" Kayo just kept walking this time.

Ed walked toward an open space with several chairs around. He stopped just short of the doorway, where they could see inside. There were five men sitting around talking and drinking coffee. Ed motioned with his head for Kayo to come beside him and look.

He hesitated. "I don't know, Mister Morrow."

"Aww, c'mon, Kevin," he said, almost laughing. "I came here and watched for years, and they won't even notice you!" He took Kayo by the arm and pulled him beside him. "'It is sometimes advantageous to be unseen, although it is most often rather wearing on the nerves.'"

"Ralph Ellison," Kayo said, looking at the group of men in the room.

"Those are the big wheels in this company right there in that room."

Kayo watched their seemingly heated conversation. "Yeah, I can just hear the ideas churning!"

"Me too. Sounds like somebody kicking a tin can around. Ha ha!"

"Ssh! They'll hear you."

"Don't worry, the millions of dollars they're thinking about has soundproofed their room and turned it into part of the twilight zone!"

Kayo watched them go at it. Two of the men seemed in pain, two others were listening intently, while the fifth seemed to hold court.

"What is your favorite sport?" Ed asked.

Kayo didn't hear him.

"What's your favorite sport?" Ed asked again, this time a little louder.

"Huh, um, basketball."

"Good. Think of them as the Boston Celtics of investment banking."

"What? I'm confused."

"Good. I don't like a man who thinks he knows everything. And I like even less a man who is confused and refuses to admit it. Now listen carefully. Those men there are the Boston Celtics." Ed looked at Kayo. "See that little guy in the corner with the freckles?"

"Yeah, I see him."

"Well, he's Danny Ainge. He's the hacksaw player in the game. Leans on clients and makes them tired, he bullies a deal. He has a total disregard for his person when he's playing. His deals are clumsy and sometimes awkward but they work. Makes money—he scores!"

"Okay, I get you!" Kayo smiled.

"Now, standing off to the side in the blue-and-grey tie is Kevin McHale. He is quiet and always thinking. He's the worker in the bunch, the setup man. He gets the deals down the court where they're workable for an easy score for the company.

"Okay!"

"Now, the man sitting down next to him is Dennis Johnson. He's smooth, but not quite as good as he thinks—but since he's in good company, that helps him out."

"Gotcha."

"That gentleman leaning over holding the pad is Robert Parish, the big man in the hole. He waits for folks to get a deal down to the wire, then he snatches it away and powers it through for the big one. Now, last but not least, the gentleman holding court is Larry Bird. I mean I don't care what the deal is, what the circumstances are behind it, or how far out it is, it's money in the bank with him. The man can hit from anywhere with any deal." Ed stepped back. "Watch them when you can and do what you will with the lesson. Now go back to your class."

"Aren't you coming back down?"

"And miss the rest of the twilight zone? No thank you. I'll see you later in the week."

"Okay, I'll come see you!" Kayo turned and started jogging down the hallway. He turned, looked back, and smiled.

Chapter 9

STEVE'S tie was slung across his shoulder as he strutted down the hallway toward Connor's back. He spun Connor around. "I'm in deep trouble."

"You're always getting worked up over nothing!" Connor spoke calmly. "C'mon, let's go." Steve's heavy breathing followed him like footsteps. "Will you calm down?"

"How?"

"Get in here!" Connor said, turning into his cubicle area.

"I'm sweatin' like a pig! Got any more shirts?"

Connor was already pulling out a shirt from his bottom drawer. "I'm losing a fortune giving you all my shirts!"

Steve took it and shook it out with a pop. "Well, if you help me out this time—I'll buy you a dozen shirts!"

"That's what you always say. Steve, you can't keep getting worked up over every little thing."

"This is a big thing," Steve said, taking off his damp shirt.

"I've got a presentation tomorrow morning at nine and I haven't done shit."

Connor whistled. "Nothing?"

"Zip," Steve said, buttoning up the fresh shirt. "Man, I was working on that Mitchell deal up until last week. Kicked major ass on that."

"I heard! I heard!"

"Yeah, well, the old boy needed a break after that one. Man, I've been cruising the bars, picking up the hottest babes."

"For a whole week?" Connor said, sitting down.

"I'm single. I'm supposed to be buck-wild!"

"Yeah, well I know you milked a lot of cows back there on the farm in Minnesota, but shit, you're lucky you can stand up."

"Hey, I'm saving just enough so that when I get married I can keep my wife happy and keep the family line going with a few kids. Until that time, this boy is sowing some *wild* oats! I picked up this one girl last night in that sushi bar on 52nd . . . and whoa, she couldn't get enough."

"Dog-gish!" Connor howled.

"I mean, multiorgasms! What could I do?"

"You could've left that piece of ass in bed, gone home, and started work on your presentation."

"Fuck her and leave? That's rude, and besides, I said multiorgasms. I had to test that out again this morning."

"Well, when you're a CEO somewhere, I'll know you fucked your way to the top."

They both laughed.

"So, you gonna bail me out or what? It'll be just like school. At Princeton, I was always pulling all-nighters."

The phone rang.

Connor picked up. "Bellington. Hi, Kayo."

Steve waved.

"Steve says hi. Yeah, a big client from Dallas, huh? No, no, don't take him to that Southern-style restaurant," Connor said quickly. "He can get that at home. Take him to Twenty One. Yeah. Tonight?"

Steve put his hands up in a praying fashion.

"No, I can't tonight. Call me after lunch and let me know how it goes." Connor hung up the phone.

"Important lunch?"

"Yeah, Kayo's real green about those kind of things."

"Well, I'm starting to feel kind of tired. Maybe I need a zap of coke to pick me up."

"You need something to eat, probably," Connor said.

"Alright, a hit and some food. I'm buying lunch," Steve said, backing out of the cubicle.

Connor came from behind the desk. "Yeah, and you're buying dinner too and all the late-night snacks and I don't want any caffeine pills or zap cola."

"Are you kidding? I heard that shit kills your sex drive!"

"Boy," Connor said, slapping him on the back, "it'd take an M-80 to kill your sex drive!"

Elizabeth was stretched out on the short beige loveseat propped against her living room wall. Without turning her head or scanning with her eyes, she could see most of her apartment: the small kitchen sink with the swan's neck faucet and wooden cabinets; the dip in the dull wood floor and the big grey windows facing the apartment building across the street; the shiny glass mirror in the newly rehab'd pearl grey bathroom; the small potted plants that practically blocked the narrow hallway leading to the front door. The walls were covered with mounted posters of Styx, the Rolling Stones, and Michael Jackson. The posters were hung at an odd angle to cover creases in the thin walls. On Friday and Saturday nights the heavy bass sounds of reggae music could be heard dancing the ceiling in the apartment downstairs. Elizabeth reached into the Ziploc snack bag she now clutched between her bare breasts. It was almost empty. In the corner, Elizabeth found enough coke left to fill two of her fingernails. First the index, then the middle finger. She sniffed hard and felt shotguns going off in her head.

It had started months ago. She had worked four weeks

straight without a day off, and still she had another day to go with her next shift beginning at five A.M. Despite that, she dragged herself to a going-away party for one of the techs heading for the network bureau in London. Someone there had said she looked tired. And she knew her eyes were droopy. Someone else had said she looked depressed. By then Elizabeth was on the verge of crying. Someone else took her aside and said she needed a pick-me-up and that they had just the thing. That was the first time she used cocaine and it had all the jittery excitement, frightened wonder, and pure giddiness of all her other firsts put together: the roller coaster ride at eight, her menstrual cycle at thirteen, and sex at sixteen.

Elizabeth could hardly move now. She focused on the little bark-colored house mounted on the wall. It was a twenty-year-old cuckoo clock Michelle had given her the last time they had dinner. That was two months ago. There were little tree branches carved on the front of the clock and leaves painted in fall colors around the lower edges. It was one minute to nine and Elizabeth anticipated the bird, tiny, fragile, accurate, and boisterous, popping out of the little shutter. Elizabeth loved to hear the cuckoo when she was high; it sounded like music. She braced herself for it, seeing the shutter doors flutter in the darkness, but instead she heard a banging on the door.

"Elizabeth? Elizabeth!"

Elizabeth looked back up at the clock just in time to see the doors snapping closed. "Fuck!" She got up and headed for the door. "Yeah, coming!" she said, stopping to wipe her face with her hands before opening the door. "Hi!"

Michelle didn't say a word. She just looked at Elizabeth's bulging eyes, her tousled hair, and her runny nose. "Do you have company?"

"No-um-no," Elizabeth said, using her fingers to comb through her hair. "Why?"

Michelle stepped past her and shut the door. "Because you're in the dark, naked from the waist up, and it took you forever to answer the door."

"Oh, well, I was"—she sniffed—"asleep."

"You slept through our dinner date," Michelle said, reaching in the corner to turn on the torch lamp.

Elizabeth flinched at the brightness.

"You look like shit!" Michelle said.

"What? Hey, I'm sorry about dinner, but hey, I overslept! I *work*, remember?"

Michelle saw a faint powdery ring around Elizabeth's nose. She frowned. "What have you been doing?"

"Nothing, just trying to rest."

Michelle saw the bag on the table. She walked over to the loveseat and picked it up. "Coke? Elizabeth, you're into coke!"

"Who the hell are you, coming into my apartment accusing me?" Elizabeth snatched a T-shirt off the bathroom doorknob. "What are you, the police, or the FBI, or my mother or something?"

"I'm your best friend, remember?"

"The one that I hardly see anymore? That best friend?" Elizabeth said sarcastically, pulling the shirt over her shoulders.

"Elizabeth, I keep telling you this Ph.D. program is kicking my butt. But that doesn't have anything to do with this. Girl, I'm telling you . . ."

"That's the problem—you're always telling me something. Anything. Anything to run my life. I just wish you'd stop preaching."

"Being concerned is preaching?"

"No, walking in here snooping is preaching. Always up on your better-than-thou soapbox is preaching, just like in school."

"In school we never had problems talking."

"Well, school is still in for you but it's real-world time for me. And let me tell you, it's rough out here."

"Well, what the hell is so rough that you gotta use coke? Huh? I mean it can't be that bad."

"See?" Elizabeth slammed her hand against the wall. "There you go again! Look, there's a lot of pressure and stress—I've got to make it, okay? See, there's a lot of competition out here and you don't know shit about it and you can't even imagine it until you're out here up to your neck in it."

"But you're better than this," Michelle said, balling the bag up and sitting down on the loveseat.

"Better than what? You act like I'm an addict or something! You don't listen. Didn't I just tell you that there's a lot of pressure? What are you, deaf and dumb or something?"

"Right now I wish I was."

"Aww no! I'm not gonna let you make me feel guilty."

"I'm not trying to make you feel guilty, I'm trying to get you to see that this is dangerous!"

"I just snort a little every now and then . . ."

"That cocaine sneaks up on you, Elizabeth!"

". . . *Every now and then* I said, to help me relax and deal with the pressure. I don't do it on the job . . ."

"Not yet."

"*And* I don't do it all the time!

"Not yet. But you just keep on."

"What-what no-no, who made you an expert on life? That's *all* I fucking want to know here tonight is *who* made you an expert on life? God, if I can ever figure that out I'll die happy!"

Michelle didn't say anything for a long moment. "Promise me you'll try to cut back."

"Cut what back? I hardly ever do it, I keep telling you!"

"Promise me!" Michelle said again stronger.

"No! No, you're trying to make me do what you want and . . . and admit to a problem I don't have! Screw that! No!"

Anger boosted Michelle up out of her seat and she didn't stop walking until she was toe to toe with Elizabeth. "Fine, screw yourself up. I don't care, okay?" And she turned away, walking to the door.

"Taking your ministry to the streets?" Elizabeth asked sarcastically.

The door slammed.

Elizabeth fell back against the wall. "Damn!"

* * *

I don't believe it!

Kayo pushed the rolled-up sleeves of his shirt all the way up around his biceps. The skin on his arms was now streaked with white. He leaned over his desk, fists down, almost reeling. I should be on the Reynolds project! A disgusted feeling filled his body. He had been working more than seventy hours a week. Kayo shifted from foot to foot. What is it? he asked himself. Kayo needed to talk to someone. He picked up the phone and dialed Connor's number.

"Yes, Conrad Bellington the third, please," Kayo said into the receiver with urgency. "Okay, would you tell him Kevin Watson called and that it's important? Thank you." Kayo sat down, then stood back up. The problem was nagging at him, not allowing him to be still. He felt on edge and decided to take his own initiative and do something about it.

Kayo turned and walked quickly out of his cubicle. He knew that Lampdon would probably be in Manchester's office. They usually had lunch together. He was determined. I'm just going to tell Lampdon that he fucked up—not putting me on that assignment. Kayo made a quick turn and headed around the corner past a narrow stretch of hallway that the secretaries used to scan the floor when they needed to find one of the analysts. Kayo glanced down over the balcony. The cubicles with desks were all evenly marked off in rows. The people inside, at the desks, were hunched over their phones and computers. He thought of the galley scene in *Ben Hur*: "We keep you alive to serve this ship . . . row well and live." Kayo watched as the people below him strained, many of then frantic, almost urgent. The plastic yet rhythmic sound of their toiling rose. Kayo whispered: "We keep you alive to serve this company . . . make money and live."

Kayo slammed his palms against the railing and then headed down the hallway. Manchester's secretary, Fran, was sitting at a desk outside his office door. A delivery man with several packages piled high in his arms was standing by the desk. As Kayo walked closer, he could hear her strained, irritated voice.

"Sir, Mister Manchester just went to lunch with a colleague and will not be back for a couple of hours. Now, I know you said you were to deliver these by hand, but I can take them."

The delivery man almost stuttered, his voice tired: "I-I was told to hand-deliver. This is my first job since moving here and I don't want to take any chances."

Kayo wasn't sure whether or not Fran was blowing the man off.

"Will you *please* give me those packages!"

Kayo eased past the delivery man's back, knowing Fran would stop him if she saw him.

"Lady, I just don't know!"

Kayo stepped inside the office. Empty. Suddenly he realized what jeopardy he had just put himself in. Suppose Manchester and Lampdon were there? He was angry and maybe he might say the wrong thing! Kayo turned to leave, but the beauty of the office stopped him. He looked at the view of the skyline, the concrete and steel shining like marble against the pale blue sky. He walked over to a wall full of small oil paintings in ornate frames. Kayo admonished himself for not taking the time to go to some of the museums around the city. He moved over to two hulking bookcases full of books and fingered the frail old bindings: *Moby-Dick, Paradise Lost, Little Women.* The man was a collector.

The door . . .

Kayo turned to hear a growing conversation.

"Fran, I forgot to get a folder I'll need later. You can go ahead and go to lunch."

Manchester!

Kayo felt his heart start to pound.

"Fran, let me take those packages for you."

And Lampdon too!

Kayo frantically searched for a hiding place and spotted the closet. He lunged at the gold Victorian handle, stepped inside, and shut the door. The sound of clanging hangers exploded in his ears as the cold metal stabbed him in the back of the neck.

"Just put them on top of the desk, Larry. I'll get that folder. By the way, I think that team you put together for the Reynolds project is a real winner."

"Thanks, Paul. You know, I really wanted to put Watson on the team but it's such a delicate project socially that I didn't want to chance it."

Kayo pressed his forehead against the door.

"I know what you mean. He's not versed in the finer things. No polish. He's just . . . there's something very unrefined about him, and the Reynolds project will call for special team meetings with the clients and I'm not sure how well he'd handle himself."

"Exactly! That's what I thought. I mean, I've seen him joking in the halls with the shoeshine boy—can you believe it? And he's a Yale man too."

"Aaah, Watson is Yale smart, but he's not Yale bred. Here's the folder. Let's hurry or we'll lose our reservation."

Kayo heard the door close, but couldn't move. Yale smart but not Yale bred. "Ain't that a bitch!" Kayo said, snatching the door open. A wave of cool air hit him. Dizziness wrapped itself around his forehead like a bandage. Kayo stepped out and took a deep breath to steady himself. He walked to the door and slowly peeped out. Fran had left her desk, and he moved quickly.

Their words, heavy and smelly, stayed with Kayo as he walked, as if he was lugging a sack of mud on his back. His eyes burned and the words put the uneasiness of an elevator ride in his chest. Kayo was glad Ed's secretary had already gone to lunch. He walked into Ed's office and sat down, shoulders slumped, hand to mouth, eyes downcast. "Ed, I think . . . I don't know, Ed."

Ed looked at him and saw himself more than twenty years ago and instantly he became angry; angry at how the company would sap the strength, crush the eagerness, and just shake the foundation of a young black man. "What did they do?" he asked.

Kayo leaned forward and for a second felt too embarrassed to even repeat it. "They didn't put me on the Reynolds project after all the good work I've been doing. And when I went to ask about it, I heard Lampdon and Manchester talking and man, Ed, they said they didn't pick me because I was Yale smart and not Yale bred."

Ed watched Kayo wring his hands. Then he leaned back in his black swivel chair and said, "Kevin, let me tell you a story. And it's real important, so listen carefully. I was born in Hope, Arkansas, in a sharecropper's shack after three days of my mother's hard labor. She almost died having me and the midwife told her to stay in bed for a couple of weeks to rest. Well, my father was real excited about his first child, me being a boy and all, and didn't pay attention to what he was doing in the fields. He accidentally tripped over a harness and threw his back out. Now he and my mother both were in bed. My grandfather would come by every day after working in the fields to cook and clean, trying to nurse them both back to health. They didn't have colored nurses or hospitals back then, and nobody could afford to stay in from the field to care for them. One day, when everybody was out in the field, a big storm rolled in. They say the sky turned black quick as a finger snap and lightning started up too. A bolt hit the shack with me, my Mama, and my Daddy in it. The first people in from the fields say they saw my Daddy drag his body along the front step with his hands, and me, in my diaper like a swing, being carried in his mouth. They said he dropped me off the porch and then drug himself back in the house that had caught fire. By the time they got inside the front yard, lightning hit that shack again and folks down there say that's the closest thing to a bomb exploding they had ever seen.

"So, I didn't know my mother and father. My grandfather raised me. He was a great guy. Worked three jobs to make sure he saved enough money for me to go to college. He'd put the money in a big mason jar that used to have raspberry preserves in it. The money would be all sweet-smelling. The education jar, he called it. Well, by the time I'd been accepted and was ready to leave for Grambling, he had worked himself to death. It seemed to me that he waited until he knew he had enough saved to see me through before he let himself die. He called me into his room in that shack, a week before I was to catch a bus to Louisiana, and said: 'Boy, the white man ain't gonna let you run his world. No sir, he ain't. But if he's feeling generous, he just might let you have a little bitsy corner. And boy, if he lets you have that corner, I want you to be ready to run the hell out of it!' That night . . . he died." Ed stopped, as if he was hearing the words all over again in his head. He looked at Kayo. "This is gonna be your corner, and I'm going to show you how to run it."

The moonlight was like slivers of glass sprinkled all over the sidewalk. The cars were dirt-covered and made a washing sound as they rolled over the slick streets. Walking through the night, Connor listened to the sounds becoming fainter and fainter as he walked up 119th Street. The misty weather annoyed him. He had to be careful walking up the satiny front doorsteps to Michelle's apartment building. Connor had a bottle of Dom Pérignon in one hand, his briefcase and a rolled-up *Business Week* in the other. Wet, grainy dirt splattered across the sleeve of his Paul Stuart trench coat as he rang the buzzer.

"Connor?" Michelle said, her voice hissing and popping over the intercom.

"Me." He was already leaning on the door when the buzzer sounded and the door popped open with a click. Michelle was standing in the doorway waiting.

"Hi babe," Connor said, walking past her.

"Do you realize what time it is?"

Connor threw his briefcase, coat, and magazine on the chair. "Two o'clock. But I knew you'd be up."

"Connor, I've been working all day." Michelle spoke while walking back to the bedroom.

Connor began undressing as he headed into the kitchen.

In the bedroom, Michelle was sitting at the head of her bed in an extra-large, sleeveless grey sweatshirt. Books and papers blanketed the bed. Michelle tiredly pushed up the student lamp clamped to the bed. The red funnel pitched the brightness up to the ceiling.

Connor stopped in the doorway, flute glasses in one hand and the Dom Pérignon in the other. "What are you doing?" he said, covering his eyes from the harsh light.

Michelle saw that he had his shirt off and that his pants were unbuckled. She yanked the funnel down.

Connor walked over to the edge of the bed. "Move your stuff."

"Why?"

"So I can get in bed. Michelle, I'm telling you I had a wild day today."

"You didn't ask how my day was," she said, crossing her arms.

"You gotta hear about what happened to me first."

"You just assumed that I would be up and just dying to hear about your day?"

"Will you move this stuff? I'm so tired I'm about to fall out," Connor said, putting his knee on the bed.

"No, Connor! You just come in here at two o'clock in the morning, take your clothes off, and start telling me about your day!"

"So what?" Connor saw that she was really angry. "Okay, fine. How was your day?"

"You take me for granted."

"I do not," he said, putting the glasses and the bottle on the nightstand. "Why are you trying to pick a fight? You're in a bad mood. You and Elizabeth have a fight?"

"That has nothing to do with this. And I'm not trying to pick a fight. You take me for granted and I'm sick of it."

Connor moved over to the bed and gently climbed on, paper and pencils crunching beneath his knees and elbows. He took her hands in his and said softly, "If I have taken you for granted I apologize." Then he began to slowly run his tongue along the top of her knuckles. He knew she would tense and when she did, he began to suck her fingers. "Tell me . . ."

Soft, wet sucking.

". . . what you want me to do . . ."

Michelle felt a melting of her insides.

". . . to make it up to you." He moved his hands along the backs of her knees, on up to the insides of her thighs. "Tell me."

Pleasure began cruising through her body and his question stayed in her mind. She answered truthfully, "Tell your family about me."

Suddenly the warmth rolled away.

"You want to fight, then let's go at it!" Connor said, getting up off the bed.

"I just said it, Connor," Michelle said, wishing she hadn't, missing the warmth. "It just came out."

"I keep telling you that I will tell my family when the time is right, so don't push me, okay?" Connor said, stepping back from the bed. "Why you gotta push me?"

"I'm not pushing you! You asked me . . ."

"Get off it! All damn night you've been itching for a fight, Michelle."

"You asked me, Connor!"

"Fuck it!" he said, backing out of the room. "You didn't want me here tonight anyway."

Michelle wanted to yell for him to wait, to stop, to come back and finish what he had started, but she held her tongue. The front door slammed and she grabbed one of the glasses and hurled it against the wall. It thundered and burst into pieces and she covered her head and eyes with her hands. He acts like it's my fault. My fault! I'm picking a fight with him? She kicked the books off the bed, then the papers. Michelle picked up the phone.

"Kayo? I know it's late, but something is really bothering me."

Kayo leaned up on his elbow and cradled the receiver between his shoulder and ear. "What's the matter?" he said sleepily.

"I just went a few rounds with your buddy."

Kayo leaned up more in the water bed to tilt the clock toward him. "Can't you and Connor fight at a decent hour?"

"I'm trying to talk to you."

"Okay," Kayo said, sitting up. "What happened?"

"Well, he came waltzing over here, ringing my doorbell at two o'clock in the morning with a bottle in his hand. Comes in the bedroom with his shirt off and some glasses, just ready for a party!"

"My man!" Kayo said, laughing.

"What *did* you say?"

"Nothing. Go ahead, I'm listening."

"Well, it's like he just takes me for granted all the time, you know?"

"Yeah, that's how you feel?"

"Don't you think he takes me for granted?"

"You're asking me?"

"What the hell do you think I'm calling you for? Kayo, what do you think?"

"I think that people in general get used to things. If you let somebody treat you a certain way, that's how they keep on treating you, out of habit."

"Meaning?"

"Meaning, you let Connor take advantage, he'll take advantage. See a sucker, lick it."

"That's tacky. I'm getting tired of this secrecy too, you know? I mean, not being able to tell anybody about our relationship—it's stupid! It makes me wonder," she said after a silent moment.

Kayo sighed. "I understand. You know that Connor loves you."

"And I love him, *you* know that."

"I know that. But you can't love him more than you love yourself. You have to take the lead some. Be stronger and let him know exactly how you feel. Okay?"

"That's what I've been thinking too. Okay. Thanks, Kayo."

"Feel better?"

"Yeah, I do," Michelle said, settling down in her bed. "There's something else too."

"What?"

"I saw Elizabeth last night."

"Oh, we're having lunch tomorrow."

"Well, Kayo, she's really gotten deep into coke."

"How do you know?"

"She stood me up at a restaurant. So I went to her apartment. She looked out of her mind. There was an empty coke bag on her cocktail table."

"Well, a lot of people toot a little now and then," Kayo explained.

"Kayo, I'm telling you she looked like shit! She didn't look like it was just a little fun."

"C'mon, Michelle, you know how conservative you are."

"Conservative! I'm talking about Elizabeth getting herself into something she can't handle. We had a big fight about it."

"So, y'all not speaking now, huh?"

"I want you to talk to her about it when you see her tomorrow."

"So she can get pissed off at me too?"

"No, so she can see she's headed for trouble!"

"Okay, I'll talk to her. I promise," Kayo said with a loud yawn escaping. "Now may I go to bed please?"

"Yes, you may go to bed." A little laughter crept into her voice. "Good night . . . and thanks again."

Kayo ordered another beer and checked his watch again. Elizabeth was already twenty minutes late, but fortunately he had set aside extra time for lunch. The restaurant was crowded. The low murmur of controlled, businesslike voices filled the room. The lights were low but the decor was cool and bright with the varying shades of white and the big, satiny tropical plants. Kayo played with the rim of his glass and let his mind wander back to the work piled on his desk. He had an important presentation coming up. Most of the company's top managers would be there. Ed was grooming him for it the way a trainer would his prime steed. Kayo thought of how close they were becoming and smiled. "Daydreaming?"

Kayo looked up and was surprised at how worn-out she appeared. Her cheeks were hollow. Her skin was blunt. Elizabeth's gaze was flat. "So how's it going, really?" he said as she sat down at his table.

"Well, I'm not getting enough rest. There's plenty of job stress, too." She gave Kayo that knowing look. "And no, I'm not hooked on coke. I get a little buzz every now and then, to relax."

The waiter came over. Elizabeth ordered a Screwdriver. Kayo held up his beer. The waiter nodded and left.

"I know Michelle called you up and told you I'm a crazy coke fiend."

"No, it wasn't that bad. She's worried, though. You do look tired—lost some weight, too."

"Kayo, you look tired too. It's the long hours. I mean, do I sound like I'm dying or something? I mean Michelle just came in my apartment and just took over."

"That's Michelle. She lets you know just how she feels."

"Unless you're her precious Connor," Elizabeth cracked.

"Yeah, we talked about that last night too. She's says she's going to let him know more about how she feels about their relationship."

"I'll bet! She made me so mad." Elizabeth looked away.

The waiter brought their drinks. Kayo picked up his glass and sipped. "Well, that's what friends are for, to bug you. Sometimes Michelle goes a little overboard. You just make sure you get some rest. I know how those long hours can cut you down."

"Yeah, Michelle doesn't have a clue about how tough it is out here," Elizabeth reflected, then smiled. "But we're going to kick some ass—huh Kayo?" She picked up her drink.

"I'll drink to that," Kayo said, clinking her glass.

Elizabeth dropped her head back and downed the drink in one gulp.

"God, you downed that like a champ!" Kayo wrinkled his face.

"Aah it's no major." Elizabeth shrugged her shoulders.

"Me and the guys at work go out drinking after the late show every now and then."

"Just watch it—bad habits can sneak up on you real quick."

"You joining the Michelle Howard ministry too?"

"I'm just saying, alright?"

"I'll be careful. Um, how's work going for you?"

He played with the label on his beer. "It's going pretty well. It's a ton of work. I'm getting ready for a big presentation right now. Big-big-*big*!" Kayo stopped to take another sip. "Elizabeth, if I can pull this off, I'll definitely be pegged as a player in the company. I just have to wow 'em."

"You can do it, Kayo," Elizabeth encouraged. "Competition's tough?"

Kayo whistled through his teeth. "Yeah, but I gotta leave everybody in the dust to get on the prime deals."

"Is there anybody there to help you? Ya know, to cue you in on things?"

"Yeah, Ed's been real helpful."

"That's the black guy that was there first?"

"Right. I told you guys about him. He's been really taking care of me like blood and everything. Ed's so astute. He knows the industry, the people. He is really sharp. That's why I get pissed when I hear people talking about how he's lost his edge."

"Well, what do you think?" Elizabeth asked, motioning for the waiter.

"Not Ed Morrow! They're just not giving him the respect he deserves and he seems to be holding back. It's like the big boys have forgotten about Ed. I don't know why. But that's okay. Ed'll show them all. I'll bet he's been working on some big deal that'll just blow everybody away."

"He sounds like a winner to me."

"Yeah, I don't need to worry about him." Kayo looked up at the waiter heading toward their table. "I'm starving!"

Elizabeth nodded. "Me too—'cause you're buying!"

They both laughed.

Chapter 10

THE fluorescent lights gave off an ivory haze in the absence of competing sunlight. Ed's enormous oak desk was covered by four different piles of papers. Two of the piles were held down with bronze eagles lifting their wings for flight. Another pile was held down by a grey tape dispenser, the last one by a large, round plastic ball. Ed sat, horn-rimmed glasses at the edge of his nose, reading. Kayo was tired and his body was settling deeper and deeper into the soft part of the chair.

"Sit up, Kevin. You can't concentrate like that," Ed said without looking at him. "Remember, body language is important."

Kayo scrutinized the dark chiseled face. "How'd you know I wasn't sitting up?"

"I heard your shoes sliding on the carpet," Ed said, still reading.

"We've been at it a long time now, huh?"

"Very long," Ed said, stopping a moment to give that grand smile of his.

"Yep. Um, what do you say we make it an early one tonight?"

Ed took off his glasses. "If I didn't know you better I'd take you seriously, but I know you're not going to let an old man like me outlast you!"

"Of course not. I was trying to give you a break, is all."

Ed went back to the report he was reading, chuckling to himself.

"Oh yeah," Kayo said, putting the report down. "Look what I bought to wear during my presentation." Kayo pulled out two small jewelry boxes. He opened the first one: a diamond tie clip. He opened the second one: two gold tie stays.

Ed took them in his knobby hands. He tilted the boxes back and forth, watching as the light ricocheted off the fine jewelry.

"Classy, huh?" Kayo said proudly.

"Won't do," Ed said, snapping the boxes shut one right after the other. "Take them back."

"Why?" Kayo said, taking them out of his hand. "These are expensive as hell! I've seen Manchester with a tie clip like this too."

Ed leaned forward. "Kevin, you want to look sharp, conservative, but you don't want to outdress them! Look good but not too good. Let them know that you're hungry. Later you can buy the tie clip. And as for those tie stays, that's a waste of money. Don't spend two hundred dollars on something you can't even see."

"Well, okay. But I want to keep the tie stays. And you yourself just said you can't see them. I can't stand to have the ends of my collar turned up—looks so tacky!"

Ed smiled. "You want the tips to lay down?"

"Yeah, you got some on," Kayo defended.

Ed flipped up the ends of his collar and pulled out two paper clips, bent like capital S's. He lifted his collar tips up and slipped them back in. "See, serves the purpose for less than a penny a piece. Now I can take my two hundred dollars and buy some nice shirts instead. Get it?"

"Got it."

"I'm from the old school, Kevin. I've learned some hard lessons. Some hard lessons. Many at this company."

"I'm going to run this company one day, show 'em all."

Ed reached out and shook him. "Kayo, this is a truth and don't forget it. No matter how hard you work, you're never really in the inner circle. There is no room there for blacks. They may let you stand close, and look in, and some people actually think they're a part of it, but when it comes right down to it—they're not."

"Aw, Ed."

"Kayo, they've got built-in support groups. Hey, if one of them makes a huge mistake, it's hush-hush. If you or I make a mistake—*Holy Jesus, call the po-lice.* See, it's an old game and the rules haven't changed. Think of the loss . . . it's like baseball with the color barrier still intact."

Kayo didn't want to hear any more. He knew things weren't fair but he thought surely he could be the exception. Ed's words stirred a fear inside him that he refused to acknowledge.

"C'mon, let's get back to these reports."

Kayo looked back at the pages in his hand and the words seemed to smear in front of his eyes. He rubbed them. "You know, who thought of this divisional report anyway? No other company does this and I mean, this is crazy. This is a helluva lot of pressure to put on a guy."

"You know, they started this mess five years ago. Selecting three of the analysts to give reports on each of the different departments. Well, the reason they did it was to see how the people they think are the stars will hold up under pressure. All the managers will be there."

"I know, I know," Kayo said, feeling a little nervous in his stomach. "I heard two of the guys last year did a lousy job and they got let go six months later."

"Yep," Ed said, turning a page. "The doorknob hit 'em where the dog should of bit 'em."

Kayo faked a laugh.

Ed took note of the nervous sound. "Kevin, they selected you from all the other analysts to give one of the presentations. You know why? Because you have worked your behind off. I've watched you getting better and sharper and smoother."

"Ed, you know I couldn't do it without you."

"Boy, I haven't done anything but smooth out some rough edges." Ed put the report down. He got up, walked over to the desk, picked up a round plastic ball, came back and handed it to Kayo.

"What is it? Looks like a big pool ball."

"It's a carnival eight ball. Tells your future."

Kayo squeezed it and a white liquid floated in a triangular opening.

Ed explained: "You spin it around in your hands real fast and ask it a question. Then you squeeze it hard and the answer pops up in the triangle. Try it."

"Naw-aw!"

"Watch," Ed said, taking the ball from Kayo. He spun it around in his hands, then asked: "Am I wasting my time working with Kevin?" He stopped and squeezed. The triangle filled with a white liquid and the word *No* in big black letters. "See? The eight ball knows all!" He handed it back to Kayo.

Kayo took it and spun it around in his hands. The rough plastic stung his palms as he twirled it faster and faster. Kayo looked at Ed and asked: "Am I going to do well on my presentation?" He stopped and his elbows stuck out and the veins in his arms tensed. The white fluid floated up. The black letters said *Yes*.

Ed clapped his hands. "Yes!"

Kayo looked at it and laughed. "But Ed, this is only a game."

"Life is a game, Kevin." Ed took the eight ball out of his hands and gave him another report to read.

Kayo took it, sat up, and settled back in to work.

* * *

Dozens of newspeople were staking out the Brooklyn Covenant Building. The gleaming panes and lacquered shutters had been built by the muscle of political patronage. It was a small return on a 75 percent voter turnout for the current City Hall administration. A house for crack babies. It would be long on political mileage for City Hall: babies, anti-drugs, jobs for folks living in the neighborhood—they had planned well. Now fifty or so of the neighborhood people were standing around in their best clothes. They didn't care that Mayor Anton Callo would be coming out at any moment, but rather they were enthralled by the possibility of being on television: television, that rarely showed people like them unless they were being arrested or victimized.

The newspeople were getting cranky. They'd already been waiting for more than an hour. Men and women took off their heavy gear and sat on the handles of their cameras. Reporters found shade that was provided by the antennas on the huge minicam trucks. Elizabeth was too anxious to be bored. The station had been short on reporters and the managing editor had asked her to field-produce. She held the mike tightly in her hand, trying to remember everything she was told: Fuck this Mister Goody stuff and the crack playpen. Everybody there will be banging Callo with questions about that Queens property he bought while borough president eight years ago and sold to the city last year for twenty times the value. That's the story. Hold the mike in his face. Don't let the other reporters muscle you out of position. Stay with the cameraman. Keep the mike in his face!

All that was rolling around in her mind along with the realization that her father knew the Mayor. They had grown up together in New Haven and had been best friends until they were fourteen and Callo's family moved to Queens. Elizabeth's father had often told her stories about the old neighborhood and all the kids there, including Callo whom they nicknamed "Cookie" because of his love for sweets. He was a chubby kid, picked on, until little Mike Nickelson began feeling sorry for him and put a stop to it with a few well-placed punches.

Suddenly, the doors of the building swung open. In the

doorway, Mayor Callo stood holding a baby. The two were a contrast: Callo's big mitt hands palmed the baby's bald, fragile head that teetered back and forth with wide, frightened eyes. Callo, his wiry brown hair blowing in his eyes, was dressed in a tailored, vested blue suit. He looked full and confident, eyes staring straight ahead. "Brooklyn Covenant House is a haven for the oppressed and weary. These are children victimized by parents who abused drugs!"

By now all the crews were in place, jockeying for the best position. Elizabeth did well, anchoring a spot in front with her mike hoisted high.

A voice from the crowd of newspeople shouted,"But what about all the money you made on the Queens property? Did you use your clout to make money?"

"No comment!" Mayor Callo shouted callously and the baby in his arms began to wail from fear. He turned to one of the workers standing behind him and handed the woman the child. His face was flushed but like any good politician he recovered and cracked a smile. "No comment."

As he began walking the newspeople eased backward, boxing him in.

"No comment."

"But Mayor . . ."

Callo snorted, then waved to the residents standing out in the recesses of the sidewalk.

They cheered at the recognition. "Yeah!"

Elizabeth walked backwards, her arm aching from holding the mike up. In an erratic move, to avoid a puddle, Mayor Callo stepped far to the left in Elizabeth's direction and for a moment their eyes locked. Elizabeth blurted out, "Hi, Cookie!"

Mayor Callo stopped. "What did you call me?"

Elizabeth swallowed and said as easily and cheerily as possible. "Cookie. My father, Mike Nickelson, grew up with you in New Haven."

"Mikey! Yes! Yes! You're his daughter, huh?"

"Yes," Elizabeth said.

The cameraman breathed in Elizabeth's ear. "Ask for a comment about Queens."

"Um, could you give us a statement about the Queens deal? Something," Elizabeth said, an edge of pleading in her voice.

Mayor Callo smiled and looked around at the crowd of reporters. "Because she reminded me of the old days, I will give you one statement. That Queens deal is legal and was not any political payoff or favor. That's all I have to say on that matter today." And he walked off.

"Good! Good for you, kid!" several of the cameramen could be heard saying to Elizabeth. Many of the seasoned reporters just rolled their eyes at her.

Later, back at the station, people kept stopping by Elizabeth's desk to congratulate her for weaseling a comment out of the mayor, who was known for being tight-lipped. She felt proud and part of the team.

Just then, Helen began making her way across the room. She crushed the loud din of the newsroom under her heels. She climbed the assignment desk and pointed a stiff finger at Gordon. "We missed the live shot! Every-fucking-body-else is on the scene and live at the top of their show except us!"

Gordon leaned over the desk and tried to whisper, "Helen, we couldn't get the signal in."

"Fuck a couldn't. You chew those guys a new asshole and we better have it right tonight or else!" Helen reared back on her heels, turned, and stormed away. She stopped midway and motioned. "Elizabeth, got a minute?"

Elizabeth fell in step behind her and just as Helen turned the corner, she heard Gordon bark: "What? Can I make a silk purse out of her ear? Now she's going to be pissed at me for the next week!"

"Maybe not," an intern sitting at the assignment desk said.

"Are you kidding? That bitch holds a grudge like I hold my dick in the john! Give me that phone! Unit Three, get your shit together A-S-A-P!"

Elizabeth turned the corner and stepped into Helen's office. Helen was standing behind her desk breathing heavily, her face flushed and twitching. Elizabeth sat down.

Helen glanced up and looked surprised, forgetting already that she had even called Elizabeth. "I heard about the good job you did today. You've got promise and I just wanted you to realize that one good coup does not make a career. This business is tough, particularly for women."

"Most careers are."

"No, but it's tougher in broadcasting because there are so few women like you and me who are behind the scenes. I'm the boss and that really bugs a lot of the guys out there. I've got to be tougher and better than a man would be so the men out there will respect me. The problem is, then I become a nasty bitch with an attitude. If I try to take a nice encouraging approach, then I'm a pussy out of place. It's tough. You want the guys to respect you but also see that you're a woman, too. A lot of them try to seduce you, and if you turn them down then you're a stuck-up bitch with a sex problem . . . if you give in, then they believe you've screwed your way to the top. There's a fine line to be walked. Watch your step."

Elizabeth fiddled with the edge of the chair.

"You do good work. I just called you in here to tell you to be more aggressive. Push yourself more. You've got to put all you have into your career to get everything you want out of it. I think you have the potential to be one of the best. Go for it!"

"Fletcher came to my desk the other day and asked me if I had any ideas for a sweeps piece," Elizabeth said.

"Pitch something. Fletcher does all the promoting and you're his hire, too—if you can meet his challenge, you'll be a rising star in this company. If you don't, you'll be stuck. Work on it."

"I will."

Suddenly, Helen lost focus as if someone had popped the tape out of the video recorder. She sat down and picked up the phone as if Elizabeth wasn't there.

Elizabeth got up, feeling like a zombie as she walked back to her desk. There were no co-workers, no noise from the typewriters, no yelling and screaming except that which was going on inside her head. *I've got to prove myself.*

The Webster Conference Room of Baker and Neiman was the largest room in the company. There were flat silver lights all around the ceiling border. The room itself was painted an odd shade that could be best described as a milky gold. Seats mounted in a semicircle were made of plush yet firm gold-colored material. State-of-the-art audiovisual equipment lined the north wall.

The conference room was almost full now and Kayo stood in the hallway and watched as the company's top managers and executives filed through.

"Kevin Watson?" one division manager asked, shaking his hand. "I've heard a lot of good things about you."

Kevin shook his hand firmly. "Thank you, Mister Halston. I really admired how you handled that bidding war over Shearson & Howell. Those guys thought they could sneak in and snatch it right out from under you."

"Thank you!" he said, then repeated Kayo's name: "Kevin Watson."

Kayo continued to greet people. He was wearing a deep blue Brooks Brothers suit, a white shirt, and a blue and red striped silk tie held in place with a Yale tie clip. Kayo leaned his head into the conference room and saw that most of the seats were taken. He nervously touched the tips of his collar, feeling the paper clips. "Where is Ed?" he whispered to himself before deciding to check Ed's office.

Kayo stopped at Nancy's desk, just outside Ed's office. "Hi," he said smiling at her.

"Big day!" she replied with her lingering Irish accent. "Go on, Mister Watson. I'm sure he'll want to see you."

Ed was sitting behind his desk, reading over a report. Smoke from a cigarette cut a grey streak down his face. His dark brow was wrinkled and Kayo had to say his name twice before he responded.

"Yes, Kevin," Ed said. He checked his watch. "Your presentation starts in ten minutes! What's wrong?"

"Nothing. So far, it's been going real smooth. C'mon, I've been waiting for you!"

"I'm not going."

"But I-I . . ."

"I'd love to come, Kevin. But I've got to clean up a big mess here. They gave me this chump-ass deal last month and I gave it to someone else to handle and they screwed it all up. I should've just done it myself, after all. Anyway, I'm mopping up here."

"People will talk if you're not there."

"I don't care, Kevin." Ed took his hands to his ears. "God didn't slap these on the side of my head for nothing! I've heard people saying that I've lost my edge. But it's what I know in my heart that counts. Now, go on!"

Kayo felt a little sick. He turned back to Ed. "But I wanted you to be there for moral support!"

Ed grinned at him and stood. "You don't need moral support, you've got skill!" He held out his hand.

Kayo shook it.

"You come back later and tell me all about it over dinner?"

"Okay, Ed."

When Kayo got back to the Webster Room, it was just about full. He came in with the last five people and took a seat at the conference table in the front of the room. He was glad he would be the first to give a presentation. He wanted to set the standard.

Kayo stood up. "Good afternoon, and thank you all for coming to our latest movie, Watch the Rookies Sweat."

They laughed.

Kayo smiled and opened his briefcase. "I always believe in tackling the toughest obstacles first." He walked over to the light switch and dimmed it. "So, I will use the projector to show you a segment of the Mergers Division that had some difficulty this first quarter. Here are the figures for this first quarter on the right and last year's quarter in the center and our top competitor Blakey and Barnum on the left. Now we are up ten percent from last year at this time and twelve percent ahead of B and B, but ladies and gentlemen, I challenge us to do better. We have to get tougher. . . ."

The longer Kayo talked the more confident he became. He was like a rising sun that grows more brilliant with time. His momentum built with each winning point. His hand gestures, his other body movements, emphasis at the right time, all were working together. When he finished, there was a silence resounding with respect and admiration.

Kayo could hardly sit through the other presentations. He knew he had achieved his goal, set the standard. Inside, he was jumping around like a kid holding the ribbon at the end of a foot race. Wait until I tell Ed! He's going to be so proud of me! I did it! I smoked 'em. On the outside, he looked intense, interested in the others.

Afterward, everyone shook his hand and patted him on the back. They did so with the others, but they held his hand longer; patted him on the back just a little harder. He jogged back to Ed's office, stepped inside, and shut the door. Kayo met Ed's anxious stare. "I killed 'em!"

Ed jumped up and came around the desk. "I told you that you would."

Kayo ran in place and waved his arms. "Man, they didn't know what to do or to say!"

"Didn't know whether to smile or fart, huh?" Ed said, egging Kayo on. "What about Lampdon and Manchester."

"Aww, Ed, they were the first ones to shake my hand. Yale smart, not Yale bred. I showed them!"

Ed held out his hand.

Kayo flipped it, palm out, and slapped Ed a high five.

Ed laughed. "I like that!"

"Whoa! Ed, let's go to dinner now. I'm dying to tell you every detail."

"I'm dying to hear. I've got one quick call to make. You go get your stuff, come back, and I'll be ready."

"Yeah, yeah!" Kayo felt the blood speeding through his veins. "Alright!" He spun around and got to the door. As soon as he opened it, he straightened his suit coat.

When he got back to his desk, there was a message from Connor and that reminded him that he had forgotten to call. Kayo picked up the phone and dialed the number quickly. "Connor? Man, it went great!"

"That's wonderful!" Connor said happily. "I thought you would of called me to get some help on it."

"Naw," Kayo said, picking up his trench coat, "Ed helped me. Connor, he is brilliant. The man is the greatest, okay?"

Connor felt warm in the face. "Well, I don't want to hear about him—I want to hear about how you did."

"Well, I'm just getting my coat. I'm taking Ed out for dinner and drinks so I can give him the juicy details! I'll call you tomorrow sometime, okay?"

"Sure," Connor said, hiding the hurt he felt. "No big deal."

Kayo hung up the phone and grabbed his briefcase. He was still putting on his coat as he walked down the hallway. Kayo was so pleased with himself that he hardly noticed Lampdon and Manchester coming toward him.

"Kevin," Lampdon said, stopping him. "Once again, I just wanted to tell you what a great job you did on your presentation."

"Yes, outstanding," Manchester confirmed.

"Thank you. I worked very hard on it. I'm glad the work was apparent."

"Well, we don't mean to hold you up. But we both think that you have a very bright future ahead of you," Manchester said.

"I've always known that," Lampdon added.

Kayo smiled. "Thank you, sir."

They stepped aside and let him pass. When Kayo was out of earshot, Manchester looked at Lampdon. "You know, we were wrong about him. I think we've got something here. He's still a little rough, but he's definitely a player. We've been waiting to get rid of Morrow—now is the time. There are other blacks we can shift up who are alright, Jefferson and Olgen, but that Watson is going to be a star."

Lampdon nodded. "When are you going to tell Morrow?"

"Well, he loused up that Jemlon Steel deal and is in the process of cleaning that up. When he's done, he's out."

* * *

Michelle wound her fingers around the straps of her purse, wrapped her feet around the sides of the chair. Her mind was on a note she had just found in her mailbox: "Michelle, please stop by my office after your classes. It's important. Professor Kingman."

She was now sitting outside his office on a wooden bench facing three secretaries. Michelle could barely see the eyes of one woman who had a stack of letters piled high in front of her. The woman grabbed a letter opener and began ripping apart the envelopes like a missionary cutting through the brush.

Michelle inventoried the reasons why she could have been summoned here: I was late getting those papers back to my class. I had to get an extension for that Victorian Lit presentation which he hated anyway.

"Michelle, Professor Kingman will see you now," the secretary said, pointing the letter opener at her.

Like a toy winding down, Michelle walked to the last door on the right of the short hallway. She took a deep breath and stuck her head in cautiously.

Professor Kingman was sitting at his desk, thumbs under his chin, his massive hands framing his face. He kept reading.

"Professor Kingman."

"Sssh!" The command slithered from in between a gap in his front teeth. The top of his shirt collar was stained from the sweat that was dripping down his face.

Michelle pictured him in the seminar making literary comparisons, emphasizing each word to the class with pinched fingers as if he was holding the beauty of it all right there for them to see. Michelle walked over to the chair in front of his desk and sat down. She tapped her foot and tried to read upside down what had trapped the attention of Professor Kingman.

Finally, when he did look up, Professor Kingman's gaze wrung her out to dry. "You were late getting papers back to the class you're TA-ing. And your presentation was late and below standard. Michelle, as your adviser I must be candid with you."

She crouched in her seat, her knees now far from the firm lap of the chair.

"I am the only black professor in the Ph.D. program and you are one of two black students. I think you show a great deal of promise, which is why I agreed to be your adviser." He paused and looked at her like a star pitcher staring down a big hitter before throwing a beanball. "*But* after your recent performance I'm having second thoughts."

"I did get behind . . ."

". . . and did a poor-ass job to boot," he said, stealing the words right out of her mouth.

She balled up her fists. "I *got* behind and did a poor job and there's no excuse for that. It won't happen again."

"This Ph.D. program has a tremendous drop-out rate, so you better be careful! Remember, I'll be watching you."

"I'll be watching you." Michelle was repeating that to herself long after their meeting was over as she walked to clear her head. She headed for Morningside Park. Many students were afraid to cut through the park, fearing robbers and rapists. But Michelle always felt good cutting through in the afternoons when she wanted to get away from Columbia, the posh Upper West Side, her studies, Connor, and back to a feeling of singularity. So now, once again, Michelle walked down through what she and Val had dubbed The Looking Glass, and found herself in Harlem.

Change washed over her as she inhaled incense and listened to the sounds of street sellers hawking their goods: "Tapes! Three for twelve!" "Earrings! Gold chains! Chokahs!"

She studied fresh okra, beets, cabbage, and collard greens on a wooden cart hoisted high on top of a truck; sculptures of Malcom X and Martin Luther King, Jr., atop an old station wagon. The doorways of shops were crowded with people going in to buy, coming out with bags, and those impatiently rocking back and forth as they waited for buses. Music—gospel, reggae, rap, blues—billowed the souls of the regulars and the visitors drifting up and down the Harlem streets. Michelle turned the corner, feeling revived, when out of the doorway stepped a man in tattered clothes, his beard frosted, his hair coiled in fuzzy dreadlocks, his mouth crusty. "Food?" he said, thrusting slender hands with small grey nails into Michelle's face. She froze with a memory from years before, hands like these reaching out to her . . .

"Thank you," Friar Pete said, taking the tray from Michelle. She had slipped out a back door of Commons with the food. Friar Pete took it, squatted, and began shoveling peas into his mouth with the metal spoon. "Pardon me. My army days made me a bit of a slob when it comes to supper."

"You were in the army?"

"Briefly. The army in the sixties wasn't a great place for a Negro man. I was stationed in Houston and had a sergeant as ugly and hateful as a mule. He had it in for me so I got it in for him—right in the mouth. Discharged."

"Well, what did you do after that?"

"Worked on the oil rigs and got rich, or thought I was. I married a charming girl with eyes as black as the oil gushing out of those wells. I worked double shifts on the rigs to buy her things. Look," he said, showing Michelle his fingernails. "That grey there is permanent. I scrubbed them for hours at a time for six straight weeks after I got laid off. Scrubbed my nails and listened to my wife and baby cry."

"I didn't know you had a family."

Friar Pete dropped his eyes and complained, "Spaghetti's too salty . . ."

Michelle backed away from the outstretched rusty palms. She forced the memory of Friar Pete away. The knot in her stomach began to ease as she stepped into the narrow opening of the African Antique Shop.

Inside, the familiar surroundings calmed her. There were aluminum racks along the wall full of multicolored dashikis—men's, women's, and children's sizes. A box of shoes, flat and of beaten leather with short straps across the toes, marked "For walking in the sands" filled one corner. Behind a glass case luscious handmade jewelry—clay, gold, and ivory—satisfied the eye. Michelle walked over to the counter now and spoke to a woman hunched over, half her body inside the case, arranging the necklaces and earrings with big, soft brown hands.

"Can I help you?" the woman offered, standing straight up with a smile.

"Is Kofee here? My name is Michelle."

"Oh, Michelle. Kofee says you're one of his best customers. He's not here. I'm his wife, Coreen." She had on a blue T-shirt, Tye-dyed with reds and yellows as if the sun was rising on her slim back. Her soft brown hair was held in place by a gold clip. Her faded jeans were tattered around the ankles and her rubber Bass deck shoes squeaked against the tiled floor. "Kofee says you're in all the time."

"Yes, I love browsing in antique shops."

"He should've been back by now with some more new items," Coreen said. "There's a box over there on the floor. A guy brought it in yesterday. He said he was cleaning out his grandmother's house somewhere on Striver's Row. She just passed away and he'd found a lot of things in the attic. We haven't had a chance to completely go through it. But if you see something you like, I'll price it special since you're a regular."

"Okay," Michelle said, bending down over the box and sifting through. It was mostly carvings and cloths. She picked up a bolt with swatches of teal, orange, and yellow. It was filthy and dusty.

"You find something?" Coreen asked.

"Yes, this cloth." Michelle walked over and handed it to her. "I could make some things out of it. How much do you want for it?"

Coreen examined the bolt. "Doesn't look like much and it's pretty beat up. Ten dollars for our regular."

Michelle reached into her purse for a ten, handed it to Coreen.

"Thanks, Coreen. I'll see you next time, maybe?"

"Okay, enjoy!" she said, waving good-bye.

The inside of the cafe was well lit, its hanging drop lights fashioned like microphones with bulbs in the ends. The wooden tables were small and very square. There were straw dividers, hand-painted with Japanese symbols, separating the tables.

Michelle and Val walked through the door, spoke to the host who then led them to their table.

"Well, it's about time," Kayo said, smiling.

Connor and Elizabeth were sipping white wine. "Hi," they said one right after the other.

"Everybody, this is Val," Michelle began the introductions. She pointed around the table, "Kayo, Connor, and Elizabeth."

"Hi," Val said smiling.

"Starving!" Michelle said, reaching for a chair.

Val looked at the chair next to Kayo. "Michelle, do you want to sit here?"

"No, this is fine," Michelle said, sitting down next to Connor.

"I'm glad I'm meeting you all. Michelle has told me a lot about you."

"Same here," Connor said.

Val opened the menu. "You all will have to recommend something because I've never had sushi."

"Really? Never at college?" Elizabeth asked, surprised.

"No, sushi isn't on the menu at Spelman," Val said, laughing.

"Huh, that's very narrow of them," Elizabeth said snootily.

"Well, I'll bet you guys didn't have soul food at Yale."

"Wrong!" Kayo said. "We had Soul Food Night every year and this boy over here," he pointed at Connor," used to try to climb in the pots and eat all the greens!"

The rest of the evening they ate and drank white wine and imported beer. Throughout the evening, Val and Kayo would catch each other's eye. She would drop hers and turn the conversation back to Michelle. Elizabeth, Connor, and Michelle locked into a debate over foreign policy toward the Middle East. Kayo pretended to be listening but really he was feeling quite annoyed that Val was fighting her interest in him. He saw the desire in her eyes but she would quickly turn them away.

Val stared into her glass. I can't believe the way he's looking at me, and right in front of Michelle! Val played with the lime in her drink, squeezing it until all the pulp was floating on top like flower petals in a pond.

Not one to pass up a challenge, Kayo leaned forward and

moved his body over so that he touched her leg with the side of his.

"Um, Michelle, show me where the bathroom is?" Val asked.

"Okay," Michelle said, sensing that something more was going on. "Come on." Michelle led the way and Val followed, trying to whip her apprehension into courage before they got to the bathroom. How can I tell her? she thought. I don't want to ruin our friendship. But what kind of a friend would I be if I didn't tell her that her boyfriend was making passes at me?

Val caught the door with a stiff arm. "Something's going on here and I don't really understand it."

Instantly, Michelle thought Val had picked up on her and Connor. She felt a bit relieved. She actually wanted Val to guess the secret so she would not break her promise to Connor. "What is it?"

"Um, Kayo has been making passes at me."

"So?"

"So! I've been playing him off all night. I wouldn't mess around with someone you were seeing."

Michelle stopped Val with a flood of giggles.

"This is funny to you?" Val asked, leaning down and looking up into her face.

"There is nothing between Kayo and me romantically. We're just friends. Totally, pure and simple, best friends. Period."

"Really?" Val said surprised. "How could you be around a guy that sexy and not go for him? What's the deal, is he gay or what?"

"No, he's not gay, and there's nothing wrong with him. He and I never, I don't know, we've just always been friends, is all." Michelle smiled. "You like him?"

"Yeah, and he seems to like me. Are you positive you don't have a thing for him?"

"I'm sure," Michelle said firmly. "Go for it, girl."

Back at the table, Connor had his jacket in hand and Elizabeth was standing ready to go. Kayo was swirling around the last bit of suds in his glass.

"You guys were going to leave without us?" Michelle asked teasingly.

"You know we wouldn't. But I've got to get up early and get to the office and Elizabeth's got a project she's working on too," Connor said easily.

Val sat down next to Kayo.

Kayo ignored her as she had ignored him earlier in the night.

Michelle leaned forward on the table to say, "Hey, you want to hear something funny?"

Connor walked around the table. "I'm ready."

"Me too," Elizabeth said.

"Shoot," Kayo said almost as a whistle down into his empty beer bottle.

"Val thought that Kayo and I were, well, an item."

Connor started laughing first, then Elizabeth, then Michelle and Kayo. Val smiled uneasily.

Kayo made eye contact with Val. "Listen, I can take Val home."

"Okay, I'll see you guys later," Connor said.

"Ready?" Kayo asked Val.

"Yes," she answered.

Kayo gently kissed her on the neck as he quickly undid the buttons of her blouse. He grabbed Val's collar with his teeth and began slowly peeling it off her shoulders while stripping away his own clothes.

Val slipped out of her skirt and panties and slid seductively underneath his body. The wiry hairs rubbing against his skin aroused them both even more.

Kayo admired her round, smooth, dark breasts with a stroking hand. He cupped them, leaned her body back, dropped his head and began nibbling until the tips swelled against his tongue.

Val ran her hands down the rugged groove in his back. She dropped her head, ran the tip of her tongue across his eyelids around to his ears, then whispered, "Condom."

Kayo kissed her underneath the edge of her chin and whispered back, "Un-uh, unnatural."

Val lifted up his face with her fingertips. "Condom."

Kayo stared into her eyes and stroked her hips with his hands as if to massage his point home. "I have some but I trust you. And it's so much better without."

"It's not a matter of trust, it's a matter of being careful. Safety can be very sexy for the both of us. Let me show you."

Kayo smiled, liking her aggressiveness.

She responded by easing him back onto the bed. Val tore open the package with her teeth and circled her tongue along the edge of the condom. Then she stroked him with the condom palmed in the base of her hand. Stiff with an erection, the rough and smooth texture made him loom even larger. When her hand and the condom felt as one, Val began slipping it on. The fullness in her hands was like a flaming candle; the plastic seemed to melt under the sweltering vapors Kayo's body was throwing off. Once the condom was on, Val began giving him a steam bath with her tongue. She swirled the soft, hot wetness down the middle of his chest, toweling the neglected insides of his navel, scouring the jutting bones of his hips. She left no spot unclean. And Kayo felt damp and amazingly refreshed; a cry of pleasure gurgled in the juices running rampant through his body.

He lifted her up on top of him, sliding their bodies together like the missing pieces of a puzzle.

Michelle opened the apartment door and immediately took off her jacket. Connor followed her in. Her bulky purse dropped to the floor. "You've hardly said a word since leaving the restaurant."

Connor grunted.

"Okay, what's the matter?" Michelle asked sleepily. "I'm tired, Connor."

"So am I, but I want to talk to you."

"What are you mad about, huh?"

"I'm not mad really," Connor said, his eyebrows arching. He sat down on an ottoman. "I-I'm, I'm not sure what I am."

"I'm about to check out any minute, so if you want to tell me what's wrong, you'd better hurry up."

"See, see, that's part of it right there. All of sudden, it's like you have no patience with me or anything. You just seem so pushy and demanding now."

Michelle eased down on the floor next to him. "I'm just telling you how I feel, Connor. I don't want to play guessing games at this time of night."

"Fine. Did you tell Val about us?"

She threw her head back and sighed, "What do you think?"

"I don't think you did."

"Then why are you asking?" Michelle jeered.

"Because I just wanted to check is why," Connor said defensively. "You've got an attitude problem."

"Fine," Michelle said, an angry streak cutting through her. "This is my attitude and my apartment."

Connor stood up, grunted, gave her an immense, fed-up look, and left.

When there was no sound her senses quaked with anxiety. Michelle cautiously reached for the phone and dialed.

"Hello?" Kayo said, glancing over at Val who was sleeping next to him.

"Kayo, would you believe that Connor asked if I told Val about us? I mean, this is getting to be a nightmare! It's like he doesn't trust me."

"Not now, Michelle," Kayo whispered.

"Why are you whispering?" Michelle asked.

Kayo looked at Val and hesitated. "Because."

"Because what?" Michelle asked.

"Because I have company."

"I'm sorry. I wasn't thinking."

"I know you weren't. When it comes to Connor, you don't think."

"Well, excuse me," Michelle said curtly.

Kayo gripped the mouthpiece tighter. "Don't get mad, I'm trying to help."

"I'm-I'm sorry, Kayo. Look, go back to bed," Michelle said, hanging up the phone.

Chapter 11

ELIZABETH sat inside the office, hugging her elbows, waiting for Fletcher. The gritty sounds of the newsroom filtered their way down the corridor and into the corner office. She had an idea to pitch.

Fletcher walked into the office in a tousled, coffee-stained suit. He made no eye contact with Elizabeth before sitting down in the squeaky chair, lifting a half-smoked cigar. "You got something for me?"

"I want to do a sweeps piece on the history of the Long Island Symphony. I know it sounds boring—"

"Yep! And when we try to tease it our viewers will think so too. 'Coming up next: a special report on how the stiff-ass Long Island Symphony is still fiddling away!'" Fletcher laughed. "I'd tune out, how about you?"

"Yeah, I'd tune out if you promoted it like that. But there are better ways to get the audience interested."

"Like what? Give me a tease off the top of your head."

The request took her by surprise, but she said what she had practiced anyway. "Um, the piece will work because our audience is open to other subjects besides Elvis, fires, and murder, stories like that. This piece would do well during sweeps."

Fletcher cut her off: "Listen, TV is about getting an audience and keeping it. So you don't waste any more of my time, that's it in a nutshell. We've got to be well written, flashy, grabby, and still be appealing to the average viewer. Other Yale grads might be interested in the symphony, but Joe Construction Worker doesn't give a shit. He doesn't give a flying shit. When he gets home, he wants meat and potatoes on a plate in front of him and on the tube when he turns it on. Basic news: what happened today, who screwed whom and why, and who's trying to fuck him over with more taxes. Features have to be easy and basic like that as well. Elvis got good ratings because there are a hell of a lot of Elvis fans and plenty of folks who think that the fans are fanatics and who want to turn on the tube and marvel at them. Now, for whatever reason, as long as they're turning on the tube our job is done."

"So anything of substance is not worth it?"

"I did not say that, Elizabeth. You've got to give the people what they want and the symphony ain't it. I know television news like I know my own name, you're just learning, so don't feel bad that you pitched a dumb idea—it happens."

Dumb? Elizabeth couldn't stop the angry look that spread across her face.

Fletcher loved generating tension. He was of the school that believes pressure inspires creativity. "When Helen told me about it the first time . . ."

"What!"

"Yeah, Helen told me about what you were pitching. I told her it was dumb and she agreed but asked me to talk to you anyway."

Elizabeth felt angry and betrayed. Helen had told her she loved the idea. Elizabeth stood, not knowing what to do with herself except get the hell out of that room.

"I'll tell you what, kid," Fletcher offered. "You bring me

one of your highbrow ideas as an *exclusive*—something nobody else has done or has, and we'll do it. Exclusive. Bring it, and kid, I'll eat crow like it was pecan pie."

"Okay," Elizabeth said, walking out the door. She finished the sentence in her mind: *and I want you to be prepared to eat the whole fuckin' pie!*

That night, Elizabeth drew the thin lines of white powder out on her nightstand. It was the third time that week she felt the need to get a pickup. She looked at the neat white rows and heard Michelle's voice: "Promise me you'll cut back." Elizabeth flopped down hard on the bed. She felt the jolt in her breasts and hugged the pillow for comfort. She hesitated, then reached over the lines of coke, picking up the receiver to dial Michelle's number.

"Hello?"

"Hi Michelle," Elizabeth said, finding the simplest greeting difficult.

"Hi Elizabeth," Michelle said, finding it just as difficult.

For a long moment, sound seemed lost.

Michelle felt herself getting irritated. She was so tired and in the smallest places; the bend in her elbow, the nape of her neck, the soft corners of her eyes—all those places ached. She didn't want to talk, looking at the papers in front of her on the desk. "Listen, Elizabeth. I'm swamped. I've got a paper due tomorrow and I just can't talk. I'll call you later."

Elizabeth wanted to say No! Not later, Now.

"Talk to you," Michelle said and hung up the phone.

The dial tone echoed in Elizabeth's ear, "Fuck you, then!" she yelled into the receiver. Elizabeth fell back on the bed and made the whistling sound of a dropping bomb: "Pughdge." She leaned down until her nostrils touched the table, snorted twice, making a sound similar to the striking of a match.

There was an explosion inside her head. The top of her scalp burned. An invisible hand pulled her by the hair down onto the bed. The room was spinning. Suddenly Elizabeth heard a crumbling sound—my teeth!—and she grabbed her mouth. Then a calm, silky easiness covered her body. The familiar goodness soothed her. She lay there, sheets sticky, her mind resting in the coolness. Elizabeth closed her eyes and unconsciously started flapping her hands like a kid splashing water in a wading pool. Wide, saline ripples left her hands and crashed against the recollections of her mind. Ramming. Battering. A memory was unhinged . . .

Elizabeth, laden with a square cardboard box, walked briskly down the campus side street. A pile of red, glossy pamphlets cemented her steady gaze forward. She had to get the pamphlets to the battered women's shelter before the six P.M. meeting for new counselors was to begin. The sleek folds of paper collapsed, spilling against her hands and dashing against her feet. "Shit!" Elizabeth moaned as she knelt and began shoveling the pamphlets back into the now empty box.

From the dusk emerged Friar Pete. "I'll help you," he said, offering as well a smiling portrait of soft, decaying teeth. He used hard-edged nails to peel the pamphlets from the moist ground. Suddenly he stopped, staring at the cover: a tall, almond-colored woman and child, their eyes of deep black fixed in a frightened, longing gaze and their lips pursed in confidence wanting to speak of hope. "Shirl and Matt."

"You know them?" Elizabeth asked, watching the twitch pounding away at the bags beneath his eyes.

"No!" Friar Pete flipped the pamphlet over, burying the people beneath his knee. Elizabeth watched the reflection of herself in the inky pupils of his eyes. The reflection began dissolving away to reveal an invisible consciousness that settled in the finite space between them.

"No. They just reminded me of my wife and baby. I'd gotten laid off my job and started drinking a little too much. I was worried and feeling less than any living person had a right to feel. God knows I was a bastard, but she could have stuck with me. I was going to make it up to her! I brought home two pearls for her that night. Pearls as white as cotton . . . and all that was left on the walls was a calendar showing November and it wasn't even November yet, just October . . . guess she wanted me to look ahead to a life alone."

"Did you look for her?" Friar Pete heard the consciousness ask.

"For years I looked. And I've been a wandering man ever since . . ."

Ever since. Ever since. The reverberations echoed in Elizabeth's mind as she drifted off into a dizzying high.

The light from the funnel-shaped lamp cast a crooked beam across the open book. Michelle's shoulders were hunched over and aching from the long hours. She greeted the words with enthusiasm as she passed them on the page but they were distant like a rush hour crowd on a city street.

"Just stop!" Michelle sat back, fingering the neck of a Perrier bottle. She used both hands to massage the back of her neck, to pinch her eyes, and to wipe away tears of fatigue. Michelle stretched her hands out in front of her and touched the bolt of cloth she had bought at the antique shop. She unrolled some of the material, fingering it. A small journal fell out. The leather cover was old and had strange markings. The edges of the pages were curled a bit. "This is handwritten. This is somebody's journal."

> Little Master Bob give me this book to do his figures in but I told him I lost it so I could keep it He told me I was only to do his lessons & if I tell a body I will get whipped I just want this book to teach Pa how to read and write so us can talk

Michelle adjusted the light and continued to explore.

> I tryed to teach Pa how to write today after they all came in from the fields He looked so weary I asked him to look at the marks I make on the cabin floor I told him thats my name Joshua and his name Will He be angry & started waving his hands & stomped out the letters & boxed my ears So evil That stands to reason why all the slaves are afrayed of him & call him the bad luck afrikan My Ma died because he stopped Auntie Sue from helping birth me His tongue is cut out for calling me afrikan name I just wanted us to talk is all Pa don't want to talk I just have to talk to this book

It seemed to be a slave narrative. Michelle kept the page with her finger and looked at the cover. No real marks except some strange scratches in the right top corner.

> Little Master Bob is sick again I sit quiet in the corner by the cathole watching the doctor give him that bitter medicine Master Whittnower says for me to stay with little Bob cause hes liable to wake up & want to play Auntie Sue say the lord gonna get Master for making me stay in with little Master Bob when hes sick I am not afrayed I never get sick and I get ginger cake from the kitchen that Auntie Sue gives me Master Whittnower says to Doc the prices in Dade County is going way up Doc tell Master Whittnower that when he went to Washington he had to send back to Virginia for more money Very xpensive Doc say theres a new sewciety that wants the niggas to be free Master Whittnower say its the doings of that grey sun He say that grey sun on the rise and got to be stopped and soon I never saw a grey sun but I sho would like to be free I figure to look for that grey sun tomorrow

Michelle was breathless. She felt herself getting excited, unable to put the journal down.

> To day Master Jerimah got all the slaves together to watch Lula get whipped She ran away her bow was gonna be sold his master hung hisself after he gambled away his plantation Auntie Sue say Master Whittnower saw it all in the newspapers I cry when she got whipped She screamed til her voice sound horse like old Uncle Tim Master Jerimah grin & laugh & lay it on more That was five days past Lula still down low sick The blood still on the ground

The lamp cast a hollow, yellow beam of light across the pages. Michelle adjusted it and quickly read on.

> I begged Pa to give me back this book He caught me writing in it & took it Pa scratched afrikan hoodoo on it and then hid it But lord, Master Jerimah found it Master Jerimah came in

> our cabin & the first words he say who this belong to Me and Pa didn't say nary a sound I was too afrayed Pa couldn't Master Jerimah hit Pa in the eye with the whip handle I started to run to get help but Master Jerimah said to stay put He opened the book

Michelle flipped through the rest of the pages and seeing blood on them, felt wounded with the haunting feeling of what might be ahead.

> I know he knows it belongs to me but no Master Jerimah cannot read just like Pa Master Jerimah says he sees that funny afrikan writing on the front & he says he gonna take Pa to Mister Whittnower & he gonna get sixty lashes cause that's the new law Pa look at me & jump on Master Jerimah just a fightin I close my eyes & I hear them fighting When I opened them again pa was laying there I know he was dead he looked different Master Jerimah is laying there too But I know hes still alive he still look evil I must run I look for that grey sun to lead me north then I can be free

There was no more. Michelle closed the book with trembling hands.

Kayo threw his elbow against the office door. It slammed against the wall. Ed popped up from behind the desk.

"I just heard," Kayo said angrily. It was then that he noticed that all the bookshelves were empty. That the pictures of Ed's mother and grandfather were gone from the desk. The prints were down and facing the walls they were now propped against.

"Hello, Kevin. Would you hand me that empty box right there by your foot?" Ed asked.

Kayo stared at Ed. He felt hurt that he had to hear about his firing in the elevator, a piece of buzzing gossip in between floors.

"It's there by your right foot, son," Ed said, pointing with his head.

Kayo bent down and picked up the box. He held it stiffly in his hands. "Why didn't you tell me?"

"You found out, didn't you?" Ed said simply. Then he smiled. "Are you going to give me the box?"

Kayo walked over to him. Ed had on a Grambling Tigers sweatshirt and a pair of jeans. He handed him the box.

Ed grabbed it, but Kayo refused to let go.

"Let's talk," Ed said, melting under Kayo's stare. "Sit down."

A worried look crossed Kayo's face as he glanced around for a chair.

Ed walked over and pulled up two boxes marked "Books." He sat on one and motioned for Kayo to use the other. Before Kayo could barely bend his knees, Ed started: "Listen, I think that you are a very strong young man and that you have a bright future in this business." Ed paused to think back to their very first conversation, then smiled. "Kevin, the Boston Celtics are cutting me from the team."

"But why?" Kayo said, confused. Then he remembered. "Ed, you know more than all those fools put together."

"I may *know* more but I don't have more *power*. Remember that Kevin—power, sad to say, wins out over knowledge in this world."

It felt as if someone was closing a fist around Kayo's throat. "But they're taking care of you, right? A lot of stock aside for you?"

"Hell no, they're just letting me go. They offered a party, a watch, but I declined—I'd rather go quietly, unnoticed."

"But what will you do?" Kayo said, distressed. "You've got some private business deals in the works?"

"As hard as these folks drive you? I didn't have time to have a family. I didn't have time to work up any private ventures. When would I have time? I was the first black here—the colored showpiece that had to be displayed at all times. But that's over now. I, um, I do have a small venture that I think will well suit me, though."

"What? I'll bet it's something sharp, too."

"I'm going to operate a Fotomat store in Jamaica. It'll be right there on the beach. I'm the owner and the manager. I'll send you a postcard—you can even come visit," Ed said, forcing a smile.

"Bullshit, man!"

"Aww, Kevin, Kevin," Ed said, rocking back on the box. "Don't take it like that—I'm not. It doesn't hurt but you taking it like this does. Stop it."

"Naw, Ed. They don't have a right to do that!" Kayo shouted. He was standing now.

Ed frowned. "No, now. You're making me think that you're more angry because you've lost your mentor rather than because I've lost my position."

"No Ed, that's not it at all. We're friends, man. We-we're home boys," Kayo said, sitting back down.

"That's better. Now, I want you to remember something that's very important. I thought I would have more time with you, but I don't."

"The dirty bastards."

"Kevin."

"I'm listening, Ed. Okay?" Kayo said, leaning forward and staring hard into his eyes.

"Kevin, after I'm gone I want you to keep pushing. It's especially tough for a black man now because everybody wants to make him a casualty in life. People steal your heart and make you walk around searching for it until what is left of you just rots and drops. I made my mistake way back when they first hired me on. I thought I was smart, so when they came for mine, I sold my heart, thinking that was better, cause hey, they were gonna get it anyway. I thought I was really getting something out of it—but I got duped on the deal and I've been empty ever since. But that's not going to happen to you, Kevin, 'cause you're strong and can fight. I want you to get under their skin, son, and suck out everything that's dear to them. Get it all: their power, their knowledge, their money, and their ideas. Then, boy, when they're dried up and weak I want you to spit it back in their faces until they are sick and tired and wondering what the hell hit 'em. Understand?"

Kayo shook his head like a pitcher shaking off a sign. The emotion of Ed's words seemed to be sucking all the air out of the room.

Ed leaned over and clutched Kayo's arms. "It's their choice of weapons—wear their armor but keep *your* heart inside."

Kayo felt Ed trembling but couldn't find the words. He nodded his head yes.

"Good," Ed said, patting Kayo's arms and squeezing. "Good."

Kayo's face was now the color of broth. His thoughts were scrambling but he kept a clean, firm stare on Ed.

"You better get back to work," Ed said, nodding toward the door.

"Well, let me buy you a drink later and we can talk—"

"No, I need some space, Kevin. And really, there's nothing to talk about."

Kayo nodded and extended his hand. Ed clasped it and pulled him up and in. He hugged him and patted him on the back. He whispered in his ear, "Don't forget?"

"Never," Kayo said, turning to walk out. He went straight to the bathroom and waited until he was in there alone before clutching the cold ceramic basin. Kayo felt his insides ringing and popping with questions. How can they just put him out like that? They take care of other people! Did he piss somebody off? Maybe somewhere down the line, over the years, he pissed somebody off? Ed, though? Naw—just can't figure it. But they take care of all the other old boys—what's so different about Ed? Kayo shook his head and looked up. He saw his reflection in the mirror. Kayo grabbed his face the way a prisoner clutches bars. Aww, man . . . man! Beads of sweat drove up and over his fingertips and sped down the backs of his hands. Steady man, steady. Kayo dropped his head and forced his hands down. They slammed against the basin and the mirror rattled. Look back up, man. His neck wouldn't move. Kayo strained: look up. Inching up, his neck throbbed with pain. Kayo tilted and turned his neck as if he was adjusting an antenna. Look at you! Just sweating and trembling like a sissy! They'd be calling you a punk back home, for sure. Kayo shored up his emotions, determined to finish out the day as if nothing was wrong. He took one last long glance, then headed out the bathroom door to finish his day.

The New York skyline was a cauldron of mist-covered buildings trying to take over the night. Streetlamps and car lights, conjuring the effect of sparks, dazzled the eye. Kayo took in the view and reasoned that it alone had sold him on his apartment. Back home in Chicago, he had always hated looking out the window. The rundown houses and drab, empty lots looked like a big Monopoly board some kid had crushed beneath his feet. Kayo sipped a martini and continued to gaze out the window. The view to him meant progress, change, movement, a different way of life. It usually made him feel good, but not tonight. Kayo pulled down the shades and the coarse white plastic barred the moonlight from inside the apartment. Kayo walked over to the middle of his living room and took a seat in his favorite chair, a black recliner made of soft leather. There was a bar made of cedarwood and posters from his days at Yale mounted on the walls. Kayo felt powerless, angry, and threatened deep in the leagues of his soul. He called Val and she was on her way.

"Are you okay?" she asked, stepping into the dark room.

"I'm really bummed out," Kayo said, walking back to his chair.

She sat down on the ottoman next to his chair. "So, they just let him go?"

"Yeah, just like that. I mean there was nothing he could do about it."

Val rubbed Kayo's leg. "He probably didn't want comfort. If he's half the man you've been saying he is, he wanted to deal with it himself. Alone."

Kayo took another sip.

"You can't drink him back to the job," Val said.

"I know, Val. I just-just want to go up to Manchester and just punch him." Kayo balled up his fists like a street fighter. "I could just kill that SOB."

"You've got to make that anger work for you, Kayo. Holding it in will just weigh you down. Burn it up, turn it into energy that you can kick ass with at work. Show Manchester that you are the best."

"But it's like they're threatening me by what they did to Ed. What's to stop them from chewing me up and spitting me out no matter what I do?"

Val took her hand in his. "You can't let them scare you. Dare them. Be strong and dare them to come at you with anything, and you'll be able to take anything and still come out on top."

"I'm going to miss Ed. I mean he was a good friend, a mentor. God, Val, just the way he said good-bye to me . . . I know that I'll probably never see him again. It really, really hurts."

"You know, anytime you lose somebody it's painful. I mean, Kayo, I can't tell you how to get rid of that hurt. You just have to work with it. My grandmother lives in Baltimore and when my grandfather died three years ago she didn't cry at the funeral. She didn't say much of anything to anyone the whole time. Nothing to my Daddy or Momma, or me, and I'm supposed to be her favorite grandchild. She had always hated to cook but all of a sudden she just started baking bread all the time. And Kayo, she would work that dough to death, punching it, kneading it, slamming it on the counter so hard that flour dust would cover her face till she looked like a ghost. She did that until she was able to break down the anger that was holding back her tears, and she just cried and cried. You have to just wait, honey, and work it out."

Kayo leaned forward and looked at her for the first time since she had come into the room. Her olive blouse matched her skin perfectly and he noticed that it was misbuttoned at the top. He looked down at her black lace-up shoes and saw that they were tied sloppily. "You rushed right over? Dropped everything for me?"

"You need a hug," Val said, moving onto his lap. Kayo hugged her tight and rested his head between her breasts.

Michelle sat at the desk, combing through the pages of the slave journal again. She had decided not to tell anyone about her find until she had authenticated it. Michelle was excited by the challenge. She was taking notes on a small legal pad, notes on things she thought would help her. Michelle deduced that when Joshua wrote "Master Whittnower says for me to stay with little Bob cause hes liable to wake up & want to play," that those were Master Whittnower's exact words. He called his son "little Bob." And all the other times Joshua called the young master "little Master Bob." Michelle was sure that the boy was named after his father. So the plantation owner's name had to be Robert Whittnower. Next to his name she wrote down all the other names: Joshua, Will, Auntie Sue, Doc. The plantation was somewhere in Virginia, because the doctor had mentioned sending back for money. Michelle also wrote down "Dade County," from when Master Whittnower had complained to the doctor about prices going up.

Michelle looked at the few notes she had made, flipped the pad over, grabbed her jacket, her bookbag, and headed back to the antique store where she had found the journal in the first place.

Michelle could see Coreen leaning against the black metal crisscrossing the front of the store window. Michelle came up behind her, spoke, and began helping her.

"You're here early," Coreen answered, welcoming the helping hand.

The gate slipped back at ease in the corner and Michelle followed behind Coreen as she unlocked the shop door. "We've got some nice items in." She hung up her coat and stepped behind the counter.

"Listen," Michelle said. "I didn't want to shop today. I

wondered if you had the name and home information of the guy who sold you that box of antiques I looked at the last time I was here."

Coreen began rearranging the jewelry in the glass case. "Is something wrong with what you bought or something?"

"No, I remembered you said he had a house on Striver's Row and I was doing some research on the area for my Ph.D."

"Oh, okay." Coreen pulled out a ledger and flipped through the pages.

Michelle felt herself getting tense with the possibility of her first link to the journal's past. "Here," Coreen said, writing the information out on a slip of paper. "It's his name and the address. He didn't leave a phone number. Good luck with your work and don't forget about us."

Michelle took the paper and clutched it in her hand. "I won't."

Outside she jogged to the corner and hailed a cab to 139th Street. The brownstones were beautifully kept. There were plants on the front ledges. The cab turned the corner and pulled in front of the last house on that block. It was a drastic contrast to the other homes. This brownstone was run-down with large cracks in the windows. From the inside of the cab, one could see that the bricks were loose and that the steps were crumbling. As Michelle paid the driver she could barely get the money out of her purse, she was so shocked at the disarray of this one house. She clutched her bag tightly and prayed, "Please let him be here!" Michelle took a deep breath and climbed the steps gingerly. She touched the wall to brace herself and one of the bricks gave way.

The front door opened. "I thought I heard someone out here."

Michelle looked up and there was a tall, young black man just a few years older than she. His skin was extremely fair and his hair was short and wiry. He wore jeans cut off just above the knees and a plain green T-shirt splattered with different colors of paint. He walked toward her in floppy sandals that left a path of loose concrete behind him.

"You must be Andre Hinton," Michelle asked.

"That's me," he said, helping her up. "I know you're here to look at the house, but it's just been sold. I'm just trying to clean out the last of this junk."

Michelle thanked him and began, "No, I'm not here for the house. I'm a student at Columbia and I'm working on my Ph.D. I wanted to talk to you about your grandmother living here on Striver's Row. Research. I got your name from Coreen at the antique shop."

"Oh, well, you can come in but I don't know much of anything," Andre said, heading back inside the house.

Michelle looked at the high ceiling and the beautiful wooden floors and stairwell. Andre pulled up two chairs. He dusted off one of the chairs with a rag he had in his back pocket, then held it out for Michelle.

"My grandmother was a recluse. I didn't really even know her."

Michelle removed a pad from her pocket.

"She was my father's mother. They moved from Washington, D.C., to New York when he was a baby after his father died from TB. She was always a little nutty, it seems. Grandma Johnson didn't like my mother and disowned Dad when they married. No one talked to her for years, even when my parents were killed in the plane crash—nothing. I got a notice from an attorney after she died a few months ago saying I was her only family and that she had left me this house. When I got here from California there was junk piled up to the ceiling. I mean junk, like tin cans, old magazines, old shoes of all sizes—it was a mess! The neighbors say she would go through garbage cans and save stuff, go into stores and buy things nobody else wanted. She let this house go to pieces and the neighbors complained something terrible, I hear. I've been cleaning the place out for months, just trying to get things straight enough to sell it. I just finished getting the last stuff out of the attic. I was lucky enough to be able to sell some of it to the antique shop."

Michelle looked up the stairwell. "What did she have in the attic?"

"Just old clothes. Nothing but old clothes—shoes, jackets, blouses, cloth—just sloppy junk she never even wore!"

The journal was in the cloth and she probably didn't even know it, Michelle thought. Her heart sank.

Andre noticed her disappointment. "But I don't know what this has to do with Striver's Row."

"Well," Michelle quickly said, "there are different kinds of people here. It's interesting history, how and why people come to live here."

"Oh," Andre said, leaning back on the box, "Well, I was raised by my mother's parents after my parents died. We never talked to Grandma Johnson or saw her or got any letters. All I know is what the neighbors told me about her collecting junk all the time. That's it."

Michelle felt as if someone had closed a door in her face. She stood up. "Well, thanks Andre, I appreciate you taking the time to talk to me."

"Sorry, wish I could help more. Maybe the neighbors?"

Michelle opened the door and paid no more attention to him. A dead end. She walked down the steps and stood in front of the house for a second before walking up toward the main avenue. Michelle only had a half hour to get back to the class she was the teaching assistant for. She had promised the Victorian Lit students their papers back today but she had been so busy going over the journal she hadn't had time to finish grading them. Professor Kingman was making it tough on her. If her performance didn't improve, he had warned, she would be kicked out of the Ph.D. program. Michelle thought of the words, of the power behind the journal and what Joshua's one story could mean to literature and history. Her heart told her that she was on the verge of something important that could salvage her school problem as well. Should she gamble? Should she blow off her Ph.D. work to research this journal? Michelle's gut made the decision. She began walking to the Schomberg Library at 135th and Malcom X Boulevard.

The black woman standing behind the desk had on tiny round spectacles and her hair was long and as grey as a shell salted over by ocean waters. She looked at Michelle with big, friendly brown eyes and said, "May I help you? My name is Sally."

Michelle felt at ease for the first time that day. "Yes. I'm trying to find proof that a person existed as a slave on a plantation."

"Trace the roots," Sally said. "Everyone's been doing that for years and years now, ever since Alex Haley wrote *Roots*. Do you have any time frame in mind, the year they probably lived?"

Michelle stared at her blankly. "I don't know."

"Well," Sally said, her laughter low and explosive like a cork popping out of a bottle, "this is going to be tough."

"I know," Michelle said. "I don't even know the name of the plantation they lived on! All I know is that it was somewhere in Dade County in Virginia." Michelle thought and offered. "I know the name of the plantation owner! If I could prove that somehow, I'd be on my way."

"Now, that's something. Let's see, I'll bring you some census rolls for Dade County in Virginia."

"They had censuses way back then?" Michelle asked.

"They've been doing them every ten years since 1790," she said, writing down the information. "I'll bring you the censuses for Dade County in Virginia. Now, nothing is in alphabetical order or anything; the census takers went from door to door, so you just have to look until you find what you want."

Michelle understood and thanked her. Then she walked over to where the microfilm machines were. A few minutes later, another clerk brought her the microfilm rolls with the censuses on them. The big, flat screen looked like a sandbox until the page rolled up. The machine magnified the scrawled handwriting.

The first column said "Head of the families" and underneath was a vertical column of names listed. Then there was a heading that said "Free White" and under that there was a section for Males and Females. Next there were vertical listings for ages: under five, of five and under ten, of ten and under twenty, and so on up to of one hundred and upward. Under the ages were little boxes with numbers in them. Then there was a column for slaves with the same headings and columns. Michelle sat back, confused. She looked back and saw that Sally was free and motioned for her.

"I'm confused by all this," Michelle said plaintively.

"I used to be too a long while back." She pointed to the screen. "The early censuses just gave the name of the head of the household. Now that column for free whites is to list himself, his wife and children, and any other white people living in the house. Now, see Hinton here?"

"Yeah."

"Well, under his name they put the number one in the column 'White males of thirty and under forty'—that's him. Then they put the number one by 'White female, of thirty and under forty.' That's probably his wife. Under that they put the number two in the male column and indicated 'of five and under ten.' Those are two white boys, probably his sons."

"Okay," Michelle said, understanding now. "And for the slaves, this means he had three females between the ages of twenty and thirty, one male between the age of sixty and seventy, and two males between the ages of fifteen and twenty!"

"Right!" Sally said. "You catch on fast!"

"I got it," Michelle said, turning back to the screen.

She spent several weeks going over the rolls, day after day, several hours without fail. She began to adjust easily to the chaotic change in handwritings as some census takers seemed eager to scrawl the names without care. She started to spend less and less time on her classes at Columbia and more and more time at the Schomberg. Michelle told herself this was her ticket, that this was more important than anything else she had ever tried to do or achieve. So, Michelle searched with the light becoming duller and duller as the hours wore on. Sometimes she could swear that she saw the name Whitt-nower, but upon closer examination it would be Whitt or Whittaker. When that happened, Michelle wanted to punch her fist through the screen, shatter it into a thousand waxy pieces, rip out the names of others that were like shrouds over the one name she was determined to find. And it was on one of those days, six hours after her nine A.M. arrival, that the back-aches, eye aches, heartaches, and utter frustration soaked her to the skin. Michelle was now on the 1830 census and the more she looked at the big, flat, dull screen the more her eyes lost their focus. Michelle turned the knob hard to the left and then pressed the button on the side but the document just whirled out of control, as if the machine itself had turned into a wild, screeching ghost taunting her eyes with white, wobbly blurs and her thoughts with doubt. Michelle bowed her head and was trying to block the grinding noise out of her mind when suddenly it stopped. She looked up at the screen and the first name there was: Robert Whittnower.

Michelle pressed her fingers against the screen and let her nail scan the letters. Robert Whittnower. In the white male columns there was the number one by the age of thirty and under forty. Michelle saw he had one white male, ten not yet twenty, living with him. That's Master Bob, she thought. She scanned over to the slaves and counted up the totals: forty-eight. He had forty-eight slaves! Michelle checked the notation for males slaves age ten, not yet twenty—and there was the number eight. Joshua is one of those eight, she guessed. Suddenly, Michelle was overjoyed: "Yeah-yeah-*yeah*!"

Several voices around her hissed.

"Sssh yourselves!" she popped back. Her face was flushed with delight.

"Michelle," Sally said, touching her shoulder. "What's the matter?" Michelle pointed to the screen. "That's the name you were looking for?"

"Yes," Michelle said. "Finally! I just wish they'd put the names of the slaves!"

Sally smiled at her. "Honey, you're not thinking. Why would they list us on a census? We were only property to them."

Michelle said thoughtfully, "Now, I need to go to Virginia. Probably check the county records there."

"Everything okay?" another clerk came over and asked. He was short, very fat, with a flabby bubble of skin under his chin.

"Yes, Pat, everything's okay." Sally patted Michelle's shoulder but spoke to Pat. "Michelle just got a little carried away with her good fortune. But she just has a lot more work to do."

"Oh, okay." he said, shrugging his shoulders. The sweater he wore was worn at the elbows and he shoved his hands deep in his pockets and turned away.

"Pat!" Sally called, stopping him. He turned back. Sally spoke to Michelle. "Pat's from Virginia."

Michelle looked at him and rubbed her eyes. "I've just found the census information for Robert Whittnower at a plantation in Dade County."

"Did you say Whittnower?" Pat asked, stepping over closer to the screen. "That's got to be one of *the* Whittnowers."

Michelle leaned forward. "Well-known family?"

"Yes, but not as well known as the Lees or anything, but fairly well known. A few descendants have held public office in the last few years—congressmen. Nobody's in office now, though. But there's a Whittnower Collection that dates back to 1825, letters and ledgers and stuff, at the University of Virginia."

"Charlottesville," Michelle and Sally said at the same time.

"I just know there's something there!" Michelle looked again at the census sheet on the screen. She pressed a button and two copies of that page slid out of the machine. "Thanks, both of you!"

"Good luck!" they said.

Michelle felt high: her first discovery. Surely, if the plantation owner was real, so was Joshua and his story. She knew she needed more, had to have more, but in her heart Michelle knew she would find it.

Chapter 12

STEVE walked over to Connor. His shirtsleeves were rolled up and the initials "CB" on the upper right-hand collar were barely visible beyond the wrinkles. He smiled at Connor, who was looking more haggard than he. "No, I didn't come to bum a shirt."

All Connor could manage was a quick nod. His tie was a ball of color at his right elbow and his left elbow served as a paper weight, holding down a stack of files. "I'm up to my ass in it, man!"

"I know. I just finished up," Steve said, checking his watch, "and it's close to eleven."

"I'm nowhere near finished," Connor said angrily. "I'm working with Needham on this!"

"Whoa! Prime time. I heard he's a big pri—" Steve stopped, remembering how they first met.

Connor did too. It was the first time he smiled all day. "What is he?"

"I heard he was a tough businessman, a real player!" Steve laughed.

"You are learning something around here, huh?" Connor leaned back and closed his eyes, resting them.

"You work tired and you'll fuck something up just as sure as I'm standing here, buddy. C'mon, let's grab something to eat—my treat since you kicked my butt in racquetball last Saturday."

Connor's eyes stayed closed, but he smiled. "Tore you up, didn't I?"

"Yeah, then. But as tired as you are now—I'd massacre you!"

"You're right."

"Listen, we'll grab something to eat—no pizza or gyros—some real good food, and we'll both come back here and work a couple more hours and put a real dent in this pile of shit!"

"You've got work of your own."

"No pressure! I'll grab my coat and be back in a sec," Steve said, turning and jogging out the door.

Connor glanced at the phone. He had been trying to call Michelle all last week with no luck. Neither Connor nor Elizabeth had heard from her. When he did talk to her this morning, all she said was that her Ph.D. work was getting more involved. She told him she had to do some research at the University of Virginia. Connor knew the trips would be over weekends, the only time they could ever spend an evening together, it seemed. He had gotten angry, angry that she was more interested in her classes than in spending time with him. The conversation ended abruptly, with him cutting her off without even telling her to have a safe trip. Michelle had said she was taking the midnight train because it was cheaper. Connor looked at the phone now and knew she was packing.

"Yo, let's move!" Steve said slipping on his jacket. "Italian!"

"That sounds good!" Connor said, standing up, slipping on his suit jacket. "Italian it is!"

* * *

Michelle felt the gentle movement of the Amtrak train as her eyes feasted on the light of the rising sun. She checked her watch. Her seven-hour train ride to Virginia was almost over. Michelle propped her feet up in the seat across from her and tried to stretch. Her eyes were stinging from being up most of the night before. Michelle's inability to sleep was a combination of things. She and Connor had argued again, and Michelle was nervous about what was ahead of her. There was a mystery riding on this train trip in the form of the spirit of a father and son's past. There was anxiety and desire to prove that past and to bring what had somehow gotten buried in some old woman's attic to the attention of the world. Michelle gathered her things as the train pulled in and steeled herself to what would be a long day.

By the time she had found a cheap motel room and gotten a cab to the campus, it was ten o'clock and a balmy sixty degrees. Michelle had a backpack stuffed with notebooks and paper and a minirecorder if she needed it. She entered the Alderman Library, registered, and headed for the rare books and collections department.

Michelle asked to see the Whittnower Collection and the clerk told her it was in two sections, letters and financial ledgers, and that she could only view one at a time. She decided to alternate back and forth. The collection began in 1825 and ended in 1870. The clerk brought her a large black book, the cover rough and gritty. She delicately opened it and looked at the inscription in the upper left-hand corner: Robert Whittnower, The Rosebloom Plantation, 1825.

Michelle scanned the first page. It was dated in the upper right-hand corner and there was a description of the transaction as well as the costs. She saw that on Tuesday, January 15, 1825, Whittnower sold a male slave, twenty-five, silversmith, to Frank Atwald of the Sandstone Plantation for $2,000 . . . and so on. There were notations for trips to Richmond and how much he spent on food, lodgings, and gifts for the family. Michelle read down further. There was an entry for Thursday, March 13: John, twenty, hurt in field accident. Right hand smashed. Damage to property, $500. It was detailed bookkeeping. By the end of the day, Michelle had only gotten a quarter of the way through the business ledger. The next day she was there when the library opened to read more, switching to the letters section. By the time the weekend was over and it was time for her to catch her train back to New York, she was worn out and hadn't found a thing. But Michelle wasn't discouraged. She knew it would take time. So, riding back on the train she made plans for the next several months, noting days when she could come back and continue working to find the answers.

The leaves slid off the trees with the wild abandon of children coming down a slide. Val reached out her hand and gently caught one on the tips of her fingers. The soft, fleeting touch lasted three full seconds before the wind whisked it away.

"That was pretty impressive!" Kayo said, as they continued to walk along the pathway hand in hand. He had taken off his suit jacket and slung it across his right shoulder.

"When I was a kid, my father and I used to bet taffy apples on who could balance a leaf the longest," Val said. She was dressed in a navy suede jacket with several zipper pockets. Her hair was pulled back, the way Kayo liked, accenting her keen features. "We always played the game on Sundays when we took our walks in the parks back home in Baltimore."

"Yeah? I'll bet he won," Kayo goaded.

"You'd be right. He always won everything—our bets, all his court cases—he beat everything but that stroke."

"Was it rough?" Kayo asked.

"Yes, but it's okay now," Val said, concentrating on the falling leaves. "Daddy worked much too hard. He was a corporate lawyer, not like my grandfather who was a civil rights attorney. Daddy wanted to make lots of money and he worked like a dog to do it. I'm not sure why, really. My grandfather wasn't poor—he left my grandmother well taken care of and even left me and my brother Willie a trust fund. Anyway, Daddy had the stroke when I was thirteen, my brother Willie was seven. He's in a rest home in Baltimore."

"I'm sorry," Kayo said softly.

"Oh, it's okay. It was a family decision to put him there. My mother just couldn't give him the professional care he needed. He's fine. We'll drive out to see him tomorrow when I get home."

Kayo squeezed her hand, then tilted his arm to glance at his watch.

Val caught him at it and jerked his arm down hard. "Don't look at your watch when you're with me! We haven't been together more than an hour yet."

Kayo gave her a pained look, partly due to the ache in his shoulder and partly to the thought of how little time they were spending together. "We've got to spend more time together. You're studying all the time and I'm working! Hook up with me tonight."

Val released his hand and turned around to face him, walking backward. "I told you that I have to study tonight—then I'm going home tomorrow."

"Study! Study! You never want to give me enough time," Kayo said, feeling frustrated.

"Well, you too! You're the one looking at his watch."

"It's easier to skip studying than it is to skip work."

Val stopped him with an outstretched palm to the chest. "I try to give you time—you're the one not giving up any time."

"I gotta go!"

"See?" Val said, getting angry now. "Case in point—you bring up something important, then you blast out of the picture before we can really talk about it."

"It's not all my fault. And you know what? I can prove it. See me tonight and I won't go back to work for another hour!" Kayo knew she would say no.

"You know I can't. You're being an asshole!"

"Asshole? Okay!" Kayo said disgustedly. "This asshole is out of here!" And he stepped into the street and threw up two fingers, waving to a cab that was speeding toward him. As the yoke-speckled vehicle churned and spurted, Kayo waved harder and faster. When the cab was within fifteen feet, the white cab driver slammed down the visor just above his head so that the sign NOT FOR HIRE lingered in Kayo's realm of vision as the cab sped away. Another cab, empty, sped past him. Kayo tried not to be discouraged; his arm stiffened and he waved faster, more creatively, in whips and loops. Another cab approaching began to slow. This time the driver was black. Kayo glanced over triumphantly at Val, lowering his arm to reach for the door. The brakes whistled and the wheels squeaked and Kayo damn near lost his arm as his fingers caught on the latch for a second as the car rolled by to pick up a white man just ten feet away. The man had on cords, a dingy New York Giants half-T, and schoolboy glasses. Kayo looked at his own Calvin Klein slacks and tie. "I hate that!"

Val, who had been watching all along, felt sorry for him and began walking toward Kayo. "Maybe one will stop for me."

"Maybe nothing," Kayo shouted, lashing the ground with his suit jacket. "Why can't a black man get a cab in New York City? I'm going to get me a cab if it kills me!"

And with that, Kayo lunged out into the street, blocking one lane of traffic. A cab turning the corner almost ran him down, but the rattling chassis jolted to a halt.

"Hey, crazy, you tryin' to commit suicide or something?" the cab driver yelled through the open window.

Kayo yanked open the door.

"Hey, look, I'm not going to Harlem. I've been robbed up there three times."

Kayo glared at him and thought about slamming the door in his face, but he knew Val was still watching and he didn't want to lose this battle in front of her. "We're not going to Harlem," Kayo said through clenched teeth. He turned to Val and ordered, "Get in!"

"Go on, you're the one in a big hurry."

Cars were backed up threefold behind the cab that was straddling two lanes. "Let's move, buddy!" the driver snorted.

Val rolled her eyes and turned away.

"Forget it," Kayo said, hopping into the cab.

For the rest of the day at work, Kayo thought about the fight in the park. Why is she saying it's my fault? I send her flowers. I take her to dinner. I love her and she chumps me off? Man, the nerve. And black women are always hollering about there aren't enough good black men out there and she can't find the extra time to spend with me? Fine. Kayo was in the middle of this last thought when Anna stopped in front of his desk. She was a young woman in her late twenties who worked in the mailroom. She was buxom and hippy and always dressed in tight clothes that gave her a much too provocative look. Anna didn't wear any makeup and her skin was smooth and taffy-colored. She had a Brooklyn accent that always seemed to shatter whatever conversation she entered. Anna had often flirted with Kayo when she picked up the late-night Federal Express packages from him and usually he wasn't interested, but tonight when she suggested in that falling-off-a-limb accent, "Let's go grab a glass of wine at your place," they did.

"Nice apartment," Anna said, hardly able to take the glass as she scrutinized the place. Kayo eased down next to her on the couch. "Yeah, I think it's cool," he said, feeling comfortable, bragging a little bit about the apartment he was so proud of.

Anna took a sip of wine. The outline of her bottom lip left a lipstick print on the glass. "You never paid much attention to me at work before. I thought you didn't like me."

Kayo had already taken off his jacket and tie, now he loosened his collar. "No, that wasn't it. I was so busy I didn't have time to give you the kind of attention you deserve." Kayo scooted over closer and dimmed the lights.

"Cozy and quick," Anna laughed. She had spotted Kayo the first day he started work. She saw his hips and thighs poised in a leisurely lean across a desk as he asked one of the secretaries a question. They had been too far away from each other to say hello, so he winked at her instead. Ever since then she had nursed a burning desire for him and the more he ignored her advances at work, however politely done, the more she wanted him. Anna usually got whatever man she wanted, but Kayo was a challenge. She wanted to know what had won him over. "Why'd you say yes today?"

"I told you I never really had time until tonight," Kayo lied. He inched over and ran his hand underneath the tight blouse Anna wore. Quickly he snapped open her bra. When she didn't resist, he let his right hand slip down to unzip her skirt.

Anna leaned over and kissed Kayo softly at first, then she worked her tongue deep into his mouth, kissing him hard.

Kayo returned the kiss with the same fervor while quickly undoing his shirt. He tossed it over his head and buried his head in Anna's neck, biting and sucking.

Anna rubbed his head in a hand-over-hand motion that aroused Kayo to the point of shivering. Then she slipped her hands down between his legs, squeezing and rubbing before sliding her hand up to his waist and unbuckling his pants.

Only Kayo heard the lock on the front door tumble over. "Oh shit!"

"What's wrong?" Anna moaned.

The front door swung open. Val walked in with a big grocery bag in her hand. "I slipped past Hal to surprise you. I've got strawberries for daiquiris—" She stopped in the center of the room, just as Anna was trying to close her blouse.

"Val!" Kayo said, jumping up, still closing his pants.

Val stared at Kayo, then Anna. Then she tossed the grocery bag at him. "Good-bye!"

He caught the bag and put it on the floor in one swift motion and had just enough time left to grab Val's arm. "Let go of me. I'm not one of your bitches!"

"Wait, Val!"

"Who are you calling a bitch?" Anna balked, now off the couch, nearing Val and Kayo.

"Anna, get your coat and go!" Kayo pleaded.

"What?"

"No, honey, you can stay, I'll go!" Val said, trying to get her arm loose.

"No, you stay, she's going!" Kayo said, holding Val even tighter now.

"Fuck you!" Anna said, grabbing her coat off a nearby chair. "She can have you."

"No, thanks!" Val said, trying to follow Anna out the door.

As soon as she slammed it, Kayo raced over by the door and blocked it with his body.

"If you don't get your lying black ass out the way, I'm going to scream my head off!"

"Who's a liar? Not me," Kayo said, becoming angry now himself. "You're the one who said she didn't have time and she was going to stay home and study, not me. You're the one who is sneaking past guards and checking up on people."

"Nig-ro pa-lease! Don't even try and blame this on me! My Momma didn't raise no fools, okay? You got caught, busted, and I'm getting the hell out of here."

"Caught what?" Kayo said, planting his feet firmly on the floor, bracing the door.

"You don't think I'll scream?" Val said, her eyes narrowing. "Boy, I sang first soprano in children's choir. You don't wanna hear that high note!"

"Don't-don't scream, Val. I just want us to talk."

"Why? You obviously want to lift every skirt you see—baby, I don't want no leftovers and no diseases."

"Fine, then say what you mean. Don't come in here and blow up at me when the rules for our relationship weren't clear." Kayo was thinking fast and hard now, afraid he was going to lose her.

"You know I haven't been seeing anyone else."

"I don't *know* that," Kayo said defensively.

"Well, we *know* that you've been stepping out. If I hadn't come by you'd be screwing your brains out now."

"All I'm saying is, is that you're always talking about fairness and justice, right? Now, we never said we weren't going to see other people, did we?"

Val shook her head violently. "No-no, you're trying to turn this whole thing around."

"I am not! Listen," Kayo said, stepping away from the door.

Val went for it.

Kayo fell back and grabbed her wrists. "Listen!"

"I don't wanna hear that poor-black-man-I-gotta-have-it-all-the-time, sow-my-wild-oats mess."

Kayo shook her wrists until their eyes met. "And I don't want to hear that all-black-men-are-dogs bullshit from you either. I'm saying we never set the rules—whether this was going to be one on one, a just me-for-you and you-for-me relationship."

"You understood, Kayo," Val shouted.

"These are the nineties. There are no understandings. Everything has to be said and agreed on."

"And I guess that means it's okay to pick up some bitch off the street."

"She's not a bitch!" Kayo said not sure why he was defending Anna. "She works in the mailroom at my job."

"Reaching kind of low, huh?"

"C'mon, that's not fair!"

"Don't give me that fair bull! I caught you up here with some bitch . . ."

"She has a name."

"What is it?" Val asked, tapping her foot with impatience.

"Anna, her name is Anna."

"Okay," Val breathed. "I catch you up here with some bitch named Anna and you try to tell me about fairness in the nineties? Kayo, you're wrong."

"I was wrong, I didn't give our relationship the respect it deserves. I'm sorry, Val. If I could undo it, I would. I—I was just frustrated about this afternoon, feeling real unappreciated, okay? I want to feel wanted and needed, just like you do. I swear this was the first time I ever had anyone else up here since we met."

Val stopped struggling and Kayo dropped her hands and moved away from the door.

"I want us to keep what we have, and go on, 'cause it's good, Val, you know it's good. I'm saying I made a mistake . . ."

"You sure the hell did."

". . . a mistake *you* helped me make."

"I did what?"

"*You* helped me make it a little bit. Now, we can make something even better out of our relationship and you can be a part of that too. If you want to go, go. I'm not going to beg you to stay, Val. I don't have to beg. But if you stay, you will have a commitment from me."

Val felt torn. She was angry and she loved him. Finally, she took a deep breath and spoke. "Commitment. Just you for me and me for you."

"I promise. Cross my heart and hope to die," Kayo said, moving to embrace her.

Sweat rolled down Connor's brow as he stretched his right arm over his head, clutching the metal strap of the subway car. People were planted in the subway car like a mess of wild flowers. Connor sniffed hard, drew in his cheeks, and sucked in the malted air as if he were breathing through a straw. The subway car jerked, forcing his body to swing over an elderly man sitting in front of him.

The man eyeballed Connor while playing with a single strand of grey hair near the front of his face. Muddy spots were tracked all over his chin. The plain white T-shirt he wore made the nipples of his chest look dark and pointy. Connor sniffed hard again, trying to get air. The man mistook his efforts for a coke habit. "A shame!" he whispered. He rolled his eyes, crossed his legs, and opened a crumpled paperback book entitled *Shakespearean Sonnets.*

Without warning, Connor pictured Friar Pete sitting on his doubled-up blazer outside the Yale Co-op reading from a small book of sonnets. Connor got a sick feeling in his stomach and quickly averted his eyes to the subway map on the corner wall. He stayed in that trance until the train pulled into the station.

Connor turned to the left with the crowd and moved in small steps with them to the doors. Through the glass, the opposing force could be seen. Their faces were tight, drawn, and determined. Some shifted from foot to foot in anticipation. Those inside tightened up their ranks. Finally the doors popped open. Connor dropped his head and felt his body surge forward uncontrollably as if they were all chained together. When he cleared the door and stepped into the dank, dimly lit station he smiled with triumph. Connor turned a congratulatory glance to those around him, but they were expressionless and scattering in all directions.

Once outside, the air was cleansing. The street was full of people rushing about. Their crumpled suits, work shirts, and school jackets signaled the end of the day just as well as the little drag in their steps and the shortened swing of their arms. Connor thought as he crossed the street, I don't know why I'm even bothering to show up for this. Michelle and I are barely speaking. All Kayo wants to talk about is how much he misses that Ed guy on the job. Elizabeth is moody as hell every time I talk to her. I had a bad day and it's tougher on me than it is on anybody else. Connor stepped through the doorway of the bar.

The atmosphere inside the bar was like a badly mixed drink: anxious gaiety on top with tension forced down on the bottom. The bar was filled to capacity. There were two counters. Bartenders were serving drinks and the rest of the room was full of square metal tables covered with hand-embroidered cloths. In between the stitches of cloth there were beer labels from Corona and Molson Golden sewn in. Big, hand-painted domed lights that barely lit the room hung from the ceiling. On the walls, oil paintings begged for interpretation. The banter about deals, the latest jazz releases, and jokes hung in the corners of the room like cobwebs. The owner was one of the youngest and most successful real estate developers in New York City who also had a developing eye for the arts. The only person in the bar over thirty was the waiter opening oysters at the happy hour seafood buffet.

"Connor—here!" Michelle called from a table just a few feet away.

Michelle was sitting next to Kayo wearing all red, from the scarf around her neck to the bangles on her wrists. She always looked particularly beautiful in red, and Connor just had to smile. Next to her, Elizabeth had on a grey silk blouse and a black skirt. Her makeup looked a little too heavy and she was sitting back in the chair, her head tilted a bit, her eyes tired. Kayo was in the middle, his shirt wrinkled around the elbows and shoulders. He sipped his beer quietly and Connor knew from past experience that he was not in a good mood.

Connor sat down next to Michelle and greeted everyone at the table.

Michelle's voice was timid and distant. "Hi, you're late—rough day?"

"I've had a bitch of a day! I can't believe how hard I've been working. I mean I stayed up all last night getting stats together for this buy."

Kayo looked away toward the people at the bar.

Connor spoke directly to Kayo. "Needham has been riding me on this deal."

"Needham?" Kayo asked, turning back around. "Isn't that the guy who used to row crew with your Dad at Yale?"

"What's that have to do with it?" Connor was annoyed, but continued. "So, like I said, he's been riding me on this deal."

Kayo sighed and offered what he could, "That's rough, Connor."

"Why'd you say it like that?"

Elizabeth sipped her brandy and spoke up. "Here we go."

"Stay out of it," Michelle cautioned Elizabeth.

"No, I mean, Kayo, why'd you say it like that?" Connor repeated.

"Like what, man?" Kayo said.

"Like it was no big deal! I'm working my ass off—"

"Man, you're in your old man's company. I mean, you're going to get a lot of help other guys starting out cold just don't get. But all the time you're moaning about how rough it is."

Michelle slumped down in her chair. "Round one."

Connor glared at her, then pointed a stiff finger at Kayo. "Hey, it's harder for me than it is for you! I've got a family reputation to live up to! You're just cranky because I told you I was tired of hearing about that Ed what's-his-face."

"Ed Morrow was one of the best investment bankers there."

"If he was so great, he'd still be working!" Connor said with a cynical laugh.

"Ed helped me a lot, showed me a lot of things!" Kayo snapped back.

"I helped you too. Then it was like you didn't need me anymore—everything was Ed this, Ed said that!"

"Sounds like you're jealous," Elizabeth said.

"Stay out of this!" Connor barked.

"Don't talk to her like that!" Kayo warned. "You're mad at me, come to me with it!"

"Connor's right, it's none of her business," Michelle interjected.

Kayo looked at her.

"You can't tell me what to do!" Elizabeth told Michelle.

Kayo ignored them. "You didn't even want to meet Ed, man."

Michelle snapped at Elizabeth, "Don't be so touchy!"

Connor defended himself to Kayo: "I was busy."

"Touchy? You're just trying to run everybody's business again!" Elizabeth snapped at Michelle.

"How busy? You're just being silly, Con," Kayo said.

"I'm not trying to run anybody's business—I'm trying to stop *all this fighting*!" Michelle shouted.

Everyone stopped and looked at her.

Connor spoke first. "I just think we've all been on the edge lately. I've really got a lot of pressure on me."

"Connor, listen," Michelle said, leaning over to try and comfort him.

"Michelle, you—" Connor stopped. "I'm tired."

"We're all tired," Michelle said, looking around the table. She stopped back at Connor. "Stop thinking of yourself so much. I've been studying for hours—going to Virginia to research—" Michelle stopped short of talking about the journal. She still hadn't told anyone about it yet, wanting to prove its authenticity first.

"Big deal. School isn't hard like working!"

"Well, if it's so easy then how come you were so rotten at it?"

"I'm sure you're working hard, Michelle, in your own way," Kayo said, taking another sip of beer.

Michelle turned toward Kayo. "What's that supposed to mean?"

"Nothing. I said you're working hard studying," Kayo offered meekly. "What do you want, a medal?"

"No-no, you said that like . . . I don't know . . . like you were throwing me a crumb or something," Michelle said angrily.

Elizabeth joined in. "Stop making something out of nothing! It's like I've been telling you, Michelle, working is not like going to school—I'm sorry—it just isn't!"

"And some jobs are more pressured than others," Connor took a jab.

"What?" Elizabeth balked.

"I mean TV news? How hard can that be? You just tell the facts and you're only on for about two hours or so a day. When the show's off you're done!" Connor said.

"You don't know what the hell you're talking about!" Elizabeth snapped.

"All that fluff stuff—how hard can it be?" Michelle said sarcastically.

"You only get that kind of stuff during sweeps. And not all of the special reports are like that."

"There was one called, 'Where Is Elvis?,'" Connor pointed out, laughing.

"Elizabeth slammed her glass down. "You guys are being real jerks today."

Michelle felt guilty. "You know, we all decided to get together here to have some fun, to catch up with each other."

"And it ain't working," Kayo said, thumbing his tie.

"Look, we've been in the cooker all week, all day today,

and you expect us to emerge like Prince Charmings? See, that's what I meant about not knowing how tough it is on the job."

"You start that again and I'm leaving," Michelle said, pointing her finger at Connor. "And I mean it."

"So what? Leave."

Michelle stood up over Connor and glared. "Go to hell."

Kayo played the scene in his mind before it happened, like a director making a film. Now Connor, you get dopey-eyed and sorry real fast.

"I didn't mean anything by it, Michelle," Connor said, softening his eyes. "C'mon, I'm sorry. I tell you what, let's just go back to your place and relax, okay? I'm just worn out. Kayo, you'll take Elizabeth home?"

"Of course," he said, looking disappointedly at Michelle.

She caught it and chastised herself. Why do you always give in to Connor?

Maybe it was the way Kayo had taken up for Elizabeth during the argument in the restaurant; or maybe it was the way he held her close, shielding her from raindrops slipping underneath the umbrella they shared while trying to get a cab; or maybe it was the caring way he got after her about drinking and cocaine; or maybe it was the way he took the keys out of her hand to open the door, or now the way the muscles in his back were flexing as he struggled with the lock; maybe it was all those things, Elizabeth wasn't sure. All she was sure of, was how differently she was seeing Kayo now.

"You know," Elizabeth said, watching Kayo work the lock, "if it was anybody else, I wouldn't dare let them see my apartment like this."

"Got it!" Kayo smiled over his shoulder. He held the door open for her. "It can't be worse than mine! Val says I'm a pig."

She walked in and turned on the torch lamp. "Here goes."

There were clothes all over the loveseat and shoes on the floor. A crumpled bath towel was on the floor by the lamp. Papers were strewn all over the cocktail table.

"Yep, it's worse than mine."

Elizabeth smiled. "I'll take that as a compliment if you don't mind."

"No problem," Kayo said, knocking some of the clothes off the loveseat with his hand. He sat down. "It's smaller than I remember."

Elizabeth kicked off her grey pumps and walked into the kitchen. "It looks smaller when it's dirty like this."

Kayo heard glasses rattling. He got up off the couch and walked to the kitchen doorway and stood behind her.

"I'm having a little drink. Want one?" she took the bottle out of the cabinet drawer.

"Elizabeth, you had enough at the bar," he said from the doorway.

Elizabeth opened the bottle and looked over her shoulder. "Just a little one," she said, pouring the brandy in the glass. She forced herself not to look at him, fighting the budding desire she was feeling.

"No," Kayo said coming up behind her, reaching for the bottle.

Elizabeth squirmed away, holding the bottle away out in front of her. "Stop, Kayo."

He reached over her back to get the bottle.

She felt his firm chest against her shoulders and the front of his thighs against her butt and hips.

"Give me that," Kayo scolded, taking the bottle out of her hand.

Elizabeth let him, leaning her body back, absorbing all the warmth.

Kayo began pouring the liquor from the glass back into the bottle.

Elizabeth glanced up into his face. She saw his eyes, determined, bright, and she felt herself begin to melt away. She turned around, threw her arms around his neck, and kissed Kayo with all the desire, fear, longing, and love her heart could muster. She felt him tense, so she worked her tongue deeper into his mouth.

Kayo stepped back.

Elizabeth felt a scalding sensation in her chest. She reached down and tore open her blouse.

Grey beads rocketed around the kitchen.

Kayo yanked her hands down, taking another step back. "What are you doing?"

Elizabeth stopped, speechless.

Kayo felt embarrassed and angry. He looked at her full breasts, doughy and pert. "What's, what's going on?" he asked.

Elizabeth saw the confusion in his eyes and instantly became afraid. "Kayo, I need somebody who really cares about me to love me."

"Elizabeth, of course, I love you—"

She dropped to her knees and started to unzip his pants. Kayo grabbed her by the hair and jerked her head back. "Stop acting like a whore."

Elizabeth grunted and pushed him away as hard as she could.

Kayo fell back into the door.

Plaster crumbled from the wall.

"Get the fuck out!" Elizabeth moaned.

Kayo looked at her. He was near tears. "We're friends. I love you because you're my friend!" he pleaded.

Elizabeth panicked. Her eyes got big and her insides were smarting from the rejection. "I guess you think this is funny, me throwing myself at you."

"No!"

She grabbed the edge of the counter and pulled herself up. "You and Val and Connor and Michelle can have a big laugh!"

"No, this is between us and nobody else."

Elizabeth grabbed a glass and flung it at Kayo.

He jumped away and the glass splattered against the wall.

"Get the fuck out!" Elizabeth said, barely able to get the words out as she began to sob. "Just go, Kayo!"

He backed away and grabbed his coat off the couch. "I'll talk to you later."

Elizabeth beat her hands against her thighs. "Get out! Get out! Get out!"

* * *

The tips of Connor's fingers caressed the nape of Michelle's neck as he undid the red scarf. It fell and landed on top of her blouse, making even larger the pool of red softness at her feet. Connor ran his hand up along her long, slender neck and cradled her delicate chin in the palm of his hand as he traced the top of her lips with the tip of his tongue.

Michelle undid the buttons of his shirt and slipped it down around his waist. She moved to his waist and listened for the light clicking of the metal buckle and the swishing sound of the leather whisking through the belt loops. She shuddered. Her tongue filled the inside of his ear.

Connor pressed his body against hers and unzipped the back of her skirt. He kissed her hard as her skirt dropped on top of his bare feet.

Connor stepped out of his pants easily. And to a silent tango, they stepped backward to the bed. He braced the small of her back with firm fingers and eased her down on the bed. The moonlight climbed through the partly opened window and slid down the curtains onto the bed with them. The smooth sound of their breathing was drumming a soft beat in the darkness. Connor took his tongue and ran it along the nape of Michelle's neck. He heard her catch her breath and he felt himself begin to tingle inside. His tongue skipped along the familiar path between her breasts. He squeezed her shoulders and swallowed down her salty taste.

The soft hairs on his chest tickled her stomach as he began kissing her harder, lower. Michelle ran her fingers through his hair. Connor let his head be pulled back until only the tip of his tongue touched her body. The hot air from his nostrils slammed against her stomach and bounced back into his face in short blasts.

Her fingers squeezed the back of his thighs as he moved back up her body. He alternated with kisses and deep sucks that caused her skin to fill his mouth for a second, then snap back down with a pop. "Feels real good!" Michelle whispered.

The words arrested him. Connor hovered over Michelle,

letting the nipples of his chest touch those of her breast. Michelle squeezed his hips, forcing his body down slowly. Connor tensed with the erection and Michelle feeling him rise forced him down harder and faster.

Her body wrapped up tightly in the sheets, Michelle snuggled underneath Connor's arm. He was on top of the spread, drying in the love-scented air.

"Good?" she asked.

"Great," he said, squeezing her shoulders. "Sorry about all the fights?"

"Yeah."

"I knew you'd come around," he said, slipping down into the bed.

It took a moment for the words to sink in. When they did Michelle leaned up. "What do you mean, I'd come around?"

"Just that. I knew sooner or later things would get back to normal," he said, patting her back.

Michelle jerked away. "This didn't mean anything!"

"What?" Connor said, sitting up straight.

"Same old relationship, huh? No demands."

"Let's just enjoy each other."

"No! This is bothering me *again*," she said. "Connor, I want you to take me to your house for dinner to meet your family."

Connor spoke nonchalantly. "Okay, I'll check with Elizabeth and Kayo to see what they're doing, then I'll set a date with Mom. She'll be glad 'cause she's been asking about you guys."

"You make me sick when you play stupid!"

"What?"

"You know darn well that's not what I meant, Connor! I want you to tell them that we are going to be married!"

Connor let his body fall back on the bed. "Why are you forcing us to fight, *again*?"

"I'm not forcing anything but what's right! We've been going together for years and I don't know your family and you don't know mine!"

"You've met my family and I've met yours plenty of times . . ."

"That's surface stuff! If we're going to get married, it's got to be deeper than that!"

"When we get married, your family will grow to love me just like mine will grow to love you because we'll be together."

Michelle softened. She leaned over close. "Then why don't we get the ball rolling now, and make things easier? Tell your parents about us and I'll tell mine."

"No!" Connor shouted, slamming a clenched fist against the bed. "Didn't I tell you that things aren't going well at work? When I make it big, when I get a well-placed foot there, then I'll tell Dad about us. We can announce our engagement and then get married."

"You keep saying that, but it just keeps getting farther and farther away. I'm starting not to see it, Connor. I swear, I'm really starting not to see it," she panted on the verge of crying. "Go home."

"Go home," he repeated. Connor looked up at the ceiling, "What's this 'go home' business?"

Michelle started to rock, clutching her elbows. "Go home, just go home."

He tried to turn her toward him. Michelle jerked back. "Go on now!"

Connor rolled out of the bed and began putting his clothes on. "This is crazy. All we do is fight and half the time I don't know what we're fighting about!"

Michelle kept rocking.

Connor watched her for a second before leaving, "You're nuts! Nuts!"

Kayo was sitting in his favorite chair, his legs swinging over one arm and his head and arms falling over the other. He had been in the position so long his armpits ached. This is deep! I had no idea she was that emotionally unstable. I can't tell Connor or Michelle and Lord knows I can't tell Val! Kayo was angry with himself for handling Elizabeth so roughly. "You called her a whore!" He swung his legs until the whole chair rocked. "Dumb-dumb!" he whispered. That's all she needed. Kayo slammed his fist against the wall.

Suddenly the phone rang.

Kayo hesitated before answering.

"Kayo?"

"Elizabeth?"

"No, it's Michelle," she said, clearing her throat. "Kayo, Connor and I just had another fight! I threw him out. Kayo, it wasn't my fault."

"Michelle!" Kayo shouted. "You've got to make up your mind, 'cause I'm getting tired of being your Dear Abby, okay?"

"Well, I was just calling you because I thought you understood!"

"You called me to get sympathy! I'm tired, okay? You know what you want out of your relationship and you know the direction it's going in!"

"Why are you yelling at me?"

"Because *all you do* is take more and more bullshit off Connor and come crying to me. Now this has gotta stop! Do you respect yourself?"

"Yes."

"Huh!?" Kayo said, getting out of the chair, pacing.

"Yes."

"Well, act like it!"

"You're right. I know you're right. I've got to make a decision."

"Do whatever you've got to do, but don't do it for me or for Connor, do it for Michelle. 'Bye." Kayo slammed down the phone.

Chapter 13

ANXIETY jolted Michelle's body as she paced the living room. It was fifteen steps across. She stopped at the window and looked out, but there was nothing to see but the fire escape of the building next door. I've made the right decision. She sighed and turned back, pacing. Drudgery was like shoes on her feet.

There was a knock on the door.

Michelle walked over, checked the peephole, and opened the door. "Hi."

Connor had on a faded navy blue and white crew shirt from freshman year. His jeans were baggy at the knees and in the back. He had a red scarf around his neck. "I saw the sign to just come up. Buzzer's broken?" he asked.

"Yeah, it happened last night sometime."

"Oh," Connor said, walking past her over to the big wooden desk in the living room corner.

"You should have on a jacket, you catch cold easily."

"Don't need it!" Connor said confidently. He hopped up on the desk and slid out the chair. He propped his feet up in it and crossed his arms. "Mom said you called and said it was urgent."

"It is urgent. Connor, we've been fighting a lot lately."

Connor patted his feet. "Way too much!"

Michelle walked over to the center of the room, "Connor . . ."

"Michelle," he said, suddenly wanting to speak first.

"I need some space to think about our relationship. I want us to give each other some space for a few weeks."

Connor felt stunned, irritated, and afraid all at the same time. He squeezed the edge of the desk and his tongue seemed stuck in his mouth. He examined her carefully. She looked like the same Michelle: same eyes, mouth, lips, hips, and breasts. He felt himself getting aroused and he knew that this was the same woman he had loved for years but her words, her thoughts, her actions lately seemed to come from someone else. "You want to break off the relationship?"

The words made his lips an ugly sore. "I'm not saying that."

"Good!"

Michelle closed her eyes. "I'm saying I haven't decided. I don't know what I want and I don't think you know what you want. Both of us need to think about it, *hard,* and the only way we can decide what's best for both of us is to make our minds up separately, apart, without any pressure or influence from the other."

"I know what I want."

"*No*-you-don't *no*-you-don't!" Michelle said, shaking her head so hard the bones in her neck popped.

"Don't tell me how I feel!" Connor shouted, stomping the chair seat with both feet.

Michelle felt the jolt. "I'm not trying to tell you how to feel, really, I'm not. That's why I said we need to have some space, away from each other, so we can decide on what we each want."

Connor walked over and grabbed her shoulders. "Michelle, just wait, okay? Please understand how tough things are for my family now. My Dad is really on my case and everyone in the firm is watching me. I mean, it's pressure with a capital P! Mom is up one day and the next day she's crying with pain. That's why I didn't get an apartment with Kayo—I wanted to stay home and be near Mom. Not now. One more thing, Michelle, and I think I'll just bust. Just be a little more patient. Hang in there just a little while longer, huh?"

Michelle's eyes remained closed. She spoke through dry, cracked lips. "I need the space. I'm going to have the space."

He released her. Michelle wrapped her arms around herself. "I'll call you in a few weeks."

"Alright," Connor said tenderly, "but I know what I want."

The sound of the door shutting softly seemed to snap her heart in two, leaving one piece aching there inside her and the other floating away numb with him.

"Mama, please!" Kayo fumbled with the papers on his desk and spoke as low as he could into the receiver. "What are you balling me out for?" He frowned, now turning over his feet, looking at his his new golf shoes.

"Baby, you know I need the rent money by the fifth," his mother said.

"I sent it special delivery. It's guaranteed to be there the next day by twelve, okay? Hang on another hour and if it's not there, call me."

"Well, you stay home then so I can call."

"No, I'm at work. I always work on Saturdays."

"Poor baby," his mother said softly. "I didn't mean to yell. Mad?"

"No, I'm not mad at you, Mama." Kayo shook his head. "Don't worry about anything. Talk to you later."

Kayo hung up the phone and leaned all the way back in the chair and reached for the golf clubs behind him. This sure is an expensive game. But the golf had been paying off. Kayo smiled to himself as he remembered the first time he invited himself to a golf game with Lampdon. Lampdon and a few other management types were talking at a reception. He had just walked up to the group while they were planning their golf date and just invited himself along. "Pick your mouths up off the floor, motherfuckers"—he said now what he had thought then. Kayo had spent hours in the library the weekend before the date, reading about golf. He was going to try to wing it, lie, and say that he knew what he was doing. But after renting a car and driving up to the course in Greenwich he changed his mind. Instead, Kayo had catered to their egos. "Oh, I've always loved watching the game and I knew that watching you guys play would help me learn. Real pros." He laughed about it now. They ate it up! He started clearing his desk. Playing this golf is helping break the ice some, but I need something else to break the ice with the big guy, Kayo thought. I want that big bonus. I know they're still not really comfortable around me. I've got to be one of the boys.

He heard a rattling sound.

Kayo stood up and peeked over his cubicle wall. A tall, young black man with slender legs and torso and a hulking stride was walking down the aisle pushing a cart. There were long, thin towels each stained a different color from shoe polish hanging like flags from the edges of the cart. Danny's hair was cut short with three thin parts on the side. His T-shirt had a big ice cube in front and was silver grey like his high-top sneakers. Danny's father had shined shoes for the building's executives for years. When the old man died from a heart attack, the business had passed on to Danny.

Kayo turned around in his chair and began fiddling with a pencil. He had been putting off playing ball with Danny to play golf with Lampdon. They used to talk a great deal but Kayo wasn't taking the time to do much of that anymore.

"What's up, Kayo?"

"Hey Danny. How are you?"

"How am I? Man, what's this okey-dokey shit? You don't play ball at the Y with me and the fellas. You see me in the mornings and just say, 'Hello Danny' real quick and keep walking. And it's like there's a fence in your voice, saying, 'Stay outta my yard.' What's the deal, man?"

"Sssh! Lower your voice, people are starting to come in!"

"So?" Danny stepped back and started talking with his hands in sharp up-and-down motions. "So what? This is about us, not them."

Kayo shook his head. "Look, Danny. I'm trying to have a certain image here. I need it to move up. You've got to present a certain image—just like we all wear the same types of suits and ties and shoes—I have to wear a certain image at work too."

"Aww, Kayo, I'm just for being real—no playacting."

"Look, I'm trying to explain . . ."

"Noo-noo! I hear you. You've turned stiff and grey like these other black folks around here who don't speak and who look down on me and the black secretaries and stuff."

"I don't think of you all like that."

"Hey, no sweat." Danny threw up his hand. "Look, I know the image you want. Fine, it's cool, but you know, I thought you were real, man."

Kayo pleaded with him. "Look, Danny, one day I'm going to have my own company and man, you can have any position you want in it. What would you want?"

Danny started turning his cart around. "I'd like to be in charge of kicking grey niggers' ass."

He moved away from Kayo with a long, urgent stride. "I'll see you Monday, Mister Watson. I hope you mold yourself into shape, brother."

The accusation snapped the pencil in two. Kayo dug his nails into the broken halves as a flashback shattered his consciousness. . . .

A red ace appeared and disappeared.

Kayo watched as he walked toward the crowd of white students surrounding Friar Pete as he performed his magic tricks. Friar Pete grinned, making the card reappear behind ears, necks, and from beneath the cuffs of their slacks. All the while he talked: "This trick proves that things are never as real as they seem. You will think one thing is happening, when really something else entirely is going on. Magic is like life—full of illusion." And he drew the card from behind the broken bib of a student's blue-and-white Yale cap.

The crowd cheered.

"You're really good," the student laughed, reaching in his pocket, pulling out two dollars.

Kayo sneered, doubling his pace as he jaunted past.

Friar Pete glimpsed Kayo in the peripheral mirror of his vision. "Excuse me," he said, taking a slight bow before sprinting after Kayo. He reached him, spun, and began jogging backward so their confrontation would be face-to-face.

"There's something ugly between me and you."

"I don't have a problem with you," Kayo said in a stiff voice.

"A man faces his problems. A boy runs away."

Kayo stopped. "Oh, I'm a boy. You're the one standing around this campus ducking your head, performing for the white folks."

"I'm no Tom," Friar Pete said, releasing gravelly laughter.

"You find it funny?"

"Yes. I've lived through worse racism than you've read about or seen on TV. I know what it's like to stack up one way and have the world size you up differently because of the color of your skin. I like magic tricks. I do a few and talk to the students around here, black and white, and I tell them what I think, pulling no punches. I'm not trying to be what anybody else wants. I'm me and I'm here."

"But you don't belong here!" Kayo shouted angrily.

Friar Pete laughed again. "I think the real question bothering you is do *you* belong here." He produced two dollars and grinned. "Bet two dollars, do you fit in?"

Elizabeth looked at the small bag of coke on the cocktail table. You don't need to get fucked up every time you feel stressed out. Elizabeth grabbed the bag and pressed the white powder between her fingers. She took enough to fill the thick nail of her middle finger and inhaled. Elizabeth blinked hard and the pit of her stomach ached. She folded the bag over and tossed it aside. Last night she had dreamt of Meghan and of the accident. Elizabeth fell back and dropped her head on the soft cushion of the loveseat. She reached down and grabbed the black princess phone. She dialed quickly and stuffed it under her ear.

"Hello?"

"Hi, Michelle."

"Hey, girl," Michelle said, stuffing clothes in an overnight bag.

"You sound out of breath."

"I am running a little ragged today. I'm packing for Virginia." She picked up a jacket, considered it, then tossed it over her shoulder onto the bedroom floor.

"More Ph.D. stuff?"

"Um, yeah," Michelle lied.

"Oh, well, I can let you go if you want," Elizabeth said, biting her bottom lip.

"I am really rushed, but are you okay?"

Elizabeth curled her body up even tighter. "Well, I'm feeling a little stressed out lately."

"Join the club!" Michelle checked her watch. "Hey, I really have to go."

"I know. Hey, did I tell you my Dad called the other night and said he's going to run for mayor in New Haven?"

"That's great! Your father would make a great mayor! You must be excited!"

"I really am. I'm supposed to be trying to come up with some catchy slogans and stuff for him. It might be fun. . . . Well, call me when you get back?"

"Okay," Michelle said. "I know we haven't been talking much and we need to catch up. I'll call you as soon as I get back and we can probably catch a movie or something."

"Okay. Talk to you soon."

The second floor of the Alderman Library was almost empty.

Michelle was sitting at her favorite corner table with her head buried in a financial ledger. Several hours had passed and she was tired but still she continued. Michelle had gone over three years in the different ledgers and she was now up to the year 1828. She pinched her eyes and swallowed. Her throat was dry and catchy like before a good cry. Suddenly there was a sound like someone cracking their knuckles and Michelle's neck would no longer support her head. The words now made as much sense as the bottom of a doctor's eye chart.

She decided to take a break and that's when weariness and doubt began teasing her. She imagined her father's face, twisted and disappointed. Cupped palms now caught her falling tears.

"Where is your faith?"

Michelle heard her father's voice and tried to stop crying but couldn't.

"Lord, church, where is your faith?"

She pictured him in the pulpit, the tip of the mike looking like a ball balanced on top of his clenched fist. His mouth wide open and red: "Now, y'all have faith in them jobs, in them Cadillacs you drive, in them fine houses you live in. And I'm here to tell you that you need to let all that pass away!"

The congregation sat silent; only the hum of the fan could be heard.

"Y'all mighty quiet up in here this morning! Y'all want be dead, he'll sho take you out!"

The row of deacons responded: "Amen, Doctor!"

Michelle watched her father point a finger, sweat dripping from the tip: "Have faith in Jesus and in yourself. Call on Jesus and he'll see you through."

Michelle moved her hands away from her face. God, please . . . just a sign, a help of some kind. Michelle leaned back and took a deep breath. Her mind responded.

> Doc say theres a new sewciety that wants the niggas to be free
> Master Whittnower says its the doings of that grey sun

Michelle concentrated on the words. New society—grey sun. Grey sun? Her mind was working now—Greysun or Grayson—no, no! Garrison! William Lloyd Garrison. The abolitionist who founded the New England Anti-Slavery Society. She didn't dare think any more. Michelle ran to the stairwell and headed down the steps.

The back of her heels ached from the force of her stride. A loud rattle and shrouded handprint marked the door as she passed through. She knew every inch of the library by now and she headed straight for the aisle she needed. Michelle hit a chair with her hip. "Excuse me!" she said, touching someone's shoulder as she continued on, turning the corner. Michelle stopped in the middle of the third aisle, remembering the beginning call letters PY216. Where is it? Finally, the creased red binding seemed to shout its title to her: *The Life and Achievements of William Lloyd Garrison.* She just flipped to the back of the book and scanned the Index. Michelle could hardly hold the book still, her hands were shaking so badly. "The New England Anti-Slavery Society, 1832!" Listed directly under that was a notation for an article written in the *Richmond Enquirer* criticizing Garrison. Michelle was speechless. It was as if a hand struck her deaf and dumb and in that world of true solitude it came to her. "Of course! It'd be in the papers! A slave killing an overseer? Yes!"

Michelle stuffed the book under her arm and ran toward the door. She headed back upstairs, taking two steps at a time. She burst through the heavy metal door with a crash and people glared at her as she reached the front desk. Michelle asked the clerk for specific microfilm rolls for the *Richmond Enquirer.* Her hands trembled as she opened the first box and slipped the microfilm on the machine. It emitted a hot, dull hum and an irritating glow. Michelle started turning the handle slowly, scanning the headlines on each page. Nothing. CLOTH PRICES UP. Turning—turning. The pages started to whirl past in mixed-up-looking bunches, then faster and smoother, like liquid in a blender. Michelle put on another roll, then another.

Her eyes started to water. She felt her jaw starting to tighten and ache.

> *Wednesday, November 28, 1832*
> OVERSEER MURDERED BY AFRICAN SLAVE
>
> William Jeremiah died after a violent fight. Jeremiah had been a Plantation overseer for more than fifteen years. Jeremiah was brutally attacked by an african slave named Will and his ten-year-old son Joshua two weeks ago. Jeremiah had apparently caught the slaves reading and writing. He was able to kill the wild african but not without suffering the soon to be fatal injuries that he hence succumbed to. The boy Joshua, also a party to the act, was later caught attempting to flee north. He was shot to death by slave catchers. The Honorable Robert Whittnower of the Rosebloom Plantation of Dade County is generously providing for Jeremiah's widow. He is also displaying the journal at the slave quarters as a reminder to the other slaves of the evil that can come from learning to read and write.

Michelle beamed with renewed energy. She pressed the button four times repeatedly and the copies shot out one right after another, landing in her lap. Michelle stuffed the copies in the book and clutched it in her hands as she ran back downstairs. She was out of breath by the time she reached the research desk. "The financial ledger for 1832, from the Whittnower Collection."

Michelle sat down on the floor right there in front of the desk and just started thumbing through, searching. Her chest felt tight and she had trouble catching her breath. Her eyes continued down the columns . . . nope, no, no. Michelle took a deep breath and flipped to the next page. The date November 19, 1832, was scrawled in the corner. She scanned the transactions, and the next-to-the-last item on the page read:

> African slave Will, 40, and son Joshua, 10, killed for writing in journal. Loss, $2200. Paid to Jeremiah widow, $2000. Total loss: $4200.

She covered her mouth and a wild giggle vibrated her fingers. "I knew it!" Michelle dropped her hand from her mouth and all the tension, fatigue, anguish, and excitement spilled out of her body in deep, cool, rolling laughter. Those around her turned in their seats and sent down annoyed stares, but by the time they reached her they were falling on a numb body.

A cool breeze wafted through the window. The small living room was sparsely furnished with a beat-up wicker couch and chairs with beautifully colored cushions. There was a planter in the corner with exotic plants growing all over each other. On the couch, Val's feet were folded up neatly behind her while her hands were clasped underneath her right ear. Kayo was sitting on the hardwood floor, the top of his head just shy of her chin. He stuffed popcorn in his mouth as Val watched the sides of his jaws work. She reached out and grabbed the top of his head. "Chew, boy!"

Kayo ignored her, grabbing another handful, sucking it down.

"You are so stubborn—even on the littlest things!" Val said, reaching and turning him around to face her. "You're just like a kid!"

"My mother is in Chicago!"

"Well, she needs to be here to tell you about your bad eating habits. It's a wonder you haven't come down with something—eating junk all the time, working so hard on the job!"

Kayo reached his hand up and stroked her thigh, "That's not what I work hardest at."

Val smiled. "Is that *all* you ever think about?"

"Mostly. But there is something else—ah, have you reconsidered?"

"I told you, Kayo, I'm taking the job in the Public Defender's Office."

Kayo dropped a handful of popcorn back into the blue Tupperware bowl. "Val! Why are you turning down a seventy-five-thousand-dollar-a-year job with the biggest firm in New York to be a public defender?"

"I've told you."

Kayo slammed his body back against the couch. "Tell me again, because I like fairytales!"

Val leaned up on one elbow. "Look! I think it's important to give back to the community. Somebody has to defend the rights of poor black people so that they can get a fair shake in the justice system."

"Alright, I'll give you that, but let somebody else do it. You're too bright, aggressive, to get buried in those problems! They'll eat you up until you don't have anything left."

"Dig you—'Let somebody else do it.' Somebody else less qualified—that's why it's all screwed up now. And you should know, if your brother Ben could get a decent public defender you wouldn't have to spend all your money on getting attorneys for him."

"Forget Ben. This is not about him. He's a royal fuck-up and always will be. This is about your career. If you take the job in the firm, you'll make a shitload of money and super contacts. You might be able to start your own practice one day! You could be such a success, Val, I hate to see you throw it all away."

Val laughed. Her body twisted over and her soft, fleece shirt rose and wound candy-wrapper tight around her body. "You think a specific job paying a certain amount of money is success?"

"What is so comical?"

Val leaned up and over, looking down at Kayo. The anger in his eyes sparked more laughter from her. She fell back on the couch clutching her sides.

"You know what your problem is?" Kayo said, raising a cautious finger, the crest of his Yale ring firmly in place. "You think you can solve all the world's problems. Why is it that all you black college grads from Morehouse and Spelman think you're Martin and Coretta King?"

Val stopped laughing. "See?" She pointed her finger.

"You're talking foolish. That's why I laughed at you. Kayo, what do you want me to do? Work myself to death trying to get ahead in somebody else's money game? I want more than that."

"If you have money and an influential position, you can make changes. How are you going to change things from the outside?"

"Kayo, you don't put a roof on a house first. You build the foundation. Until there's a solid foundation, freedom of choice and expression for all people, there's no need for anything else. I'm going to be feeling real good about myself when I get up in the morning. I'm going to be smiling in the mirror 'cause I'll be doing something important and something that will make a difference, a difference that will help black people. I'll be doing something I like! I'm not going to be worrying about how much money the guy sitting across from me is making, will I get this next promotion, playing that political game. It's not that important. I want to love what I do."

"All that's talk." Kayo shook his head. "Just wait till you get out there. Life isn't like that, Val. You've got to get ahead of the other guy and be a star in the marketplace to get anywhere. Being underpaid in a thankless job is not the way."

"You can't see it my way at all, huh?"

"Nope, and I don't feel like arguing anymore—your mind is made up. How 'bout this, though?" Kayo grabbed a handful of popcorn and shoved it in his mouth. He pointed his finger: one chew, two chews, three chews, four chews, and five chews—swallow!

Val smiled at him. "It's a little thing, but it's a start."

Elizabeth sat and thought about Michelle. She said that she was going to call me back after her trip and she didn't. I know she's back. What kind of a best friend won't call a friend and check on them? She should be able to tell from my voice that I need her.

"Rrrng!"

Elizabeth looked at the phone, then at the clock. It was

twelve o'clock. She knew it was her father. Elizabeth bent down and grabbed the receiver. "Hello?"

"Hi, baby," her father said cheerily.

"Hi, Daddy," Elizabeth said, playing with the cord.

"You're off tonight, right?" he questioned.

"What'd you say? Our connection is always bad!" Elizabeth said, straining.

"I know, I never should of switched to that bandit long-distance company. You speak up too," he said.

"Okay, that's better. I'm a little worn out tonight and I don't feel like watching our news and I don't really feel like going out either." Elizabeth yawned.

"You know, the other night when I called, you sounded strange."

"Really? It was probably nerves and being really tired," Elizabeth lied, remembering how high she had been.

"Yeah, yeah, that's what I thought. But I just want you to know that I'm very proud of you. You're handling yourself really well there in New York all by yourself. You've told me how stressful it is for you at times, and I want you to know that I'm behind you one hundred percent. If you need anything, just let me know. You're going to make it big there, I just know It!"

"You know, you always give me confidence and cheer me up—I don't know what I'd do without you, Daddy!"

"That's my girl! Say, how are Michelle and the guys?"

"I think everybody's okay. We're all just so busy now with our jobs and Michelle with school. We're starting to drift apart a little."

"No, it's probably just your imagination. You guys are so close, you just don't have the time to spend, is all. Hey, listen. There's a big political rally weekend after next. If you can come, it sure would be nice."

"Big day, huh?"

"This is really important to me. At first I wasn't too keen on the idea. But with the old guys on the force backing me, Mayor Simmons retiring, and an open field of candidates, I could take it. I'd be the second kid from the old neighborhood to make it, just like old Cookie there in New York. Have you run into him again yet?''

"No, not since that time in Brooklyn.''

"He's a good guy. Still owes me a favor or two from the old days,'' Nickelson chuckled.

"He's a good mayor too. Just like you're going to be!''Elizabeth said excitedly. ''Mayor Nickelson. Sounds good to me!''

True excitement and joy were emanating from every extension, every pore of Michelle's body. Her hair gleamed and bounced around her shoulders as she rushed around her apartment. Her eyes twinkled and sprinkled everything she saw with good feelings. Michelle's arms were light and full of extraordinary energy as she spent most of the evening cleaning and decorating her apartment for the party she was having for herself, Connor, Kayo, and Elizabeth. She could hardly wait to tell them about the journal, about her work on authenticating it. Professor Kingman had almost fallen out of his chair when she showed him the journal and her findings. He was a bit angry at first that she hadn't told him about what she was doing. Kingman even said that he was preparing to drop her from the Ph. D. program because her work had suffered so badly and had been so incomplete. But now, all that was over and only the best of times were ahead. Michelle and the Professor were going to make a surprise showing of the journal at the Schomberg Library Saturday at the National Convention of African American Historians. The timing was perfect. Professor Kingman was so excited he had begun to stutter. ''Yo-ou will be-be able to speak all around the country and when you do finish your Ph.D., you will be able to write your ticket to any university in the country!''

Michelle had hardly been able to believe that it was all happening. It was as if someone had granted her a wish that she wouldn't have dared ask for. She wanted to share her happiness, her joy, with the people who meant the most to her. So Michelle had called each of them separately, not telling them why she wanted them to come to her apartment, but just that they must come. They must come. And maybe it had been the excitement, the litheness in her voice, but each had agreed and she knew that all of them would be there tonight, despite the tough times they were all having.

So Michelle had filled the room with flowers, beautiful blooming roses of red, white, and yellow. Her house smelled stuffily sweet like a box of candy. She went to the bank and drew out what little money she had left in her savings account and bought a case of champagne and as much jumbo shrimp and imported cheese as she could afford. Later at home, she dressed carefully, wanting the colors she chose to express the tremendous joy she was feeling after so much stress and work; the way a rainbow clothes the sky. Michelle was checking herself in the mirror when she heard the first knock at the door. The royal blue, teal, and lavender in the blouse illuminated her shoulders and the matching slacks hugging her hips and flowed down her legs. "Come in," Michelle said, opening the door.

Connor followed her into the room. He stopped and watched her body move underneath the swirling colors. Connor was struck by how beautiful she was, and the fact that he had not seen or talked to her for several weeks seemed too unreasonable for him to have endured. "You look beautiful and I have truly missed you."

Michelle felt herself blush with different emotions. She was overjoyed about her good fortune and sorry about what had happened between her and Connor. She had meant to call him several times, to tell him what she had decided after many nights of tossing and turning, but each time she found a reason not to. "I've missed you too and I have something important to tell you, Kayo, and Elizabeth, and I don't want to talk about us."

"But why?"

"Connor, I feel great! Can't you see I feel great? Let me enjoy and let me share it with you all."

Connor saw that she looked happier than he had seen her in over a year. "When are they going to get that buzzer fixed?

It's too dangerous, people being able to just walk up to your door."

Michelle was grateful that he had changed the subject. "Don't worry, the janitor said it won't be much longer before it's fixed. Hey, make yourself useful and open a bottle of champagne."

There was a knock at the door.

Michelle opened the door and let Kayo in. "I'm glad to see you!"

Kayo walked past her and she stopped him with a firm hand on his shoulder, whispering. "I know we've bumped heads, but tonight everybody has to leave their attitudes at the door because tonight is one of the most important nights I'll ever have."

Kayo looked at her, then at Connor, who was bent over the champagne case, opening it. Kayo nodded, "Well, you know good times are for good people." He took off his suit jacket and tossed it on top of Connor's on the rocker. "Hey, old man!"

Connor turned around and smiled timidly at Kayo. "Grab a corner and pull, huh?"

"I've got some food in the kitchen, too!"

There was another knock on the door. "That's Elizabeth, last but not least."

When Michelle opened the door, Elizabeth breezed right past her and sat down on the couch. She slipped off her leather jacket and tugged up the sleeves of the oversized orange T-shirt she was wearing. Elizabeth noticed the flowers and the way Michelle was dressed. "So, what's so important? she asked nonchalantly, forcing her eyes down, not looking at any of them.

"Elizabeth, I have some great news and I wanted us all to be together to celebrate," Michelle said, ignoring her despondent attitude.

Kayo watched the way Elizabeth hardly paid attention and then he looked at the way Michelle's shoulders started to tense.

Connor pulled out one of the bottles of champagne. "Whatever it is, we'll be ready with this!"

Kayo spoke to Elizabeth. "How's it going?" That was all he could think to say, not having talked to her since that night in her apartment. Every time he had called she had hung up the phone and now she was shunning everyone in the room.

As Elizabeth stared at him, her heart sank, and the pit of her stomach cramped. She said dryly, "Okay," and turned her head.

Michelle reached over and took her hand and pulled her off the couch. "Help me in the kitchen."

Connor looked at Kayo and shook his head, whispering: "She gets moodier and moodier!"

Kayo nodded. "Yeah."

"Elizabeth," Michelle said, handing her a tray, "tonight is real important to me. I know I was supposed to call you and I didn't."

"Don't worry about it," Elizabeth said, playing with the stopper in the sink.

"I know we've all been at each other, but not tonight. I've got something important to tell you guys and I want you to be happy for me, just like I'd be happy for you."

Elizabeth felt herself soften. "What's so important? You keep hinting but you're not saying anything."

Michelle backed out of the kitchen with a wicked smile on her face. "Listen, okay, this is it. This is big!"

Kayo plopped down in a small bamboo chair in the corner, swinging his leg over the side. "Well, spill it!"

"Hey, that chair!" Michelle winced. "It's an antique!"

"Well, it's not my fault you can't stand to buy anything new. I'm tired of walking on eggshells every time I come in here!" Kayo wiggled his hips in the chair. It creaked. "Stop wasting your time hunting up junk in those antique stores!"

"I've been trying to tell her that for years, man!" Connor said, shaking his head in agreement.

"If I'd listened to you two, I wouldn't have run across the find of the century!"

"What are you talking about?" Elizabeth asked, trying to force herself to be part of what was happening.

"What?" Connor was anxious, seeing the excitement on Michelle's face.

Michelle sauntered over to her desk, opened the drawer, and pulled out the journal.

Connor tried to peek over her shoulder and she buried the journal in her chest. "What is it?" he said, laughing. You're acting like a kid!"

Michelle held the journal out delicately in her hands. "Well, it's a long, long story!"

"Ooh!" the three of them moaned.

Kayo leaned up in the chair, his elbow resting on his knee. "You're gonna bust before you get through telling a long story. Spiilll it!"

"Alright!" Michelle said, hopping up and down. "I'll tell you! I was browsing in this antique store in Harlem and I ran across this!" She gingerly turned it around to face them.

"A book? So?" Connor stared at it, squinting.

Elizabeth leaned forward. "Looks very old!"

Kayo frowned. "So you found a book?"

"It's not a book, it's a journal that's never been published. It's a handwritten journal by a slave boy named Joshua. A slave narrative about his life!"

They all sat silently.

Elizabeth whispered the words to herself, "A handwritten journal by a slave boy named Joshua."

Kayo's mind was racing now. "An undiscovered slave narrative?"

Connor's eyes got wide. "It's like you discovered the diary of Anne Frank!"

Michelle snapped her fingers and pointed at Connor. "Now, you're cooking with grease, baby." She grinned.

Connor stepped over and hugged her. "Congratulations! That's great! It must be worth a fortune!"

Elizabeth and Kayo were now making their way across the room. "Michelle, you must be dying with excitement! I'm so happy for you," Kayo said, kissing her on the cheek.

"I'm so happy! You guys just don't know! I dropped almost

all of my Ph.D. work to research this—months, hour after hour—all that money going back and forth to Charlottesville."

"So that's what all those trips to Virginia were for," Elizabeth said.

"This journal is one of a kind. There's nothing else anywhere like it. My career is made now! Professor Kingman says I'll be able to go around the country lecturing and that when I finish my Ph.D. I'll be able to write my ticket at any university. He said I'd be a shoe-in for the Huntington fellowship."

"What's that?" Connor asked.

"It's a fellowship for a Ph.D. student that allows them to study at any university in Europe for a year."

"Europe for a whole year," Connor said, his voice dropping.

"That's great, Michelle," Elizabeth said, now excited herself. "I read an article about that fellowship. It's very prestigious."

"And that's not all! I'm going to present it Saturday at the Schomberg at a national convention for black historians. It's just perfect timing and I know it'll be the biggest day of my life!"

"That's great, Michelle." Kayo examined the journal. "Man, this must be worth a lot of money."

"Probably, but it's priceless to me," Michelle said, reaching for a glass of champagne. She stopped, not wanting to get anything on the journal. She opened the top right-hand drawer of the desk and slipped it inside.

Elizabeth squeezed Michelle's hand and smiled. "Your luck has put you on easy street!"

Michelle saw something other than happiness in her friend's eyes. She saw jealousy.

They felt it themselves. It hit each of them separately, then traveled to the others like an electric shock. They each tried to hide the jealousy deep inside their bodies in a corner somewhere, where it wouldn't be able to escape again, where hopefully it would die from neglect and loneliness.

"A toast . . . to Michelle's good fortune," Kayo said, raising his glass.

The glasses clinked and they drank one bottle after the other. They all took turns proposing toasts—to Michelle, to their friendship, to the journal, to the Schomberg, to the world, to the makers of the champagne, to the makers of the cardboard box that the champagne came in, and so on until the last bottle was empty and each of them was sacked out around the apartment.

Kayo was sitting in the corner chair with his feet propped up. He cradled an empty champagne bottle on his stomach with the back of his right hand. She should sell that journal. I know she wants to donate it to the Schomberg. But man, a private collector would pay her a huge amount for that journal—somebody like, like Manchester! Manchester would die to have that journal in his collection. Hey, I-I could present it to him and he'd think I was the greatest thing since wheat bread! If I could just convince her.

Elizabeth lay on the floor face down, her crossed hands a pillow underneath her head. She stared at the rising bubbles floating to the top of the glass. Now Michelle won't have to deal with the pressures and the petty politics! No way—made in the shade. I wish I had found that journal. I'd have an exclusive special on the whole thing—a half-hour news special—I know the ratings would be great! I'd go back to the area of the plantation, have Michelle on talking about her research and the find, and I'd have experts from the field talking about it. Oh, man, it would be the exclusive that Fletcher was talking about. I'd make him eat crow for sure. But she's going to present it at the Schomberg and then it isn't exclusive anymore. I wish I could talk her into holding off, into giving it to me first.

Michelle sat in the corner loveseat with Connor. By now she couldn't hold up her head.

Connor thought about Europe and how far away it was and why Michelle would want to go that distance. That fellowship—maybe she won't get it. He looked down at her. I need you here, Michelle! I can't be without you. But I know, with that journal, you'll win that fellowship and you'll go. Connor hugged her close to him.

Sunshine burst through the window. Michelle flipped over and buried her head in the pillow, dreading the thought of getting up. Her back and arms were heavy, weighing her down in the bed. What a party! It was like old times. Too bad they all had to work today. Michelle stretched, her fingers lightly touching the nightstand next to her. She patted the table itself, then the phone, and then the alarm clock. She jerked her head up and stared at the nightstand, sure she had put the journal there. Whe-ere! Her mind started racing, trying to pinpoint where the journal could be. You put it in the desk drawer, remember? Michelle dropped her head and sighed heavily.

She moved into the living room and looked at the bottles scattered all around. "Y'all could've cleaned up!" she admonished them in their absence. Michelle walked over to the desk. There was a note on top of the empty champagne box: "Congrats again, we'll buy the next one. Love, Us!" She reached into the top right-hand drawer for the journal. It was gone. Michelle jerked the drawer all the way out and it fell. Paper, pencils, and dozens of pennies were scattered on the floor. She turned around and pulled the next drawer out and threw it on the floor. Michelle started pulling out the cushions, looking into the cracks of the furniture. Her breath was quick and hard and she ran around the room like a toddler in a new place. Michelle raced back into the bedroom and began looking under the bed. She found an earring. Michelle grabbed it and tossed it as hard as she could at the wall. It sounded like a ricocheting bullet. She tossed all the clothes out of the drawers, then ran back into the living room.

"It's got to be in here, but where?" she whispered. Michelle looked at the note on the champagne box again: "Love, Us." *One of Them took it!* No, she shook her head in disbelief. My-my best friends? It was the only thing that made sense. Michelle began to cry and the truth seemed as real as the tears washing her palms. They know how important that journal is to me and one of them stole it! Michelle slammed her fists against the cushions. "Friends!" She ground the words out from in between gritting teeth. "They won't get away with it!" Her head was aching with the painful thought. Her teeth were chattering.

"Rrrng!"

That's one of them apologizing, she thought. One of them took it by accident, was reading it and just took it with them.

She jerked up the receiver. "Hello!"

"Michelle? Girl, you sound terrible!"

"Val," Michelle said, letting herself fall forward across the ottoman, head over the side, hair falling away from her neck.

"You okay?"

"Yeah," Michelle lied, almost holding her breath. "Okay."

"I just called because I've got to cancel lunch—got a heavy-duty exam."

Michelle barely understood the words, her mind clogged with thoughts.

"Michelle," Val said, speaking louder, "We'll get together later. I know you said you had something you wanted to tell me."

"No! There is nothing! Alright?" Michelle was trembling uncontrollably now.

"Alright, I'll talk to you later."

She stood in a daze holding the phone until the buzzer snapped her back to life. Suddenly a cold memory splashed over Michelle's body. She saw his face—dark, discolored, and bleeding. Michelle trembled and whispered, "Friar Pete."

Michelle dialed the phone. "Conrad Bellington," she coughed into the phone. "Um, the son, yes."

"Hello?" Connor was sitting hunched over a pile of papers on his desk.

She tried to judge his voice: Was it him?

"Hello?" Connor voice came across cheerily again.

"This is Michelle, Connor," she said, anger starching her words.

"Hangover?"

"Yeah, I've got a hangover and an even bigger problem. My journal is gone!"

"What?"

"My journal is gone and I want it back."

"Michelle—"

"Uh-huh. Just listen, don't talk. I want that journal back by midnight tonight. Without it, I'm ruined. So, hey, if it's not back by midnight tonight, I'm calling the New Haven police and tell them—" she paused, taking a deep breath—" and tell them about the hit-and-run!"

It took a moment for the threat to hit. Connor exploded, "Michelle, that's crazy—calling the police—you'll ruin all of us!" He clenched the receiver tightly. "Listen, did you check the apartment for the journal?"

"Yes, I checked! I don't want to talk about it anymore unless you have my journal. I'm telling all of y'all—by midnight, or I'm calling the cops!"

"Michelle, I don't have it."

"Click!"

Michelle was breathing hard. She clutched her right fist against her chest, then coughed out short, hard puffs as she picked up the receiver and began dialing again. "Elizabeth Nickelson, please!"

"Nickelson," she answered in a faraway voice as she edited some copy with a pencil.

"Elizabeth, where the hell is it!" Michelle squeezed the receiver. "You took my journal and I want it back, understand? I want it back by midnight tonight or else!"

"Michelle, what-what are you talking about—you sound strange!"

"Just shut up and listen because I don't want to talk to you—to any of you, really—so just shut up and listen. My slave journal is gone—stolen! I want it back by midnight tonight or I'm calling the New Haven police and spill the beans about the hit-and-run. Understand what that means?"

Elizabeth dropped the stopwatch she was holding. It crashed onto the floor. "What?!" she shouted.

"Exclusive?" the writer next to her asked.

Elizabeth forced a smile and waved no. "Wait a minute, Michelle."

"Midnight!"

"Michelle!"

"Click!"

Elizabeth sat back in the chair, numb.

Michelle's fingers trembled as she dialed Kayo's number. Sweat was dripping onto the buttons. I'll have it back by midnight. But how can I ever trust them again? "Um, Kevin Watson, please. Well, this is an emergency. Please leave a message to call Michelle at home. It's urgent." She hung up the phone before there was a response.

Instantly, Michelle felt faint. She tried to go to the bathroom but the floor began to pitch. Her knee slammed against the floor. Michelle palmed the floor, her hair tickled the back of her hands. Friends I love . . . who I thought loved me.

"That's great, Michelle!" Connor's voice from the night before. Michelle looked wildly around the room. Connor's voice from the night of the hit and run: "I can't believe this!" Michelle shook her head as she pictured them huddled together by the river.

"I'm so happy for you." Kayo's voice. Michelle clutched her ears and squeezed until she winced from pain. "Both of you grab the ends with one of us!"

Then she heard her own voice: "No! I can't touch him!" Michelle could hardly believe it was happening, that she was reliving it.

Elizabeth's voice: "Close your eyes if you have to!"

Oh Lord! Michelle was crying now and saliva was dripping over her bottom lip. Don't-want-to-hear! The voices began again, but this time they were faster and louder. Michelle squeezed harder; her breath left her and the pain of it all shut her eyes. "Shut up! Shut up!" Michelle shouted, chasing the voices away. Finally there was nothing.

* * *

"Now, what was so urgent that it just could not wait?"

Kayo stared at Manchester with a cocky smile. "I wanted to catch you before your big meeting this afternoon. I know it could run well into the evening."

"C'mon, Watson. I don't have time for pleasantries."

"Well, I wanted you to know that I was feeling especially well this morning because I now have the opportunity to do something for you."

Manchester looked at his watch. "Really, Watson, I have very little time so if you'll excuse me . . ."

"Just another minute. I know that you have a fine collection of art—paintings and rare books. I have something I'm sure you'd be interested in. Take a look at this!"

Manchester took it and began examining it. "Hmmm, this is a very old volume."

"This journal is the story of a slave's life written by a ten-year-old boy named Joshua. It has never been published. I can arrange for you to buy the journal at a fraction of what it would go for at, say, an auction." But Kayo knew he wasn't going to sell it cheap. He wanted Michelle to make a lot of money on the deal and Kayo could tell by looking at Manchester that he wanted the journal badly.

Manchester looked up at Kayo suspiciously. "Well, how do I know it's authentic?"

Kayo's face hardened. "I have proof. I wouldn't bring you anything that was not authentic!"

Manchester put on his poker face. "Well, I might be interested in this. I would like to have someone look at it, just a preliminary examination in addition to your authentication."

Kayo forced a smile: "It dates back to 1832. Now, as I said, I can arrange for you to buy it. I'd like you to have it. But if you're not interested, I can make arrangements with someone else,"

"No-no. I just have to have it examined, for insurance purposes, you know. It'll take only a few weeks."

Kayo was stunned, remembering Michelle was to take the

journal to the Schomberg tomorrow. "Um, no. I can't let it go for that long!"

"So there is a problem then?"

"No, there's no problem." Kayo kept smiling but his stomach lurched.

"Then it's settled. Thank you, Watson. I hope this works out. I appreciate you offering it to me first," Manchester said, standing, holding out his hand.

Kayo took it and squeezed hard. His mind searched for a way to tell Michelle. His mind played it out like a hand of cards. Michelle, I took it to my boss and he loved it. I'll set the deal up, you're going to make a nice piece of change—enough to pay for the rest of your Ph.D. and then some!

"Good man," Manchester said, smiling. He waited until the door closed behind Kayo. Then he reached over to his Rolodex and began looking for a business card of the man he had met three months ago at a fund-raiser for the New York Cultural Society. He was a professor at Columbia who specialized in researching rare works and developing collections. Professor George Kingman.

Kayo felt funny as he walked back to his desk, thinking, once you tell her that you've got it set up, she can't possibly get mad. She doesn't have any money. She can pay for the rest of her Ph.D. and then some. I'm doing her a favor—she should thank me. Kayo sat down at his desk. On top of his messages was one saying "Michelle called, urgent," then "Connor called, very important." Kayo picked up the phone. He didn't think she would be up early after all the liquor she'd had. "Michelle? Kayo. Guess what?"

"Shut up and listen!" the voice was abrupt and filled with rage.

"What's wrong with you?"

"One of you so-called friends stole my slave journal. All of you knew my hopes and dreams were riding on it and *still* one of you just stole it right out from under me like a common thief!"

Her ferocity startled him. "Michelle, calm down—"

"Calm down? One of my best friends just stabbed me in the

back and you say calm down? No-uh-naw-*no*! I want that journal back by midnight tonight. Best friends—all for one and one for all? If I don't get that journal back I'm calling the New Haven police and tell them about that hit-and-run."

Kayo heard the phone click. He slammed the receiver down and grabbed his head with both hands. I didn't think she'd go nuts! I can't even tell her that I took it to help her—she'll think I'm a thief!

His mind sent him mixed signals: Call her back.

No, get the journal back.

You can't go and ask Manchester for it now, you'll blow everything!

Explain it to her.

"RRrrnng!"

Kayo snatched up the phone. "Hello!"

"Kayo, Connor." The voice quivered.

Suddenly it occurred to him that maybe Connor could talk to Michelle. "You're just the person I need—"

"Man, Michelle called about that damn journal!" Connor said, cutting Kayo off. "She thinks one of us stole it. How could she think one of us could be that rotten?"

Kayo slumped down in the chair.

"I mean, she's threatening to ruin all of us! About you-know-what. Over that journal, and I'll bet it's somewhere in the apartment! I mean, one of us wouldn't do something that low."

"Yeah," Kayo said, the lie sapping the strength out of his voice. "She called me too. Listen, can't you talk to her?"

"I tried to talk to her but she just hung up! She says she doesn't want to talk or see anybody unless they have her journal. Man, I'm sitting here shaking. I just called her back a minute ago anyway and didn't get an answer! We're in big trouble." Connor's voice started to rise.

"Well, calm down. Maybe we can talk to her."

"Maybe nothing! She can't tell that. We'll go to jail. It'll be all in the papers—we'd all go through hell. Nope, no, she's not *telling*! Do you hear? Fuck that journal—she's not telling!"

"I hear you. We've all got to reason with her. Let's give her time to calm down first. Have Elizabeth go over tonight around eleven and talk to her. You go at eleven-thirty. And I'll go at midnight. One right after another, we'll just pound some sense into her. I'm sure she'll calm down."

"How can she put us through this! How can we ever trust her again?"

Kayo buried his face in his arm on the desk. "I-I gotta go. Just talk to her and tell Elizabeth to do the same."

"Alright, but Kayo, somebody's got to do something."

Elizabeth walked down the hall in a daze. People were speaking to her and she felt herself responding but she was in a state mute with fear and anger. *How can she even think of doing this to us?* Elizabeth turned quickly down a hall containing three edit rooms. All were dark behind the grey-tinted glass doors. The screens and the desks shone and took up most of the space. Elizabeth slid back the last door and sat down in the padded chair. She knows if she tells we'll all be ruined! Elizabeth started dialing frantically. The flashing buttons were the only light in the dim room. "Daddy? Are you alone?"

"Yes, what's wrong?" Nickelson asked, leaning back at his desk.

"Daddy, Michelle called today all upset because a journal she had was stolen from her apartment."

"Burglary?" he asked.

"Not a burglary or anything. Me, Kayo, and Connor were there and she thinks one of us stole it and, Daddy, she's going nuts like I've never seen before!"

"Honey, calm down . . . she'll find it in a week or so and you'll all laugh about it."

"If it was that simple, would I be calling? Daddy, she called all of us today and threatened to call the police about the *accident* if the journal isn't returned by midnight tonight."

Dead silence.

"Daddy, did you hear what I said?"

"I heard you," Nickelson said. "Talk to her."

"I've been calling all afternoon and I can't get her—no

answer. I'm going to go over tonight and try to reason with her. Kayo and Connor say they're going to do the same. I'm just so worried and mad, Daddy! I think she really might do it. I don't know what's gotten into her lately."

"Listen, calm down. I'm sure if you talk to her, after all three of you talk to her, she'll change her mind."

"Are you sure, Daddy? Cause if she tells . . ."

"She won't tell. Michelle has better sense than that. Just talk to her, okay? Talk to her and I'll call you later, alright?"

The calm with which he was appraising the situation gave Elizabeth some relief. "Okay, Daddy. I'll talk to you later."

"Okay. I love you."

"I love you too. Bye."

Elizabeth leaned back in the chair, rolling it with the heels of her feet. She began thinking of what she wanted to tell Michelle. She would have to tell her to calm down, that they didn't take her journal and she ought to be ashamed of herself. Where does she get off making all of them worry like this? Elizabeth reasoned that her father was right, just lay it out for Michelle and she would come to her senses. Elizabeth thought, hell, if it wasn't for him we'd all have been in trouble the first time—oh! Elizabeth put her hands to her lips, realizing that if Michelle told, she'd have to include the fact that her father helped them cover up the accident. He would be kicked off the force and he'd never get to be mayor. Could he go to jail too? The Michelle I knew at Yale would never threaten us, never hurt us, but this—this is somebody else. I won't let her hurt us!

Chapter 14

MICHELLE used the pillow to wipe the tears from her eyes before burying her face in it. It was well past midnight and the night's events were too much for her to stand. She felt as if her whole world was giving way around her. Her thoughts were rambling and she didn't pick up the phone until the fourth ring. "Hello?"

"Michelle, what's wrong?" Val asked. "You sound terrible!"

"Oh, Val, I've been so upset and so worried."

"What's the matter?"

"I-I can't talk about it on the phone . . . and it's late, almost 12:30 . . . but can you come over? It's important." Tears clogged her throat and she covered the phone with her hand.

"Okay. I-I'm way up at the Med School, at one of the study halls here. I'll be there as soon as I can, okay?"

"Hurry, Val. I need to talk to somebody," Michelle managed to mumble before she hung up the phone. She felt exhausted. Numb. The phone rang again, "Hello?"

There was heavy breathing but no answer.

Michelle shrugged and hung up the phone. She sat there staring at the wall, hurting. She barely heard the knocking at the door minutes later.

"Coming!" Michelle called.

She felt her head touch the hot wood as she leaned forward, wobbling on the balls of her feet, hands on the doorknob. Michelle looked through the peephole and her eyebrows raised. She opened the door but before she could speak, the blow blacked out her eyes and sent pain rippling through her body. Michelle's head smashed against the wall and bright lights and loud bells shattered the darkness. She opened her mouth to scream but was cut off by hands clamping around her throat. She wanted to kick, but the blow had knocked the fight right out of her body.

The hands became tighter and more powerful around her throat like a wrench around a bolt.

Michelle's tongue started to swell and smack against the roof of her mouth. "Please," she strained.

Nails pierced the sides of her neck. Knees pinned down her upper arms. Haunches smashed her breasts and paralyzed her upper body.

Michelle's mind was roaring with pain. Suddenly she pictured herself as a child, mouth sucking, trying to get water from a dripping pump in the churchyard. She worked her mouth in the same way. A trickle of air crept down her throat. She reached up and scratched as hard as she could and the deadly force slapped her face. Michelle heard a rumbling inside her ears like a wall crumbling.

She saw splashing, roaring water. Michelle saw Friar Pete's body dropping over the side . . . falling. She tensed in anticipation. Then Michelle heard her father's voice booming inside her ears, overpowering the sounds of the tidal waters: "You all ought to live in such a way that when it's time to meet the Lord you have few regrets. Ask his forgiveness and he'll wash your sins away!"

God, I'm so sorry.

Convulsions. Then there was nothing. Michelle lay perfectly still on the floor. The hand of death laid her out flat like the cracked spine of a book.

Val climbed the outer steps with a long, steady stride. She heard pebbles grinding against the pavement beneath her loafers just before a siren blared off in the distance. She stopped to catch her breath after walking up the flight of stairs. Val knocked on Michelle's door. No answer. "Michelle! Michelle!" Val called, her mouth against the door. Then it occurred to her that she and Michelle had exchanged keys. Val unzipped the side of her bookbag, reached inside, pulled out a silver ring, and flipped to Michelle's key. Val opened the door and stepped inside.

"Michelle?"

She clicked the light switch.

Val's mouth dropped open and she grabbed her face with both hands, squeezing. *"Michelle!"*

Her face was plain. Almost grey. Eyes closed. Perfectly still. Papers and books were scattered underneath the body. Ugly welts of blue circled her neck.

Val shut her eyes tight. Please Jesus let me move, she prayed. She wanted to scream but couldn't. Tears began flowing down her face. She clamped her lips shut until they throbbed, and began backing away slowly with her hands out, reaching for the walls and still air. Something thick and heavy was crawling up through her chest.

Val's head hit the door, knocking her eyes and mouth open. A thick, bitter fluid gushed forth. It hurt her chest and throat and sprayed against the door and on the hallway floor as she stumbled out. The side of her face slammed against the bars protecting the apartment across the hall and she could feel the sharp edges against her face. Slowly she started sliding to the floor. Suddenly Val stopped her fall by clutching the lock; the silver, shiny, firm, safe-looking lock that was now suspended just above her head.

A hand touched her shoulder and Val turned, mouth open to scream. She recognized Jose, the janitor. "Call the police, *quick*!" Val said, motioning inside. "Michelle's been murdered."

"What? Holy Mother of Jesus."

Val sat there too weak to move, her sobs bouncing off the walls.

The hallway and the apartment were whirring with people. There were police officers, detectives who still had on their coats even though the apartment was cooking from body heat and steam from the corner radiator. The men from the medical examiner's office in their worn polyester suits and too-wide ties dragged themselves around the room, tiredly performing their duties. At a glance, they all possessed a special hardness that separated them from other people the way the look of a diamond distinguishes it from other stones.

In the corner of the room a short, muscular man stood giving orders. Authority rippled through his voice like muscles through his arm. He delivered orders like blows and then sat back and watched their effect. He was a detective named Jim Brady and his surveying eyes, his cockiness, his tenacious attitude, were the envy and fear of every other man in the room. He reasoned that that had allowed him to come to New York after being pushed off the force in New Haven. He had packed everything he owned into one suitcase and hopped the express train, a clip from the *New York Times* stuffed in his top shirt pocket. It said that dozens of officers had been arrested and convicted in a money-laundering scheme and that there was a shortage of officers, a shortage that was putting the city in peril, and Mayor Anton Callo was issuing a call to officers from other cities to come and help build the force back up. With that knowledge, Brady had come to New York to start again. He rose fast.

Brady watched the people moving about the room. The

whole apartment was in total disarray, with pillows and papers tossed everywhere and the chairs strewn about. Brady looked at the mess and the people analyzing it. His partner, Al Sweeney, a tall, stocky detective with gracious eyes, was standing at the victim's desk going through papers he found scattered on the floor. Brady walked over. "Anything interesting?"

"Bunch of bills," Al shrugged. "Student loan papers. Light bill. Telephone bill."

"Oh, that reminds me, don't forget to subpoena the MUDS for the telephone. That'll tell us who she was calling and when. Could be important."

Al sat on the desk. "She called somebody in Georgia a lot."

"Val Jemison says she's from Georgia," Brady said, glancing at his notes, then at the phone bill. "It's high—two hundred bucks."

Al flipped to the front page of the bill. "Yeah, the long-distance plus she had that automatic call-back service."

Brady snapped his fingers. "Hey!" Then he began searching the floor with his eyes.

"What?" Al asked, looking over his shoulder.

Brady found the phone and lifted the receiver. "Star 6-9. I got this service. It calls back the last number that phoned in." He covered the receiver with his hand. "It's ringing."

"Hello?"

"Who is this?" Brady asked.

"Who are you?" the voice asked back. It was male and very young. There was a great deal of noise in the background.

"I'm Detective Brady and this is a murder investigation."

"Yeah, right!" the voice said and hung up.

"Wait!" Brady said, looking at his watch and making note of the exact time. "Al, it's 2:01 A.M. on April twenty-third. The call I just made should show up on the phone records. We'll get the number off there and get the address. That number belongs to one of the last people Michelle Howard talked to. I want to know who it is and what she said to them."

"Check."

Brady stood up and his glance landed on the bookcase.

Dozens of volumes were piled high in front of it. He walked over to it, curious that the books were dumped in a pile at the foot of the case, not tossed clear across the room as a robber would do, but in a pile right there as if a person searching for something had examined them and then dropped them on the floor. Suddenly he noticed a book, a single book, upright in the upper left-hand corner. Brady pulled out his handkerchief and picked it up. He noticed the worn bindings and flipped it open to pages the color of dusk from age. He examined it carefully and reasoned it was a journal that was quite old. Instinct told him it was important. It was the only thing in the apartment in place, so he examined it again to seal it in his mind, then he slipped it into a plastic evidence bag and handed it to one of the other men. As he moved to leave the room, it struck him that there was something strange about the whole thing. This, to him, didn't seem like the case of a robber being startled by someone returning home. His instincts told him that this was different and that's what he had always relied on heavily, instinct.

In the hallway, Val was sitting on the cold top step of the stairs clutching a cup of coffee. Her hands were trembling and her nails were digging into the sides of the white Styrofoam cup. The shiny black liquid mirrored her nose and eyes as she sipped and the motion made her stomach turn, but she dared not close her eyes for fear the vision of Michelle's body would return. The sounds of the people rushing about gave her some security; the busy clicks and hard steps actually made her feel life. At that very moment, shivering in the cold, busy hallway, she realized that life was everything and everything was a part of life. Sounds and sights and smells and thoughts: all that, even the still body she had stumbled upon. Val leaned back and watched as the detective who had questioned her earlier came toward her now. He had asked the same things over and over again. Why was she there that time of night? What did Michelle say when she called? How did she get in? What did she touch? What did she see after she found the body? All those questions and then some. Val gulped down the last of the coffee to steel herself for more.

Brady stopped at her side, watching her trembling hands. "Are you okay?"

"I feel a lot better."

Brady bent down and looked right through her. He didn't suspect her at all. The way she was clutching that lock when the police got there, the look in her eyes, the cracking sound of her voice when questioned—all told him she had nothing to do with the murder but the finding of the body. "Now, you say you talked to the deceased?"

"Michelle, her name is Michelle."

"Right. You talked to her sometime around 12:30 . . ."

"I've told you everything I know!"

Brady brushed the words aside. "She was upset but didn't say why, huh?"

"Right, she just said hurry, she wanted to talk. She was upset. It probably had something to do with her Ph.D. work—her adviser, Professor Kingman, was giving her a hard time."

"Right, a George Kingman," Brady said reading his notes from earlier. "Why was he giving her a hard time?"

"How the hell do I know? Why do professors fuck with their students? Uh-ummm, because they want them to work harder . . . or they get off on it. . . . I don't know!" Val was getting hysterical. "All I know is that I came and she was dead . . . Michelle is *dead.*"

Brady stood up and motioned for an officer standing in the corner. "Brent!" he pointed to Val. "Take her home, okay?"

Val cried softly.

"I may call you later."

Walking out, all Val could think about was how was she going to tell Kayo. The sheer thought of it caused her soul to ache. She would need clear thoughts and strong lips to speak of the inconceivable—because that's what Michelle's death was, inconceivable. When they got outside, she found herself surprised that nothing had changed. The sky was still the sky, the stars were still the stars. Death changed nothing but people. Val knew this because somehow she was now changed, although she wasn't quite sure how—she just felt vastly different. And when the car door slammed and the officer asked, "Where to?" Val was only able to whisper Kayo's address through lips parched with dread.

The security guard at the front desk instantly perked up when the squad car pulled up in front of the building. He lifted up his block-shaped glasses and magnified the worry lines and age spots across his brow. He straightened up, his blue uniform decorated with iron spots, as the officer helped Val into the lobby.

With a wave, Val signaled to the officer that she was safe after seeing Harold the security guard come from behind the desk. Harold took her by the arm and, watching the squad car pull away, he asked, "You okay?"

"Yes," Val said. "I need to see Kevin."

"Do you know what time it is?"

"Yes, I mean, no." She wiped her eyes and leaned on the counter. "I-I know it's late. But it's urgent."

Harold nodded and looked back out the door at where the squad car had been, wondering what was going on. He picked up the house phone and dialed Kayo's code number. "No one's home."

"He's there!" Val shouted, then realizing how harsh she sounded, softened. "Let it ring. He sleeps soundly." Finally there was an answer and she walked toward the elevator. She pressed the button and heard herself saying in her mind, over and over again: "Kayo, Michelle is dead. Murdered."

When she got upstairs Kayo was standing in the doorway of his apartment. Standing there, bare-chested and drowsy, his hair tousled and his pajama bottoms bagging, he looked like a little boy. At that exact moment Val realized she loved Kayo and the thought of hurting him tied her tongue in knots.

"Are you going to stand in the hallway, or are you going to come in and tell me what's so important?"

Val nodded as she walked in. He tried to kiss her, not with

passion but with welcome, and she turned her head. "What gives?"

Val turned around and for the first time since finding Michelle's body she closed her eyes, fear of that vision giving way to the fear of hurt that was sure to spring into Kayo's eyes. "Kayo, I was leaving the Med School . . ."

He rushed to Val and clutched her arms. "Did somebody get after you?"

"No," she sighed.

"What then?"

"Michelle is dead. She was murdered tonight." Val felt his hands leave her. She opened her eyes and Kayo was standing by the window, staring out, his hands palming the window.

His head fell against the glass with a thud.

Val looked at his back, motionless and straight. She was feeling weaker and weaker, her body beginning to give way to exhaustion and grief. "K-K- . . ." just the first syllable of his name was all she could say.

Kayo went to Val and wrapped his arms around her as gently as if he were holding a bubble. Her sobs hurt his chest. It took a half hour for her tears to run dry, and her voice was hoarse when she told Kayo it was she who had found the body. He picked Val up, took her into the bedroom, undressed her, and put her into the bed. Kayo stayed there until a faint snore signaled she was asleep.

He walked back into the living room to the bar and poured himself a straight whiskey. He drank it down fast, hardly tasting or feeling it. The inside of his head ached as if fists were pounding and feet were kicking against the walls of his skull. Kayo stumbled over to the recliner, the glass at his side, whiskey dripping on the tips of his toes. He slumped down in the chair and let the glass slip from his hand and land on the carpet. He looked at the phone and decided he wanted to talk to the police. Kayo picked up the phone, called the operator, told her it was an emergency, and asked for the headquarters in the Columbia campus area. She put the call through for him.

"Yes, I just found out a friend of mine was . . . was

murdered . . . up on the Columbia campus, and I wanted to know what you guys are doing—Michelle Howard is her name. What? Why? Kevin Watson. She lived at 420 West 119th Street. You can tell me, she's one of my best friends. No, I want to know . . . you don't give that information out over the phone?! I'm trying to find out what you lousy-ass police are doing about her murder! Hello? *Hello!*"

Kayo looked at the receiver and then slammed it down. He chewed on his knuckles until they hurt. Connor had said he would be working late, staying the night at the office, so he dialed his number first.

"Hello?" Connor said in a tired voice.

"Man, it's me."

"What's up?"

"I've got something important I have to tell you and I can't do it over the phone. You need to get over here right now."

"Can't it wait? Jesus, I'm upset and tired," Connor groaned.

"No, it can't. Please, get here." Kayo hung up the phone, then dialed Elizabeth's home phone number.

"Hello?" she said in a quivering voice.

"It's me. You've got to get over here. I've got something urgent to tell you."

"I'm in bed."

"I can't talk about it over the phone. Please, just come. Connor's on his way now. 'Bye."

When they arrived, Kayo was tongue-tied. He had them sit down and took a long moment to choose his words. "I have some terrible news, and I don't know how to tell you guys."

Their breathing was tense.

"Michelle is dead. She was murdered tonight."

"What! No-no!" Connor said the words choppy with disbelief.

"My God!" Elizabeth said.

"Val called Michelle and she asked her to come over. When Val got there, Michelle was dead."

Kayo heard what seemed like a moan and a sigh and a cry and a gasp, all in one, from Connor, then: "What happened?"

"I don't know. I called the police and they said they couldn't give out any information over the phone, the lousy motherfuckers."

"She was mad as hell, but fine, when I saw her last night," Elizabeth whispered.

"I was there after you," Connor added. "And she was still mad about the journal but okay!"

"I saw her last, and she said she was going to bed. I don't know what happened. I just don't know!" Kayo said.

Elizabeth started to cry.

"Jesus, Michelle. Why her?" Connor moaned.

Kayo said nothing. He just paced.

"I can't believe it!" Connor wrung his hands. "What did the police say?"

"I told you they wouldn't say anything over the phone," Kayo said, his voice wobbly as if he was speaking under water.

"I'm going over there and find out what's going on," Connor said, standing up.

"I'll go with you," Kayo decided. "Maybe the two of us—"

"The three of us," Elizabeth managed to interject.

"Okay, maybe we can get some answers. Val is still in the bedroom there, asleep. She was really shaken up. Let me check on her, and we'll go."

Flashing lights, from a distance, gave the impression of lightning streaking across the dark sky. Connor, Kayo, and Elizabeth got out of the cab at the corner. There was no room to turn around on the street because of all the police cars. They walked up the block toward Michelle's apartment building.

Connor could hear Kayo's words: "Michelle is dead." And he looked up to the sky as if to ask the stars how he would live without her. A crushing weight pressed against the top of his head, the small of his back, the bend of his knees, the lids of his eyes, and all at once Connor was struck blind. He stopped to rub his eyes, to catch his breath. He stumbled backward and fell against the damp, keen edges of a wrought-iron fence. "God!"

Kayo clutched his arms to steady him. Elizabeth rested her head on Connor's shoulder. They stayed this way for a long moment. Then they walked the rest of the way together in silence.

When they reached the front of the apartment, Elizabeth stopped. Her eyes were puffy from crying. She hung back. "I feel so bad!"

Kayo and Connor were speechless.

Elizabeth came forward and just as she did, a bright light put the three of them in a brazen yellow circle. "What's going on?" the deep voice accused with authority.

All three of them covered their eyes with their hands. Kayo spoke first. "Nothing's going on!"

Elizabeth spoke up next, her eyes adjusting to where she could see the badge behind the tunnel of light. "We're here because our friend was murdered and we want to know what happened."

Brady cut the light off with a click and stepped forward. "How do *you* know she's dead?"

"My girlfriend Val told me and I told them—who are you?" Kayo said.

"I'm Detective Jim Brady. I'm handling the case."

"What happened?" Connor shouted and his voice began dropping as he went on. "We came down here to find out what in God's name happened."

"I'm sorry. I can't tell you anything about the murder investigation."

"We were all best friends! We-we went to Yale together. We have a right to know!" Kayo said.

"You don't have a right to shit!" Brady said, feeling the need to get the situation in line. "I can't jeopardize the investigation by giving out any information to you or anyone else."

Kayo stepped forward, his grief turning to anger. He pointed his finger in Brady's face.

Connor reached to stop him.

"Man, listen—"

Brady grabbed Kayo by the collar and backpedaled him against a Chevy Nova parked at the curb.

"Hey!" Connor yelled.

"Get off me!" Kayo yelled as his back banged against the car's hood.

"Look, you're gonna respect me and the law!"

"Get off!"

Elizabeth shouted, "Stop it! Stop it!"

Kayo and Brady locked eyes.

Connor leaned over and spoke softly to Brady. "He's upset. We were close." Connor touched his arm. "Let him up."

Kayo yelled his fear and disdain with the deepest part of his eyes.

Brady made him feel the same, leaning his hips in the middle of Kayo's body.

"Stop it!" Elizabeth shouted again. "Michelle is dead and you all are acting crazy."

Her words snapped Brady back to reality. "I'm letting you up. Behave." Brady eased his body back and away first and then he released Kayo's collar.

Kayo sprang up, spun, and then walked several feet away. He stopped and leaned on the fence, shoulders slumped, head bowed.

Elizabeth was pacing back and forth. "This is a nightmare! I just saw her a few hours ago and now she's dead."

Brady looked at her, then pulled a pad out of his back pocket. "What's your name?"

"Elizabeth Nickelson—I can't believe it."

"When did you see her?"

Elizabeth was standing straight as an arrow, holding herself in. "Um, a few hours ago . . . around eleven o'clock. I saw her, talked to her, she was mad but okay."

Brady was writing with broad, quick strokes. "What was she angry about?"

"Oh, she was upset about-about . . . um, her schoolwork."

"You were the last one to see her alive then," Brady stated.

"No," Connor said, leaning against the car and pinching his tired eyes. "I went over after Elizabeth. It had to be around eleven-thirty."

"You are?"

"Conrad Bellington the Third."

"Did Hothead go too?" Brady said, nodding toward Kayo's back.

"His name is Kevin Watson. He said he went over after I did. We'd like to know anything we can. I was very close to her."

"Look!" Elizabeth gasped.

Two police officers were making their way out of the front door carrying a stretcher. Elizabeth and Connor stared in silence as the body, covered in a white sheet bound with two black straps, was being brought out.

Kayo turned around, stumbled back, then just covered his eyes with trembling palms.

The whiteness filled Elizabeth's eyes and she felt as if the whole night had turned into one vast, pallid empty place.

Connor buried his eyes in Elizabeth's back, squeezing her shoulders, unable to say anything.

Brady watched them clutch each other as the officers brought the body past. He heard Elizabeth whisper, "If only . . ."

"Sssh! Sssh! It's okay!" Connor quickly hushed her by gently holding her chin from behind.

Then the two of them turned away from Michelle's body and their gaze fastened on Kayo.

Brady followed their line of vision to Kayo, who was looking at Elizabeth and Connor and shaking his head in disbelief. Then, exhausted by their exchange, Kayo bent over a car on the street, his fists down, spasms ripping through his arms that were now supporting his body against the hood.

It was the way they grieved that bothered Brady. There was something deeper here—Brady knew it, and instinct told him whatever it was would be important to his investigation.

The doors of the paddy wagon slamming shut sounded like a gunshot and Brady was sure Elizabeth was going to faint. He walked over and helped Connor rest her against the car hood. Brady gave a rushed condolence and then began asking them for their addresses and phone numbers so he could question them later.

Kayo watched the round, red brake lights of the paddy wagon as the engine cranked up loud and fierce, shattering the night. He stepped into the street and watched as the wagon began backing down his way, the red lights piercing his chest where he stood. The wagon moved closer and the street slant grew deeper and the scarlet circles loomed larger, swallowing his entire body. Kayo bent his head in sorrow, then was startled by a hand dropping on his shoulder. He jerked away from Brady. "What?"

"Look, I know that you're upset. I'm going to let you go home now but I'll need to talk to you routinely later. Your friends gave me your address and phone number. Be available."

Kayo grunted.

Brady noticed two fresh scratches on the side of his face. "It's a shame, losing a friend."

Kayo said nothing.

"I always say friends don't get to spend enough time with each other. I haven't seen my best friend in weeks. Something like this'll make me go back to the office and give him a call. Huh, when was the last time you saw Michelle?"

Kayo took a deep breath and said easily, "Day before yesterday, evening. She had a little get-together at her apartment, the four of us were there. It was happy, nice, like old times at Yale almost."

Brady watched Kayo play with the zipper of his jacket. "Well, like I say, you've got to spend more time with your friends. You never know. Well, I'll give you a call later today sometime—just routine."

Kayo nodded, wishing he would go away.

Brady walked across the street to his car and got in. He

glanced back at the three outside. Brady decided he wanted to solve this case fast. The press would have a field day with it—a pretty grad student murdered on the Columbia campus. Every alum with any power would be ringing the phones off the hook. He pictured the body and remembered that he had thought she looked familiar—they had gone to Yale together. That's where he had seen her probably, somewhere in New Haven. Brady cranked the engine, wanting to get back to the station quickly. He was giving this case the green light. He wanted every lab and forensic worker on the evidence—he wanted results fast.

Kayo waited until he pulled away, then he walked back toward Connor and Elizabeth. He stopped in front of them and spoke softly. "Listen, Connor, you'd better take Elizabeth home to her apartment and stay with her. I'll meet you guys there later—I want to go and take Val home. You know, make sure she's alright."

Connor nodded okay.

And as Kayo turned to walk away, Elizabeth reached out and touched his face. Kayo let her hand fall away as he headed to the corner.

"Professor Kingman?"

A short, round man was putting books on a shelf behind a desk. His arms were massive barrels. "Yes?"

Brady pulled the pad out of his back pocket. "I'm Detective Brady. I'd like to ask you some questions about one of your students, Michelle Howard."

"She was murdered. I know," Professor Kingman said, hanging his head.

"You do?"

"I heard the story on the radio this morning." He held out his palm toward the empty chair in front of his desk.

"Thanks." Brady sat down. "When did you last see her?"

"About two days ago. She was excited about having some of her undergrad friends over to celebrate her great find."

"What find?"

"She was browsing in an antique shop and found this

journal. After she researched it, it turned out to be an authentic slave narrative. We were going to present it this afternoon at a convention at the Schomberg Library. It was a rare and beautiful volume . . . her career was to be made on that discovery. It could have meant something wonderful for her."

"And this journal was pretty valuable, huh?"

"Yes, if you sold it to a private collector it would bring a great price. But more than that, it was art, history, culture—not to be bought or *sold*!" Kingman said, pacing.

Brady leaned forward in his chair.

"And that's what I was trying to tell her. I'd been calling her all day yesterday right after I got that call asking about the journal."

"What call?"

"I'm trying to tell you. I got a call from a man named Paul Manchester; he's an executive at one of these investment firms. I don't know him really, just met him a couple of times at receptions. Anyway, we had exchanged cards. So, he called and said he wanted to have a journal authenticated. 'Of course,' I said. But the journal he described was Michelle's! I was so angry. Manchester said a young man at his company had approached him about buying the journal for his private collection. Well, I told him that was surely a mistake since it was to be presented to the Schomberg. And he said maybe it was and he'd get back to me on it. I tried calling Michelle all day—either the line was busy or there was no answer. Now the poor girl is gone and I wonder where the journal is!"

Brady thought about the journal he had just seen in the apartment. "Do you have this Manchester's number?"

"Yes, hang on." Professor Kingman opened a drawer and flipped through papers. "Aha, here's his card."

"Good," Brady said, taking it. "Where were you last night around twelve-thirty to, oh, say one o'clock?"

He sputtered, "Surely you don't think . . ."

"I've got to ask, don't I?"

Professor Kingman's eyes narrowed. "I was at a reception for historians who are in town for the convention. My wife and

I were there from ten to two this morning. There were at least two hundred people there!"

"Okay, okay. Can I use your phone?" Brady picked it up and started dialing.

Kingman made a mock gesture. "Help yourself. I have an appointment. Surely, an ace detective like yourself can lock up." He was by the door now, grabbing his coat.

"Yeah, can I speak to Paul Manchester? This is detective Jim Brady with the NYPD. Yes, it's important. Catch him and tell him to stay put. I need to talk to him about a murder."

"What's this all about?" Manchester asked, standing behind his massive desk. He hands were poised tensely in front of him.

Brady entered the office and a stunning beam of sunshine striped his chest as he sat down on the corner of the desk. "I'm Detective Jim Brady. I'm working on a murder case. The victim was Michelle Howard."

"I don't know any Michelle Howard," Manchester sighed, relieved.

"Well, you had something that belonged to her. A journal." Brady smiled.

"I don't have it."

"I know you don't still have it. We've got it. All I want to know is, who offered to sell it to you?"

"Kevin Watson."

Brady stood up.

"He's one of our analysts here. He brought it to me offering to sell it. I, of course, told him it had to be checked out and he said I could have it for as long as I needed."

"That's when you called the Professor?"

"Exactly. Later, Kevin comes to me and demands the journal back, saying it's not for sale. I gave it to him and that was that."

Brady wrote down the last bit of information. "Huh, what kind of guy is this Watson."

"Did he murder someone?"

"I'm asking the questions. What kind of guy is he?"

Manchester hesitated. "He's a good worker. But you know, I've always thought there was something, well, streetwise about him."

Brady laughed. "Thank you for your time. I will be contacting you later."

Manchester followed Brady to the door. "Please let me know about this Watson thing. Anyone mixed up in something like this is bad news."

Brady got to the door and turned. "Let me worry about him, okay?"

Manchester fiddled with the bottom button of his suit jacket. "Of course."

Brady stopped at the secretary's desk just outside Manchester's office. He picked up the phone and flipped the pages back until he came to the phone number for Kevin Watson. Brady dialed the number with the end of the pen. It rang and rang. No answer. "Shit! I told him to hang around." Brady slammed his thumb down and dialed the number for Elizabeth Nickelson. It rang three times before she picked up.

"Hello?"

"Elizabeth Nickelson?"

"Yes, this is she."

"Detective Brady. I'd like to talk to you this morning if I can. I had wanted to talk to Kevin Watson, but he's not home."

"He's here with Connor and me," Elizabeth said.

Brady gripped the phone now with both hands. "Good. would all of you stay there? I'll be over in, say, an hour or so. I have to make a stop back at the station. It's important."

"Yes, yes, we'll be here. Have you found out anything?"

"I'll talk to all of you when I get there."

Elizabeth hung up the phone in the bedroom and walked back into her living room. She could hear Connor and Kayo still talking, their voices rising and falling. For the last few hours they had been reminiscing about the good times. Kayo was sitting on the loveseat and Connor was sitting in a chair, leaning back against the wall nearest the kitchen. Elizabeth came and sat back down in the middle of the floor.

"Hey, remember that time we were studying in the library in Trumbull and we convinced Michelle to take a break?"

"Michelle never liked to take study breaks," Connor said, remembering.

"'Cause she knew you guys—you'd break all night."

"Yep," Kayo said, nodding. "And this night, remember, that's what we did. We went to that party at the Afro-Am House and by the time we all got back to Old Campus . . ."

". . . they had locked the gates," Connor said, leaning forward and picking up the story. "And you were too lazy to walk around!"

"You were drunk," Elizabeth said, pointing at Connor. "And when we climbed the side gate everybody was over but Michelle."

Kayo snapped his fingers twice. "And her jacket got caught in the spikes."

"She was just hanging there, suspended in midair like a puppet or something. She was yelling her head off, 'Get me down! Get me down!'" Connor started to laugh.

Elizabeth and Kayo joined in. Elizabeth managed to say, "And you guys wouldn't help her and you wouldn't let me help her. Connor held my arms so I couldn't."

"You did it," Kayo said, pointing at Connor.

"I couldn't help it. I just couldn't stand to see her get down right away, it was too funny."

Elizabeth let herself fall over with laughter. "She said she wasn't going to speak to any of us for a week and she didn't either!" Elizabeth stopped laughing and thought a moment. "Do you think she would have told the police about the accident like she threatened?"

"Damn," Connor said, jumping out of the chair so fast it hit the floor. "You had to bring that up."

"It's tied to her memory and we can't forget it."

"Let him try." Kayo looked down at the floor from the loveseat. "Can't we try?"

"I mean, we can't just forget her—"

"We're not forgetting her," Connor said angrily to Elizabeth. "I don't want to talk about it, okay?"

"But I can't help but think that if we hadn't done what we did . . ."

"I was feeling better," Connor said, pacing the floor talking to himself. "I was"—he turned—"and you had to spoil it."

Elizabeth sat up. "Can't you see that everything was so good at first? We were good together and it started going wrong all of a sudden, right after that accident."

Kayo didn't want to talk about it either. "What's done is done, Elizabeth. And we said we weren't going to talk about it anymore—remember? We promised."

"I didn't break the promise, Michelle did! She's the one who called us up threatening to tell because she thought one of us took that stupid journal."

"Like we would steal from each other," Connor said, becoming angry at Michelle.

"How could she suspect one of us like that?"

"Just drop it!" Kayo demanded, hitting the side of his leg with a clenched fist.

"See, Elizabeth," Connor said, pointing at Kayo, "you got us mad at Michelle!"

The buzzer sounded impatiently.

Elizabeth got up slowly. "That's Detective Brady. He called to say he was coming over with some news."

Kayo sat back down on the loveseat, his head down. Connor continued to pace. Elizabeth came back into the living room followed by Brady. "Can I take your coat?" she asked.

"No, I'm okay," Brady said looking around the apartment. He sensed the tension in the air. He walked over to the loveseat where Kayo was sitting and dropped the journal on the cocktail table. "Why'd you steal the journal, Kevin?"

Connor looked surprised. "You took it?!"

"I didn't steal it!" Kayo said, shaking his head. "It wasn't stealing."

Elizabeth dropped to her knees and touched the journal, turning it toward him. "You stole it!"

"It wasn't stealing!" Kayo said, leaning forward, appealing to Connor and Elizabeth.

Brady jumped in. "He took it and tried to sell it to one of his rich bosses for a lot of dough—but that's not stealing, is it Kevin?"

"Fuck you!" Kayo was trembling. He looked at Elizabeth and Connor, who were staring at him. "He's trying to make it sound worse than it is!"

"Did you take it?" Elizabeth shouted.

"I wasn't trying to hurt Michelle."

"Look at him, *son of a bitch*!" Connor said, turning away and clutching his head with his hands.

"I didn't take it for me. I took it to sell to Manchester so Michelle would have some money, some security! It wasn't for me."

"You took it out of the goodness of your heart," Brady said sarcastically, egging the tension higher.

"To help Michelle," Kayo said, coming from behind the cocktail table. "You guys know me!"

"Do you know what you put us through! Huh?!" Elizabeth said, clutching the journal.

"He doesn't care," Connor said, shaking his head bitterly.

"The nightmares!" Elizabeth whispered.

Brady stood quietly in the corner, watching and listening.

"If I was just in it for me, would I have given her the journal back? I took it back right at midnight. I put it on the shelf myself."

"And then you killed her," Brady said.

Connor and Elizabeth both gasped.

Kayo looked at Brady. "Are you losing your mind! I would never hurt her. Never!"

"Yeah? Well, I asked you before when was the last time you saw her and *you lied* and said day before yesterday at an evening party she had for you guys. Your buddies here had already told me you went there around midnight. And you just admitted you were there! Jose, the janitor, who lives across the street? Says he saw you running from the apartment building sometime after midnight! That's just around the time she was killed. See, I figure you brought the journal back and she told you what a lying, cheating dog you were and she was going to tell your buddies here—and that's when the fight started. You killed her."

"That's a lie!" Kayo snorted. He looked at Connor and Elizabeth, who were looking at him as if they had never seen him before. "Don't believe him. He's lying!"

They said nothing.

Brady looked at them and continued, "He choked her to death."

"Shut up!"

"How'd you get those scratches on your neck?" Brady asked. "Bet that blood under her nails is yours."

Connor and Elizabeth stared at the small scratches on his neck.

Kayo shook his head, feeling lost and helpless. "No!"

Connor stepped back away from him.

Brady pulled out his handcuffs. "You're under arrest for suspicion of murder. You have the right to remain silent. Do you understand that anything you say . . ."

"This is not happening to me."

". . . can and may be used in a court of law . . ."

Kayo felt his hands being cuffed and he closed his eyes, pleading. "Connor, get me a lawyer. You guys gotta get me a lawyer!"

Brady jerked his arm and pulled him toward the door.

"Kayo," Elizabeth shouted in a confused voice.

"It wasn't me," Kayo shouted over his shoulder. "Connor!"

Connor just stood in the middle of the room. He felt hurt and angry and betrayed and vengeful all at once. The rush of emotions froze his body.

Elizabeth was afraid . . . afraid because she didn't know what to do. "What are we going to do?"

"I don't know, Elizabeth," Connor said, "I just don't know."

Chapter 15

THE inside of the interrogation room was crowded and bland. There was one short wooden table in the center of the room and four chairs surrounding it. Someone had kicked in part of the wall and the paint, the color of Pepto-Bismol, was cracked and spreading. A big, square window made of two-way glass was on the left side of the room. There were cobwebs spreading in the bottom corners of the floors. Kayo felt isolated despite the fact that Brady was sitting in the chair right across from him and another detective was standing beside him.

"Look, Kevin, you might as well confess 'cause I know I got you!"

Kayo looked at Brady. "Man, I'm not talking until my lawyer gets here."

"See, you lied about being there and Jose saw you running from the apartment building after twelve. That Jose is a good one too," Brady said, laughing and rubbing the palms of his hands together.

Kayo heard them grate and the sound pricked his nerves. Brady turned and looked at Al, who was assaulting a piece of Black Jack gum. "Al, Jose just got his citizenship and is dying to testify to prove he's a good American!"

Kayo looked at Al's thick arms, the mustache hanging over his top lip like a scowl, and then turned away.

Al ran his hands through his red hair. "Shit, that Mexican is gonna put this nigger away!"

Brady turned back to Kayo. "And this case is a big one too. The press is already going crazy. It's been on the radio and that means the TV and print dogs ain't far behind! This is the kind of story they love, too. Huh, after this gets in the paper—killing that poor, bright girl—any jury will throw your black ass under the jail."

Kayo just gazed straight ahead, concentrating on a spot he picked out on the wall, the one clean spot in the whole wall that wasn't cracked or peeling or smudged with dirt.

"And a pretty boy like you in jail," Al kicked in, "oh, man, they'll be gang-raping your ass every night. So, hey, make it easy on yourself."

"I've been trying to tell him, Al. But he doesn't want to talk!" Brady scooted closer to Kayo.

Kayo scooted his chair back.

"Whoa, you're setting race relations back forty years. Relax. Now, I'm going to tell you what happened and I want you to nod."

"Aww, Brady, just kick the shit out of him."

Kayo's eyes widened.

"We don't need to waste the energy. We got him. See, Kevin here is going to nod if this is how it happened—'cause I know how it went down."

The inside of Kayo's throat was boiling.

"Now, you took that journal and tried to sell it. Michelle got upset and figured one of her best friends took it. She called all of you and told you to bring it back or else—I haven't figured out what 'or else' is yet, but that's not important now. You brought it back, and you were pissed that you couldn't get your deal going. She was pissed because you ripped her off! She slapped you, scratched you, and you thought you'd slap her around some—teach her a lesson maybe—and it got out of hand and you accidentally killed her."

Kayo shook his head no.

Brady grabbed his head with both hands.

"Now, that doesn't sound like first-degree murder to me—how about you, Al?"

"Naw, that's not first-degree murder!"

"Your record is clean up until now," Brady observed. "So, give us a statement and save the city some money and we'll lower the charges."

"I didn't kill her! How many times do I have to tell you?" Kayo shouted, unable to hold the fear, anger, and anxiety inside any longer. "I didn't."

Brady sat back surprised.

"He can talk!" Al said, stepping over by Brady's shoulder, then he snatched Kayo's collar. "But he lies!"

Kayo shook the hand from his shoulder and pinned his own hands in between his knees. "That's not how it happened. I was there . . ."

"Tell me something we don't know!" Brady shouted.

"Let me get this motherfucker!" Al said, reaching for Kayo again.

"Lay off!"

"I was there," Kayo said looking long and hard into Brady's eyes. "I returned the journal. Michelle was alive when I left. I could never kill her. I would rather die myself. I didn't do it."

Brady examined Kayo for a long moment, then walked out and let Al continue the questioning.

The hallway outside the interrogation room was dark and narrow. Scuff marks lined the floor and the walls. Brady opened a second door to an adjacent room. The chief of police, Dan Vitto, and the district attorney, Hal Price, were watching through the two-way mirror. Brady took a deep breath. "I think he's telling the truth."

"Sssh!" Vitto, said holding up his hand. His suit, of common cut, was wrinkled. His cologne reeked. "Listen."

Brady heard Kayo's muffled voice over the speaker. "I told you, I cut myself shaving!"

"What, you don't know how to shave?" Al asked stupidly.

"I was trying this new shaver—for black men. Our skin is more sensitive and sometimes we get these bumps if the hair isn't shaved off properly. So I tried his new shaver and I cut myself!"

"Hear that?" Vitto said, laughing. The deep laughter seemed foreign coming from his thin, wiry body. "That's the worst lie I ever heard. Let's nail this prick."

Price was a stout, rubbery-looking man with beady eyes and bushy eyebrows. He stroked his thinning grey hair and nodded. "I think we got enough to charge him."

Brady spoke up. "Maybe we should wait."

The two men turned and stared at him.

"You were all gung ho this morning," Vitto said. "Said he lied about being there. Said you had a witness to place him there. Said you had a motive and that the forensic lab was working overtime on evidence that would link him there."

"What's that?" Price asked.

"Well, the victim had some blood under her nails and the lab is doing an analysis on it. There were also some strands from the killer's clothes under her nails as well."

"Good. That's more than enough to put him away!" Price said, sitting down in one of the small, wooden chairs.

"Even with the lab working overtime with top priority, it'll take them at least a week to get back the results!"

"So what? We've got enough to charge him now and Mayor Callo called me on this one—said he wanted it out of the way fast!" Vitto said. "Book this guy and get it over with!"

"But I've got a feeling here."

"Fuck a feeling!" Vitto said. "The press is on this and Mayor Callo is on my ass to get it closed, understand? Now, Price, can we charge this guy or not!"

"Got plenty by me, DA's office is ready!"

"Charge him!" Vitto said, walking toward the door. "First-degree murder."

"Do you think he killed her?" Elizabeth shouted. She and Connor were standing toe to toe, their voices high and vexing.

"I'm saying I don't know. I mean he lied about the journal." Connor turned away. "He lied to Brady about being there last night!"

"But kill Michelle—why? He said he was giving her back the journal."

"Maybe he tried to convince her that she should sell it and they got into a fight and he killed her."

"Or maybe she just decided that she was going to tell about the accident anyway! And he wanted to stop her."

Connor started to pace.

"Stop pacing! You're driving me crazy."

"Fuck you," Connor barked over his shoulder, swinging around, taking another step.

"He's waiting down there, thinking you're getting him a lawyer."

"I know! I was here, remember?"

"Connor," Elizabeth said, "you've got to get him a lawyer. Kayo's down there and they're grilling him on Michelle's murder and everything that happened up until then . . . about the journal, everything. He might tell about the accident."

"He wouldn't tell that!"

"We didn't think he'd take the journal either." Elizabeth's voice got sad all of a sudden. "I'm not sure of anything anymore."

As Kayo lay on the small cot, he could feel the cold metal sides against his arms, neck, and ankles. He tried not to think about how long he'd already been locked up. Maybe Connor is having problems finding a lawyer? He trembled in the piss-laden air and fixed his eyes on the topless toilet. He wished the water-stained, smelly thing would disappear. Kayo closed his eyes, took shallow breaths, and affirmed in his mind, It'll be okay. It'll be okay. He put the flat, stale pillow over his face.

"Hey, you trying to smother yourself?"

Kayo dropped the pillow and turned toward the guard standing at the cell door. His stomach was round as a bowl and hung over the belt of his pants. His face was clean, pale. His jaws were fleshy and draped off the sides of his face. His teeth were the color of vanilla wafers. A metal badge, as thin as a tie clip, pinned to his shirt said "McKinney."

"C'mon!"

Relief washed over Kayo. "My lawyer is here."

"Wrong, kid." McKinney laughed, scratching the bald spot in the top of his head. "You're going for a walk!"

"A walk?"

McKinney held out the handcuffs. "Give me your wrists."

"No! I'm not a criminal!"

"Hey, no trouble." McKinney touched the gun at his side.

Kayo held out his wrists timidly, and gritted his teeth. As the cuffs clinked, his mind begged: Where is Connor?

"Let's go, asshole!"

They walked out of the cell and started down a short corridor that led to a door.

"You still haven't said where we're going!"

A sinister laugh belched from McKinney's body.

The door opened.

There was a bright beam of light. Kayo tried to move his hands to cover his eyes.

A crowd of about twenty-five reporters and camera crews jammed the lobby.

"Why'd you kill her?"

"Do you have a statement?"

Kayo closed his eyes and shuddered as he was paraded back and forth.

McKinney sneered. "Smile, and let the folks see you!"

Kayo was sweating and trembling now. All he could hear was the sound of his cuffs rattling and his feet scraping against the floor.

Parading back and forth, back and forth.

Suddenly, McKinney stopped in the middle of the hall and jerked Kayo's head up. He felt like a slave on an auction block.

"Do you have anything to say?"

Kayo could hear himself walking again and each step sounded like thunder. He felt hot and itchy and miserable. His head throbbed from tension.

"Got enough?" McKinney asked. "I gotta get this guy back in the cell."

"Yeah, we got enough!" several voices responded.

Val stretched across her bed in a white terry robe, resting on a pink rabbit and two stuffed teddy bears. Kayo always said the only childish thing about Val was the stuffed assortment that crowded her bed. After Kayo left, she had tried to go back to sleep but couldn't, fear of the nightmares still nagging at her mind. So instead, Val had turned on the television, watching but not really watching. After a long while, she thought about a game that she hadn't played since she was a little girl. She would lie as still as she could and think of all the things that made her happy. Then it was cotton candy and rides on the roller coaster. The last time she had played the game, Val was thirteen and it didn't work. Her emotions were adult emotions. But today, she would try anything, including childish games.

Val saw herself making a quilt with her grandmother and great-grandmother on the front porch of their house in Baltimore. Their sinewy fingers guiding her hands along the pattern with firm patience. She could smell green beans and catfish cooking and their raspy laughter rang in her ears. That feeling gave way to the light touches of fingertips on her breasts and on her hips. She thought of Kayo and the touches became stronger and more soothing. Val felt herself relax and she even thought for a moment that she heard someone say his name. She heard it again. The news was on. Val sat up. They flashed a picture of Kayo handcuffed in a hallway somewhere being paraded back and forth for the media.

". . . Kevin Watson was arrested and charged with the

murder of Michelle Howard, a graduate student at Columbia University. The two were allegedly friends and police say an argument led to the murder of passion. Watson is expected to be taken to bond court tomorrow morning. We'll have the latest on the case and all the other news at eleven."

Val slammed her fist against the Off button and the picture faded quickly into a white dot in the middle of the black screen. She grabbed the phone and dialed the number for the Public Defender's Office. "Extension 314, please."

Val slipped on a pair of jeans. "Hello, Adele? Val."

"Hi," the voice said cheerily. "We were just talking about you. I was just telling everybody that I wasn't the only Columbia grad with a conscience."

"There was an arrest today for the murder of Michelle Howard."

"You know, I was going to ask you if you knew her."

"We were good friends," Val said, then she decided to skip the story about finding the body.

"Well, they bagged some guy on it already. Some investment-banking guy."

"That's Kayo—the guy I've been telling you about!"

"Oh no!"

"Adele, he couldn't have done it. I know him. They were best friends. You've got to help him! Please get down there and see who is defending him."

"Sure, Val. I'll do what I can."

"I knew that I could count on you. The television guy said he was going to bond court tomorrow?"

"Yeah, the cases are backed up. And his bail will probably be high-high, about half a million dollars! Ten percent—that's fifty grand!"

"He hasn't got that kind of money," Val said, sitting on the edge of the bed stunned.

"Then he'll just have to stay in jail and I wouldn't advise that to anyone."

"Go ahead and see what's happening. I'm going to see about the bail."

"You've got that kind of money?" Adele asked, surprised.

"You know my grandfather left me some money when he died."

"Yeah, but I didn't think it was that much."

"Well, that's about all of it."

"You trust him like that? If he skips—"

"He won't . . ."

"But if he does . . ."

"*He won't.* Adele, I trust him. He needs me now."

"Alright. I hope you know what you're doing."

Kayo was pushed through the door.

Connor was surprised at how haggard he looked, his eyes puffy and the skin around them ashy. Kayo's clothes were dirty and clung to his body with static.

Kayo looked at Connor, jerked the chair out, and sat down. "Man, how could you!"

"Look, don't take it out on me, okay? I didn't put you in here."

"And you're not helping me get out either!"

"I'm sorry you had to spend the night in jail but I got you a great lawyer!"

"I already got one!"

Connor leaned over the table. "Not like this one. The guy I got is one of the best in the country!"

"Is that why you took your sweet-ass time about finding him? I should trust him, like I trusted you so he can leave me hanging too?" Kayo put his hand out like a stop sign. "No excuses. Val got me a friend of hers at the Public Defender's Office—never lost a case. She got bond set and Val is bailing me out now."

"My lawyer is better. I'm trying to help you."

"You know the movie, *The Defiant Ones*, where the black con and the white con are chained together trying to escape north . . ."

"This is not movie quiz time, okay?"

"The black guy falls into the water and the white guy pulls

him out. The brother says, 'Thanks for pulling me out.' And the white guy says, 'Man, I wasn't pulling you out, I was keeping you from pulling me in.'"

"Fuck you. I don't have that coming!" Connor stood up and slammed his fist against the table. "Don't start that bullshit now. I'm trying to help you."

"Don't get righteous with me. I needed you and you took your time about finding me some help. And where is Elizabeth?"

"She's waiting back at her apartment." Connor saw the look in Kayo's eyes and lied. "She's in such a bad way about Michelle's death, I told her I would come alone."

"That's real gallant of you."

"Let's just get out of here," Connor said, looking around the dingy room, "and we can talk this out later."

"It isn't pretty, is it? I spent the night here! Hell, you left me in here and they walked me in front of the television cameras. My name and face are plastered all over the place!"

"I know, but once they clear you, it'll be okay."

"Don't give me that Beaver Cleaver look. You and Elizabeth think I did it. You think, 'Kayo killed Michelle to keep our secret.'"

"I've never said that," Connor challenged. "Never."

"But you're not sure, are you?"

Connor looked away.

"Say it," Kayo said, standing up. "You and Elizabeth both, neither of you are sure. Say it: 'We're not sure, Kayo. You could be a killer!'"

"Godammit, we're not sure!"

The truth caused Connor to lose his footing and he braced himself against the table.

Kayo fell silent.

Connor threw his chair to the floor. "I'm tired of this guilt trip you're laying on me—the big white man didn't help the poor black man. This whole mess would've never even started if you hadn't stolen that journal. Talk about lowlife! Stealing from your friends!"

"I didn't steal it, I borrowed it to show to Manchester to

arrange a buy for later so Michelle would not have any money worries—"

"And so you could get kudos with Manchester. It was for you, man, 'fess up, it was for you. You didn't give a damn about Michelle!"

Kayo lunged over the table. The already weak legs of the table gave way under the weight, crashing to the floor. The two rolled over on the floor, squeezing and punching.

Two police officers rushed in. "Hey, hey! Break it up!" One grabbed Kayo, the other Connor. The guard holding Kayo said to him harshly, "You keep this up, we won't let you out to that pretty girl that just posted your bail!"

"Go to hell, Connor!" Kayo said, his voice waning as the cop pulled him out the door. "I don't need you or Elizabeth! I don't need either of you!"

During the cab ride home, Val did the talking, telling Kayo what a great attorney Adele was and how she would surely get him off.

Kayo let her talk as the cars and buildings whirled by. Michelle was gone. Murdered. He was a suspect, arrested, treated like a common criminal. The people he swore he could count on the most had abandoned him. He felt more alone than he ever had before in his life. By the time the cab pulled up in front of his apartment building, Kayo was seething. He jumped out of the cab and headed straight inside the lobby, trying to get to the safety of his apartment. Val stopped to pay the driver.

Just as Kayo stepped inside the lobby, Harold the security guard looked up. There was an elderly couple waiting in front of the elevator with a basket of laundry. All three of them looked at Kayo and he swore he saw the man whisper something to his wife.

"What the fuck are you looking at?" Kayo challenged. In their eyes was fear and he fed it with his own bitterness. "Yeah, that was me on TV—yeah. Alright, I'm a jailbird!" Kayo just rambled on as he headed toward the elevator. "I'm no goddamn murderer! But after today I should be!"

The couple backed away.

Val entered the lobby and she looked at the people standing there. The elderly couple were staring at Kayo as if he was a wild animal on the loose. Val instinctively walked over and slipped her hand into Kayo's. The elevator door opened and Val led Kayo in by the hand. Val leaned out the door and said softly, "Are you coming?"

The couple shook their heads no.

"Good!" Kayo said, using his foot to push the Close button.

"Calm down. Acting crazy is not going to solve anything."

"I'll do or say whatever I want!" Kayo said, bolting out of the elevator to his apartment door. "I'm put in jail for nothing! Treated like a criminal, and you expect me to grin like nothing ever happened?" He flung open the door and Val slammed it shut behind them.

"What, because you're hurt, that gives you a license to act crazy? Get a grip."

"Me get a grip? Everybody is kicking my ass and I have to get a hold of myself?" Kayo was now at the bar pouring himself a drink. He looked away and tried to think of something else. Kayo's eye caught the answering machine. He pressed the message button.

There was a hiss and then one message—from Manchester: "Kevin, I'm sorry to have to call and tell you this over the phone. But as of today, we are giving your duties at the company to someone else. At this time, the company feels that your employment is not proper for our image. We will give you two months' severance pay . . ."

Val could feel his chest lurching wildly as she hugged him tight. "It's bad. So bad, I know. Kayo, there's more. I talked to Michelle's father and he said that they're shipping her body back and the funeral is at the end of the week. You can't go. You're out on bail and can't leave the state." Val felt his body convulse and she clutched him tighter. "Michelle would understand. I'm staying here with you."

* * *

It was a terrible day. The cries of the people inside the church seeped through the windows and backed up into the sky, turning the sun into a jaundiced eye that watched over their grief.

"Lord! Lord! Lord!"

Blue-black bunting draped over the doorways and around the pulpit bruised the eye. A full choir, in their funeral white, sat motionless, their chests vibrating from the force of the song they hummed. The casket was thick and silver and the open top was padded with white satin.

Connor was in line to view the body. He and Elizabeth had gotten separated when the line formed. He looked back for her now and, like hands, their gaze touched, then fell away. Connor turned back and saw that after viewing the body, people were stopping at the far-right pew where the family was sitting. Michelle's mother shivered in her seat. Her mouth was open and there was no sound. It was as if she was screaming at a pitch so high that only God could hear it. Michelle's father was sitting next to her gently rocking his right knee back and forth. His right arm was wrapped around his wife's shoulder and every now and then he moaned, "Lord! Lord! Lord!"

It took all of Connor's strength to face Michelle for the last time. He stumbled away, stopping in front of her parents. Guilt was like a stone rolling in front of Connor's throat as he groped for something to say.

Michelle's father didn't even look up when he said simply, "I know, son. Just go on now, I know."

And the compassion in his voice staggered Connor. He made his way down the aisle, stopping at the first empty seat he saw.

Elizabeth stared down at Michelle's hard, pale face. She dropped her eyes and her gaze came upon a row of round-toed, block-heeled shoes. Elizabeth heard the sobs of the elderly, women all clothed in the same black dresses with white roses pinned above their hearts. A little sign, taped to the side of the pew, said THE WILLING WORKERS. Then Michelle's voice from their last night together seemed to come to Elizabeth from the rafters . . .

"I'm surprised you can face me," Michelle said.

"What the hell is that supposed to mean?" Elizabeth questioned angrily.

"I mean you took my journal."

"I don't have your stupid journal, alright?" Elizabeth said, noticing that the apartment was in shambles. "What have you been doing in here?"

"I looked for my journal, so don't say I didn't because I did!" She spun around the room. "See, I checked everywhere because I didn't want it to be true. I didn't want to believe that one of my best friends would stab me in the back!"

Elizabeth was standing in the center of the room staring at her. "Stabbed you in the back! You're the one threatening us, jeopardizing all our futures over a damn journal. We've been working our asses off, all of us, except you, to get our careers going, and now you want to destroy us all?"

"I want what's mine! I mean, is it okay for my dreams, my work, to go down the tubes?"

"You know what I think? I think you lost the damn thing yourself and are just trying to pin it on us! You don't care about anybody but yourself anymore—it's just you, *your feelings.*"

Michelle walked over to Elizabeth and examined her eyes. "You're high. Coked up. I feel sorry for you. It's eating you up and you don't even have sense enough to see it."

"Aww, don't give me that. I'm fine, just fine, and I don't need anything from you but your word that you won't go to the police tomorrow."

"I'm not promising you a thing. If you don't have my journal then get the hell out."

"I don't have that journal and you better not go to the police!"

"Don't threaten me, Elizabeth. I'm tired of it all, the missing journal and everything else. I'm tired of trying to make our friendship work. I'm sick of Connor using me. I'm tired of lugging around this guilt about Friar Pete. I'm just going to tell it. Lord, I've got to make something right!" And Michelle began sobbing.

"Please, Michelle!" Elizabeth said reaching out to her.

"No! Get out," Michelle sobbed . . .

As the music in the church became louder, Elizabeth saw herself backing out of the room with slow, cautious dread and she shook her head now until she couldn't distinguish the ringing in her ears from the notes of the big pipe organ. Elizabeth closed her eyes and began saying a silent prayer as she walked to find a seat.

Michelle's uncle, Reverend Alexander Howard, cleared his throat. He was a big man, once a fullback for Fisk University. His face was taut and his skin ash-black. His eyes were glassy as he looked at his brother and began the going-home service.

"To my big brother D. Z., this day is the day that God never should have made. Michelle is gone. We were blessed with her, blessed with her for a good while . . . not a long while, like we wanted, but a good while. And amen, that's good news. And even better news than that, God now has her for evermore in His loving care. Like Job, shore up and know that sorrow don't last always. Remember her the way she was, I know I'll never forget her . . . The way she used to call me 'Unkie Al' like there was nobody in the world more special than me. Huh, Michelle had that gift about her, don't you know."

Someone in the back called out, "Yes-yes!"

And Elizabeth felt as if she were being smothered.

Connor covered his face with sweaty palms and shifted in the dense air.

"I don't know about y'all, help me Jesus, but I'm going to use my faith like a solid rock this morning. Michelle is gone but she lives on in our hearts!" And then, for the first time, he looked weak. The Reverend clutched the side of the podium and his head dropped forward, an inch from the mike. And as if he were pulling the notes up from his toes, his voice began in a clear, booming baritone: "Precious Lord, take my hand, / Lead me on, let me stand . . ."

The choir joined in: ". . . I am tired. I am weak. I am worn."

The whole church began to sing, the sound as filling and strong as ocean waters: "Through the storm and through the night . . ."

The pallbearers grabbed the casket and lifted it up on their shoulders, heading down the aisle.

"Lead me on . . . to the light, / Take my hand, precious Lord, and lead me on."

Kayo was sitting in his pajama bottoms on the floor of his living room in the corner nearest the window, as the moonlight bathed his outstretched feet. Val had fixed him his favorite breakfast, waffles with strawberries, and then taken him to a black film festival in Harlem. That evening, Val treated him to a steak dinner and later massaged his back until he fell off to sleep.

Now at eleven o'clock he had awakened and slipped out of bed, leaving Val sleeping soundly in the other room. How the hell did everything go so well, then just fall apart like this? He knew. Kayo knew the beginning of the end. And now, in the quiet darkness of the room, he could feel again the motion of the car, the jarring thud of contact. He could feel his feet cold against the wet ground as he stood over the body. Kayo heard himself say, "We gotta dump the body." That began the unraveling.

And on top of all that, the journal. I know I shouldn't have taken that journal. God knows, I hate that our last words were so hateful. But Michelle's gone and there's nothing to do about it. I'm so sorry. Kayo let those words ricochet around his mind as he slid all the way out on the floor and turned over to face the moon. He lay there quietly, hearing his throat catch with each breath, and waited for sleep to come.

It had been two days since Michelle's funeral and Elizabeth, now back home, was slipping into a slow, immense depression. She had not talked to Connor or Kayo. Connor and she had been speechless and afraid to look each other in the eye the entire plane ride home. Once home, the thought of talking to Kayo made her sick to her stomach. She sat in between her cocktail table and loveseat now, admonishing herself. You can't face him because you're afraid of what he'll say, of what you'll say! Elizabeth remembered Connor telling her what had happened when he went to the police station. That alone was enough to warrant her keeping her distance from Kayo. Elizabeth poured herself a Scotch, trying not to snort the coke that was in the small plastic bag at her side. But she needed to be numb, there was too much to think about, and the Scotch was not enough. Elizabeth reached down in the bag and made two lines. She snorted hard and hoped that the power would blow her misery to pieces. Instead she saw herself walking up to the casket in the church. Slow, slow steps and slurred sounds, leading her to the casket. Elizabeth tried to shake the vision gripping her but couldn't. Closer, each second was closer, and she tried to get up from the floor. I don't want to see Michelle again. I've lived this once—not again. Elizabeth could see the casket rising and tilting in a shroud of fog. She pulled up on the pillows of the loveseat and tried to hoist up, but her body was a heavy stick of cement. The vision was now becoming clearer and clearer. Elizabeth thought, Michelle in the casket, and braced herself. She watched as the fog cleared and there in the shiny, silver casket was Friar Pete.

"Szzzt!" Elizabeth hissed. Her hands cupped her ears and she squeezed. "Umph."

Then the phone rang and the vision, still clear in her mind, hung with Elizabeth as she rolled over on the floor and grabbed the receiver. "Friar Pete in Michelle's casket!"

"Elizabeth? Elizabeth?" her father said over the phone.

"Daddy, Friar Pete in Michelle's casket." Blood was running down the dark face. "Daddy?"

"Elizabeth, honey?"

"Friar Pete," Elizabeth moaned. She heard the casket click closed in her mind and the vision disappeared. "Daddy, it's the accident. If we hadn't done that, none of this would of happened!"

"I told you to forget about that, didn't I?" her father said firmly.

"Yeah," Elizabeth whined like a kid. "But I told you what happened that night with Michelle, when you called I told you about how we argued. It wasn't like *us*, and now she's gone."

"Listen," Nickelson said, sounding worried. "I told you then and I'm telling you now, things have a way of working themselves out. Now, calm down."

"Oh, Daddy-daddy-daddy!" Elizabeth cried.

"Elizabeth, I want you to get a hot bath and then take two aspirins and go to bed. I'm coming to get you tomorrow afternoon and bring you home for a few days."

"Come and get me, Daddy, okay? Tomorrow, okay?"

"Tomorrow afternoon." He heard her breathing relax.

"Okay." Elizabeth said, hanging up the phone. She leaned back and took deep breaths. Elizabeth stood and staggered into the bathroom. She reached over and grabbed a bottle of bath milk off the counter and poured the entire contents into the tub. She turned on the hot water and then the cold, and let the waters run over the back of her hands.

Then someone buzzed the front door.

Elizabeth looked through the peephole and saw that it was Detective Brady. She turned quickly, running over to the loveseat and hiding what was left of the cocaine in between the cushions.

"Coming," Elizabeth called as she raced back to the door to open it.

"Hello," Brady said, stepping into the apartment. Before closing the door he looked at the lock. "This is a weak lock. You should have it changed to a double bolt."

"I know," Elizabeth said, turning away from him and walking slowly back into the living room. "My Dad's a cop and that's what he says too."

"Really?" Brady was walking behind her. He noticed a teeter to her walk, then her glassy eyes, her running nose. He knew she was high. "How are you today?"

"I'm tired. I was just about to take a bath. I've had a rough week—Michelle's death, the funeral."

"I came to ask you some questions about the night of Michelle Howard's murder. You say you were there at eleven?"

"Right, um, it had to be eleven because I got home around twelve, my Dad called, yeah. Eleven."

"And she was upset about the missing journal," Brady said, walking around the room. It was a mess, clothes and newspapers scattered everywhere.

"Yes, I told you about that before," Elizabeth said, nodding. "I'm tired of-of talking about it."

"She threatened you all to get it back, had all of you pretty scared," Brady said, baiting her. "Had something big on you all. I imagine she would have gone through with it, too. She had the goods on you three." Brady stopped by a small desk shoved in the corner. He stopped and stared at a photograph on the desk.

"The threat! Huh, she was in the car too . . ." Elizabeth stopped, catching herself. Brady's back tensed. Elizabeth shook her head, trying to get her thoughts together.

Brady turned around and looked at her hard, pointing to the picture. "This is you and your Dad?"

Elizabeth sighed, hoping Brady hadn't heard her. "Yes."

Brady looked back at the picture. Mike Nickelson! I never even made the connection! His mind was working furiously now.

Elizabeth felt as if her entire body was melting. "Look, please let me rest, please."

Brady backed away from the desk and spun around. "Yeah, that's all for now. I'll talk to you later."

"I'm going home, my Dad is coming tomorrow afternoon to take me home for a couple of days. Here," she reached down and grabbed a pad and pen off the table. "This is my home number in New Haven."

"Okay," Brady said, looking at it. Then he just stared at Elizabeth.

Finally, she made a move for the door.

"I'll see myself out." Jim Brady made his way down the stairs, taking two steps at a time. He heard Elizabeth's voice· "She was in the car too." What car? When? Where? Something terrible had to have happened for them all to be that afraid. And Nickelson's daughter is involved! Brady pictured Mike Nickelson, yelling at him, forcing him out just as he was making headway on that hit-and-run. His mind screamed: *That's it!* There's some connection! Brady was in his car now, speeding back to the station, trying to recall the facts from the case. He rushed into his office to the cabinet. God, I hope I didn't throw my notes away! He rifled through the cabinet drawers. There was tremendous light in the office, his windows unblocked because of construction going on across the street. The office itself was sparsely furnished: a desk, a chair, two file cabinets. Brady found the tattered, dust-coated file he wanted stuffed in the back of one drawer.

This was the last case I worked on before Nickelson ran me out of town! The coat we found at the scene, the one he threw in the back of his car at the scene of the crime. Nickelson pulled all the good rookies off the case and left all the fuck-ups on! That stiff-ass sarge blowing me off in the evidence room. All of it fits. That's what Michelle Howard threatened them with—telling about this accident! They hit that old bum and dumped his body in the river. Brady went over his notes, over doodlings he had made of the raincoat and of the unique tire tracks found at the scene.

"Hey, Brady," Al said, walking into the room.

"Al," he said, not looking up from the file, "have you gotten the pathologists' reports or the MUDS from the phone company on the Howard case?"

"Not yet," Al said, now standing in front of the desk.

"Dammit, put some heat on it."

"Jesus, I thought we had this one pretty much wrapped up with Watson," Al said, scratching his head.

"Al," Brady said, standing, "Just do what I say, okay?"

"Sure. I just wanted to tell you that the pathologists' reports on the case will be back early tomorrow morning."

Brady glanced up, his face rigid. "I need them tonight."

"Tonight?" Al groaned.

"Tonight. Put your foot in their butts. I've got two important stops to make."

Chapter 16

KAYO touched his tongue against every soft part of her body: the silky lining of her mouth, the button of skin at the base of her throat, the ribbony stretch beneath her bulging breasts, the satiny meeting place of her thighs. Then they wrapped their arms around each other and spun until Val was on top of him. She became a necessary part of Kayo, her bobbing, soothing movements as natural as the Adam's apple lubricating his throat. They spun again and now Kayo felt the afternoon sun blazing across his bare back as he took long, deep thrusts. He cradled Val's shoulders and the heat from her breasts and eyes aroused him beyond belief. Kayo moved in harder and faster, wanting to get inside her skin, inside her mind, her body, as deep as he could and stay there.

Val felt the inside of her body becoming softer and wetter and the singularity of their bodies pushed her to the edge of complete physical pleasure. She dug her nails into his back, wrapped her legs around his waist, and squeezed.

Kayo shuddered and wanted the tingling excitement to cruise through them both forever. He knew Val was feeling it too and afraid to move, they held each other until emotions tore their bodies away in cleansing exhaustion. Kayo's head fell neatly under Val's chin and he told her candidly, "I have never been so loved by anyone else before in my life."

And like sudden rain, the words were surprising and refreshing. Val answered, "We're good to each other and good for each other."

Kayo whispered, "You've never asked me."

"What?"

"If I did it." Kayo hesitated. "If I killed Michelle."

"Don't talk about that, Kayo, we're feeling too good. Besides, I don't have to ask—I know you didn't do it." Val could tell by the way he held her that he was searching for something, that he wanted more. "I know that you cared a lot about Michelle, loved and cherished her friendship. I know you, your touch, the kind of man you are, and I know that you couldn't have murdered her."

"But Connor and Elizabeth have known me a lot longer and look at how they acted."

"That's them and this is us. People make mistakes. I know you're hurt by the way they've acted, Kayo, and I can't give you an answer for it. I just know that I love and trust you and that's all that matters."

Kayo looked at her and was surprised that he felt so safe. He wanted to tell her everything—about the accident, about stealing the journal—all of it. "Val, I want to tell you some things that did happen though."

"No. Why bring old furniture into a new house? Past is past. Let's just go on from here." Then she reached up and kissed him.

"Val, I want you to go to class today. You've been missing a lot staying here with me and I don't want you to jeopardize your graduation."

"I am a little behind, but not much. I'll be okay for the exams coming up, I think."

"No, now." Kayo said, concerned, raising up on his elbow. "If you shower and get dressed, you can make your last two classes for today."

"Okay"—she gave in—"I'll be back after the classes."

They both showered and dressed, but still Kayo had to almost push her out of the door. "Will you go on?"

"Are you sure you'll be okay?" Val stood there, her backpack bunching up her coat.

"Good-bye!" Kayo prodded, opening the door. "See you later. I'll fix dinner."

He shut the door and fell back against it smiling. Kayo walked over to the kitchen and put the kettle on. The sink was full of dishes and Kayo hardly felt like tackling them so he knelt down to get clean ones out of the bottom cabinet. Kayo's eyes caught a stack of papers in the corner, next to the garbage pail. On top was a *Daily News* from the day after Michelle's murder: COLUMBIA CO-ED KILLED. The newspapers had printed articles with pictures of him and Michelle from their Yale yearbook. Tormenting articles that quoted the police as having taken quick and speedy action in catching the murderer. Some papers took slants: "Could it have been a murder of love and passion?" Kayo grabbed the bundle of papers and headed for the garbage chute. When he opened the door, Brady was leaning on the doorjamb.

Kayo tried to slam the door.

"Now is that polite?" Brady asked, blocking the door with his foot.

"Why don't you leave me alone?" Kayo said, turning away and walking back into the apartment.

Brady came in behind him and shut the door. "I just saw Valerie Jemison leave."

"Look, what do you want?"

"Right now? A drink!" Brady said, walking over to the bar.

Kayo folded his arms across his chest. "You got a fuckin' lot of nerve! You've been dogging me out since the first time you laid eyes on me and now you come in my apartment and just make yourself at home."

"I wouldn't dare drink on duty," Brady said looking at a bottle of Perrier. "I've been meaning to try this yuppie shit. Your problem, Kevin, is that you don't know who to trust and who not to. Now. Valerie is a nice lady."

"I don't need you to tell me that."

"She's been staying with you—we watch now! But I haven't seen your friends, um, Elizabeth and Conrad."

"Fuck both of them."

Brady knew he had hit a nerve and he began egging Kayo on. "Did they even call and tell you about Michelle Howard's funeral?"

"I haven't talked to either of those assholes since I got out jail." Kayo was so caught up in his own anger that he didn't even realize what Brady was so obviously doing. "They don't care about anybody but themselves!"

"Yeah, I could tell they didn't give a shit about you, the way they looked when I arrested you. Looked at you like you were guilty as hell!"

"Me kill Michelle? Never! Everybody's pointing their finger at me. Hell, Connor's the one who treated her like shit. He dated her for years and kept it secret, afraid his old man would have a fit about him having a black girlfriend. Finally, she was starting to see the light and was getting ready to dump him."

Brady drained his glass. "Yeah?"

"Yeah!" Kayo said sarcastically.

Just then the door opened. "Kayo, I'm not checking on you, I just forgot one of my books and—" Val stopped suddenly, staring at Brady, then Kayo. "What's going on here?"

Brady picked up the empty bottle of Perrier. "I stopped by for some bottled water."

Kayo dropped his eyes.

Val's face flushed a dark color and her words to Brady were brittle. "He's not supposed to be talking to you. So unless you're going to take him down for questioning, where he can have a *lawyer*, get out."

Brady started to argue, but he decided to let it go. He wanted to talk to Connor now. "Okay, it was just a friendly chat." Brady walked from around the bar, brushed past Val, and went out the door.

"You know Adele told you not to talk to the police unless she was with you!"

"I opened the door and he just walked in and started talking."

"Kayo, Adele is doing everything to help you and you're just being stupid!"

"Hey, it just happened, alright?"

"Forget it!" She headed for the door and Kayo ran behind her, shutting the door with the force of his body against hers.

"I made a mistake. We didn't talk about much anyway. He brought up Elizabeth and Connor and I just lost it, started bitching about them. I'm sorry. I know you and Adele are doing everything you can for me. I'll be careful."

Connor sat on the edge of his bed, looking out the window. His father was at the office and his mother was downstairs with a group of her friends, planning a charity drive for multiple sclerosis. He had dressed hurriedly this morning, his blue oxford shirt misbuttoned all the way down. His pants were old, too short, and worn. He tried not to think about all the trouble, the hurt, the fear, the loneliness he was feeling. But it nagged and nagged at his being.

God, I miss Michelle! Connor lay back on the bed and closed his eyes. The memory of their last night together continued to sting and sting . . .

"Are you going to let me in or are you just going to stare at me from behind the door?" Connor asked.

"Do you have my journal?" Michelle said with cutting words.

"Let me in and find out!"

Michelle swung the door open and spun on her heels, walking away.

By the time Connor walked in, she was sitting on the floor hugging a pillow. "Where is it?"

"I don't have it. I told you that on the phone before! Michelle, I don't know why you think one of us stole it."

"Why? Because I've searched every corner of this apartment. I want it back or else."

"What's all this threatening stuff, huh?" Connor said, pacing the room. "When haven't we been able to talk to each other, huh?"

"This is not about talking, dealing with each other, this is about betrayal—cold and sure. Do you know how much time and money I spent researching that journal?"

"No!" Connor snapped. "You didn't tell any of us what you had or what you were doing, remember?"

"Good thing too! *Hell*, one of you might have stolen it sooner."

Connor looked at her coldly. "Why are you being so fucking nasty?"

Michelle stopped rocking. "I'm being nasty? My friends steal from me, betray our friendship, and I'm out of line! And you. Oh God, you. You have played me to the hilt—taking all I had to give and not giving me what I needed in return."

"Michelle—"

"Please don't give me any more lame excuses. My back is bent and I can't take any more burdens."

Connor leaned down beside her and forced a smile. "Look, baby, let's just relax and talk about something else for a while."

"You're patronizing me like always," Michelle said angrily.

"Let's have a drink and relax and you'll see, tomorrow everything will be gre—"

Michelle slapped the rest of the words out of his mouth, Connor's shoulder slammed against the couch and he held his cheek as a blazing streak racing beyond his fingertips.

"It's over, okay? I was going to tell you before all this happened. It's over. Hell, you don't want a girlfriend, you want a release—someone who can do everything for you without you giving and caring."

"That's a damn lie!"

"Is it? Search yourself, is it?! I mean you showed me no respect. Oh, you loved me, still do, like I love you, but I've decided to love myself more. I'll get over you, yeah, I'll get over you."

Connor was shocked. Her eyes seemed to tear the skin off his face. He was hurt beyond belief. His heart exploded, sending big, bulky pieces plodding through his veins. "You don't mean that."

"As sure as I'm sitting here and God is my savior, I mean every word."

Connor moved his lips and heated words hissed out. "How can you do this to me?"

"You don't get it, do you? I'm dead serious. I can't take any more. Our relationship is finished. Our friendships are finished. I can't stand this guilt about Friar Pete anymore. How can you stand it? You forget, you were driving the car."

"You-you—" Connor backed away, totally out of control now. "You *black bitch*!"

And just as the words left his mouth a crushing self-hate descended on him.

Michelle burst into tears. "Just go. Please, go on . . ."

Connor got up off the bed, his eyes stinging. He grabbed his Yankees jacket and ran out of the door, needing to get some air. Connor thought the stretch of hallway leading to the stairs had suddenly turned into a treadmill. He jumped down the steps and almost lost his footing. The jolt woke a thought hibernating in the back of his mind: *the accident.* Connor clutched the railing and it felt like a cold steering wheel. He heard a thud of contact. He saw Friar Pete's body and heard a splash.

"Are you okay?" his mother asked.

"Huh?" Connor said, a bit startled. His mother was standing by the stairs. "I'm fine, Mom. Go on with your meeting. I'm taking a walk."

The air was crisp but did nothing to boost his energy or his morale. Connor headed down the walkway. There were five cars—two Mercedeses, one Jaguar, a Porsche, and a BMW—

parked in the driveway. It was the BMW Connor's grandfather had given his father, who had given it to him. It was the car used in the hit-and-run. Connor couldn't bring himself to get rid of it, but he never drove it. After the accident, Connor had given it to Tim. Connor was staring at it now when he heard a horn honk from across the street.

Brady got out of his car and began jogging toward him.

"Fuckin' great!" Connor said under his breath. He looked back up at his house and wished that he had never set foot out of it.

"Say, Conrad."

"Connor," he said, still looking back up at the house.

"Okay," Brady said, "Connor, glad I caught you. I was just about to come in to ask you some questions."

"What do you need to know?"

Brady looked up at the colonial-style mansion and the manicured lawn. "I'd love to see what this place looks like inside." Brady nodded toward the house. "Let's go inside and talk."

"No. My mother and her club are inside and I don't want to disturb them."

"I'll be quiet," Brady said, taking a step toward the house.

Connor stepped over, cutting him off. "I don't want my mother upset, *I said, understand?!*

"Okay, okay!" Brady began feeling around in his back pocket. "You got a pen or something?"

Connor looked at him with disbelief. He felt in his back pocket and pulled out a gold Cross pen.

"Thanks," Brady said. He pulled a pad out of his back pocket. "Writes smooth!"

"Yeah, they're nice," Connor offered, not knowing what else to say.

Brady had eyed the BMW as he parked across the street. He'd noticed the Yale sticker on the back as well as the slender tires. "I just want to ask you a few questions," Brady said, intentionally dropping the pen. He knelt down and picked it up. He took the tip of it and traced the triangular tread of the tires. "Unique tires!"

Connor felt as if he were being strung out. "Yeah, they're custom-made in Germany."

Brady looked up and smiled at Connor.

"Listen, can we get this over with?"

"Sure," Brady said, standing up and dusting off his hands. "What was your relationship with Michelle Howard?"

"I told you before, we were friends."

"I know that's what you said, but it was more, wasn't it?"

"No."

"Well, according to Kevin Watson, the two of you were lovers and you were afraid to tell anyone because you didn't want, excuse me, a black spot on the family name!" Brady said with a crooked smile.

"Fucker!" Connor hissed.

"Now, I'm thinking that maybe you had a lovers' quarrel."

"I don't think we should go on with this."

"She was about to dump you and you lost it."

"Shut up!"

"You strangled her to death!"

"That's bullshit! I loved her! I could never kill her," Connor clenched his fists. "Get away from me!"

Brady stepped forward.

"I mean it. Just get the hell out of here, wasting my time with your sleazy accusations!" Connor backed away onto the lawn and began running toward the house. "To hell with you!"

Brady was just about to go after him when he heard the buzz of his car phone. He skipped backward into the street. Brady reached through the open car window and snatched the receiver up. "Yeah? The lab reports are back? I'm coming in."

"Watson did it."

"Al, just run down the reports to me," Brady said, scooting his chair from around the desk so he and Al could look at the same time.

"Here we go," Al said, opening the files. "Time of death

12:40 A.M. Cause of death is strangulation. There was a struggle. Umm, she's got bruises on her forehead, front right, as well as both arms. She had enormous handprints on her neck, but we couldn't get prints. We did find four sets of prints in the apartment. One belongs to the victim. One belongs to Watson—the match is from the ones we took when we booked him. One belongs to Elizabeth Nickelson—got her prints from a minor arrest six months ago."

"For what?" Brady asked.

"She was at that big demonstration in front of the abortion clinic on the East Side. The pro-choicers got a little rowdy when the pro-lifers blocked the clinic doors. And the last set of prints belong to Conrad Bellington, the Third."

"He's got a record too?"

"Naw, he worked as a researcher on that big government project with Poland. A bunch of companies sent teams over here for a few weeks to help them develop new business systems. The Mayor insisted everybody get clearance." Al held up a sheet with Connor's picture and fingerprints. "See? Got it from a government friend of mine."

"Okay."

"I'm telling ya, man. Watson's prints were all over the place."

"He admitted being there that night," Brady shrugged.

"After we caught him in a lie about it. Hey, the blood found under her nails? Type O. Guess who's type O?"

"Watson and half a million other people in New York!" Brady laughed.

"But none of them were seen running from the apartment at the time of the murder."

"What about the fibers under her nails?"

"It's from a material that was coated with a special spray called Ambersin. Twenty years ago, a company in Seattle discovered it and began using it on their coats. It helped bead up rain and snow, you know. About ten years ago, the spray was found to have a cancer-causing agent in it. The Food and Drug Administration banned it. Company went belly-up."

"How many coats were made with it?"

"Hundred thousand. And they shipped them all over the country."

"Any match with the samples taken from his clothes or from his apartment?"

"No." Al shook his head weakly.

"Aha!" Brady said.

"Big shit." Al shrugged. "He could have thrown away what he wore that night."

"Huh. Well, maybe . . . maybe it was Bellington," Brady said, easing back in the chair.

"Motive?"

"Lovers. And she was about to can him because he wouldn't tell his family about her. Race thing."

"No shit?" Al said, eyebrows raised. "Source?"

"Watson told me."

"Aww, he's trying to throw us off."

"Maybe, maybe not. But it's true. I cornered Bellington on it and he lost his mind. Then maybe . . . Elizabeth Nickelson did it."

"Stop pulling my dick," Al said, standing up to stretch.

"She's strong enough to have done it. Her prints are there."

"Motive?"

"Her motive is a motive that could have driven any of them to kill Michelle Howard."

Al stared at Brady who reached back on his desk and picked up the file he had found in the back of his drawer. "The four of them were involved in a hit-and-run while they were at Yale together in New Haven. They killed a bum and dumped his body in the river."

"Shit!" Al said, looking at the notes. "Your case?"

"Mine and the rest of the rookies on the force. That is, until Sergeant Mike Nickelson, Elizabeth's father, pushed me off the force to cover up the case. I think once that journal came up missing, Michelle Howard threatened them with exposure and one of them killed her."

"Well, let's call New Haven and get 'em all for that hit-and-run and smoke out who bumped off Howard."

Brady shook his head. "These are my personal notes on the case. Old Nickelson has surely done away with that evidence the way he *thought* he'd done away with me. Elizabeth Nickelson, yeah, she's a suspect too."

"But according to Watson and Bellington, they saw Michelle *after* Nickelson did."

"She could have doubled back. Any of them could have just doubled back and done her in."

The door opened and a police officer handed over a sheet of paper with perforated holes. "Here's that info from the phone company you've been waiting on. I got the addresses for you too."

Brady took the paper and quickly flipped through for the phone number of the call he made the morning of April 23. Written on the side of it was the address. Brady stood up. "Let's roll. Maybe we've got our killer."

"Our killer is the 24 Hour Gourmet Super Market," Al said, looking up at the sign.

"Okay," Brady chuckled, "so it's a pay phone. But it's around the corner from the victim's apartment. We're close. Let's talk to the manager."

They stepped inside the store that was brightly lit and painted in pastels. The aisles were narrow and the store was busy for a late afternoon. Brady spotted the pay phone in the back next to a cash machine station. He stepped over to a nearby counter and spoke to a man in a blue polyester coat with a nameplate that said "Manager."

"Can I help you?" the slim, elderly man asked.

Brady and Al flashed their badges. "Yes. We're investigating a murder that happened just around the corner from here ten days ago."

"Michelle Howard. She'd get her *New York Times* and coffee here every morning. Nice girl," the manager said, shaking his head.

"Well, on the night it happened, someone made a call from that pay phone to her house."

"I'm the only one on duty that late at night, and I don't recall anything strange."

Al pulled out a mug shot of Kayo and the government clearance sheet with Connor's picture on it. "Recognize either of these guys?"

"No, can't say that I do."

Brady pulled out the police photo of Elizabeth taken after her arrest at the rally. "How about her?"

"Yes, definitely. She came in the store with Michelle a few times, recently too."

"Was she here that night?" Al asked.

"I can't remember," the manager said, now fiddling nervously with a pad by the register.

"Think!" Al said.

"Hello!" Brady said spinning Al around. He pointed up to the corner of the ceiling. There was a video camera.

"That's for the cash station transactions," the manager offered.

Brady shoved Al toward the phone. "Make a call."

"To who?"

"Your wife—your girlfriend."

"Funny," Al said, making his way to the pay phone as Brady made his way around the back of the counter. Mounted underneath was a tiny silver screen. He saw the cash machine clearly. In the upper left-hand corner it showed the day, the date, and the time, ticking off by the second. Brady watched as Al's profile slipped into view as he picked up the phone. He whispered, "Jackpot."

The cloudless, sunless sky paled the afternoon. A slight wintry breeze scooted the crowds of people down the streets. Nickelson felt his car idling hard as he covered the brake while a woman crossed in the middle of traffic. She had her young daughter strapped to the front of her body with a long blue scarf. He watched her walk with slow, steady steps and he took particular note of the way she cradled the little girl's head close to her body, protecting her from the stinging wind. The death of

Meghan had been a terrible loss and that sorrow had changed states over the years, hardening into a fierce protectiveness of Elizabeth. Nickelson was now three blocks from her apartment and he hoped that Elizabeth would be better today, stronger and calmer than she had been on the phone yesterday.

He pulled his car in front of the apartment building. The drive from New Haven had been particularly long, slowed by construction on the highway. Nickelson got out of the car and stretched. He reached over the front seat, grabbed his lucky trench coat, and headed quickly inside.

"Hi Daddy," Elizabeth said, giving her father a big smile as he walked in.

Nickelson was struck by how thin Elizabeth had gotten. Her hair was limp and dull, her eyes dull as well. "Why do you look so sickly?"

Elizabeth tried to shrug off the question with a weak laugh. "Stress, Daddy. I've been really upset, not sleeping, thinking about all that's happened with Michelle, and now Kayo's accused of the murder and I've had nightmares about her funeral."

Nickelson walked over and hugged her. "We'll get you home where you can have a nice long rest and some good food and you'll see how much better you'll feel."

Elizabeth hugged him tightly around the waist, feeling calmer and more secure than she had in months. "Okay, Daddy."

"Get your bags."

Elizabeth skipped backward out of his arms and headed for the bedroom to get her things. "Be back in a second."

Just as she turned the corner, there was a knock at the door.

"Expecting someone?" he called to Elizabeth in the other room.

"No!" she called back.

Nickelson looked through the peephole. It was Jim Brady. He took a deep breath and opened the door. The two men locked eyes. Brady looked through Nickelson, behind his eyes into the man. He saw sternness, steadiness, and stubbornness.

He saw the man who had refused to give him a break, the benefit of the doubt, the man who had forced him out of town, humiliated him two years before. Brady struggled to control himself.

"Long time no see," Nickelson said.

Brady thought about punching him. "Hello Sarge. Long time, too long."

Nickelson said nothing.

"Well, you know I'm a detective here."

"I heard," Nickelson said.

"I'm working on the Howard murder case and needed your daughter to come down to the station to make another statement."

"Daddy? Who is it?" Elizabeth stopped just behind her father and looked over his shoulder. "Oh, detective."

"Hi, I'm sorry to bother you, Miss Nickelson. I was just telling your father that I needed you to come down to the station and make another statement for our investigation."

"Why?"

Brady addressed Nickelson. "Our department isn't small like in New Haven. We've got tons of stuff going on and one of the officers misplaced some of the files for this case. It'll only take a few minutes." Brady looked back at Elizabeth. "You said you'd do anything to help."

"Okay," Elizabeth said wearily. "Can my father come? He's a police officer."

"Sure, I was just about to ask him." Brady nodded.

Brady led Nickelson and Elizabeth toward the interrogation room. He stopped by the wooden rack and hung up his coat. He held his hand out to Elizabeth and she slipped off her coat. He motioned to Nickelson and he handed Brady the trench coat he had folded over his arm. Brady nodded to a sergeant in the corner and hung them up.

The narrow interrogation room was already full when Brady walked in, followed by Elizabeth and her father. Connor was slumped down in a squeaky wooden chair. Kayo was sitting at the other end of the table facing everyone else. Al was standing up against the wall. Brady held out a chair for Elizabeth and looked at Nickelson as he spoke. "I had the others picked up too."

Nickelson looked at him and took a seat next to his daughter.

"Man, I'm not saying anything until I call my lawyer," Kayo said, pointing his finger.

"I'm not making any statements without a lawyer!" Connor echoed.

"Two hotheads!" Brady said. "Well, in that case, I guess Elizabeth is the only one with nothing to hide."

She looked at him, startled. "No. Nothing."

Her father slipped his hand over hers and squeezed. "What's going on?"

"I'm just trying to figure this whole thing out. See, this murder case has been on my mind ever since I took it on. I was sure I had it closed when I brought Watson here in."

Connor looked at Kayo and their eyes met over a void of recognition. Kayo turned away.

Brady strutted around the room. "Give us your statement again. Tell your friends here what happened that night."

"For what?" Kayo snorted.

Brady leaned down until he was nose to nose with Kayo. He whispered so only Kayo could hear, "I'm trying to help you, stupid."

And Kayo saw something different in Brady's eyes for the first time. He swallowed hard before beginning. It was difficult so he turned away from them and stared at his reflection in the two way mirror. His voice was slow in coming, like a trickle of blood from a small wound. "I went there and it was just about midnight." Kayo's head began to hurt as the memory became clearer in his mind. He could see Michelle standing there in her living room, in the same clothes she had on the night before, her eyes like torches burning a hole through him . . .

"You did it. I can tell by looking at you that you did it!"

Kayo reached into his jacket pocket and walked over to the

empty bookcase. He stepped on top of the pile of books on the floor, pulled out the journal, and placed it on one of the shelves.

Then Michelle was on his back, beating him with her fists. "How could you!"

Kayo let her hurt him, the pain replacing the guilt, and he turned around to accept more and Michelle saw the look on his face and stopped. "How could you?"

"Let me explain," Kayo said. "I was trying to help you. See, I was going to sell the journal to Manchester and give you the money."

"The money!" Michelle said, stepping back, stumbling over the papers and pillows scattered on the floor.

Kayo reached out.

"Don't touch me," she said, snatching away. "You took something important to me—you knew it was important, priceless to me—and then tried to sell it to your fucking boss!"

"Not for me! You would of gotten the money and been able to pay for the rest of your Ph.D.! I would of made some points—what was the harm?"

"The harm is that you're a liar and a thief!" Michelle said, stomping her foot. Her clothes were clinging to her. "And the things you made me say to Elizabeth and Connor tonight. You've ruined our friendship."

"Don't say that!"

"It's true! I can't believe you! I can't trust you!"

"You're the one who went crazy. Just went nuts over this stupid journal!" Kayo walked toward her.

"You betrayed our friendship."

"Stop saying that. I wasn't trying to hurt you, swear to God!"

"Don't bring God into this. Don't you dare bring Him into this," Michelle said, standing face to face with Kayo.

Kayo reached out, wanting to touch her and hold her. "Won't you please listen?"

Michelle slapped him.

Tears came to Kayo's eyes. It wasn't the pain of the blow

but the loss of faith that the blow carried. He could feel it on his cheek, see it there in the narrow space separating them. Kayo felt he had to run, to run as if his very life depended on it . . .

"And I ran out of the apartment. I ran until my chest felt like it was going to bust and then I went home. That's what happened. I didn't do it!"

All eyes were on him in a room stuffy with silence.

"If you didn't, you won't have a problem looking at the body," Brady said, clearing his throat, pulling out a folder and flipping it open. "See these marks around her neck where she was strangled?"

Kayo dropped his eyes.

"Look!" Brady shouted.

Kayo stared at the picture.

Brady stood back up over him. "Go for my throat!"

"So you can blow me away? Please!" Kayo said sarcastically, folding his arms across his chest.

"C'mon, you've wanted a piece of me for a long, time. C'mon, nigger."

Kayo's hands shot up under Brady's throat.

"Hey," Al shouted.

"Forget it," Brady coughed, grabbing Kayo's elbow, holding it steady. His other hand braced Kayo's wrists, taking the real pressure away from his throat. "See where his fingers are? On my neck. His fingers are around to the back almost." Brady raised his knee and kicked Kayo back down into his seat.

"What's the point?" Nickelson asked.

Brady held up a police photo of Michelle's neck. "She was choked so hard, the indentations of the nails and the base of the fingers are clear. The hand marks are closer to the front! The murderer had short, fat hands! Plus, her lower ribs were broken from where the killer sat on her body and choked down!" Brady squatted and made the motions with his hands. "Like this. This is how it was done." Then he pointed to Kayo. "He's too tall—his body would naturally hit her around the lower waist, upper thighs! Someone shorter did this murder."

Brady walked over to Connor and jerked his hand up. "You've got short, fat hands."

"I didn't kill her," Connor said, snatching his hand away.

Elizabeth looked at Connor.

"Don't look at me like that!" Connor shouted at her.

"Why?" Kayo laughed. "That's how you two looked at me!"

"Shut up!" Connor screamed at Kayo.

Brady played on the tension. "Once your friend over there told me that you and the victim were lovers, I thought, Oh, jackpot, a lovers' quarrel!"

Connor glared at Kayo.

"Then I talked to Elizabeth, and she let it slip about a car and a threat. And then things started falling into place."

"I-I didn't tell you anything!" Elizabeth said, feeling ashamed, looking around the room.

"Damn," Kayo said, sinking down into his chair.

Connor was stunned.

Nickelson stared at Brady intently.

"She was so high when I saw her that she made that tiny slip."

"High?" Nickelson asked, looking directly at Elizabeth.

Her eyes remained downcast.

"Coked out!" Brady said. He grinned at the hurt look on Nickelson's face. "See, I used to be a cop in New Haven, that is, before I started working on a particular case. I remembered that case, the bum hit by a driver who dumped him into the river. It was the case I was working on when the good old Sarge here railroaded me off the force. Now I know why he pushed me off the force. See, I was making headway on the case when he dropped some cocaine in the back of my car and forced me to leave town."

Nickelson sat up in his seat, keeping his eyes on Brady.

"He wanted to protect his daughter Elizabeth. He ran me out of town, tampered with evidence to save her. And when Michelle Howard threatened to ruin you all with that secret, which would also ruin *him*, Nickelson drove to New York and killed her."

"That's a lie!" Elizabeth shouted, looking from Brady to her father and back again.

"What?!" Connor shouted.

Kayo leaned forward. "Huh?"

"It's the truth, isn't't?" Brady asked, leaning deep into the space in front of Nickelson.

He sat back and said coldly, "No."

"I figure it like this: initially, Elizabeth called you from work and told you about the threat and you decided to make a little trip to fix the situation if they couldn't talk Michelle out of blowing the whistle about the accident. You got to New York, called Elizabeth and she told you Michelle was determined to go through with it! Then you went to her apartment and murdered her."

"That's bullshit," Nickelson said with ease. "I was on a stakeout with two other officers that night."

"Stop lying. The last phone call into Michelle Howard's apartment came from a pay phone around the corner from her apartment. You were checking to see if she was there alone."

Everyone was on the edge of their seats, staring at Brady.

"See, you didn't notice the video camera. We've got your mug right on that tape just minutes before Michelle Howard was murdered."

All eyes were on Nickelson.

"There's more!" Brady said like a gloating child. "Hell, the blood typed O. Your type. And the fibers? There were several coated with a special spray that's not even used anymore. We've got your old lucky trench down there now. I'll bet my balls there's a match."

Nickelson's face was rigid.

"You're under arrest for the murder of Michelle Howard!"

Elizabeth burst into tears. "It's a lie!"

"Shut up!" Kayo said, leaning across the table, yelling at Elizabeth.

"Murdering bastard!" Connor breathed.

"Read the Sarge his rights, Al!" Brady said.

Al grabbed Nickelson by the arm and he jerked away.

"Daddy!" Elizabeth said, reaching for him as they hustled her father away.

Brady strutted down the hallway, full of the familiar self-satisfaction he always felt after solving a case. He waved at some of the other officers who were sitting at their desks filling out forms, bringing in suspects. He headed down a narrow corridor and opened the door to his office. At sunset, as it was now, the room was particularly drab. He could smell the dust sprinkling down his nostrils and into his lungs. He walked over to his desk, sat down, and leaned back in the chair, thinking of the reporters he wanted to call to give interviews to. He played with the tip of the folder as he thought. Just then the door opened and Dan Vitto, the chief of police, walked in.

"Hey Chief," Brady said excitedly, "I just closed a major case."

"The Howard case, right. The one I told you to leave alone."

Vitto's hands were shoved deep down in the pockets of his suit jacket. He pulled out a cigarette and lit it. Taking a long, hard drag, he blew smoke over Brady's head. "I'm going to lay it on the line. Kick the bust on the Howard case and drop the investigation altogether."

"What?" Brady said, sitting up. "Hey, I got Nickelson by the balls. I got proof."

"I didn't say you were wrong, I said kick the bust."

Brady looked at Vitto with a dumbfounded expression.

Vitto took another pull from the cigarette and sat on the edge of the desk. "That one phone call he made? To Mayor Callo. It seems the two of them grew up together in New Haven. Callo called me and told me to drop everything on this—it's a personal favor."

"Personal favor my ass!" Brady shouted, flinging the chair out from behind him as he jumped up.

"What's the problem here? I mean, did you know this girl, were you fuckin' her or something?"

"No, I wasn't fucking her," Brady said, slamming his fist down against the desk. "We got him. You know he's guilty."

"So what do you want me to do? Go against the Mayor to bust some flatfoot from New Haven for the murder of some college kid who'll just be another stat next week?"

"What about the press?" Brady said.

"Next week they'll all be dogging another story! This one will be old news."

"I ran the whole thing down for the people in that room."

Vitto got up off the table, flicking the butt in a corner. "So what? You were wrong, you were trying to bait them, to see what they'd say!"

"No! No!" Brady began pacing behind the desk now. "We've got the lab reports, the tape, all that evidence."

"It's going to disappear. All of it."

"But he did it! He did it to protect his daughter, to cover up that hit-and-run, just like he did before when he ran me out of town with that phony coke drop."

Vitto took a long, deep breath.

"No, he set me up." Brady slammed his fist down on the desk again. "Man, I thought about suicide after that. If I hadn't gotten this job I probably would've killed myself."

"He didn't try to ruin you," Vitto said sarcastically.

"Bullshit!"

Vitto leaned across the desk and pointed. "Did you think we took you on this force without checking out your background? Hell, we called New Haven. He said you were a decent kid who needed a change and to give you a shot. Hell, he could've black-balled you around the country if he had wanted too. Don't be a fool. You can't lock balls with the Mayor and win! The evidence in the lab, the videotape, all of it is disappearing now. Al is already with the program. It'll just be another unsolved murder case. That's it! Otherwise, who knows? You just might find yourself off this force too, for some strange reason."

Brady picked the folders up off the desk and handed them to Vitto without looking.

"Good man. I knew you'd see the light."

Chapter 17

ELIZABETH stared up at the ceiling. It had been a week now since her father was released and they had driven home to New Haven. The police had dropped the case so suddenly. All the while in the car, during the whole two hours of the ride to New Haven, Elizabeth had sat quietly, saying nothing but asking a lot of herself. Could her father have killed Michelle? Could he, to protect her, murder her best friend?

Now the questions nagged at her as she lay in the bedroom where she had sulked and played as a child. Could he have murdered her? She knew her father was capable of killing; he was a cop, and all cops had to have that hard, rigid reserve that would allow them to do whatever they had to in the name of the law. But could he kill without a moral cause? Murder without question in the name of protection—protection of her?

She thought back to the phone conversation they had the night of Michelle's murder. . . .

"Honey, have you been crying?" her father asked over the phone.

His voice was strong and clear. Elizabeth sniffed. "Where are you? You sound so clear."

"Oh, um, we finally got a good connection for a change. Did you talk to Michelle?"

"Daddy, I tried to . . . but it was like she was somebody else. Oh, Daddy, we fought something terrible."

"Do you think Connor or Kayo will have any luck with her?"

"No-no!" Elizabeth said biting her bottom lip. "They won't. I'm telling you, Daddy, the way she was with me, I know she'll be the same with them. She won't listen to anybody at this point."

"Don't worry about it, baby, okay? You just get some rest, and tomorrow you'll feel a lot better."

"But Daddy, she's going to go to the police—she is!"

"She won't, honey. Michelle has better sense than that. I promise you it'll be alright . . ."

Elizabeth rolled over in the bed and buried her face in the pillow. *Did he?* Elizabeth's mind ached with doubt. Then her heart, bristling with hurt from Michelle's death and the deteriorated friendships of Connor and Kayo, spoke to her soul: Leave it alone. Believe in him, like he does in you. And with that, Elizabeth relaxed and her body instantly lulled into a long, deep sleep.

Connor was sitting at his desk, staring at the phone. He had worked more than ninety hours over the last week. At this time of the morning, no one was in the office at all unless they were working on some kind of crash-and-burn project deadline. Connor had no deadline, he was just trying to work all his frustrations out. He had called Brady several times, asking about the progress of the murder investigation, and each time Brady had said simply, "Still working on it. No suspects." He had been surprised when they dropped the charges against Elizabeth's father. Connor heard Brady's voice explaining, "I was baiting, trying to get something going. Now we think it was a burglar. Some addict looking for cash. I'll call you when we get something."

Connor hadn't talked to Kayo at all. He knew Elizabeth was at home and he hadn't called her either. He was confused about himself, their friendship. They had lost something special over the last few weeks. And as he sat there now, Connor begged himself for the courage to do something about the splintered relations between them. He picked up the receiver and dialed a number.

"Hello?" Kayo said sleepily.

"Hi, it's Connor," he said louder, trying not to sound as nervous as he felt.

Kayo glanced over at Val, sleeping beside him. "Do you know what time it is?"

"Look, I want us all to be friends again."

Kayo sighed long and hard.

"Let's try. For Michelle, let's try. When Elizabeth gets back from New Haven next week, let's all have lunch. For Michelle, okay?"

"Call me and we'll see," Kayo said, angry that he was giving even that much. Then he hung up the phone.

"Who was that?" Val said sleepily.

"Connor," Kayo said, sitting up in the bed, staring out the window at the cascading mixture of dawn and moonlight.

"Something new on the investigation? Adele said the last she heard, they thought it was a burglar—an addict or something."

"No, it wasn't about the investigation. That bumbling ass Brady was accusing everybody in sight and wrong about everybody—me and Elizabeth's father—I don't know what the hell they're doing!"

"Yeah, it's a mess." Then Val openly wondered about Connor's call. "Then what did Connor want?"

"He wants us all to get together and be friends again. Can you believe that? I told him I'd think about it basically."

Val rubbed his arm, "Meaning?"

"Meaning that I don't know. I'm not sure if it's worth trying to fix."

Val sat up, the covers falling away from her naked shoulders. "You can't go through life holding grudges."

"He says do it for Michelle." Kayo shook his head. "Still using her even in death."

"Well, this time it's for something that might work for the good of all of you. I'm not saying it will be like it was, Kayo."

"I know it won't!"

"But bury the ill feelings that you have. Talk to Connor and Elizabeth and get it all out and go from there."

Kayo felt overwhelmed. He looked at Val a long time. Ever since the charges were dropped against him and the press had picked it up, things had begun to get back on track. Manchester had called and offered him his old job back, but Kayo had refused. He had gotten a better job offer at a competing firm and had decided to take that. He was feeling stronger and better each morning and he knew that it was all because Val had come into his life. Now Kayo looked at her and decided to say what he had been thinking about for quite a while. "Now that this is all over, I want us to get married."

Val's heart jumped. She was dying to say yes, but inside she felt a little uneasy. "Kayo, maybe you should wait before asking me that. I mean, to be sure of what you're asking. I've been there for you and sometimes people are so grateful . . ." Her voice trailed off and she prayed he would say the right thing.

"I'm not confused. I'm convinced. I love you and you love me. I want you with me always."

Val leaned up, giving with her eyes, giving her answer with pure expression, and Kayo returned that expression with a gentle caress and he knew that now the worst was over and only the best was ahead for both of them.